Son of Samson

and the Daughter of Dagon

ZONDERVAN®

The Daughter of Dagon
Copyright © 2007 by Gary Martin
Illustrations copyright © 2007 by Sergio Cariello

Requests for information should be addressed to:

Zondervan, Grand Rapids, Michigan 49530

Library of Congress Cataloging-in-Publication Data

Martin, Gary, 1956–
    The daughter of Dagon / written by Gary Martin; illustrated by Sergio Cariello
        p. cm. -- (The son of Samson; v. 2)
     ISBN-13: 978-0-310-71280-0 (softcover)
     ISBN-10: 0-310-71280-7 (softcover)
     1. Graphic novels. I. Cariello, Sergio. II. Title.
     PN6727.M374D38 2007
     741.5'973--dc22

                                         2007012420

Series Editor: Bud Rogers
Managing Editor: Bruce Nuffer
Managing Art Director: Merit Alderink

Printed in the United States of America

---

07 08 09 10 11 12 • 10 9 8 7 6 5 4 3 2 1

Son of Samson and the Daughter of Dagon

series editor: bud rogers

story by gary martin

art by sergio cariello

 ZONDERVAN®

ZONDERVAN.com/
AUTHORTRACKER
follow your favorite authors

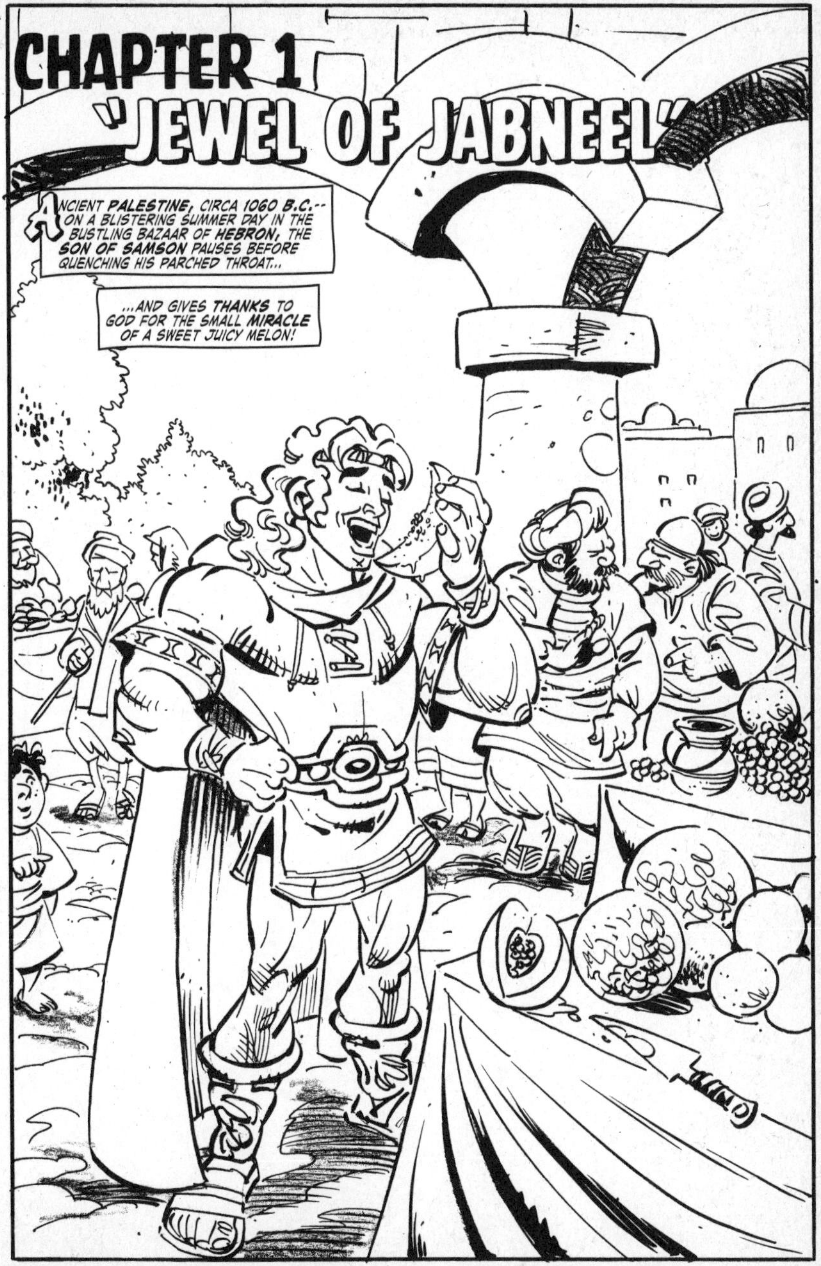
CHAPTER 1
"JEWEL OF JABNEEL"
ANCIENT PALESTINE, CIRCA 1060 B.C.-- ON A BLISTERING SUMMER DAY IN THE BUSTLING BAZAAR OF HEBRON, THE SON OF SAMSON PAUSES BEFORE QUENCHING HIS PARCHED THROAT...
...AND GIVES THANKS TO GOD FOR THE SMALL MIRACLE OF A SWEET JUICY MELON!

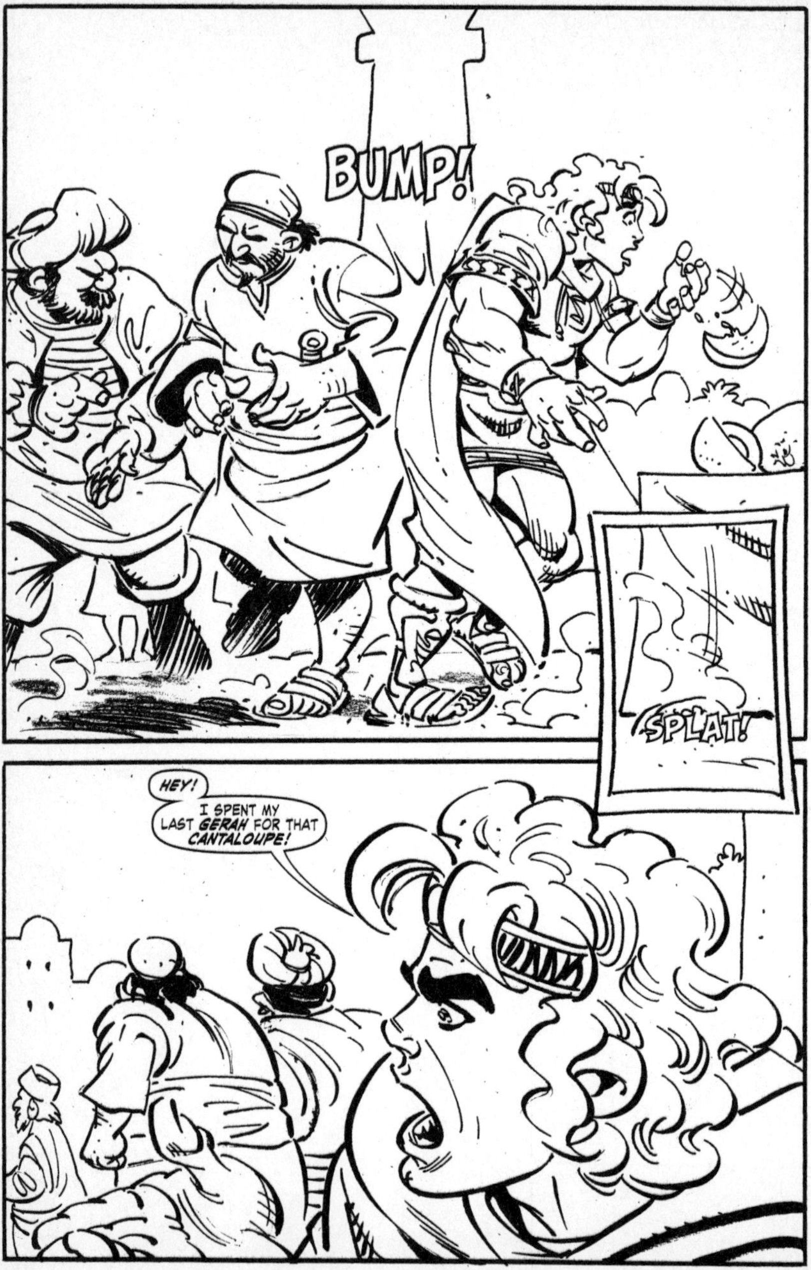
BUMP!
SPLAT!
HEY!
I SPENT MY LAST GERAH FOR THAT CANTALOUPE!

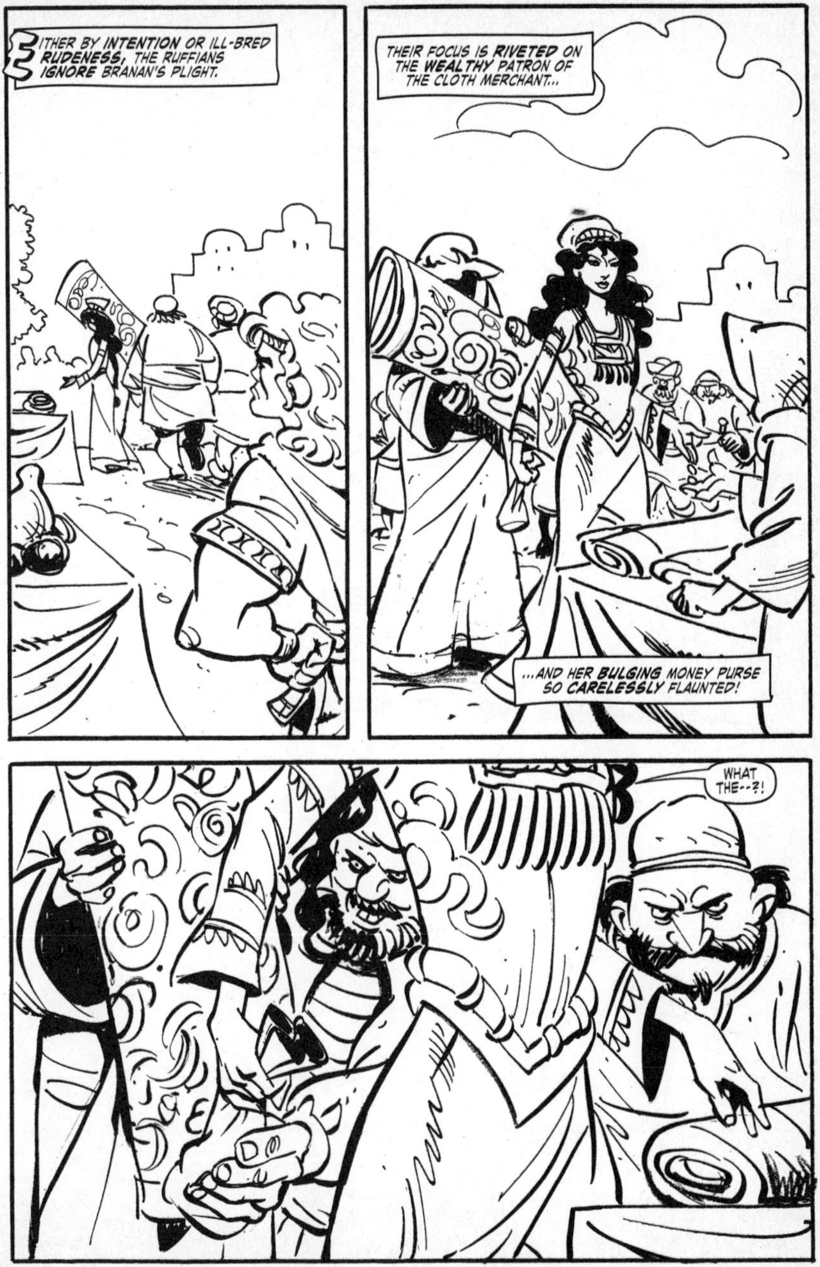
EITHER BY INTENTION OR ILL-BRED RUDENESS, THE RUFFIANS IGNORE BRANAN'S PLIGHT.
THEIR FOCUS IS RIVETED ON THE WEALTHY PATRON OF THE CLOTH MERCHANT...
...AND HER BULGING MONEY PURSE SO CARELESSLY FLAUNTED!
WHAT THE--?!

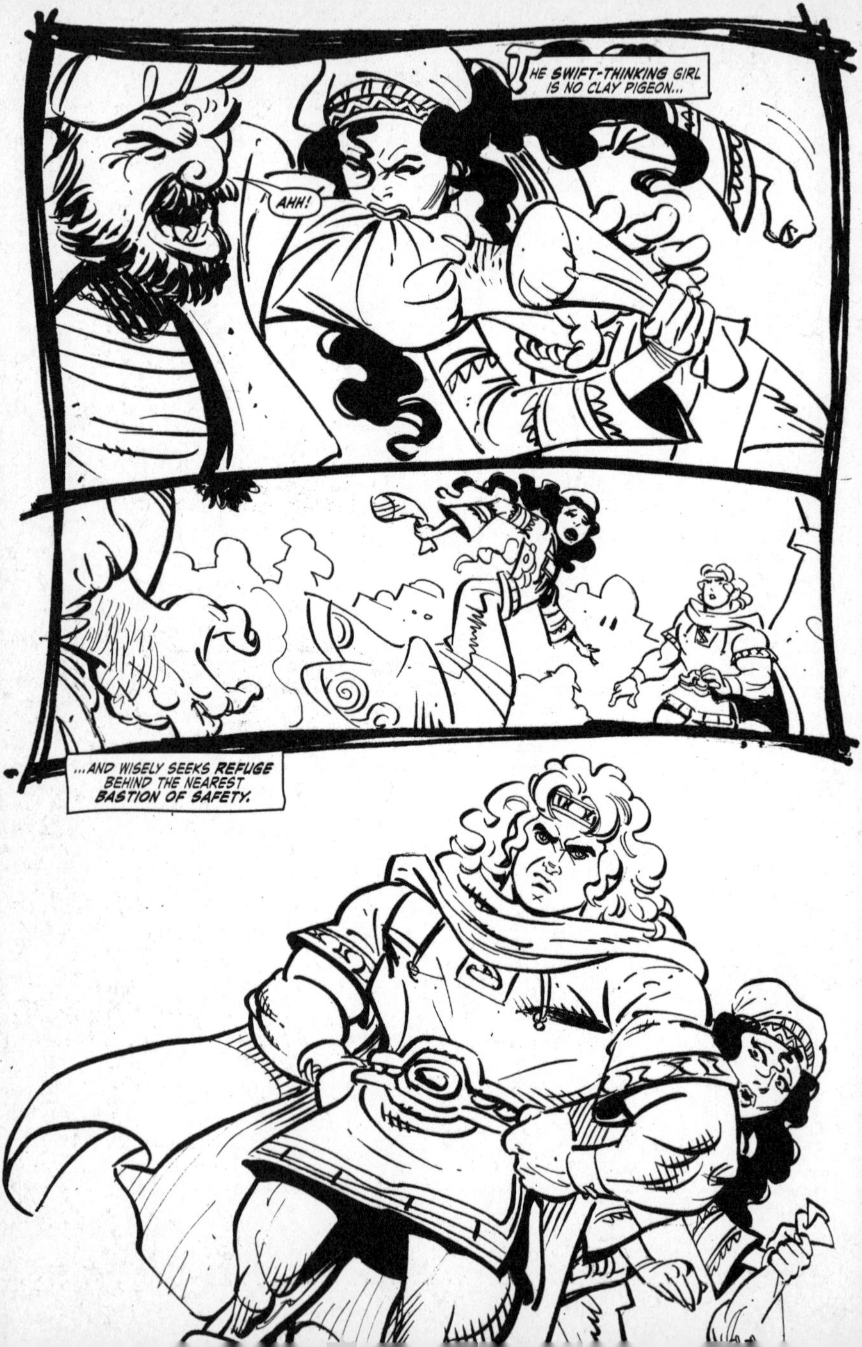
THE SWIFT-THINKING GIRL IS NO CLAY PIGEON...
AHH!
...AND WISELY SEEKS REFUGE BEHIND THE NEAREST BASTION OF SAFETY.

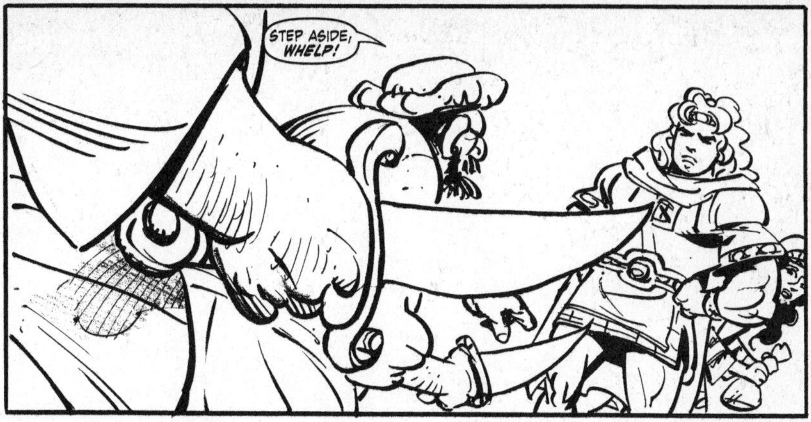
STEP ASIDE, *WHELP!*

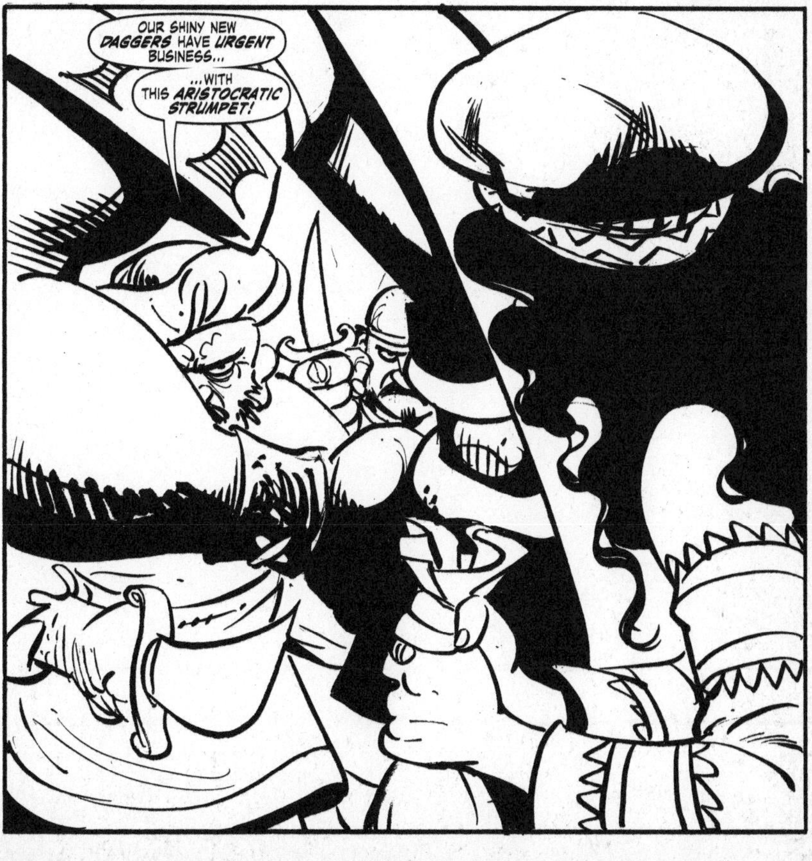
OUR SHINY NEW *DAGGERS* HAVE *URGENT* BUSINESS...
...WITH THIS *ARISTOCRATIC STRUMPET!*

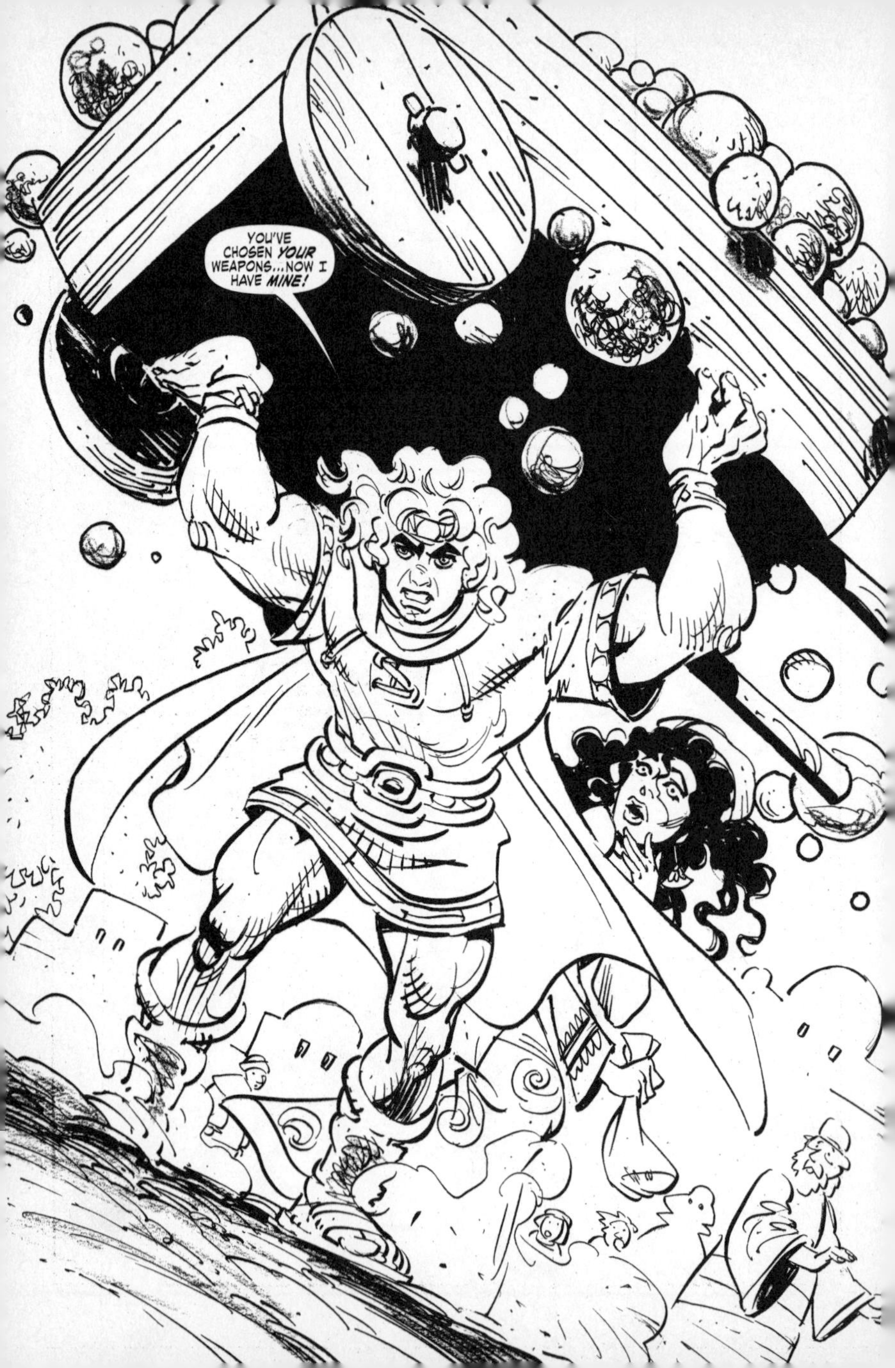
YOU'VE CHOSEN YOUR WEAPONS...NOW I HAVE MINE!

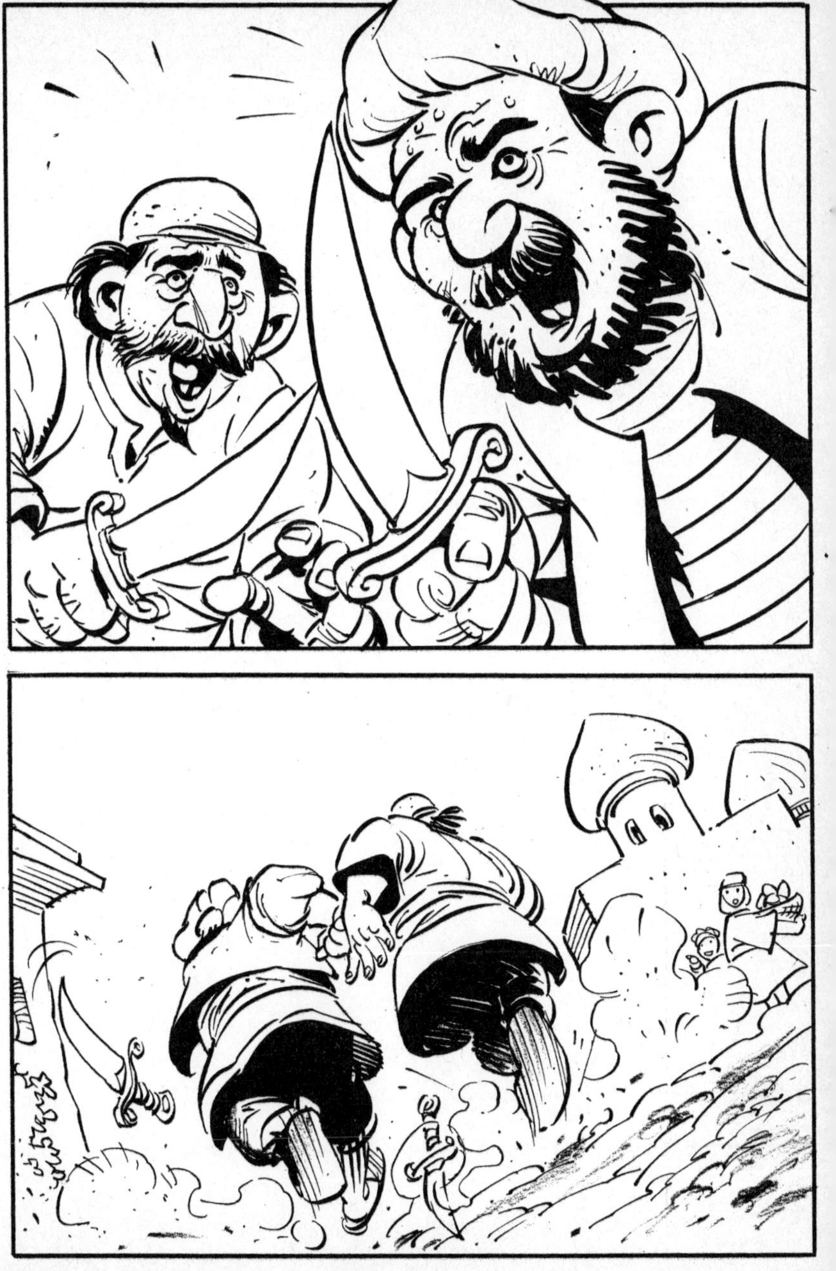

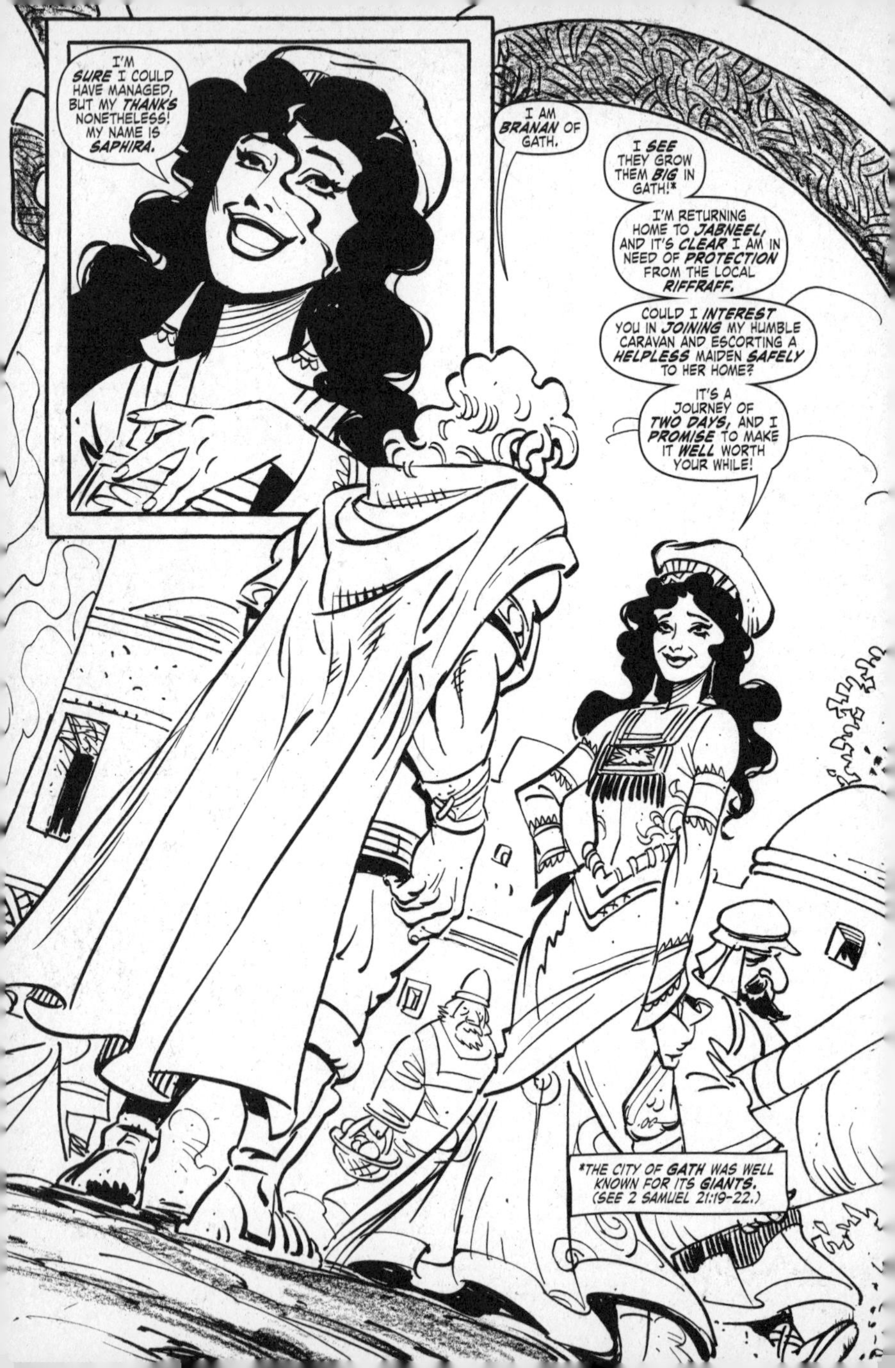
I'M SURE I COULD HAVE MANAGED, BUT MY THANKS NONETHELESS! MY NAME IS SAPHIRA.
I AM BRANAN OF GATH.
I SEE THEY GROW THEM BIG IN GATH!*
I'M RETURNING HOME TO JABNEEL, AND IT'S CLEAR I AM IN NEED OF PROTECTION FROM THE LOCAL RIFFRAFF.
COULD I INTEREST YOU IN JOINING MY HUMBLE CARAVAN AND ESCORTING A HELPLESS MAIDEN SAFELY TO HER HOME?
IT'S A JOURNEY OF TWO DAYS, AND I PROMISE TO MAKE IT WELL WORTH YOUR WHILE!
*THE CITY OF GATH WAS WELL KNOWN FOR ITS GIANTS. (SEE 2 SAMUEL 21:19-22.)

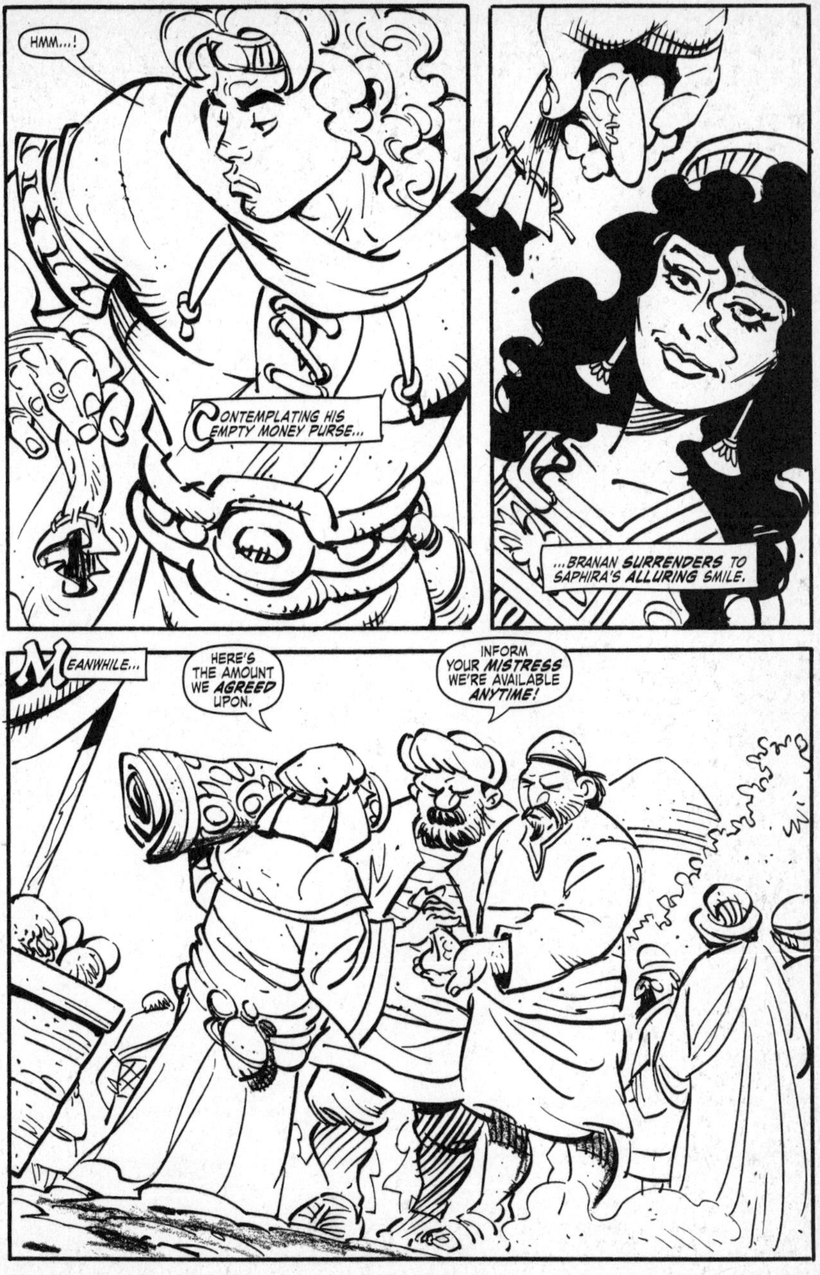
HMM...!
CONTEMPLATING HIS EMPTY MONEY PURSE...
...BRANAN SURRENDERS TO SAPHIRA'S ALLURING SMILE.
MEANWHILE...
HERE'S THE AMOUNT WE AGREED UPON.
INFORM YOUR MISTRESS WE'RE AVAILABLE ANYTIME!

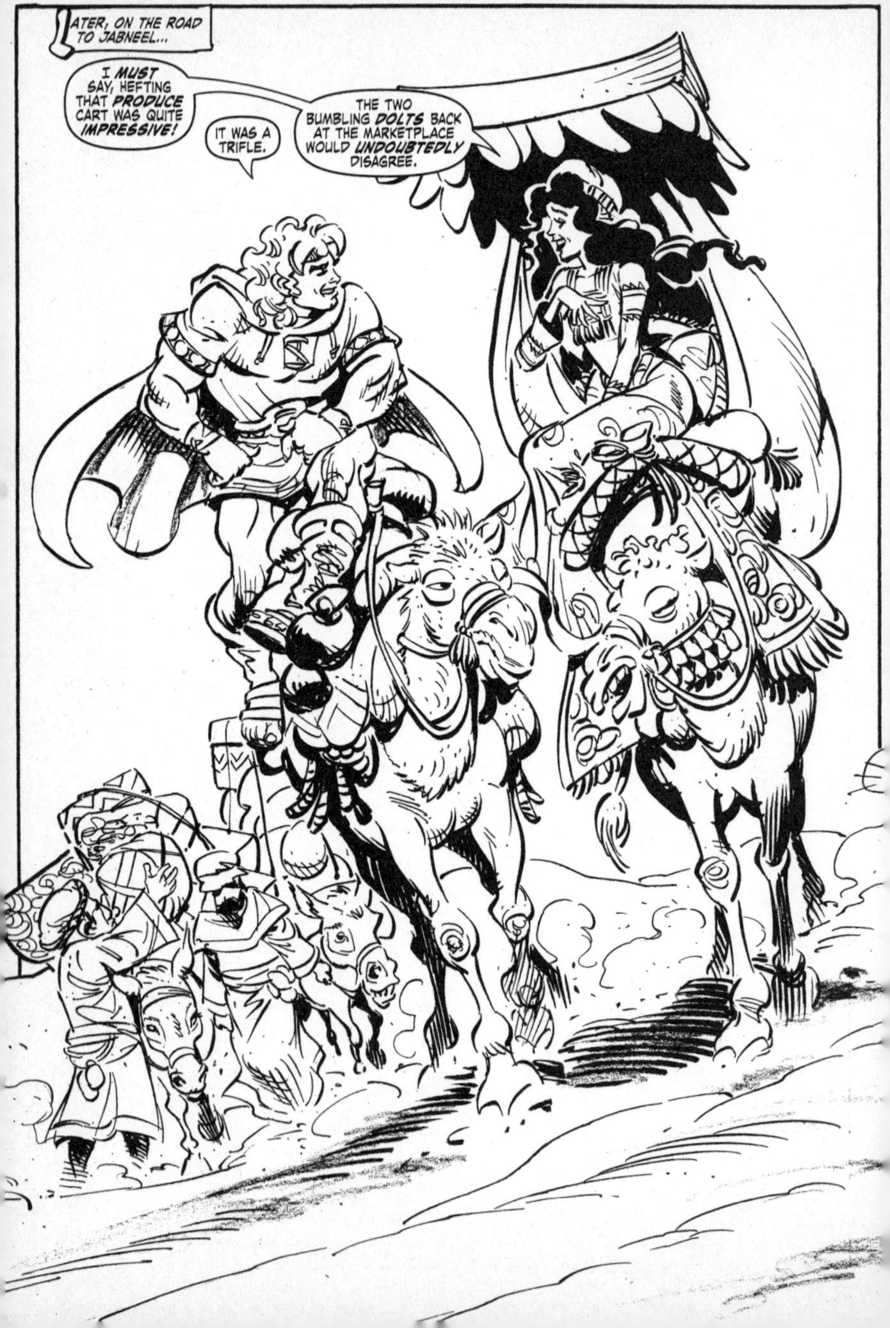
LATER, ON THE ROAD TO JABNEEL...
I MUST SAY, HEFTING THAT PRODUCE CART WAS QUITE IMPRESSIVE!
IT WAS A TRIFLE.
THE TWO BUMBLING DOLTS BACK AT THE MARKETPLACE WOULD UNDOUBTEDLY DISAGREE.

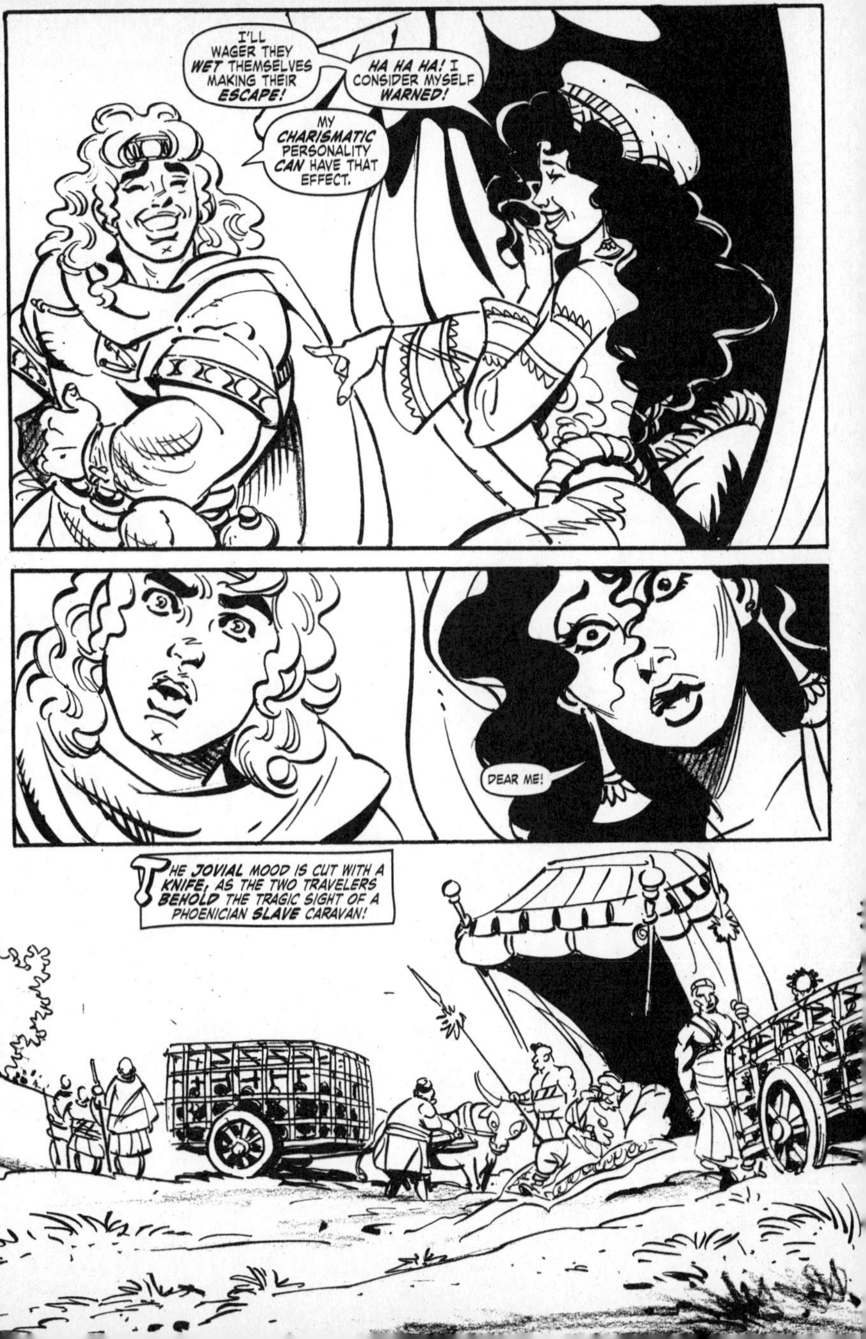
I'LL WAGER THEY WET THEMSELVES MAKING THEIR ESCAPE!
HA HA HA! I CONSIDER MYSELF WARNED!
MY CHARISMATIC PERSONALITY CAN HAVE THAT EFFECT.
DEAR ME!
THE JOVIAL MOOD IS CUT WITH A KNIFE, AS THE TWO TRAVELERS BEHOLD THE TRAGIC SIGHT OF A PHOENICIAN SLAVE CARAVAN!

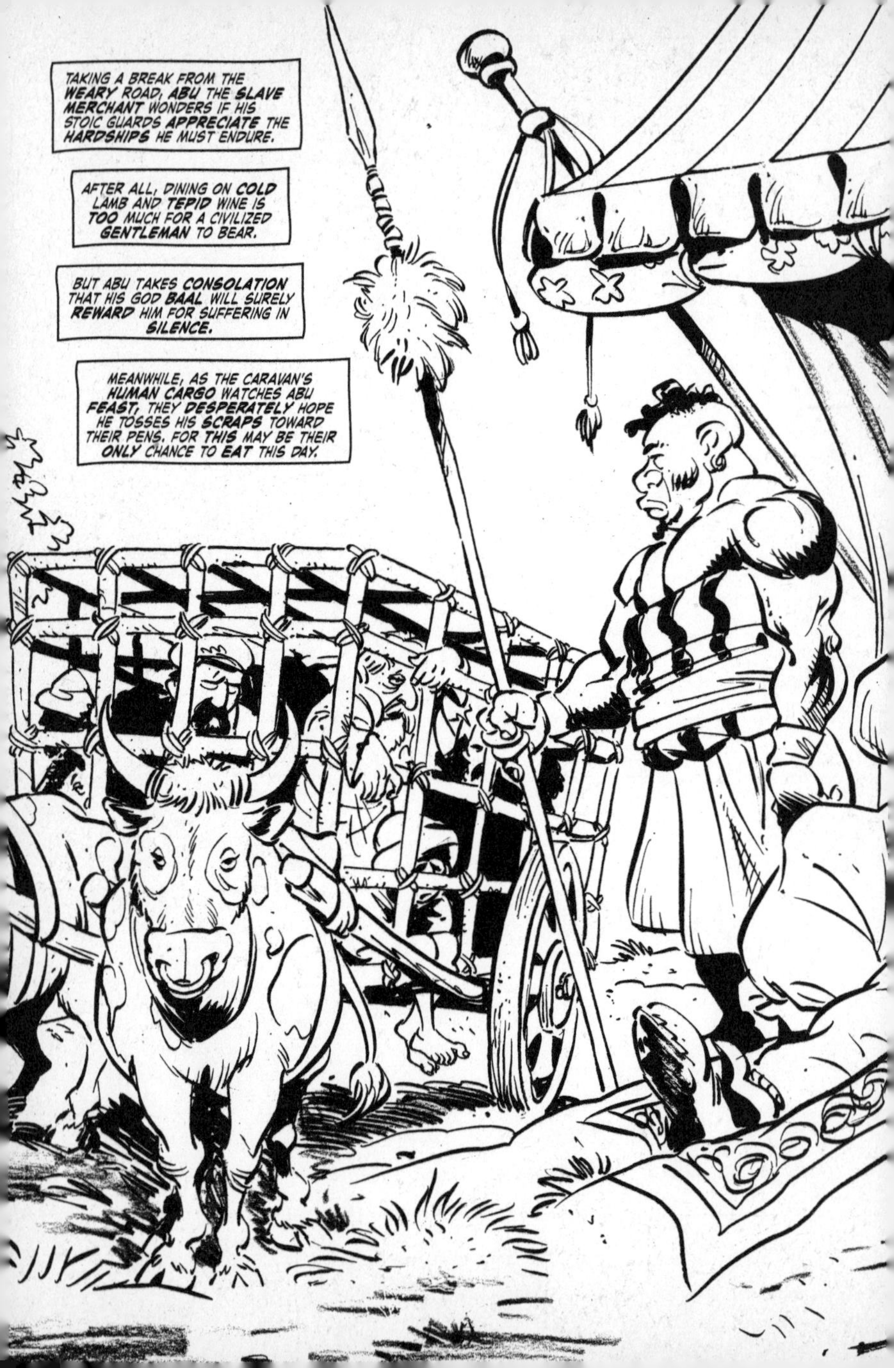
TAKING A BREAK FROM THE WEARY ROAD, ABU THE SLAVE MERCHANT WONDERS IF HIS STOIC GUARDS APPRECIATE THE HARDSHIPS HE MUST ENDURE.
AFTER ALL, DINING ON COLD LAMB AND TEPID WINE IS TOO MUCH FOR A CIVILIZED GENTLEMAN TO BEAR.
BUT ABU TAKES CONSOLATION THAT HIS GOD BAAL WILL SURELY REWARD HIM FOR SUFFERING IN SILENCE.
MEANWHILE, AS THE CARAVAN'S HUMAN CARGO WATCHES ABU FEAST, THEY DESPERATELY HOPE HE TOSSES HIS SCRAPS TOWARD THEIR PENS. FOR THIS MAY BE THEIR ONLY CHANCE TO EAT THIS DAY.

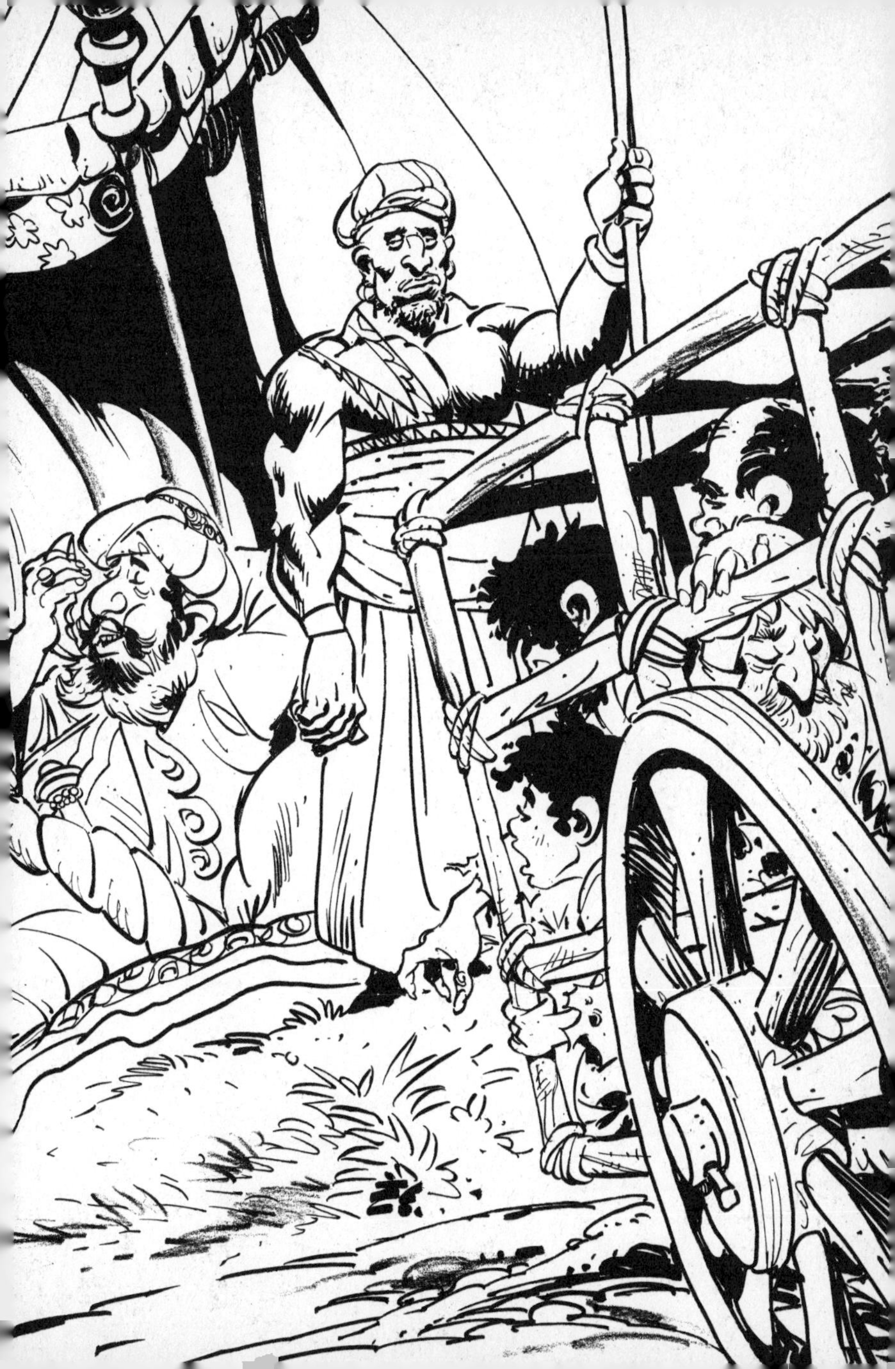

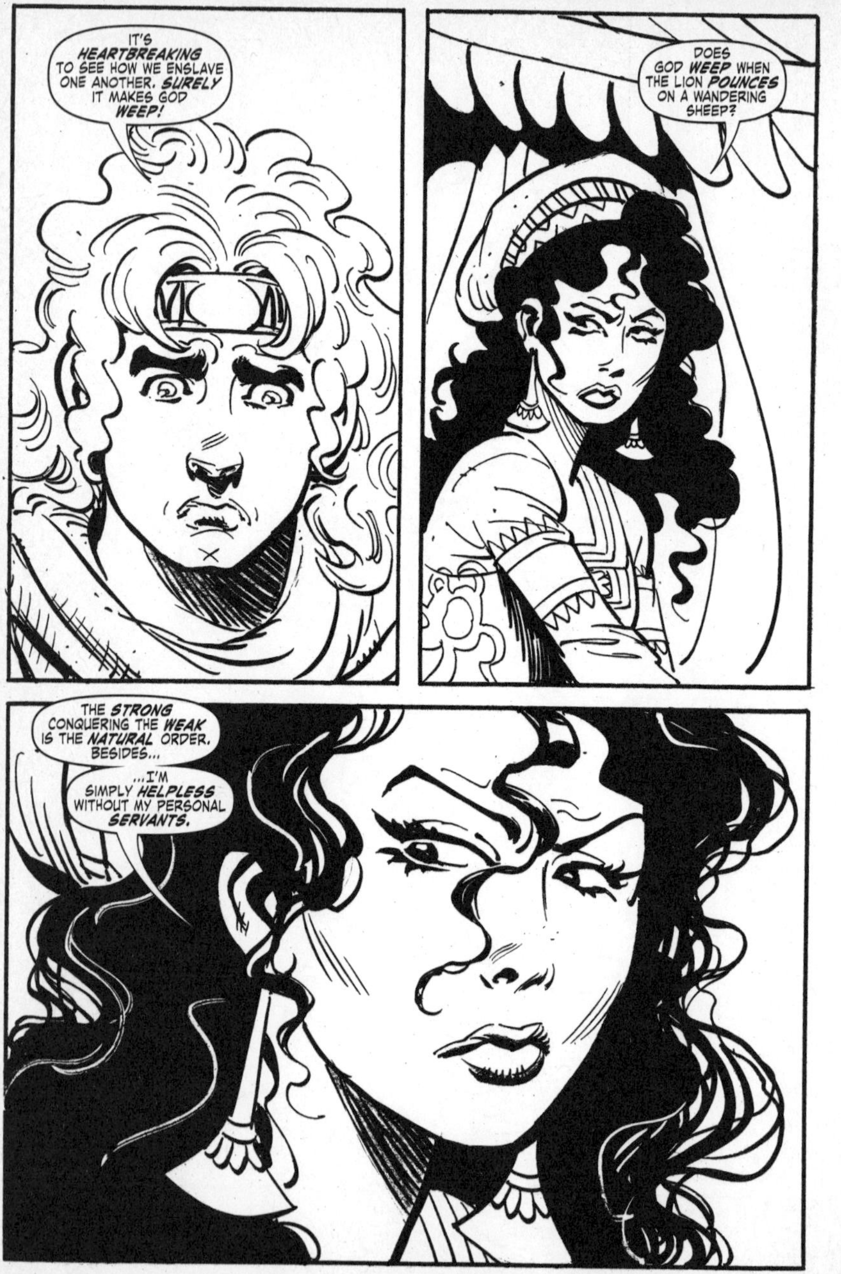
IT'S HEARTBREAKING TO SEE HOW WE ENSLAVE ONE ANOTHER. SURELY IT MAKES GOD WEEP!
DOES GOD WEEP WHEN THE LION POUNCES ON A WANDERING SHEEP?
THE STRONG CONQUERING THE WEAK IS THE NATURAL ORDER. BESIDES...
...I'M SIMPLY HELPLESS WITHOUT MY PERSONAL SERVANTS.

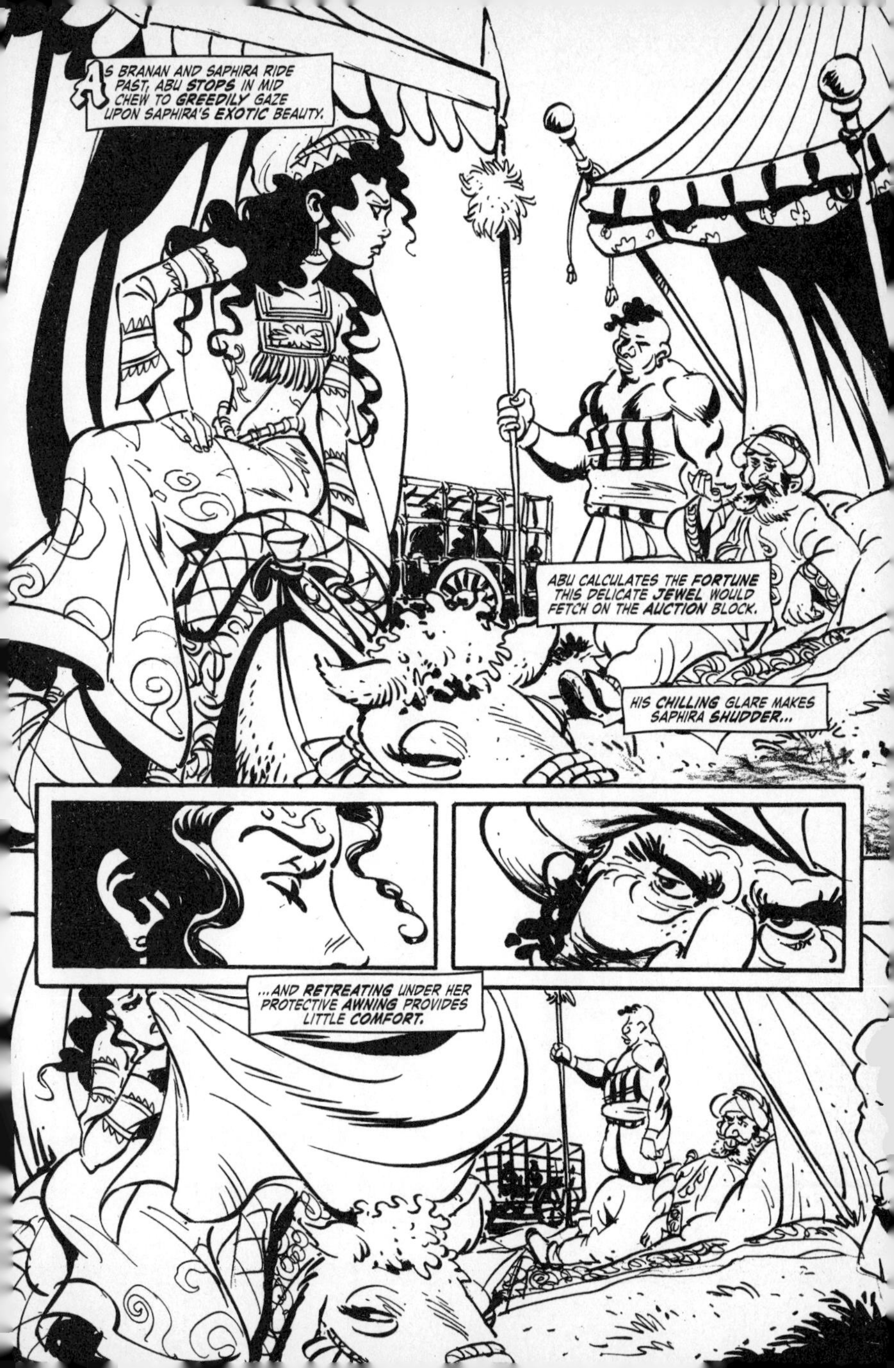
AS BRANAN AND SAPHIRA RIDE PAST, ABU STOPS IN MID CHEW TO GREEDILY GAZE UPON SAPHIRA'S EXOTIC BEAUTY.
ABU CALCULATES THE FORTUNE THIS DELICATE JEWEL WOULD FETCH ON THE AUCTION BLOCK.
HIS CHILLING GLARE MAKES SAPHIRA SHUDDER...
...AND RETREATING UNDER HER PROTECTIVE AWNING PROVIDES LITTLE COMFORT.

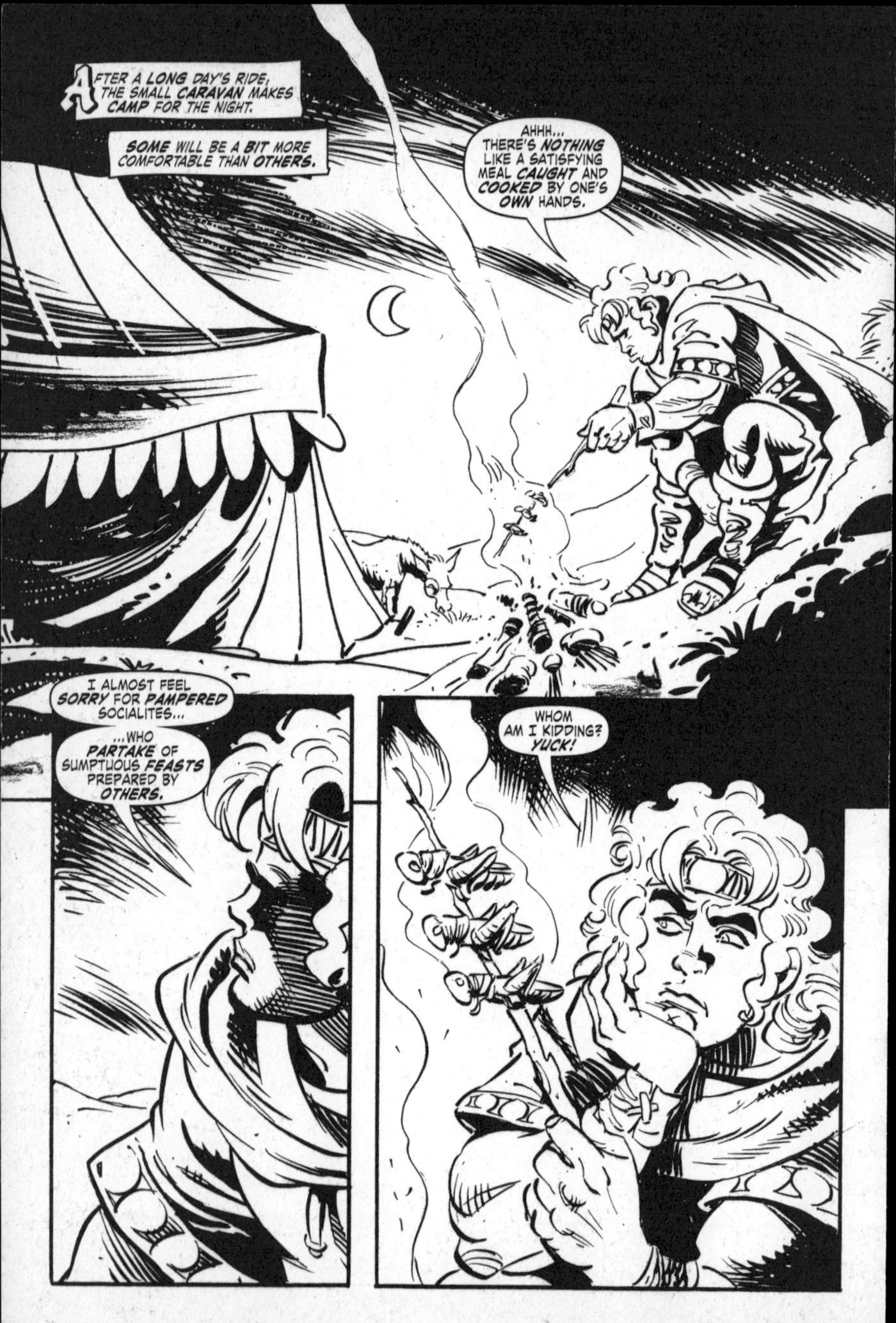
AFTER A LONG DAY'S RIDE, THE SMALL CARAVAN MAKES CAMP FOR THE NIGHT.
SOME WILL BE A BIT MORE COMFORTABLE THAN OTHERS.
AHHH... THERE'S NOTHING LIKE A SATISFYING MEAL CAUGHT AND COOKED BY ONE'S OWN HANDS.
I ALMOST FEEL SORRY FOR PAMPERED SOCIALITES...
...WHO PARTAKE OF SUMPTUOUS FEASTS PREPARED BY OTHERS.
WHOM AM I KIDDING? YUCK!

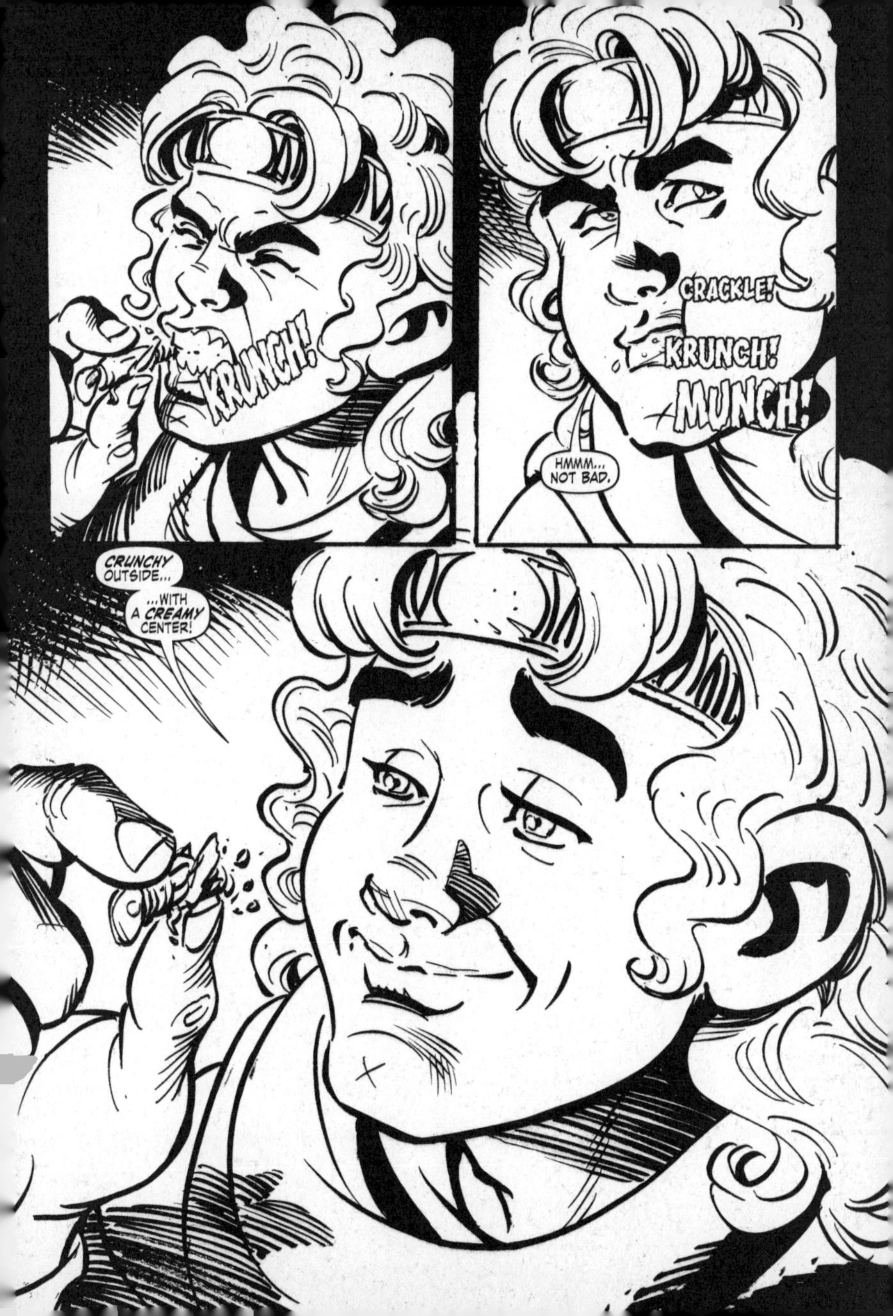
KRUNCH!
CRACKLE!
KRUNCH!
MUNCH!
HMMM... NOT BAD.
CRUNCHY OUTSIDE...
...WITH A CREAMY CENTER!

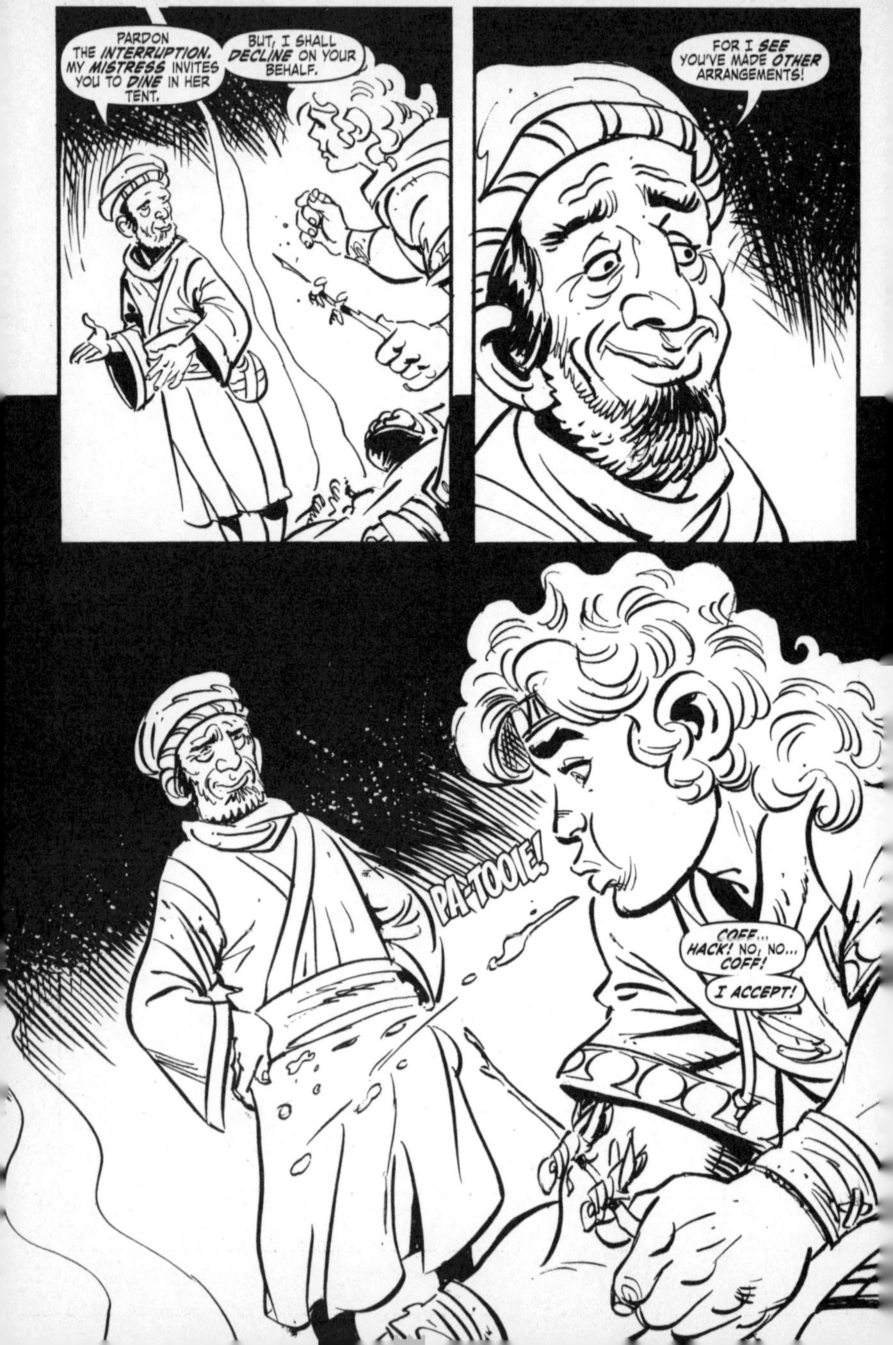

PARDON THE *INTERRUPTION.* MY *MISTRESS* INVITES YOU TO *DINE* IN HER TENT.
BUT, I SHALL *DECLINE* ON YOUR BEHALF.
FOR I *SEE* YOU'VE MADE *OTHER* ARRANGEMENTS!
PA-TOOIE!
COFF... HACK! NO, NO... COFF!
I ACCEPT!

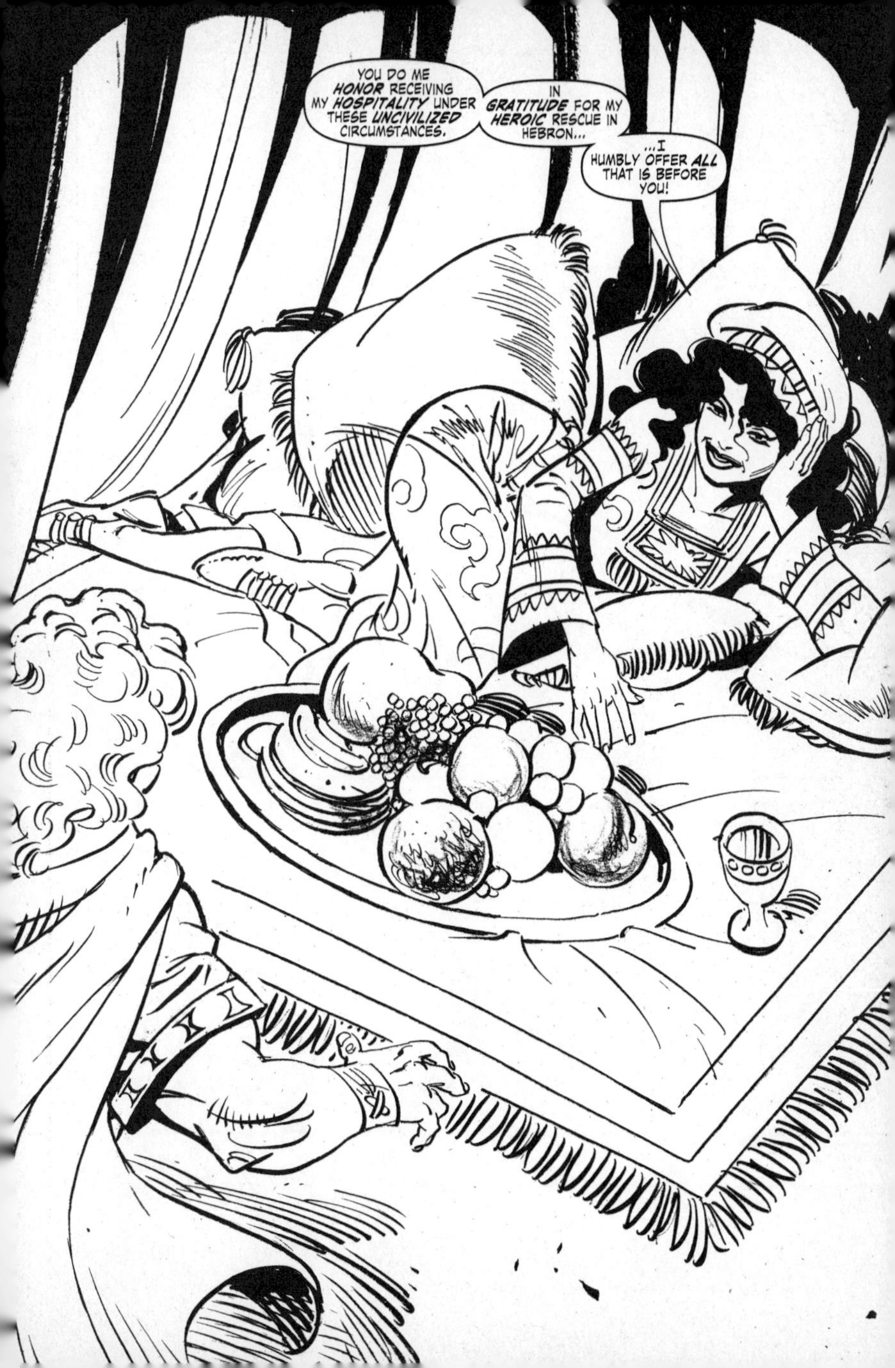
YOU DO ME HONOR RECEIVING MY HOSPITALITY UNDER THESE UNCIVILIZED CIRCUMSTANCES.
IN GRATITUDE FOR MY HEROIC RESCUE IN HEBRON...
...I HUMBLY OFFER ALL THAT IS BEFORE YOU!

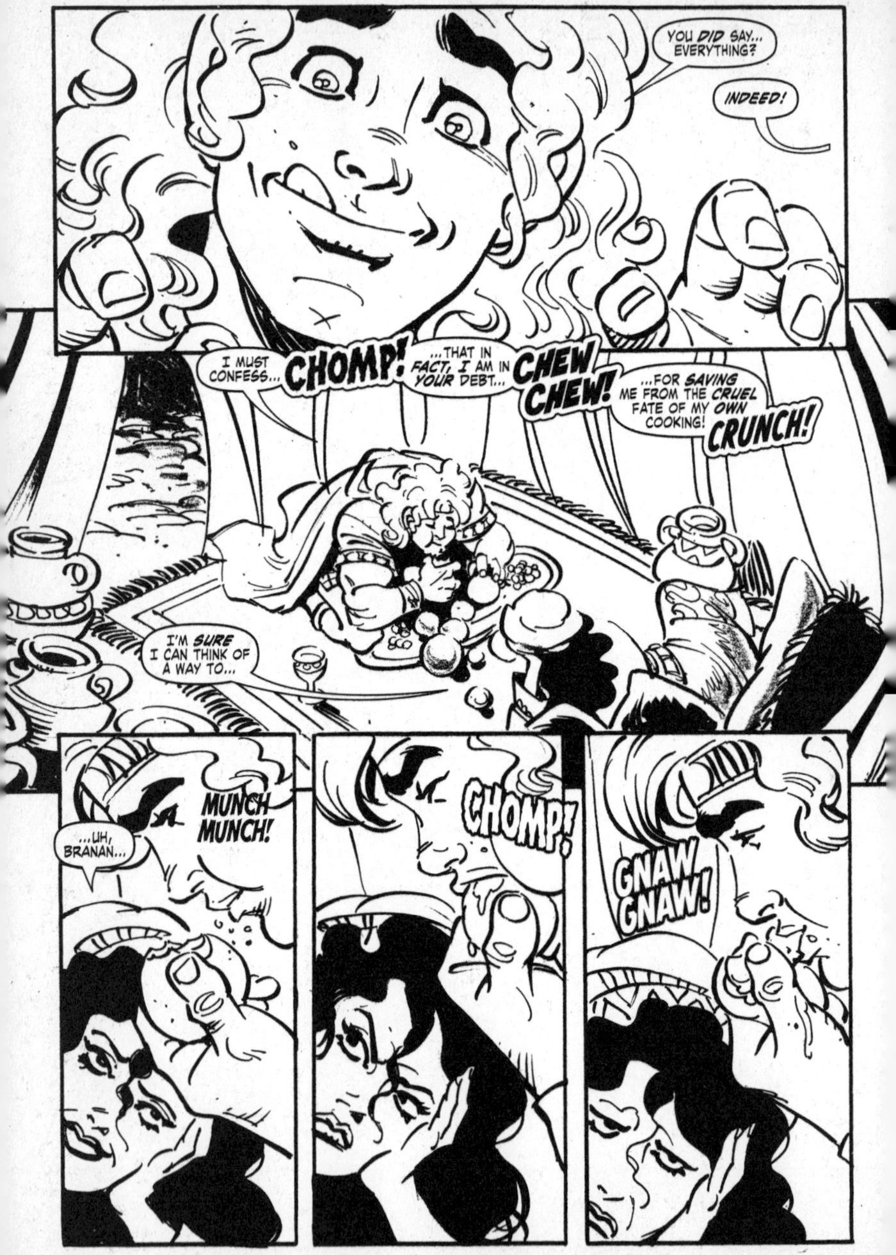
YOU DID SAY... EVERYTHING?
INDEED!
I MUST CONFESS...
CHOMP!
...THAT IN FACT, I AM IN YOUR DEBT...
CHEW CHEW!
...FOR SAVING ME FROM THE CRUEL FATE OF MY OWN COOKING!
CRUNCH!
I'M SURE I CAN THINK OF A WAY TO...
MUNCH MUNCH!
...UH, BRANAN...
CHOMP!
GNAW GNAW!

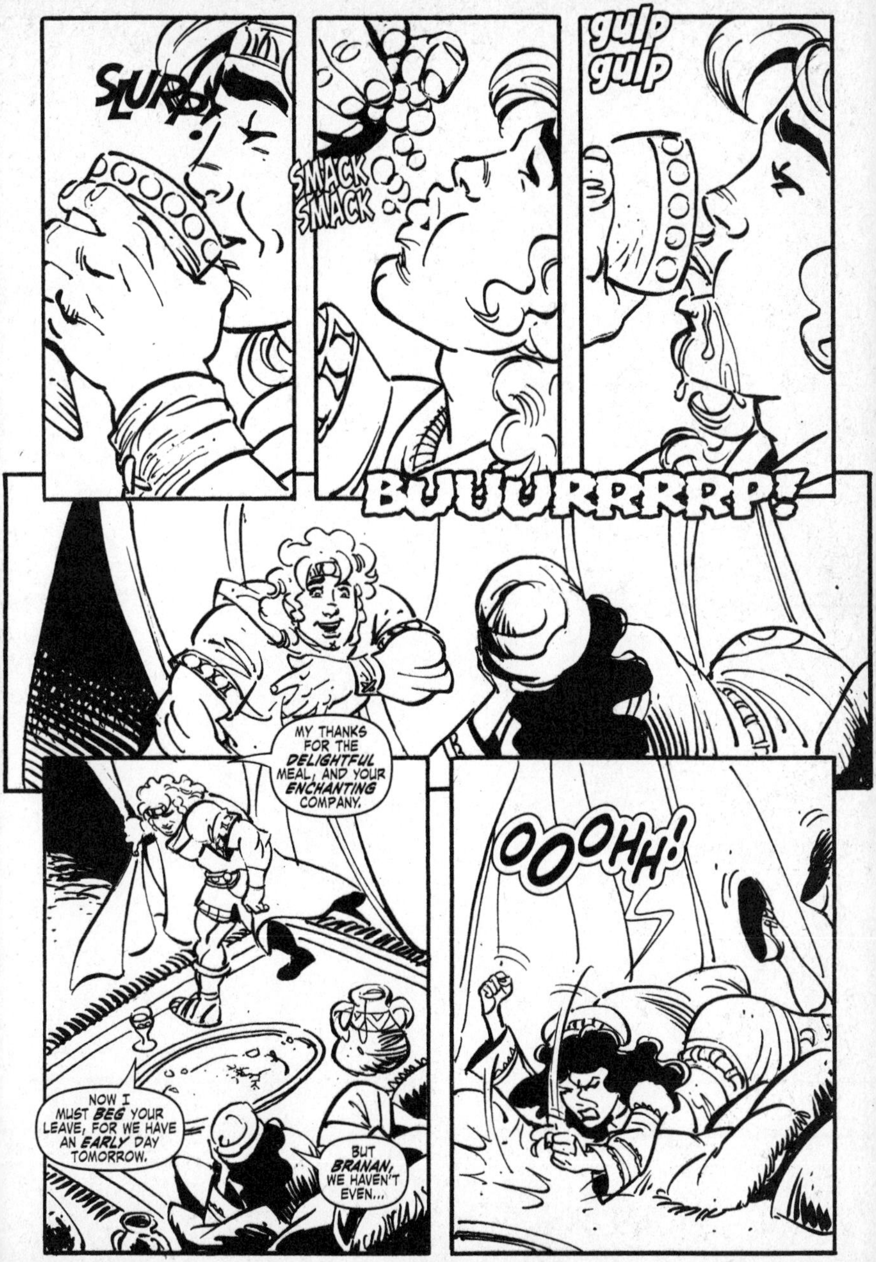
SLURRP!
SMACK SMACK
gulp gulp
BUUURRRRP!
MY THANKS FOR THE DELIGHTFUL MEAL, AND YOUR ENCHANTING COMPANY.
NOW I MUST BEG YOUR LEAVE, FOR WE HAVE AN EARLY DAY TOMORROW.
BUT BRANAN, WE HAVEN'T EVEN...
OOOOHH!

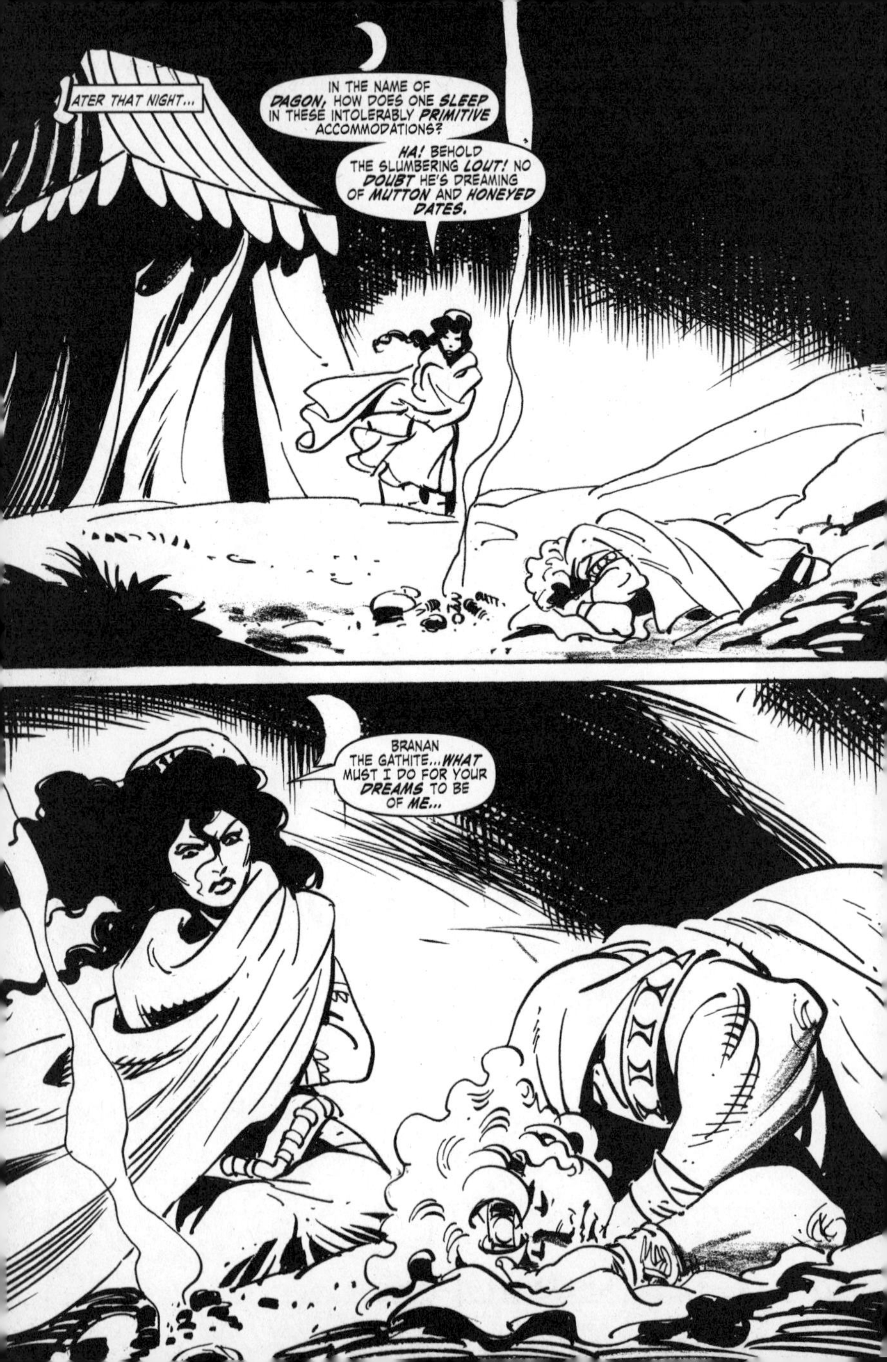
ATER THAT NIGHT...
IN THE NAME OF DAGON, HOW DOES ONE SLEEP IN THESE INTOLERABLY PRIMITIVE ACCOMMODATIONS?
HA! BEHOLD THE SLUMBERING LOUT! NO DOUBT HE'S DREAMING OF MUTTON AND HONEYED DATES.
BRANAN THE GATHITE...WHAT MUST I DO FOR YOUR DREAMS TO BE OF ME...

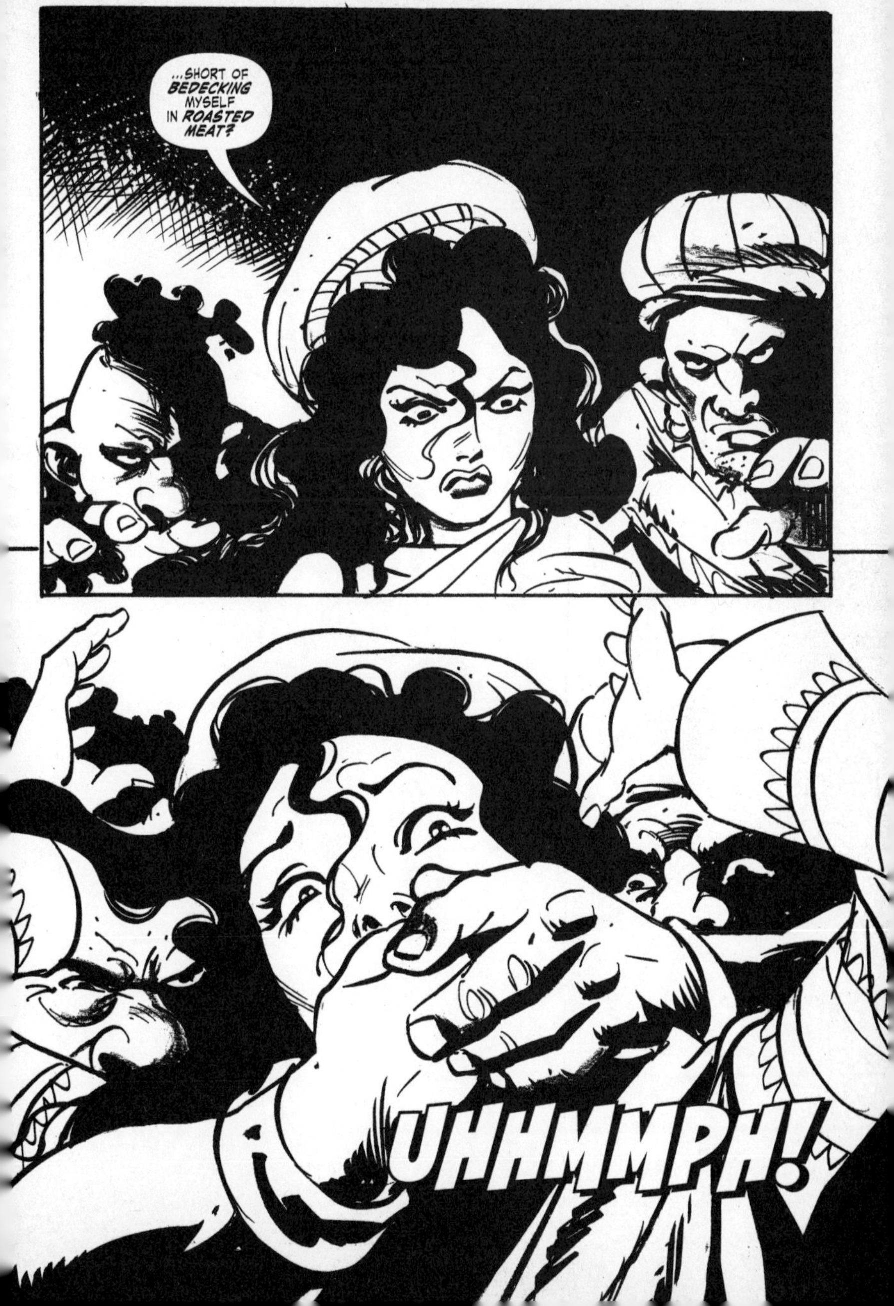
...SHORT OF BEDECKING MYSELF IN ROASTED MEAT?
UHHMMMPH!

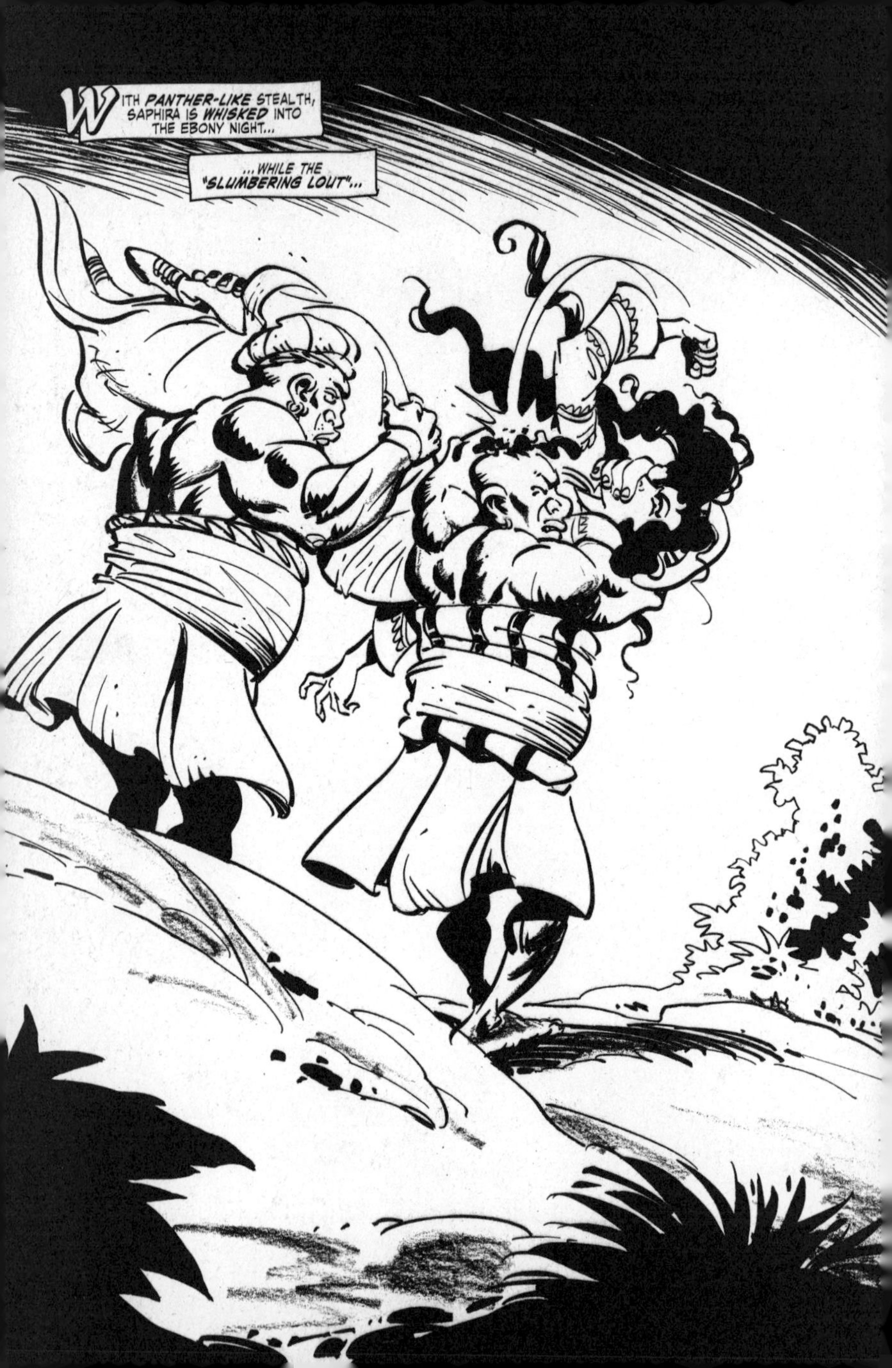
WITH PANTHER-LIKE STEALTH, SAPHIRA IS WHISKED INTO THE EBONY NIGHT...
...WHILE THE "SLUMBERING LOUT"...

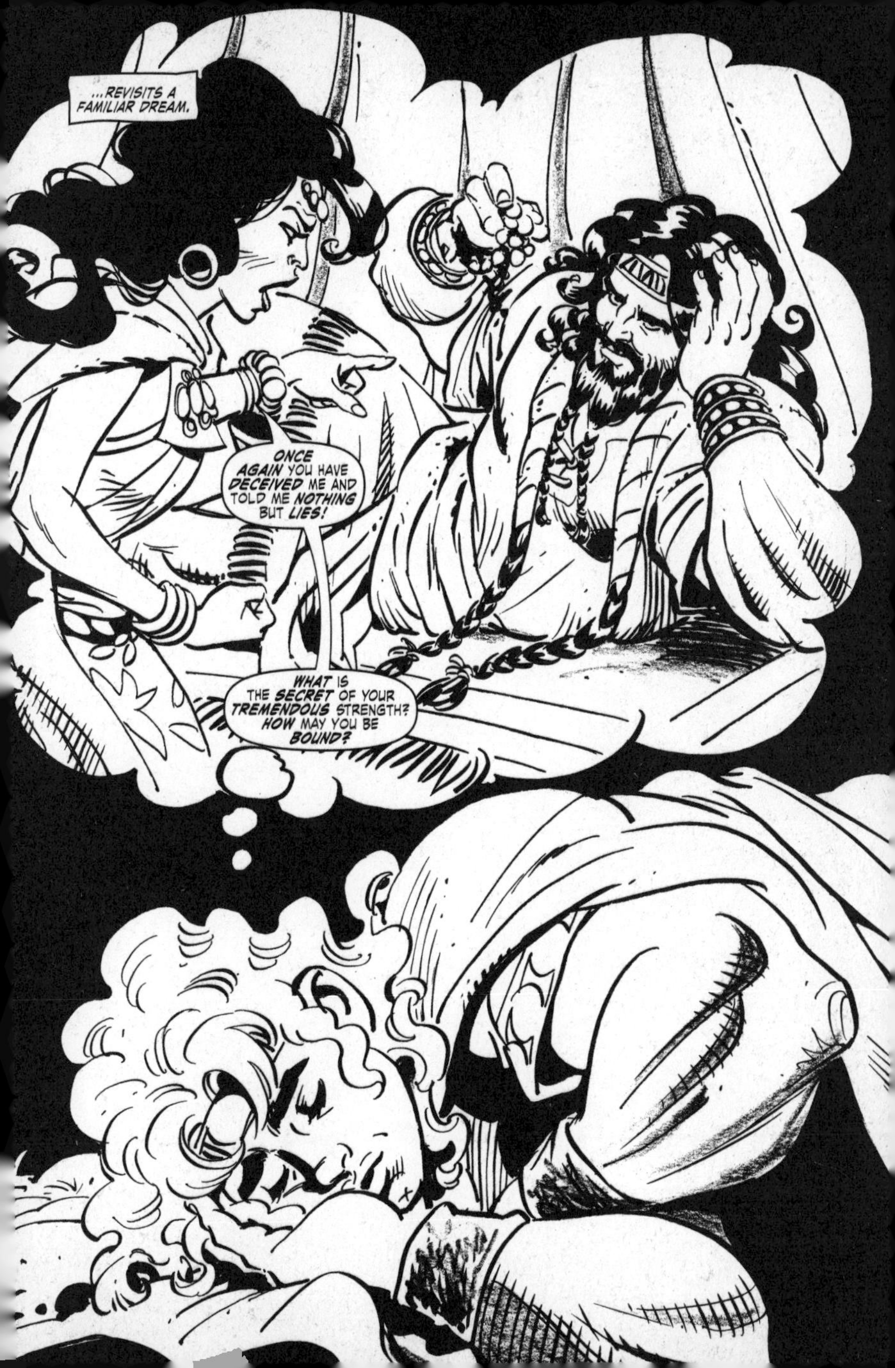
...REVISITS A FAMILIAR DREAM.
ONCE AGAIN YOU HAVE DECEIVED ME AND TOLD ME NOTHING BUT LIES!
WHAT IS THE SECRET OF YOUR TREMENDOUS STRENGTH? HOW MAY YOU BE BOUND?

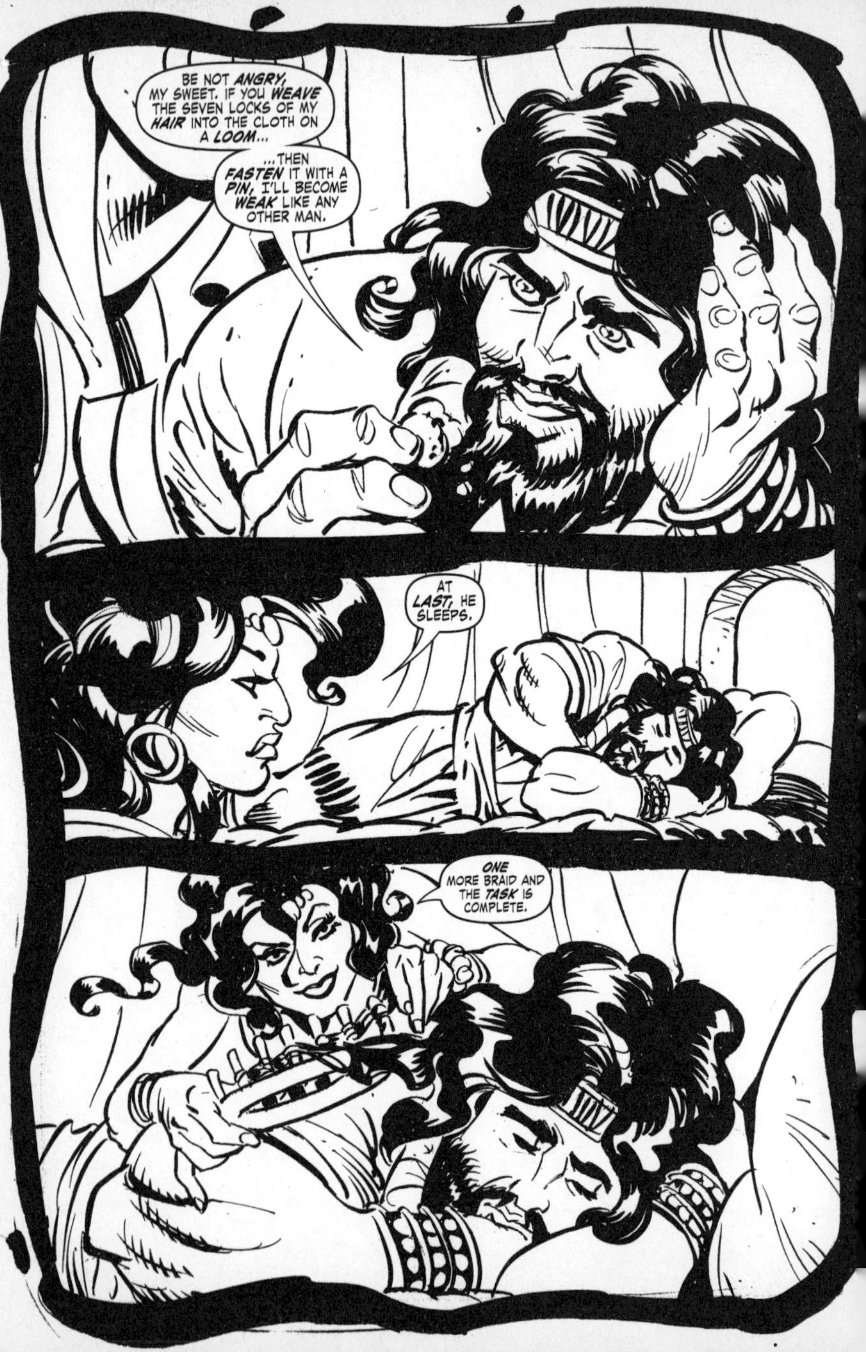
BE NOT ANGRY, MY SWEET. IF YOU WEAVE THE SEVEN LOCKS OF MY HAIR INTO THE CLOTH ON A LOOM...
...THEN FASTEN IT WITH A PIN, I'LL BECOME WEAK LIKE ANY OTHER MAN.
AT LAST, HE SLEEPS.
ONE MORE BRAID AND THE TASK IS COMPLETE.

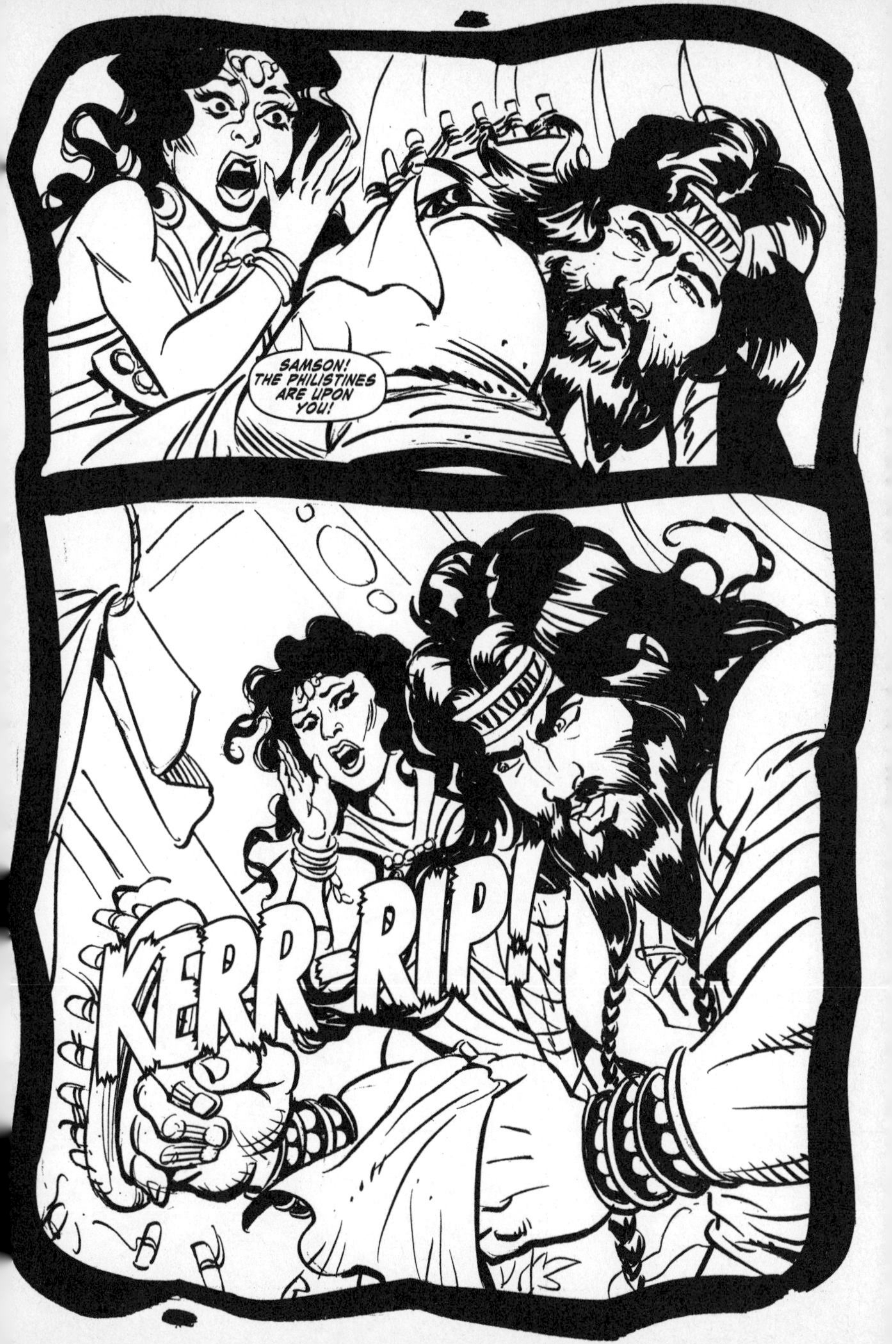
SAMSON! THE PHILISTINES ARE UPON YOU!
KERR-RIP!

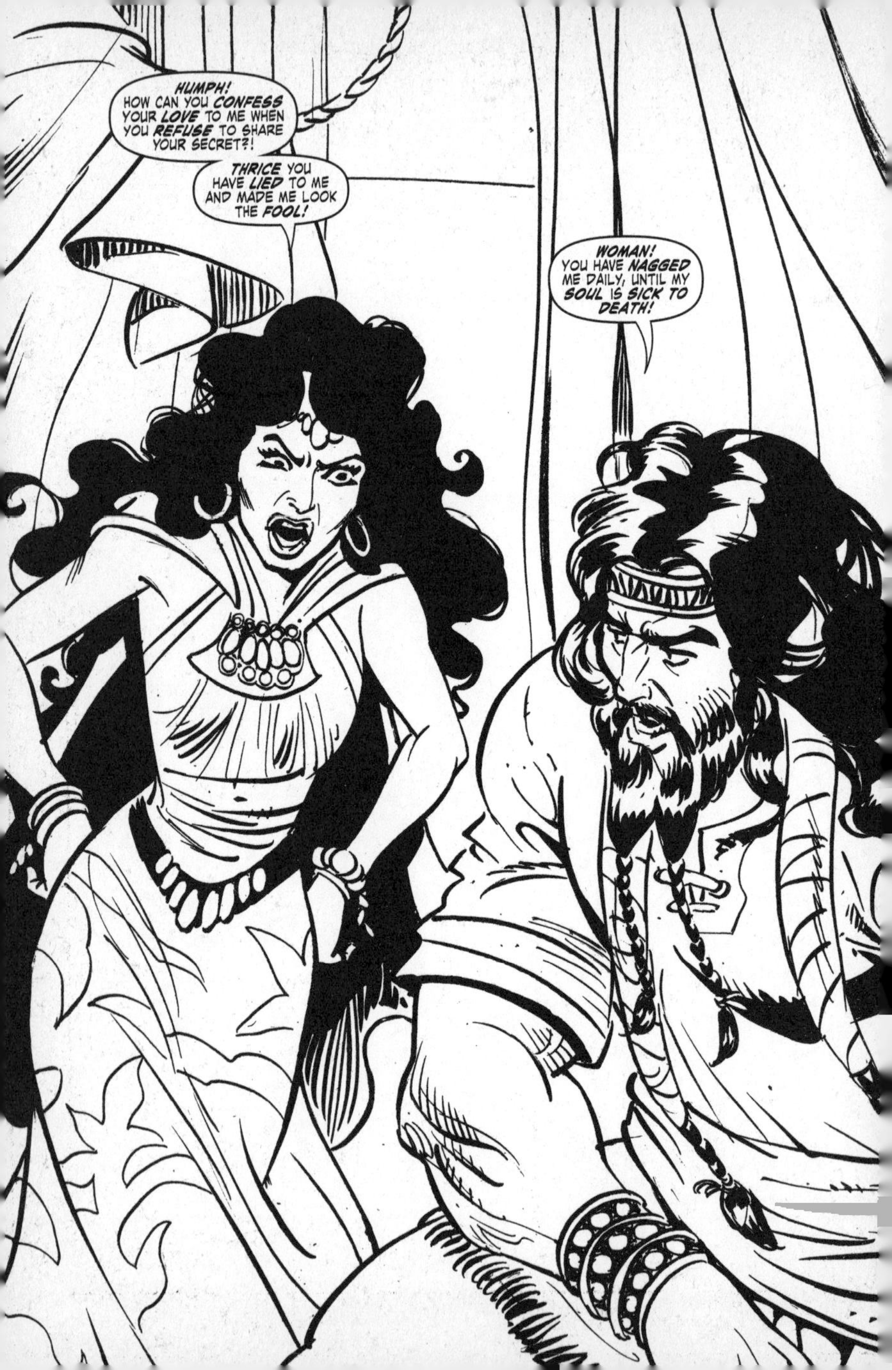
HUMPH! HOW CAN YOU CONFESS YOUR LOVE TO ME WHEN YOU REFUSE TO SHARE YOUR SECRET?!
THRICE YOU HAVE LIED TO ME AND MADE ME LOOK THE FOOL!
WOMAN! YOU HAVE NAGGED ME DAILY, UNTIL MY SOUL IS SICK TO DEATH!

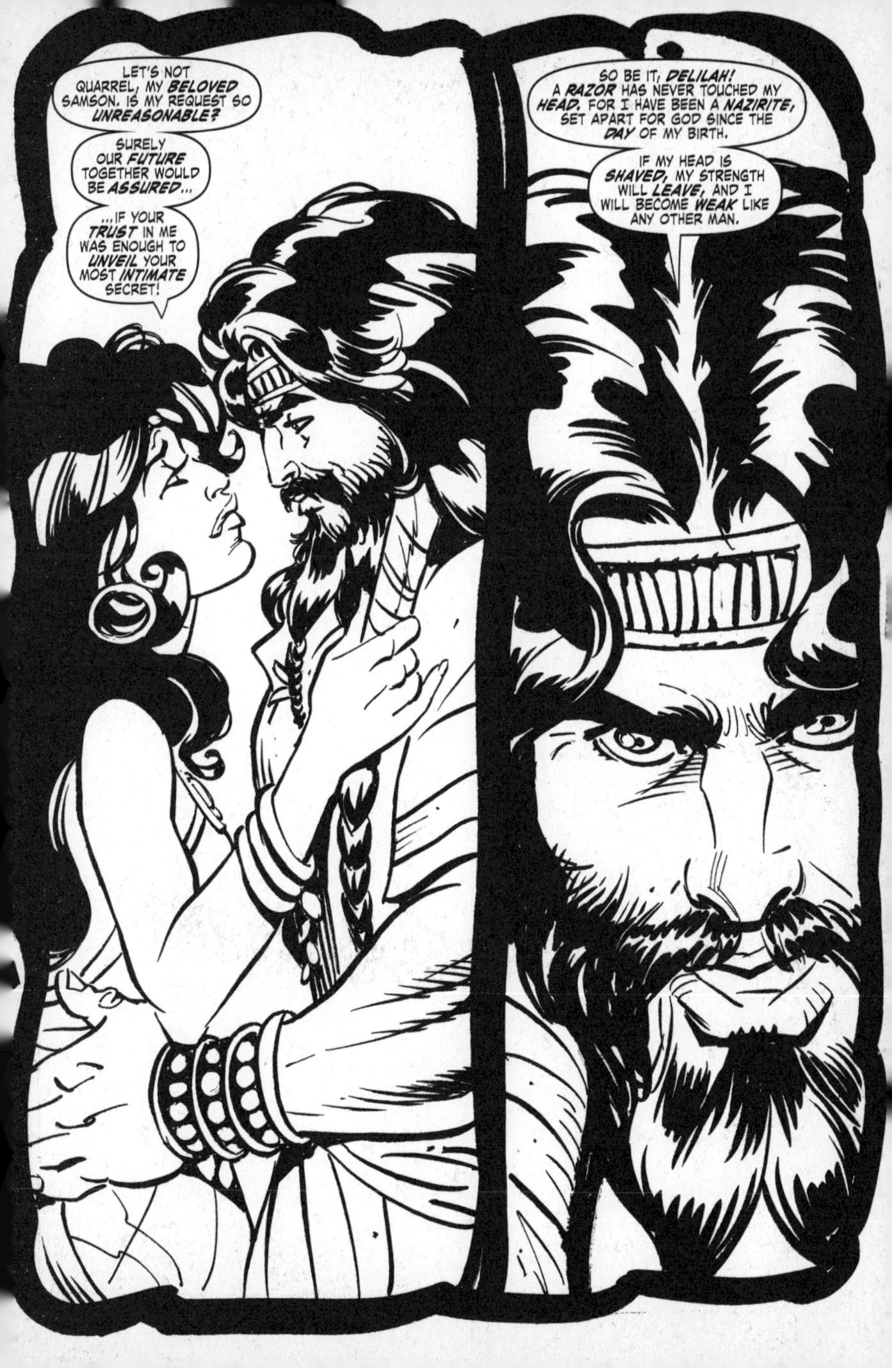
LET'S NOT QUARREL, MY BELOVED SAMSON. IS MY REQUEST SO UNREASONABLE?
SURELY OUR FUTURE TOGETHER WOULD BE ASSURED...
...IF YOUR TRUST IN ME WAS ENOUGH TO UNVEIL YOUR MOST INTIMATE SECRET!
SO BE IT, DELILAH! A RAZOR HAS NEVER TOUCHED MY HEAD, FOR I HAVE BEEN A NAZIRITE, SET APART FOR GOD SINCE THE DAY OF MY BIRTH.
IF MY HEAD IS SHAVED, MY STRENGTH WILL LEAVE, AND I WILL BECOME WEAK LIKE ANY OTHER MAN.

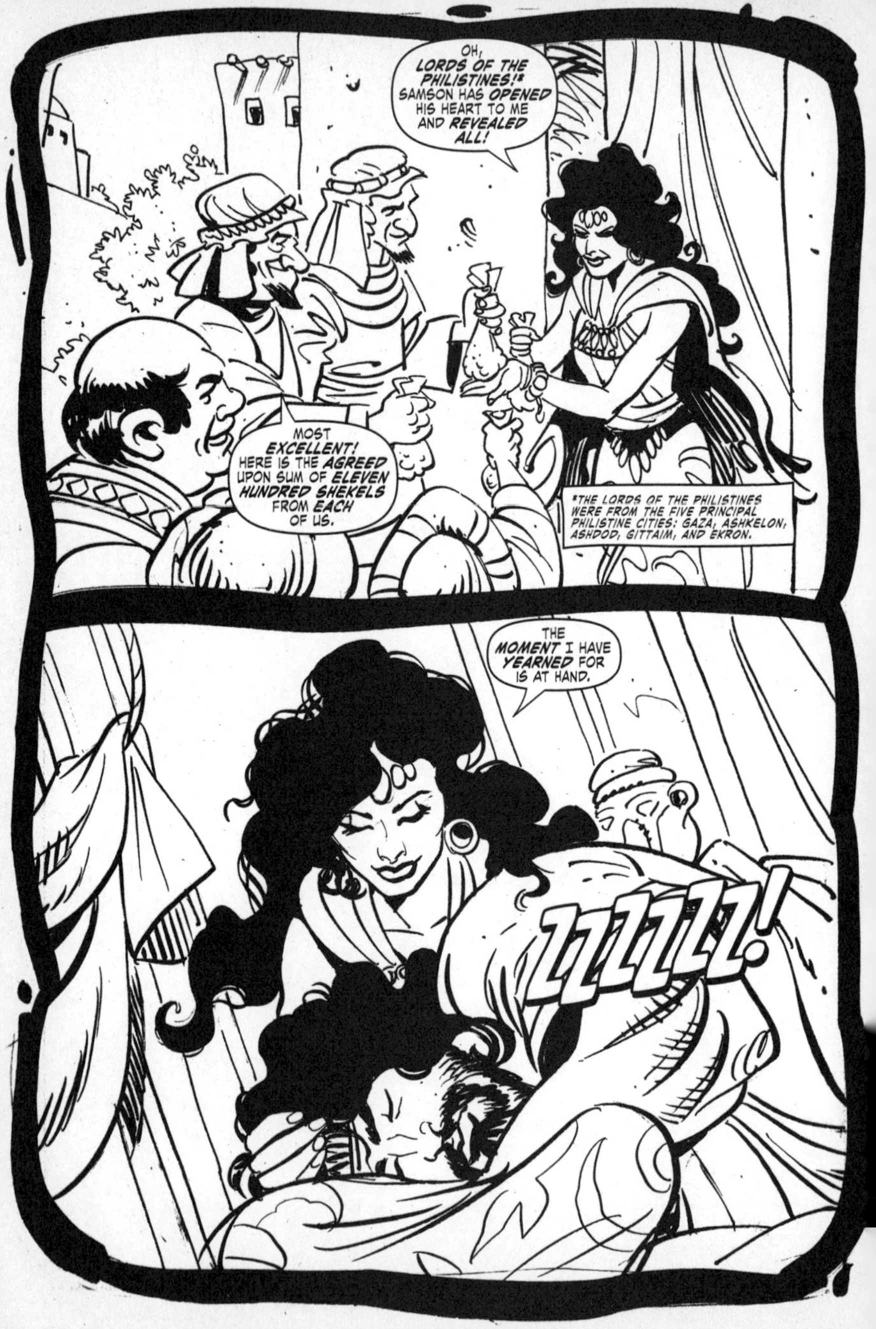
OH, LORDS OF THE PHILISTINES!* SAMSON HAS OPENED HIS HEART TO ME AND REVEALED ALL!
MOST EXCELLENT! HERE IS THE AGREED UPON SUM OF ELEVEN HUNDRED SHEKELS FROM EACH OF US.
*THE LORDS OF THE PHILISTINES WERE FROM THE FIVE PRINCIPAL PHILISTINE CITIES: GAZA, ASHKELON, ASHDOD, GITTAIM, AND EKRON.
THE MOMENT I HAVE YEARNED FOR IS AT HAND.
ZZZZZZ!

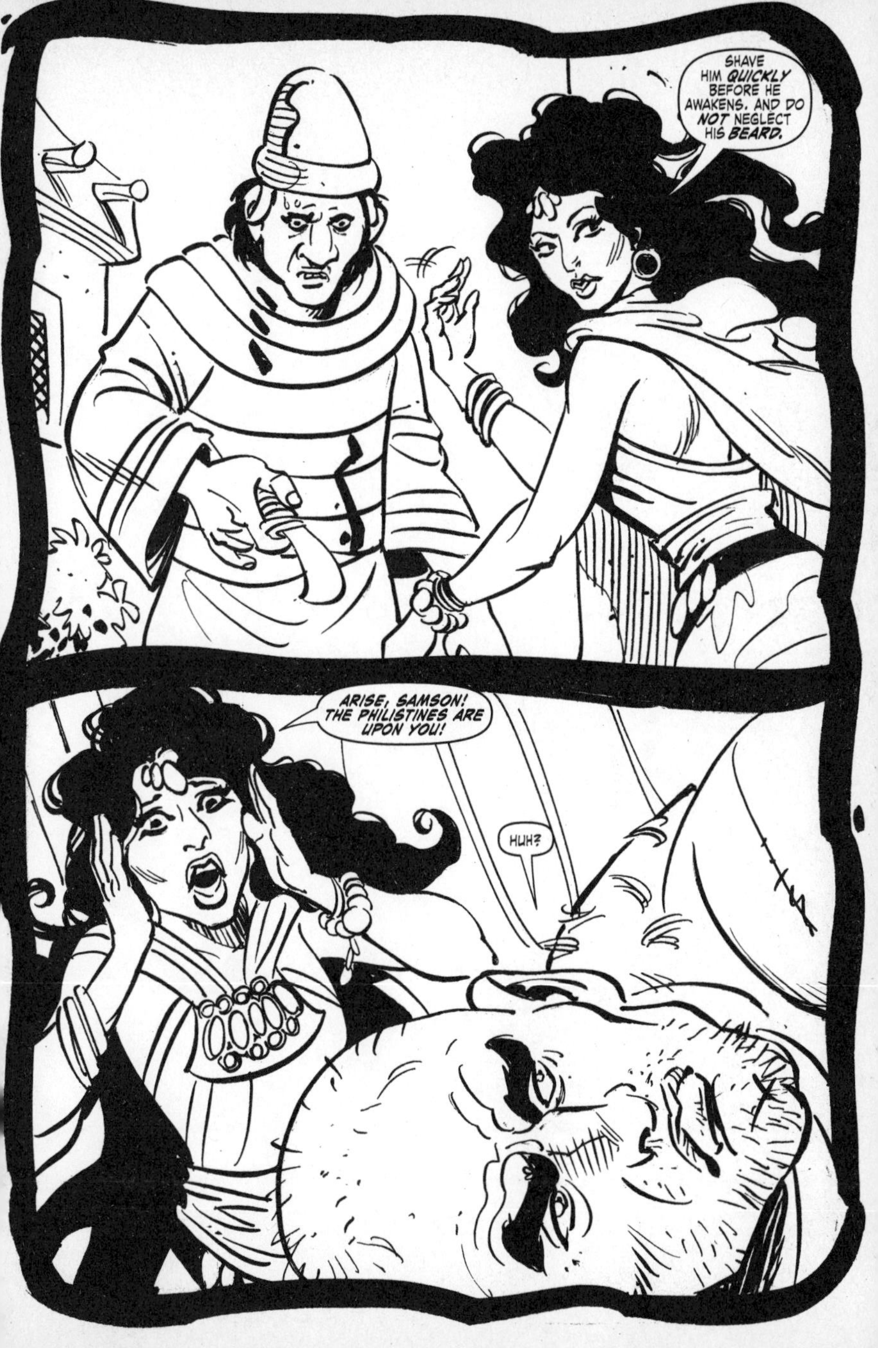
SHAVE HIM QUICKLY BEFORE HE AWAKENS. AND DO NOT NEGLECT HIS BEARD.
ARISE, SAMSON! THE PHILISTINES ARE UPON YOU!
HUH?

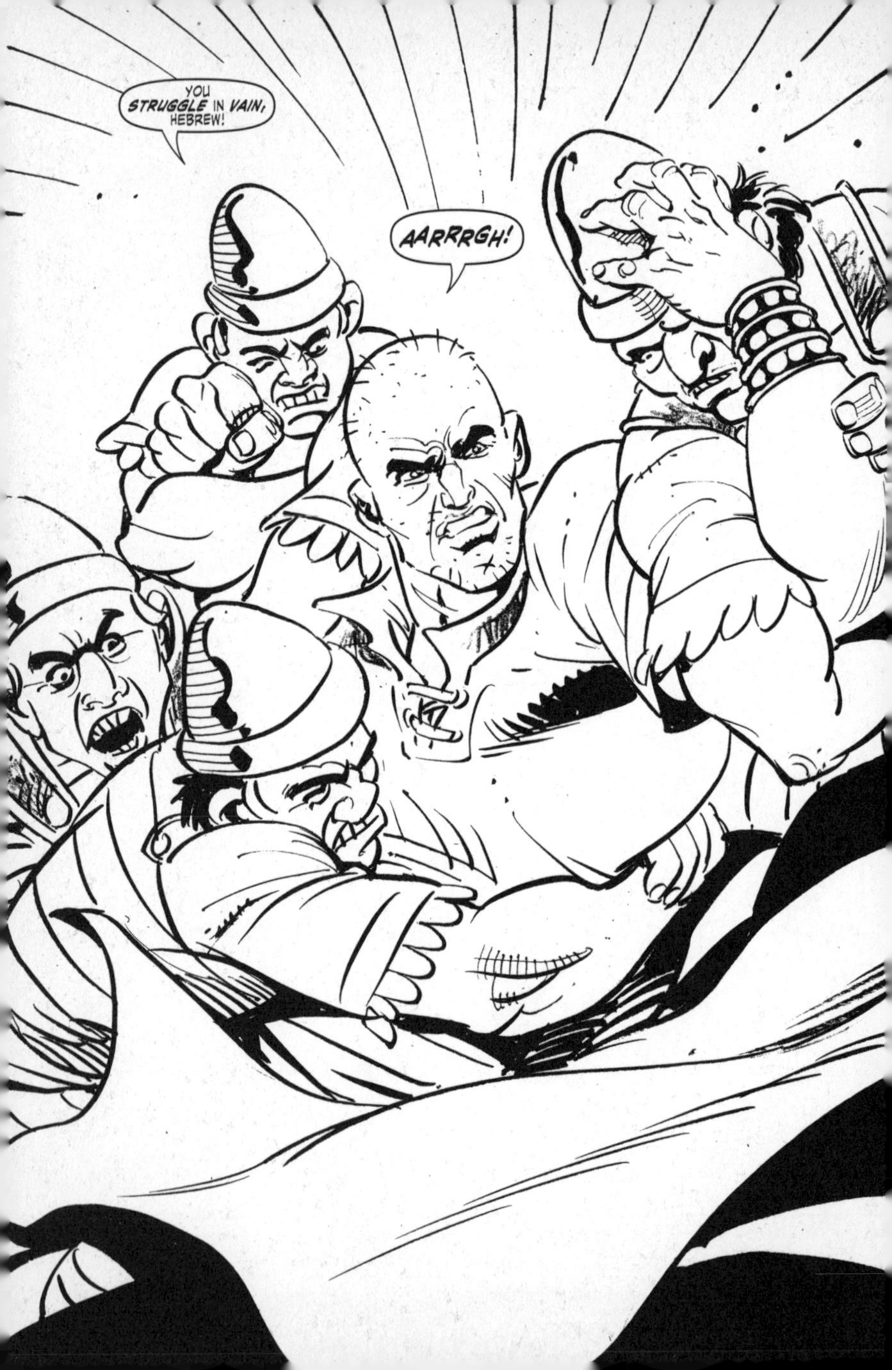
YOU STRUGGLE IN VAIN, HEBREW!
AARRRGH!

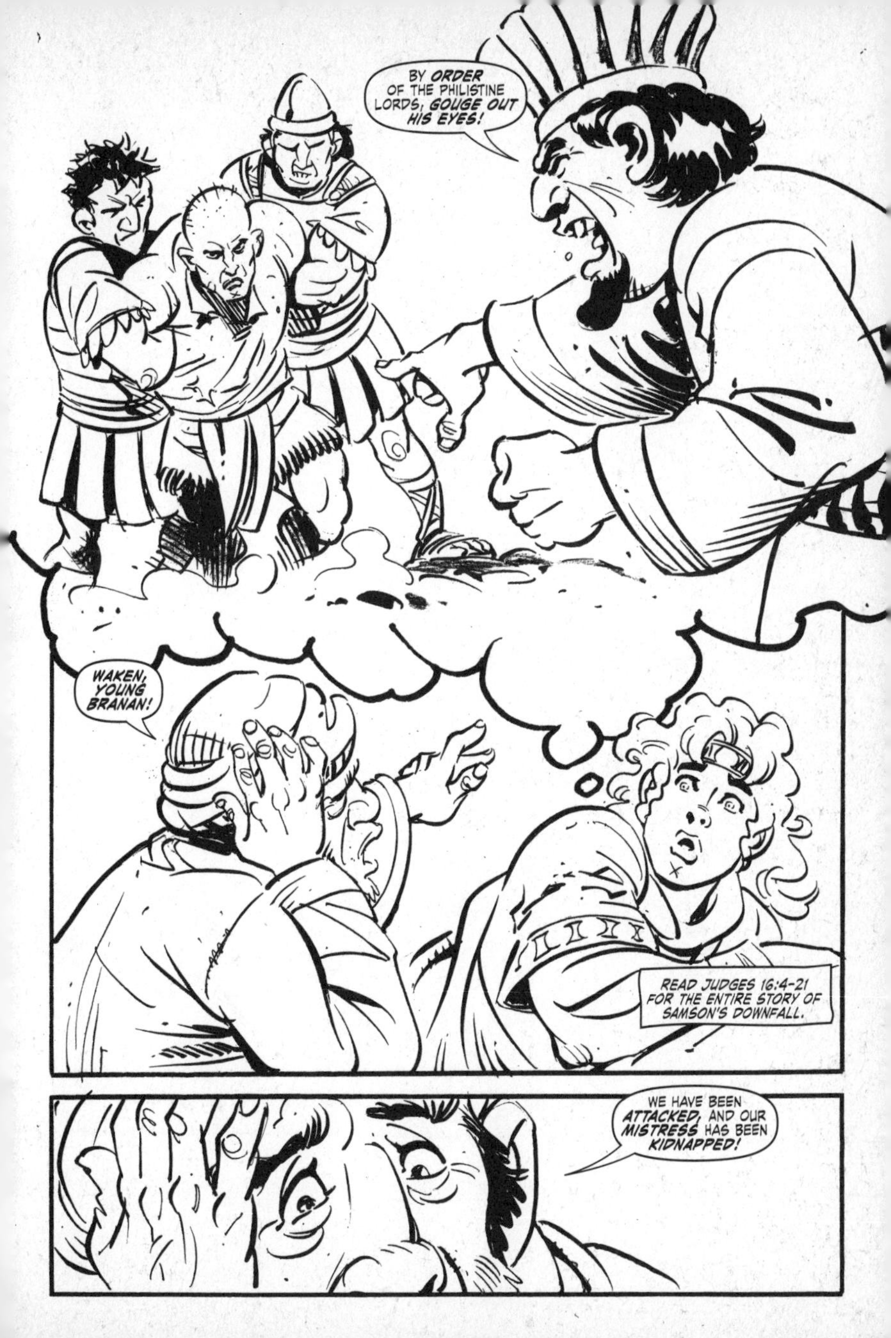
BY ORDER OF THE PHILISTINE LORDS, GOUGE OUT HIS EYES!
WAKEN, YOUNG BRANAN!
READ JUDGES 16:4-21 FOR THE ENTIRE STORY OF SAMSON'S DOWNFALL.
WE HAVE BEEN ATTACKED, AND OUR MISTRESS HAS BEEN KIDNAPPED!

CHAPTER 2
"SCROLLS OF FREEDOM"

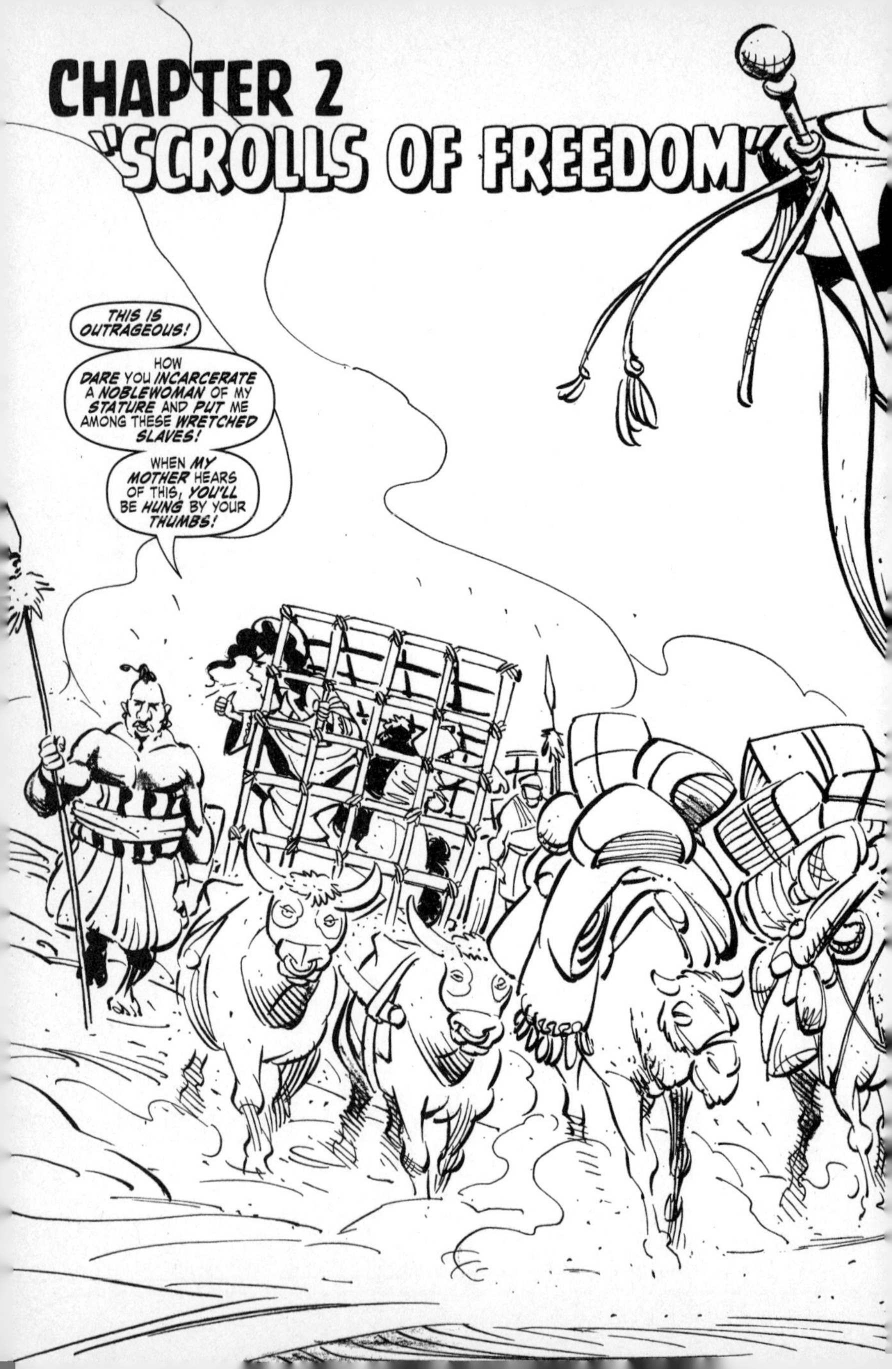
THIS IS OUTRAGEOUS!
HOW DARE YOU INCARCERATE A NOBLEWOMAN OF MY STATURE AND PUT ME AMONG THESE WRETCHED SLAVES!
WHEN MY MOTHER HEARS OF THIS, YOU'LL BE HUNG BY YOUR THUMBS!

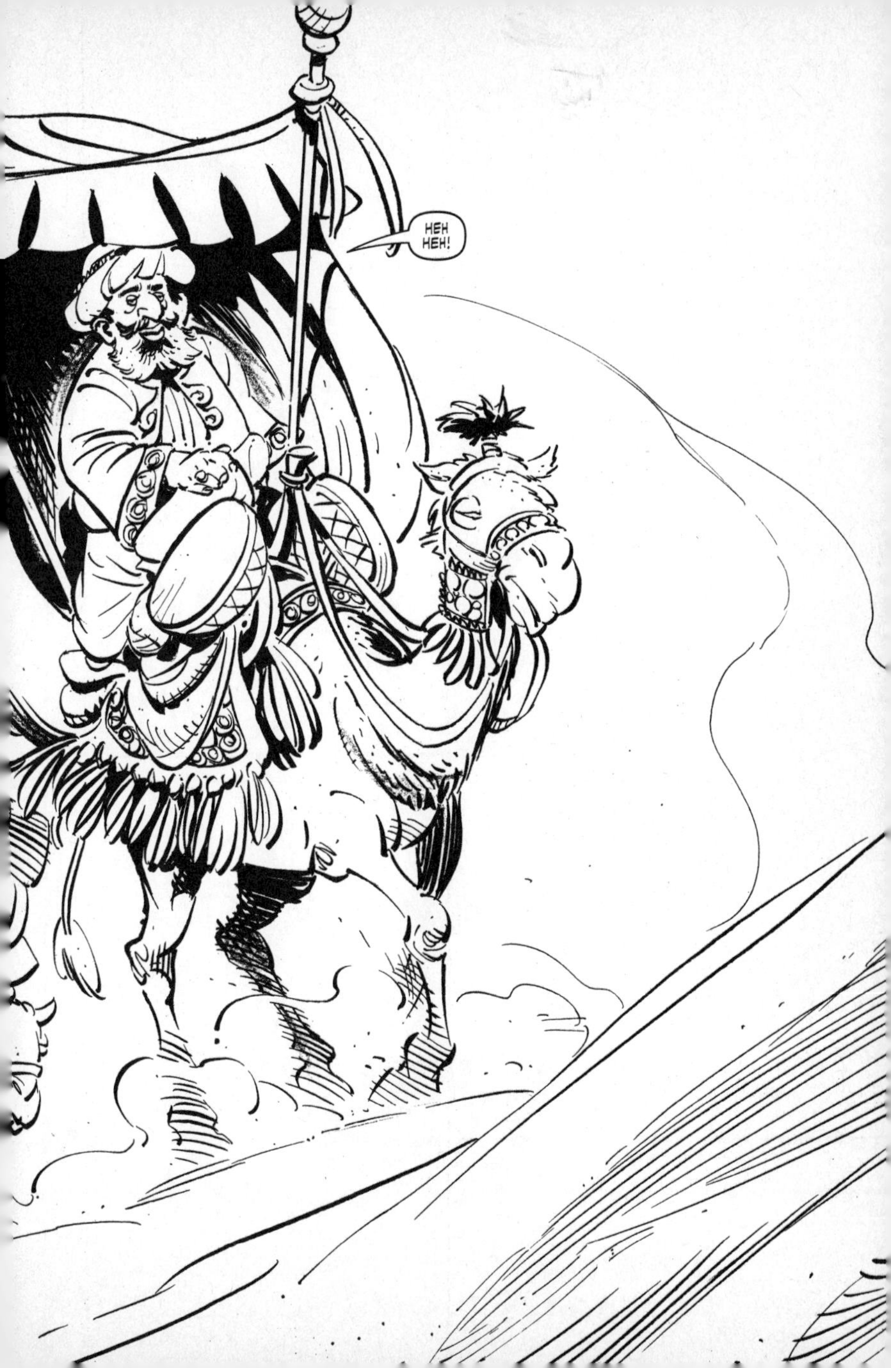
HEH HEH!

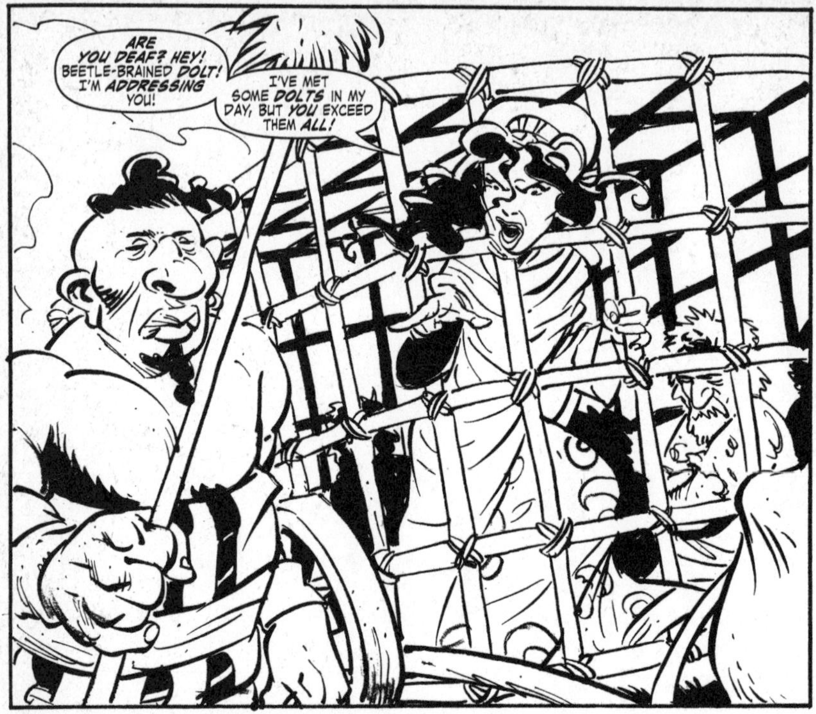
ARE YOU DEAF? HEY! BEETLE-BRAINED DOLT! I'M ADDRESSING YOU!
I'VE MET SOME DOLTS IN MY DAY, BUT YOU EXCEED THEM ALL!

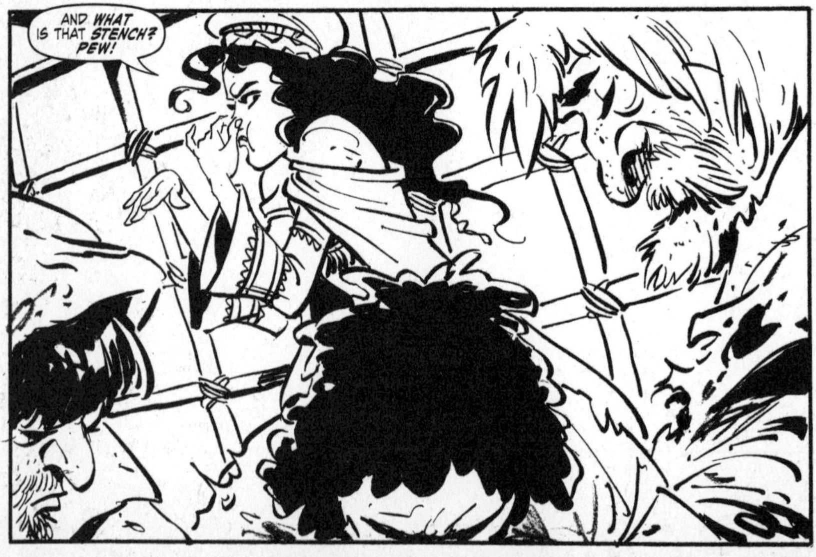
AND WHAT IS THAT STENCH? PEW!

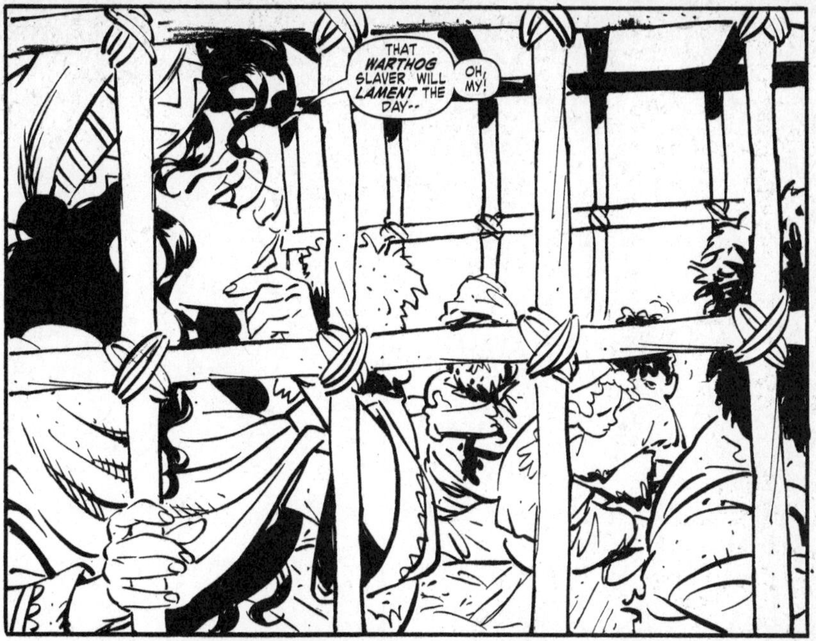
THAT WARTHOG SLAVER WILL LAMENT THE DAY--
OH, MY!

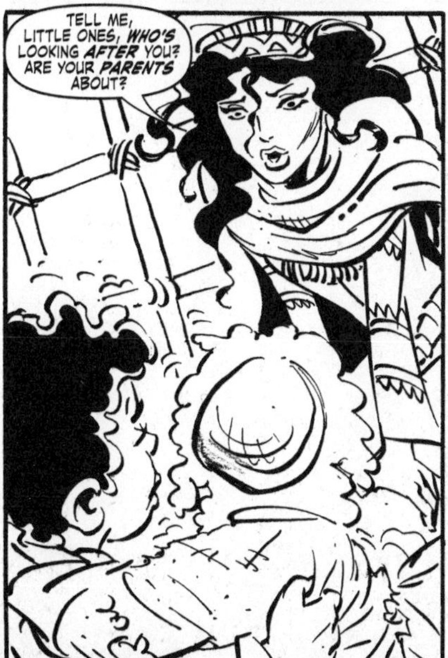
TELL ME, LITTLE ONES, WHO'S LOOKING AFTER YOU? ARE YOUR PARENTS ABOUT?

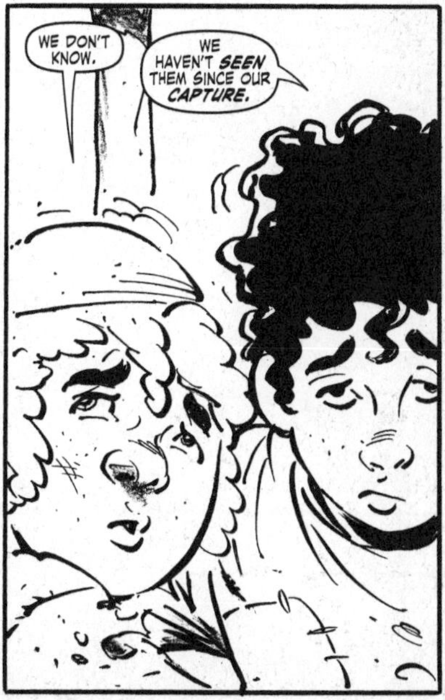
WE DON'T KNOW.
WE HAVEN'T SEEN THEM SINCE OUR CAPTURE.

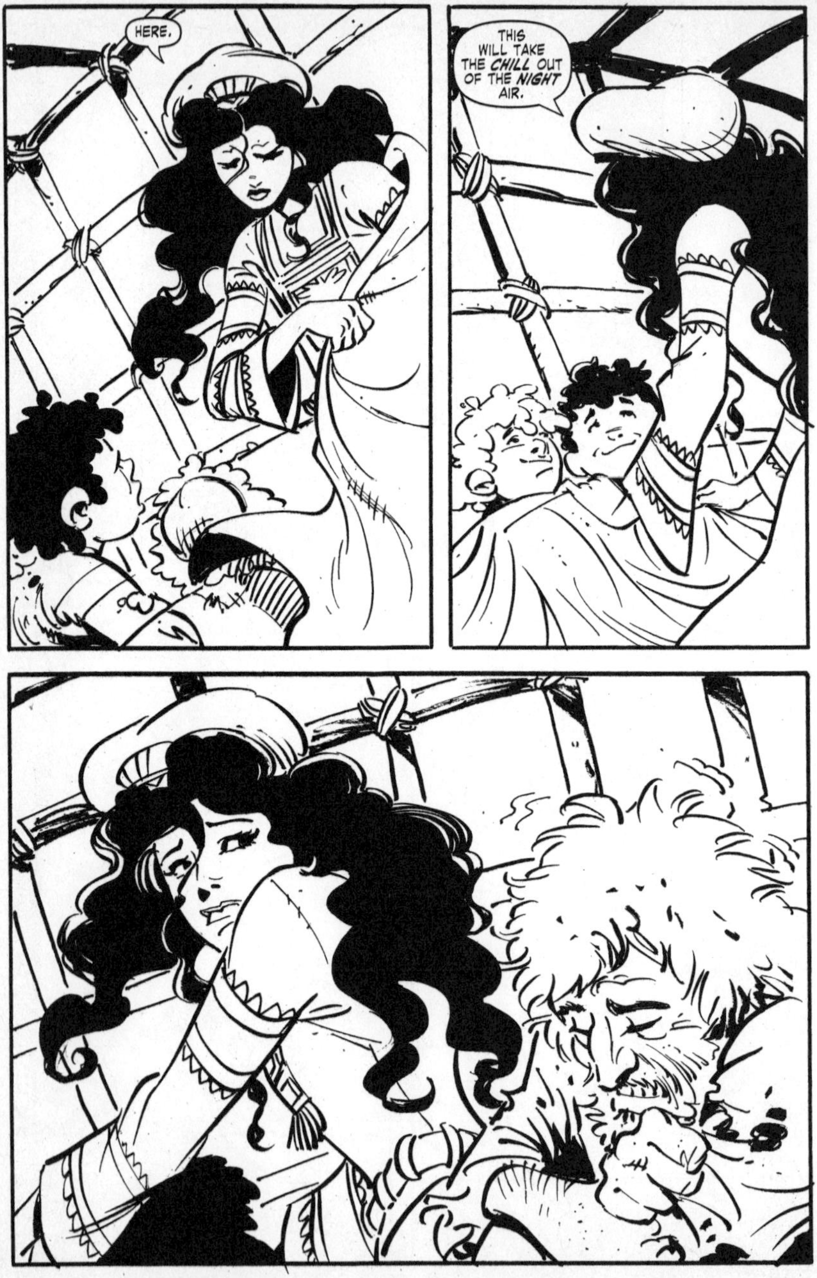
HERE.
THIS WILL TAKE THE CHILL OUT OF THE NIGHT AIR.

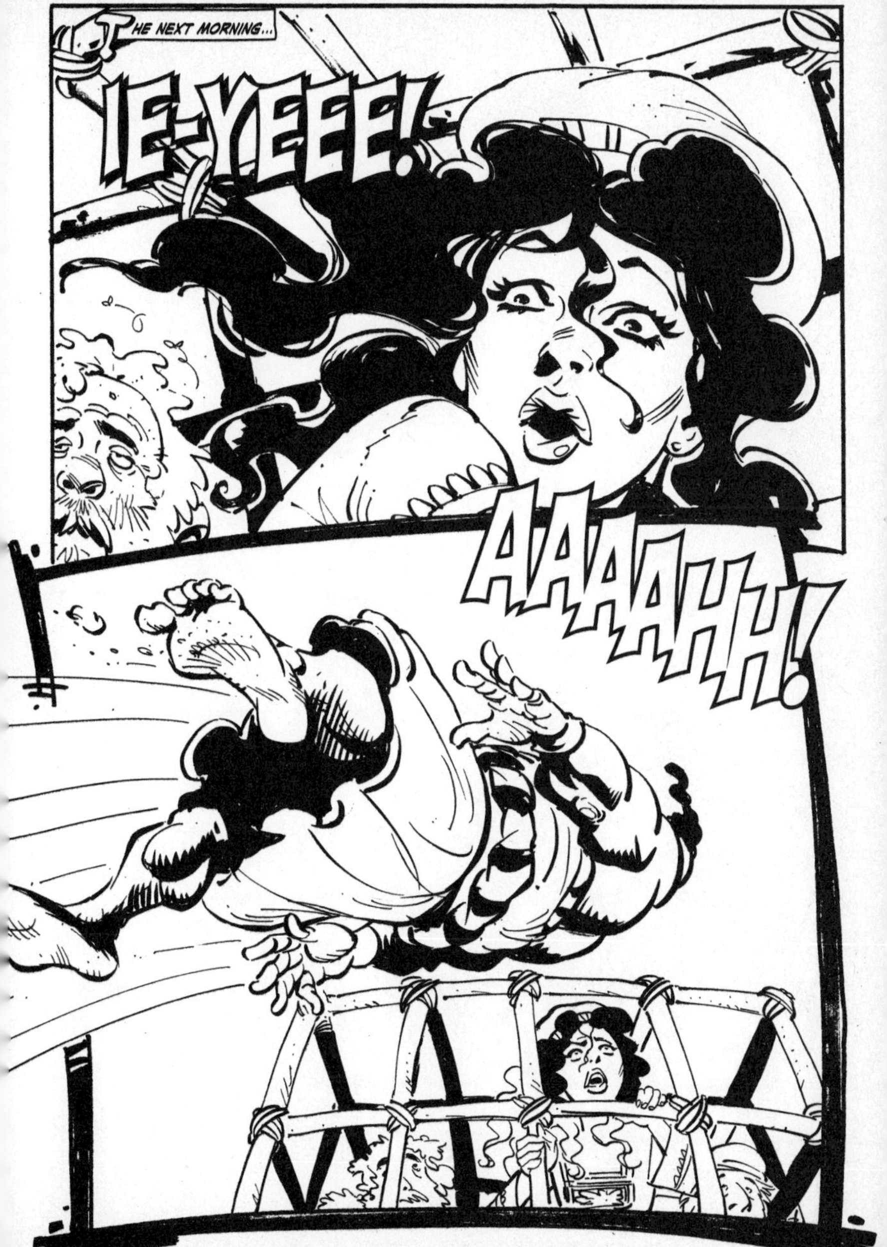
THE NEXT MORNING...
IE-YEEE!
AAAAHH!

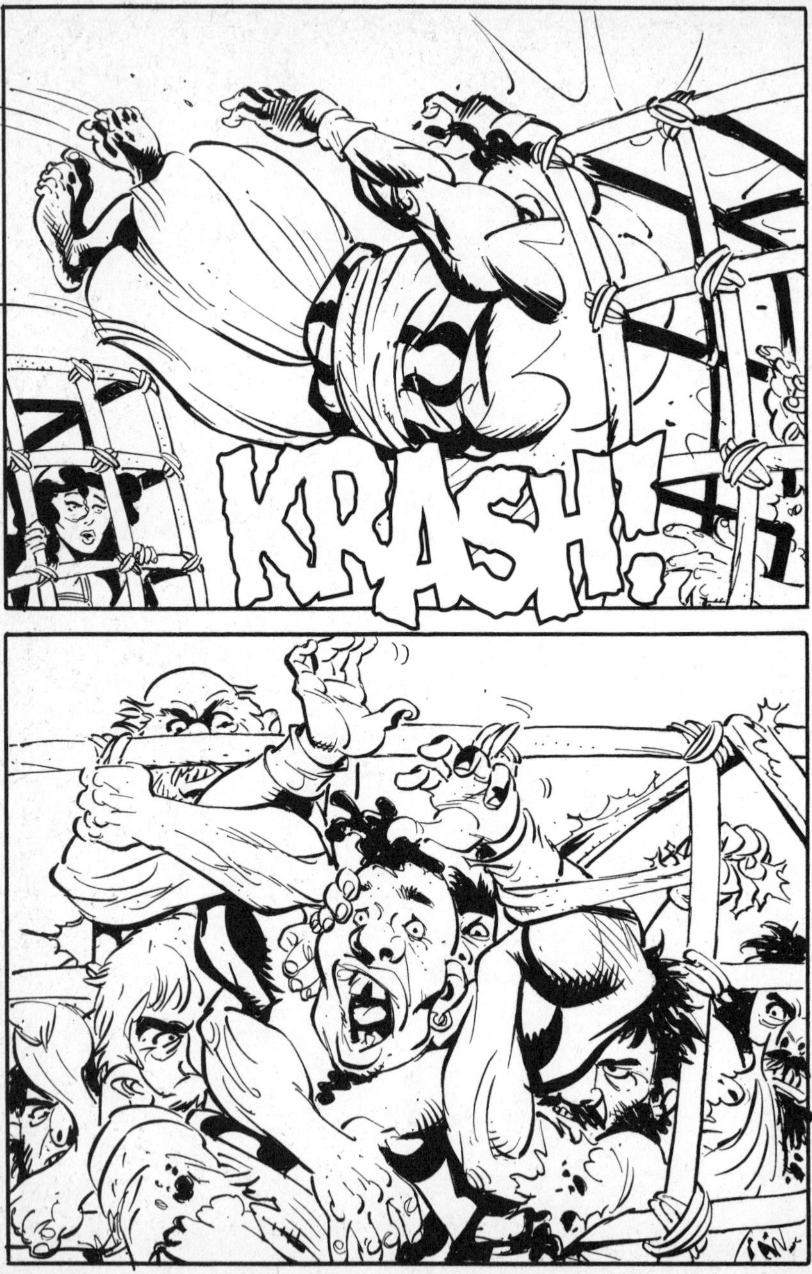
KRASH!

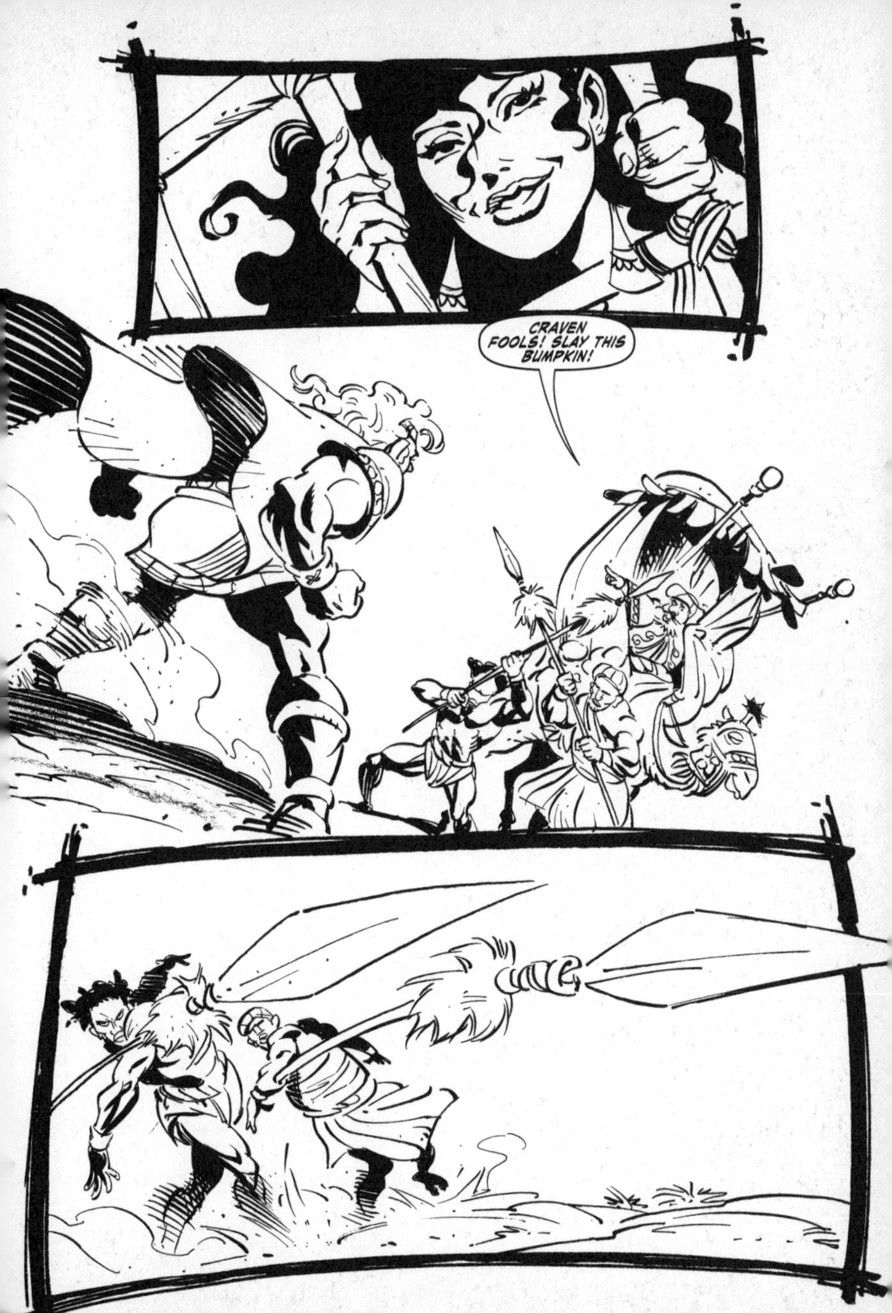
CRAVEN FOOLS! SLAY THIS BUMPKIN!

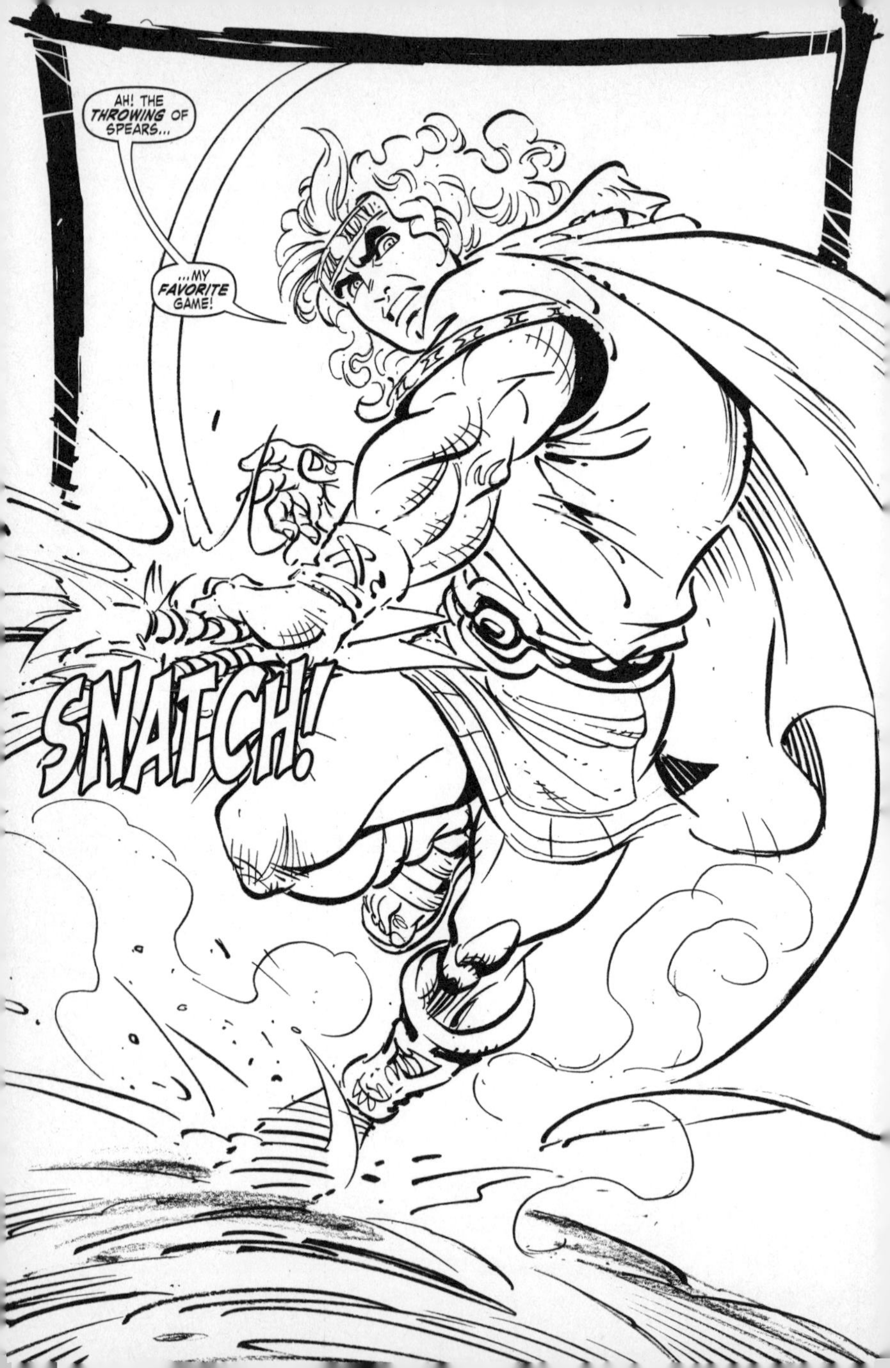
AH! THE *THROWING* OF SPEARS...
...MY *FAVORITE* GAME!
SNATCH!

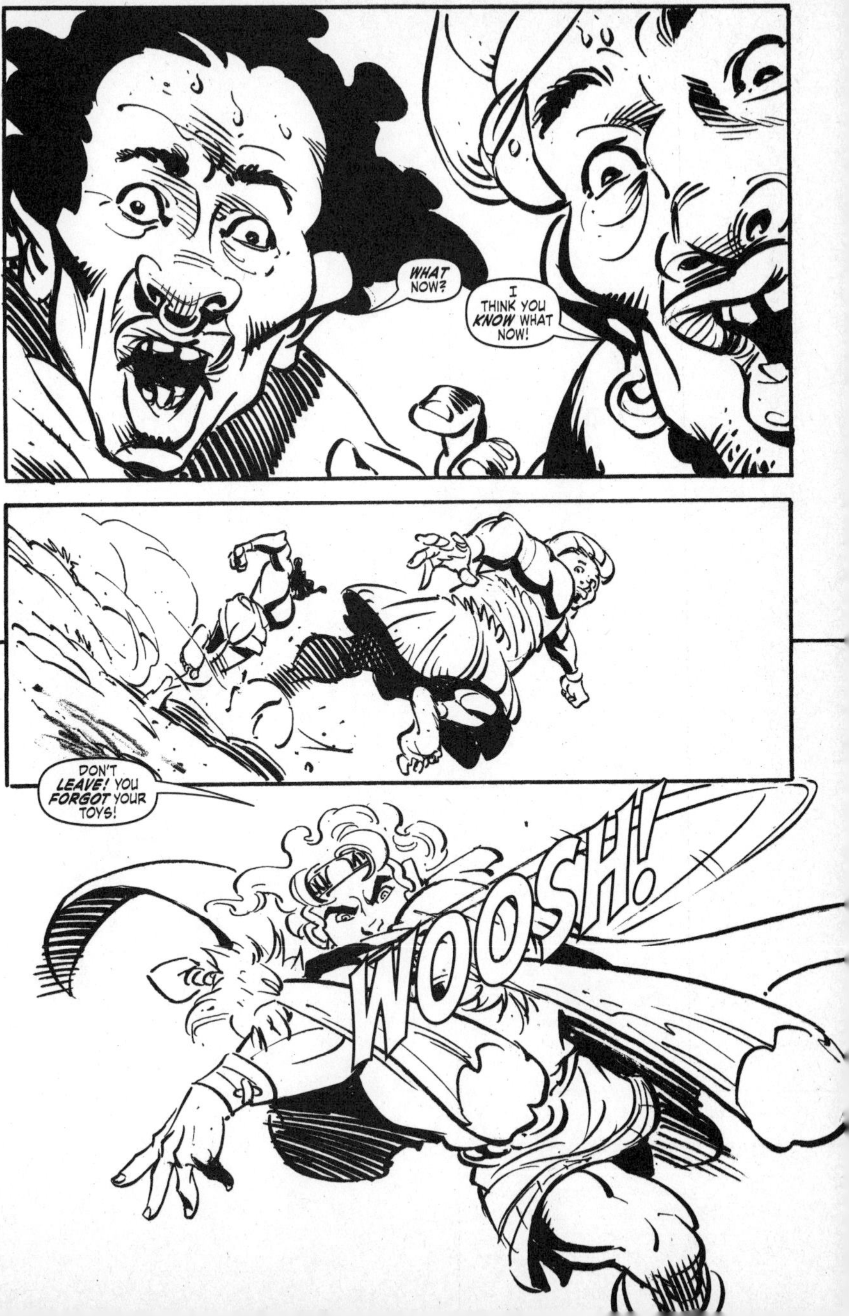

WHAT NOW?
I THINK YOU KNOW WHAT NOW!
DON'T LEAVE! YOU FORGOT YOUR TOYS!
WOOSH!

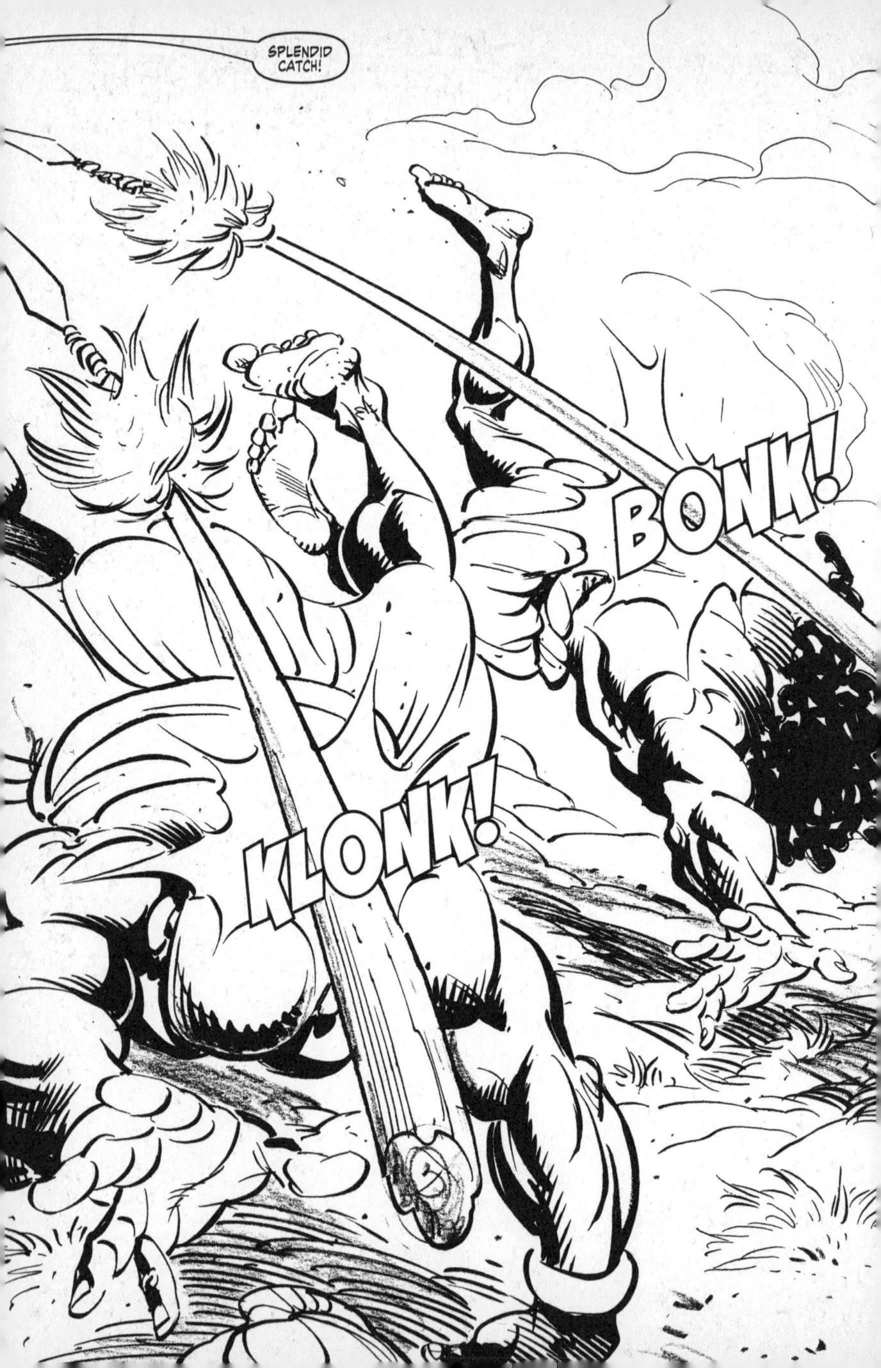
SPLENDID CATCH!
BONK!
KLONK!

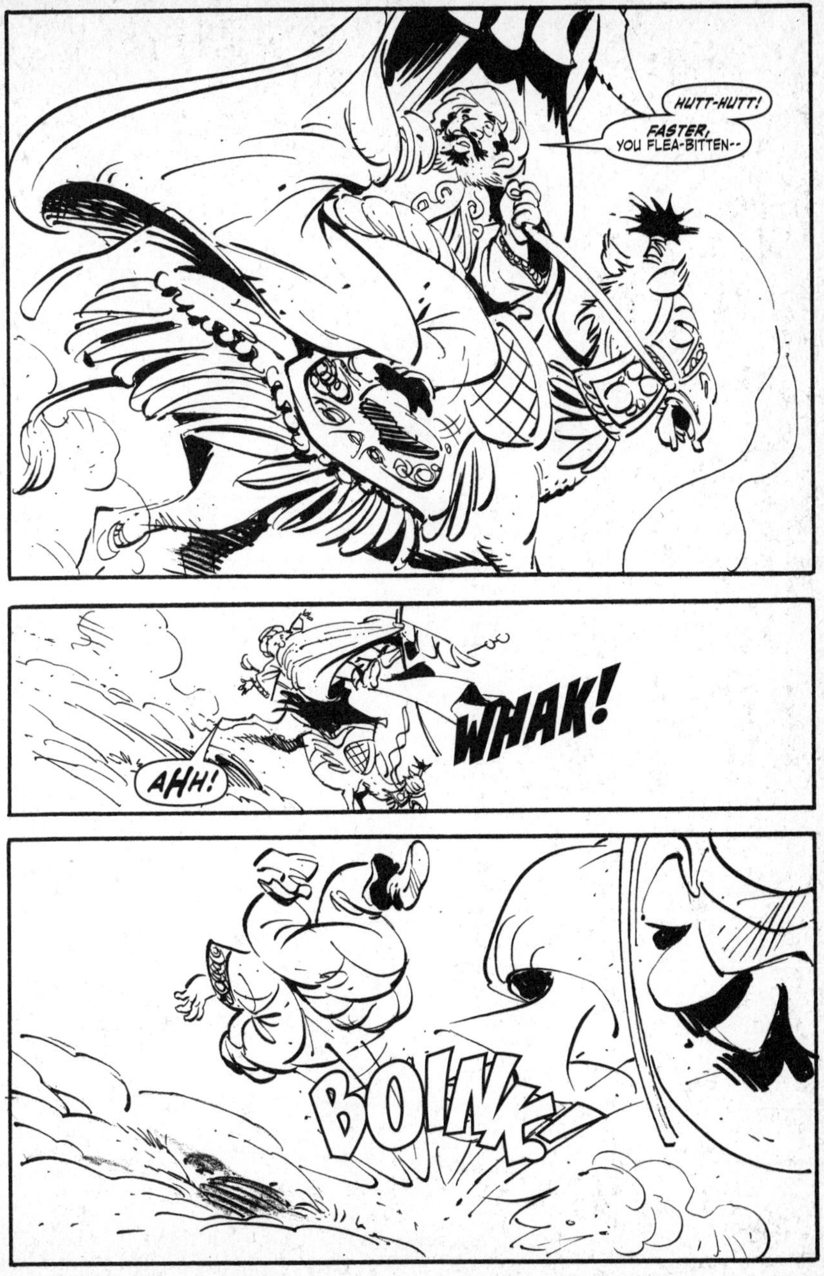
HUTT-HUTT!
FASTER, YOU FLEA-BITTEN--
WHAK!
AHH!
BOINK!

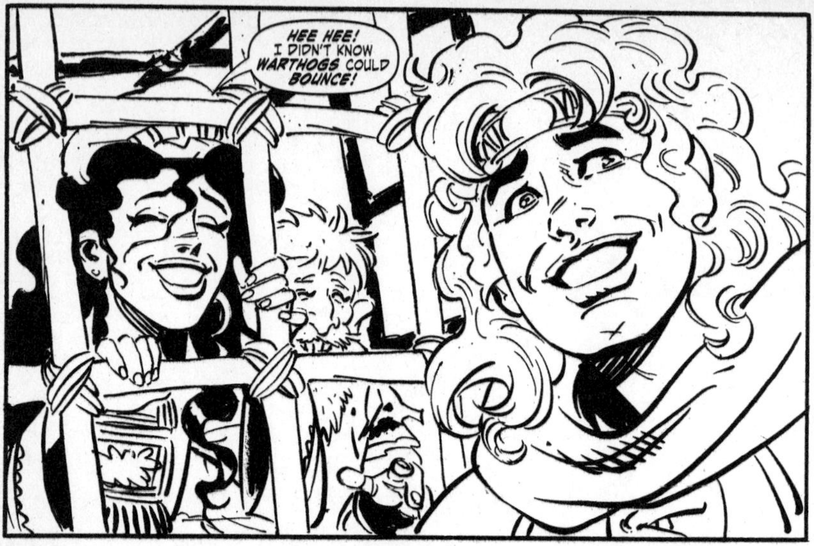
HEE HEE! I DIDN'T KNOW WARTHOGS COULD BOUNCE!

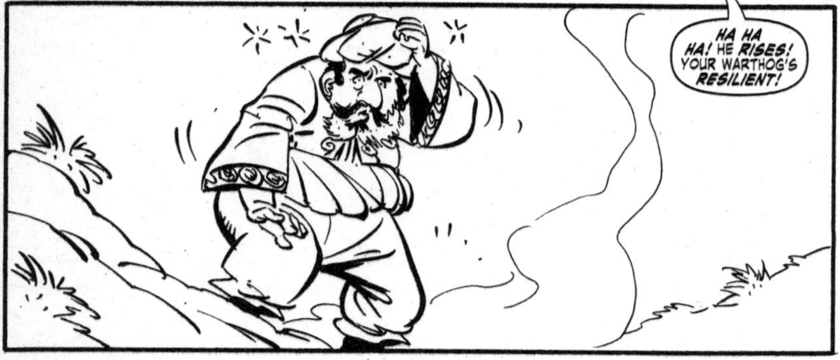
HA HA HA! HE RISES! YOUR WARTHOG'S RESILIENT!

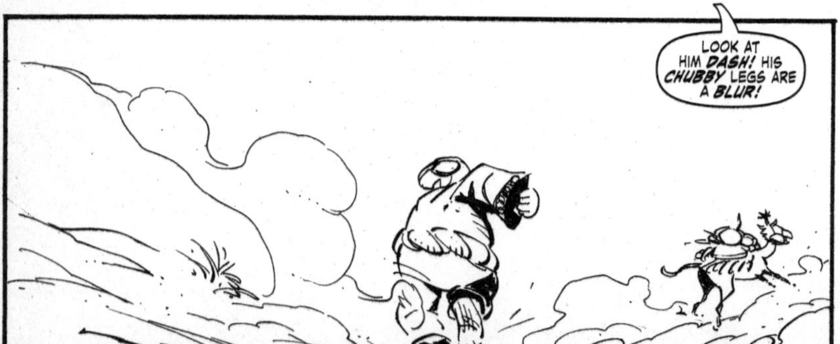
LOOK AT HIM DASH! HIS CHUBBY LEGS ARE A BLUR!

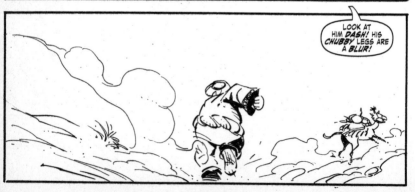

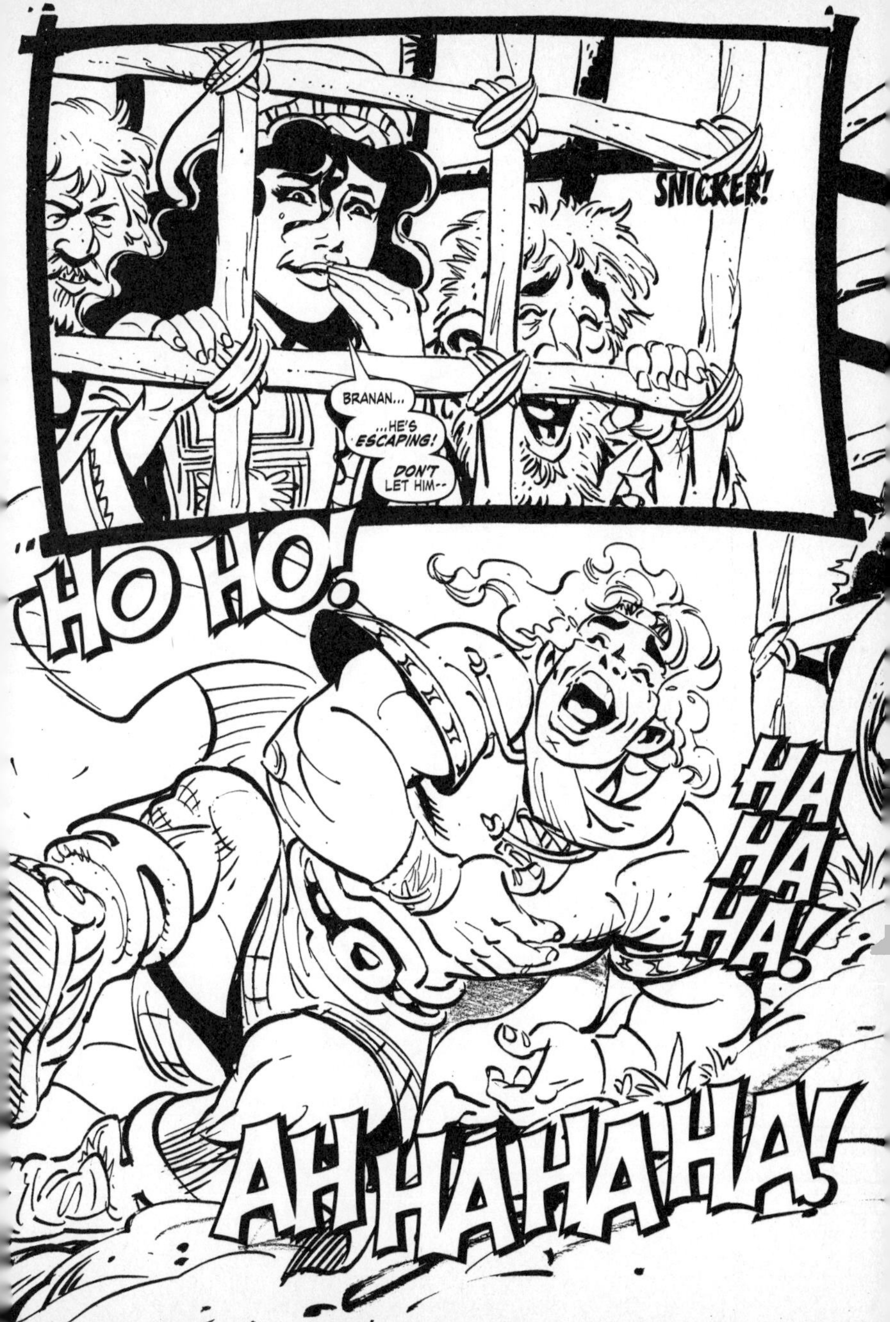
SNICKER!
BRANAN...
...HE'S ESCAPING!
DON'T LET HIM--
...HO HO!
HA HA HA HA!
AH HAHAHAHA!

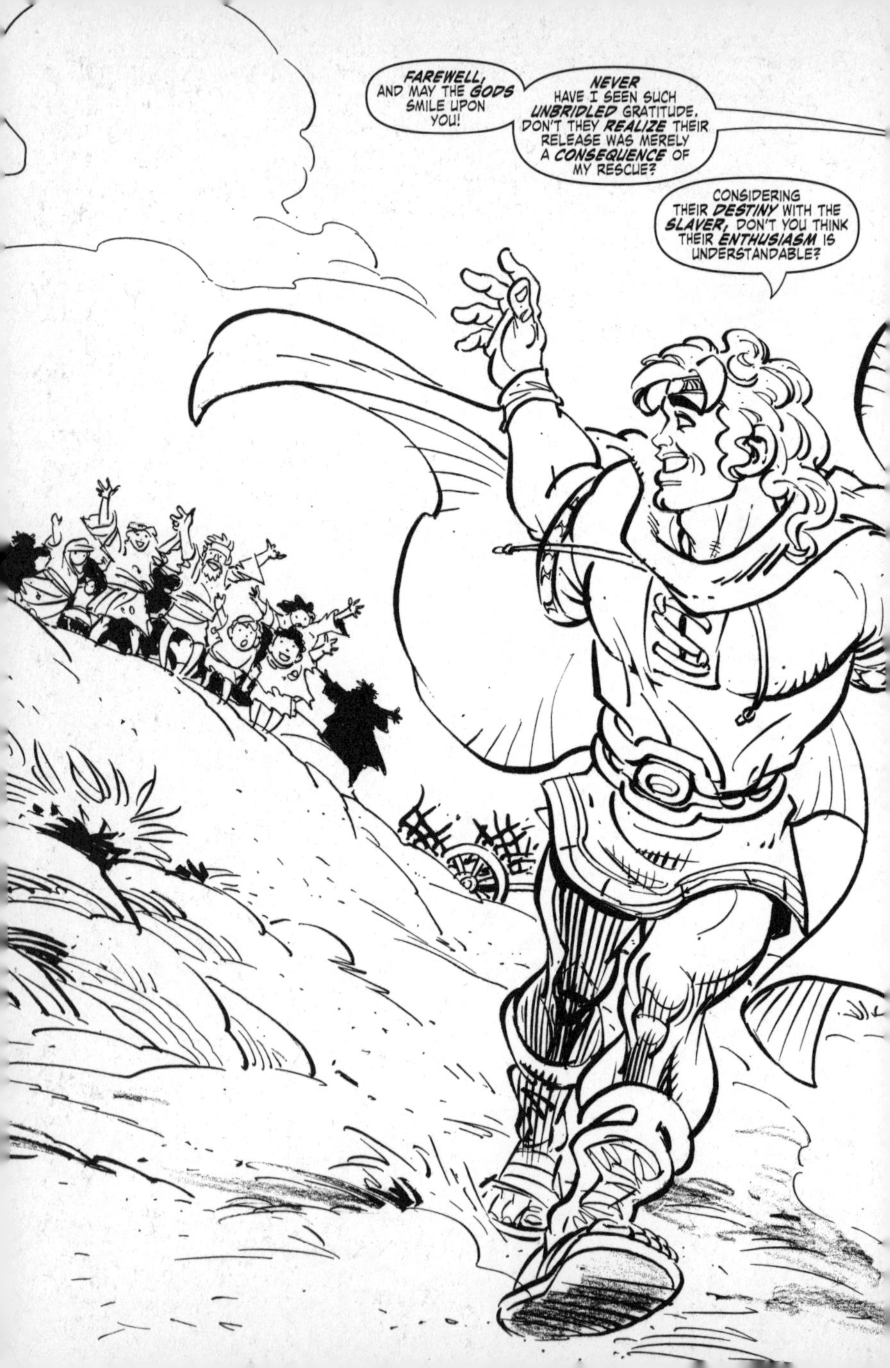
FAREWELL, AND MAY THE GODS SMILE UPON YOU!
NEVER HAVE I SEEN SUCH UNBRIDLED GRATITUDE. DON'T THEY REALIZE THEIR RELEASE WAS MERELY A CONSEQUENCE OF MY RESCUE?
CONSIDERING THEIR DESTINY WITH THE SLAVER, DON'T YOU THINK THEIR ENTHUSIASM IS UNDERSTANDABLE?

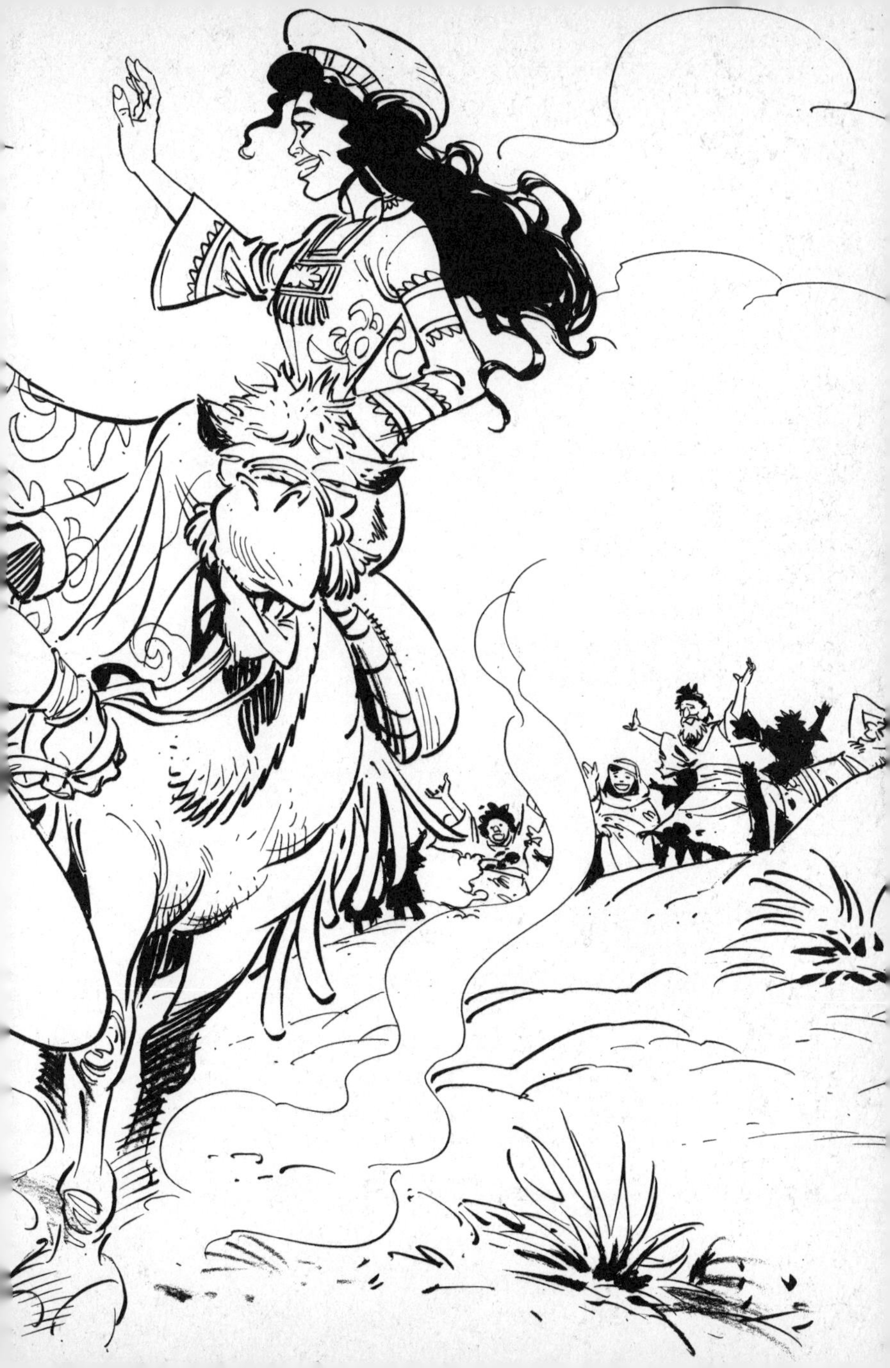

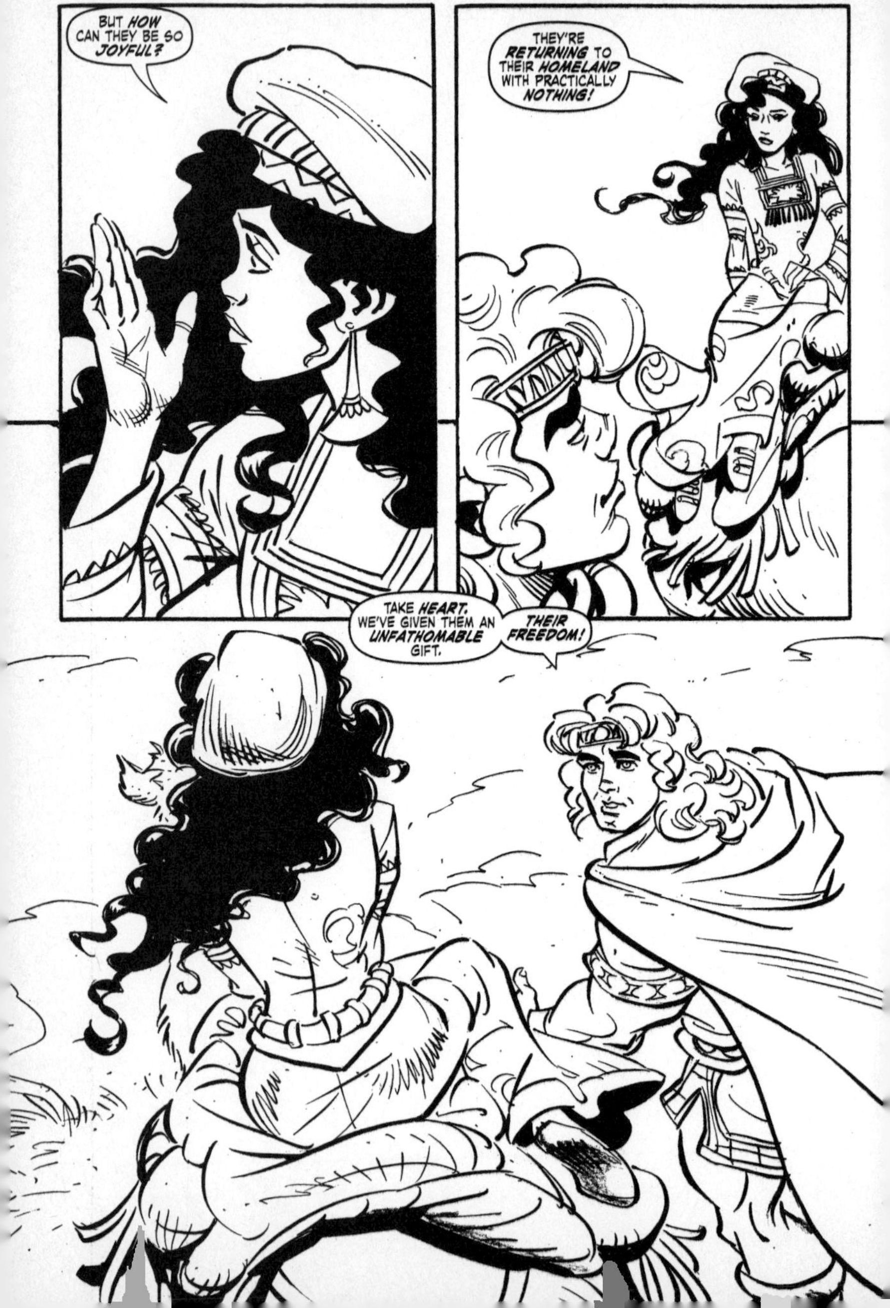
BUT HOW CAN THEY BE SO JOYFUL?
THEY'RE RETURNING TO THEIR HOMELAND WITH PRACTICALLY NOTHING!
TAKE HEART. WE'VE GIVEN THEM AN UNFATHOMABLE GIFT.
THEIR FREEDOM!

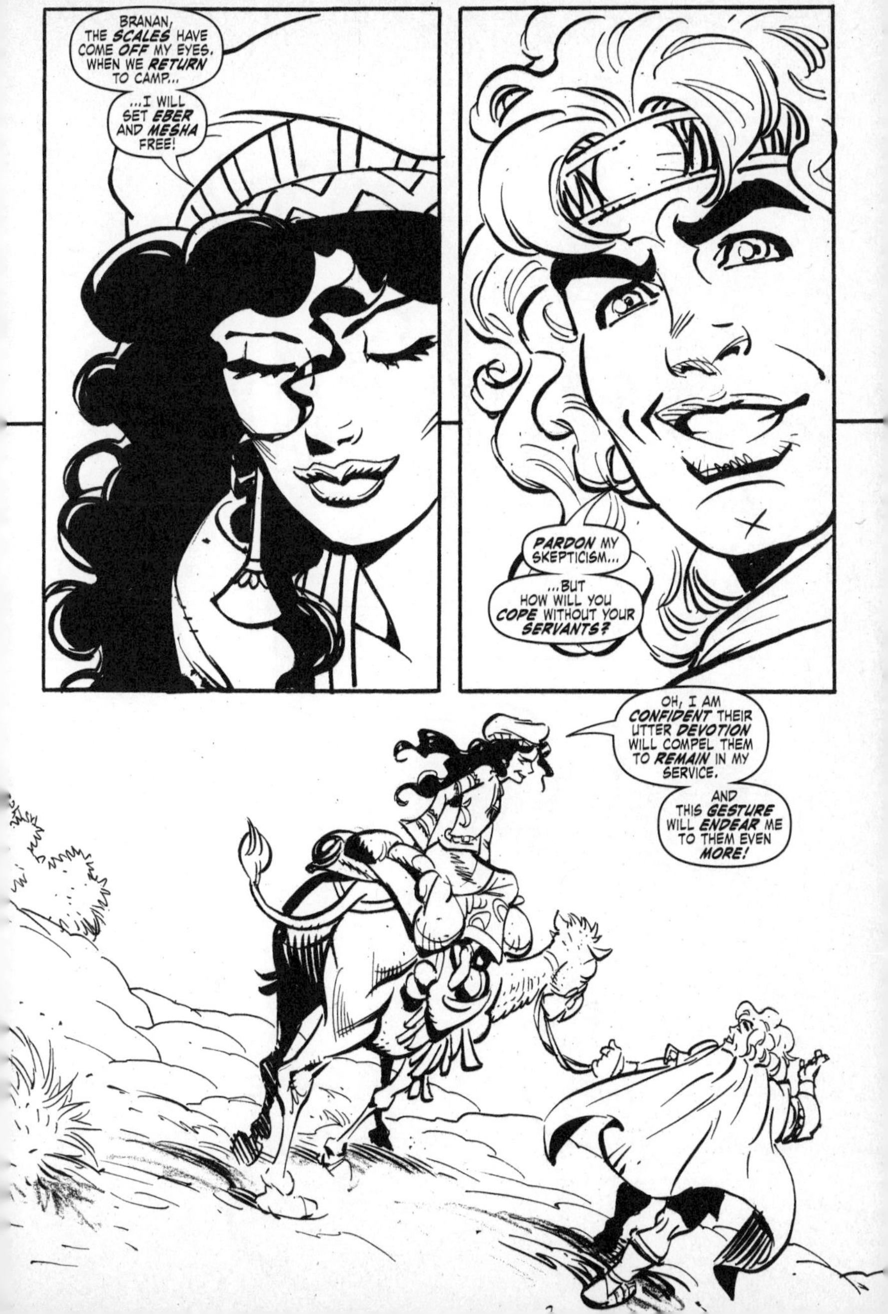
BRANAN, THE SCALES HAVE COME OFF MY EYES. WHEN WE RETURN TO CAMP...
...I WILL SET EBER AND MESHA FREE!
PARDON MY SKEPTICISM...
...BUT HOW WILL YOU COPE WITHOUT YOUR SERVANTS?
OH, I AM CONFIDENT THEIR UTTER DEVOTION WILL COMPEL THEM TO REMAIN IN MY SERVICE.
AND THIS GESTURE WILL ENDEAR ME TO THEM EVEN MORE!

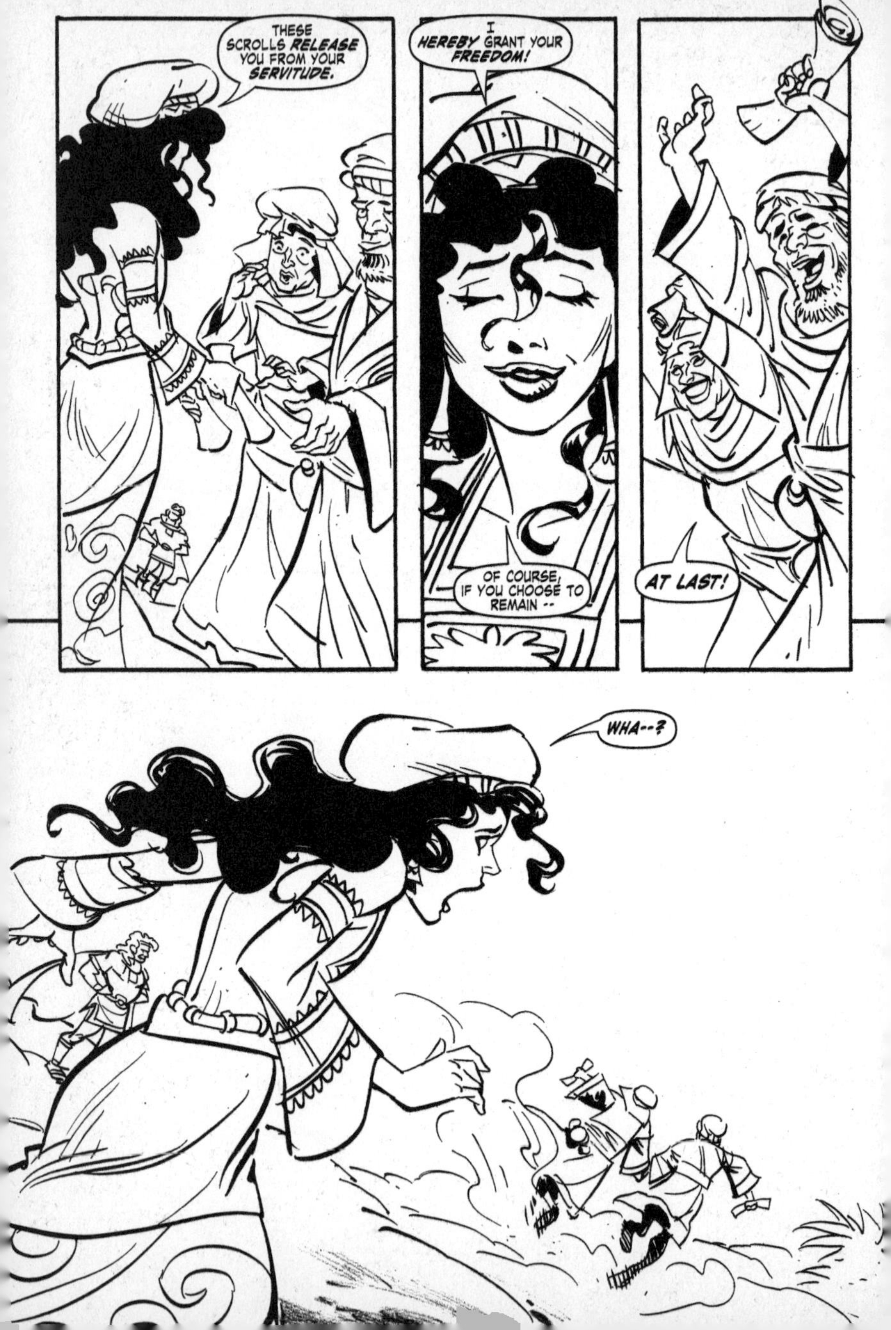
THESE SCROLLS RELEASE YOU FROM YOUR SERVITUDE.
I HEREBY GRANT YOUR FREEDOM!
OF COURSE, IF YOU CHOOSE TO REMAIN --
AT LAST!
WHA--?

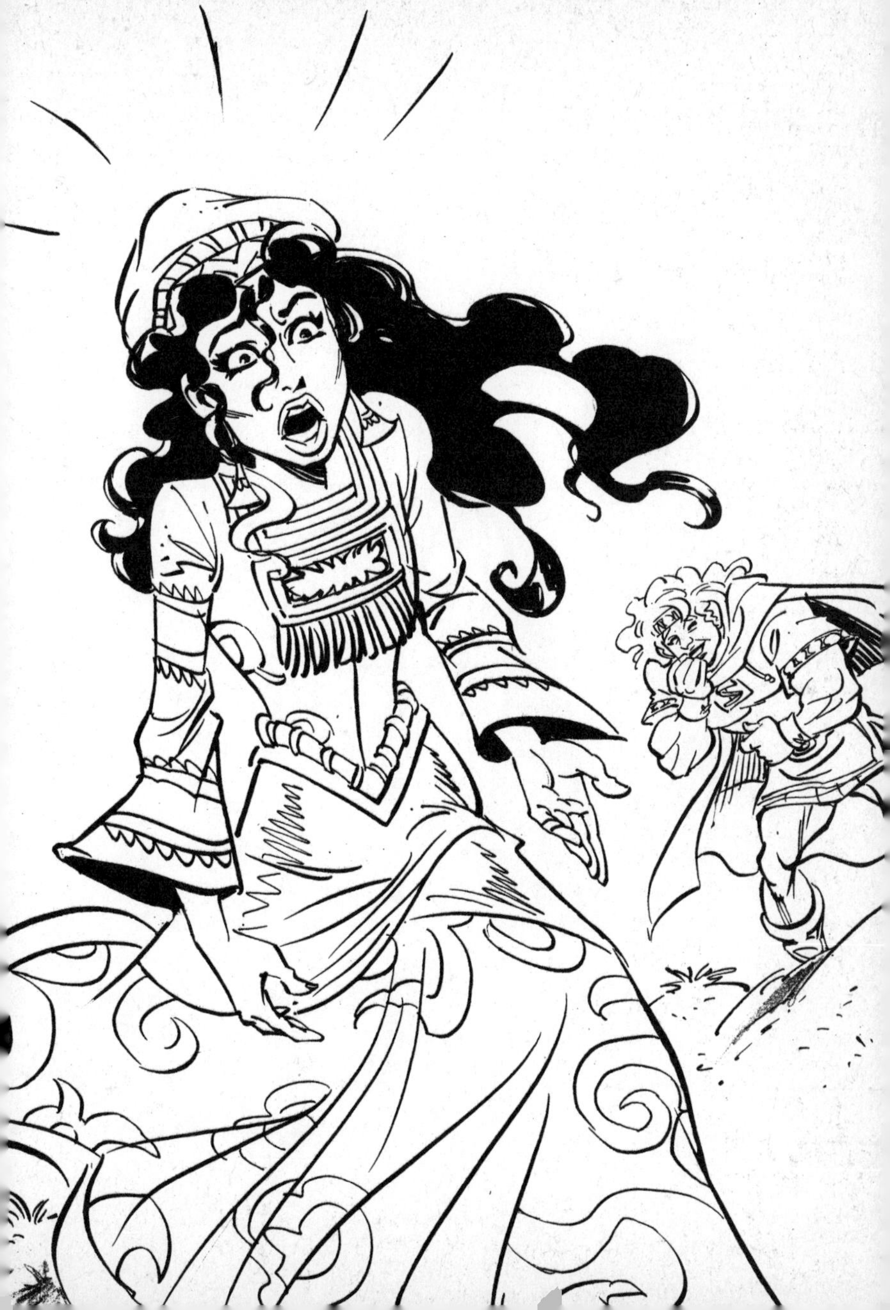

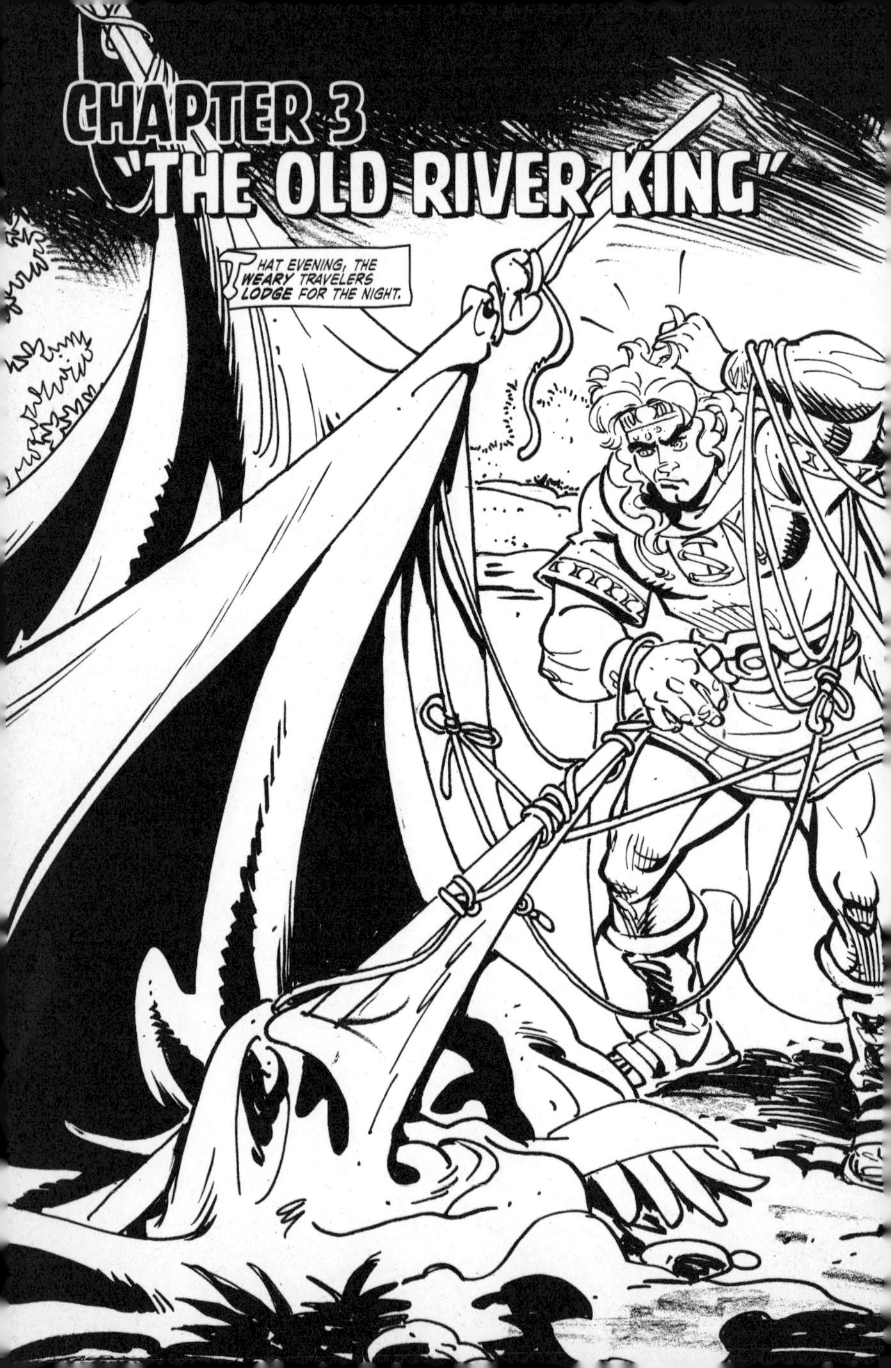
CHAPTER 3
"THE OLD RIVER KING"
THAT EVENING, THE WEARY TRAVELERS LODGE FOR THE NIGHT.

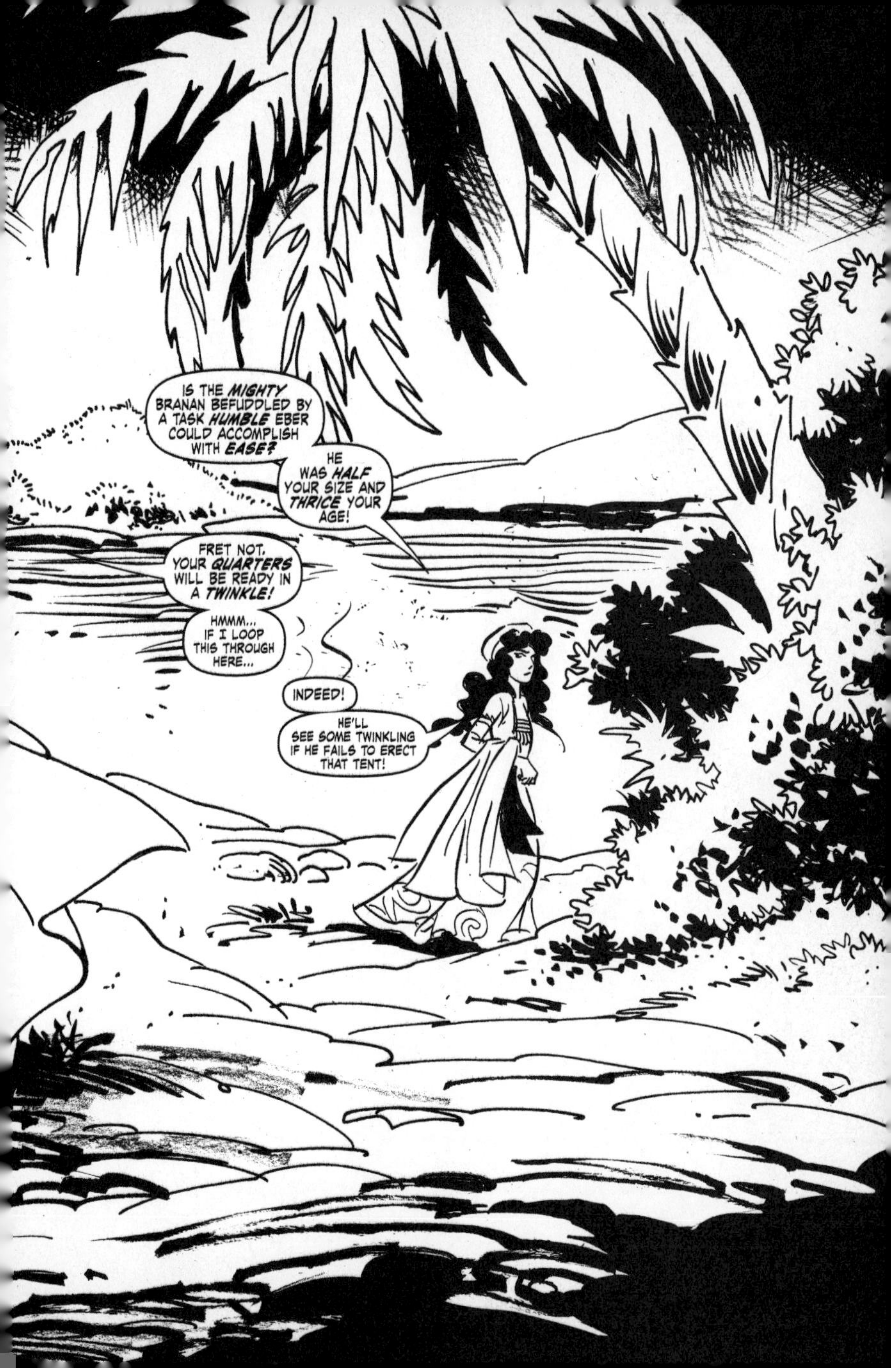
IS THE MIGHTY BRANAN BEFUDDLED BY A TASK HUMBLE EBER COULD ACCOMPLISH WITH EASE?
HE WAS HALF YOUR SIZE AND THRICE YOUR AGE!
FRET NOT. YOUR QUARTERS WILL BE READY IN A TWINKLE!
HMMM... IF I LOOP THIS THROUGH HERE...
INDEED!
HE'LL SEE SOME TWINKLING IF HE FAILS TO ERECT THAT TENT!

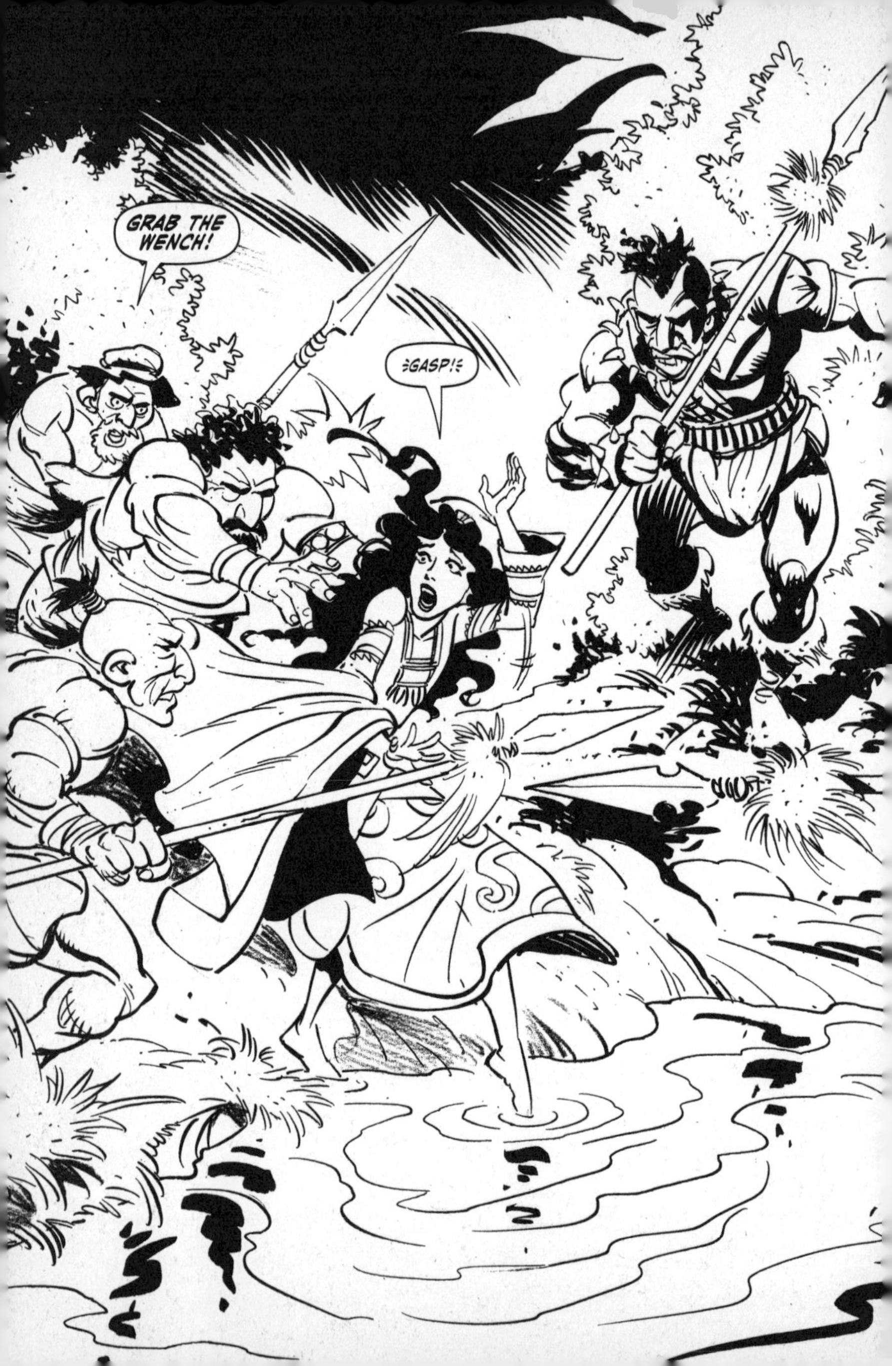
GRAB THE WENCH!
GASP!

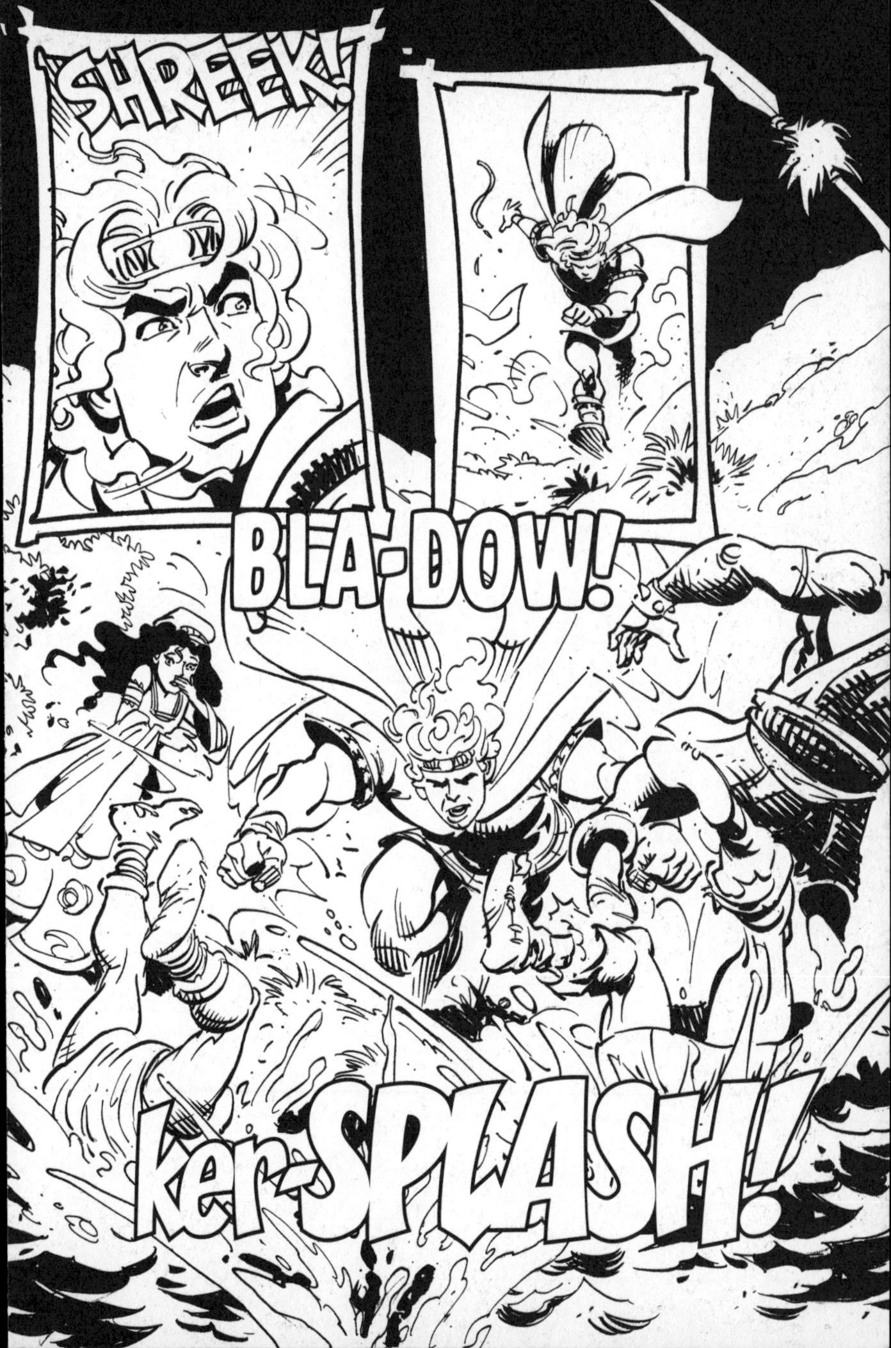
SHREEK!
BLA-DOW!
ker-SPLASH!

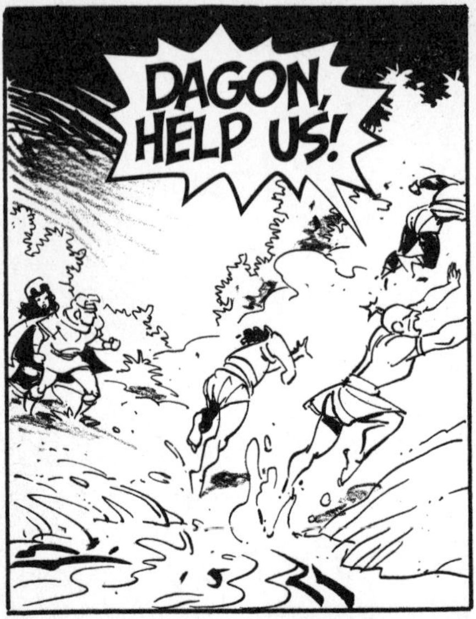
DAGON, HELP US!

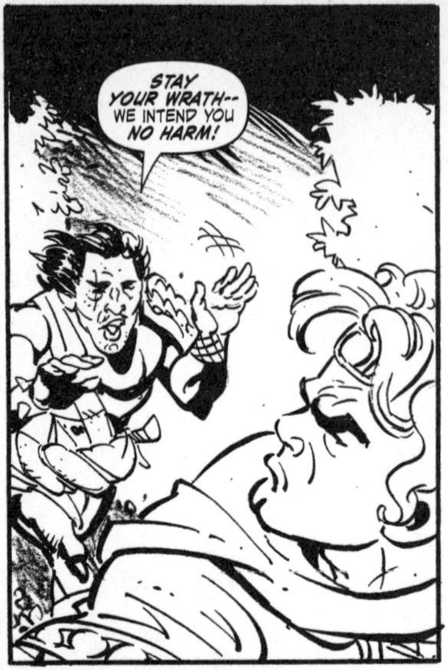
STAY YOUR WRATH-- WE INTEND YOU NO HARM!

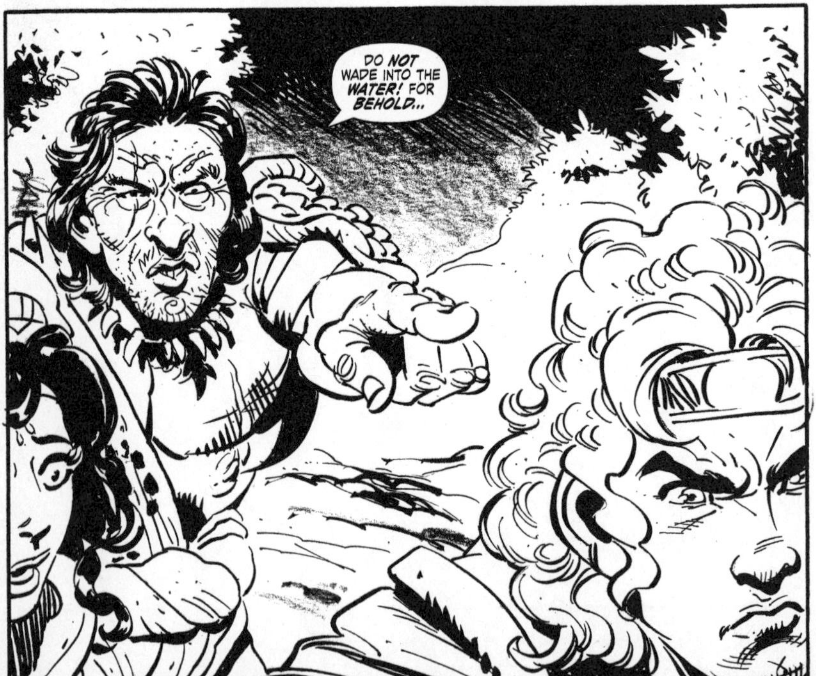
DO NOT WADE INTO THE WATER! FOR BEHOLD...

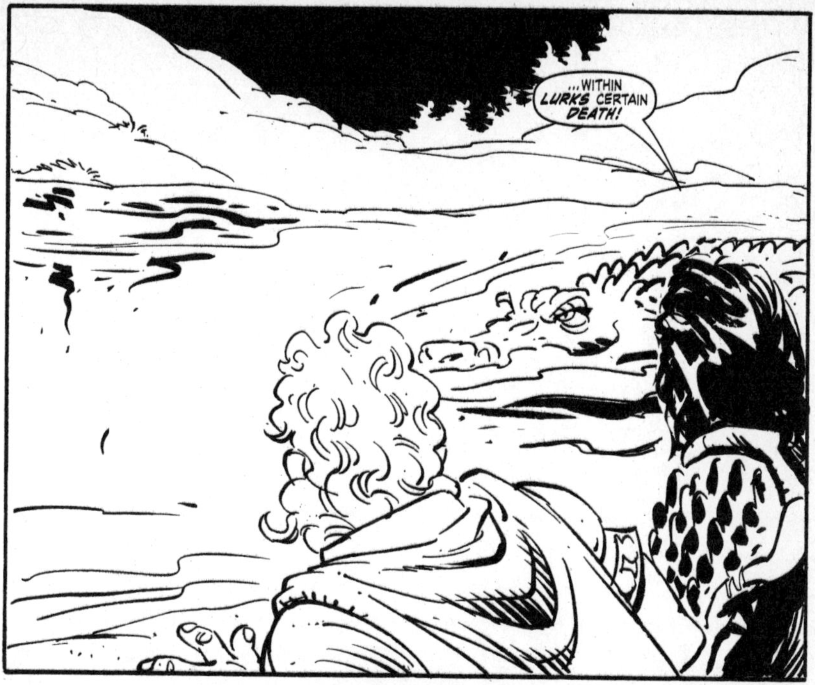
...WITHIN LURKS CERTAIN DEATH!

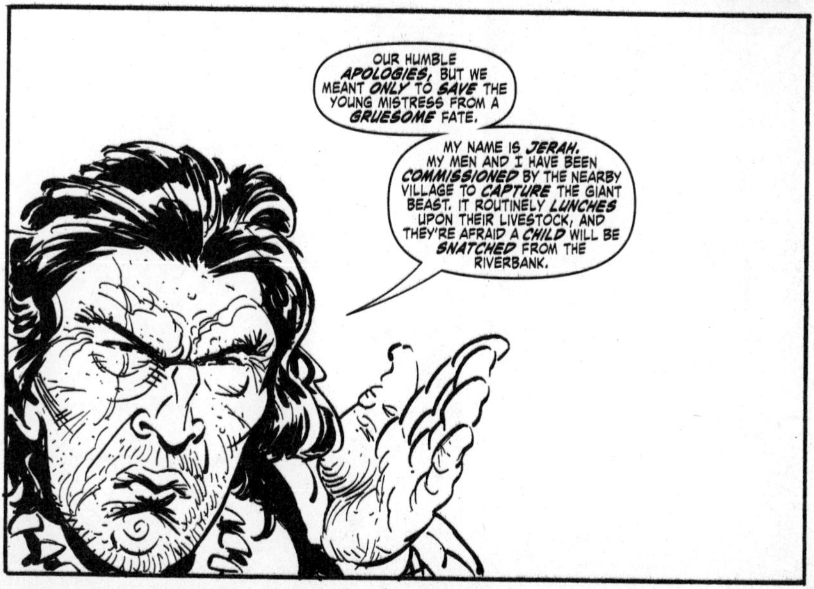
OUR HUMBLE APOLOGIES, BUT WE MEANT ONLY TO SAVE THE YOUNG MISTRESS FROM A GRUESOME FATE.
MY NAME IS JERAH. MY MEN AND I HAVE BEEN COMMISSIONED BY THE NEARBY VILLAGE TO CAPTURE THE GIANT BEAST. IT ROUTINELY LUNCHES UPON THEIR LIVESTOCK, AND THEY'RE AFRAID A CHILD WILL BE SNATCHED FROM THE RIVERBANK.

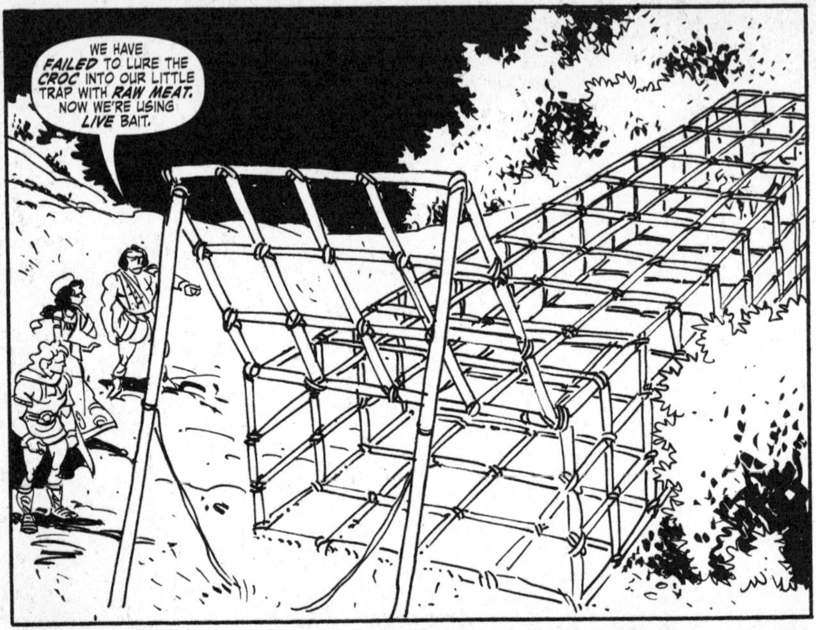
WE HAVE FAILED TO LURE THE CROC INTO OUR LITTLE TRAP WITH RAW MEAT. NOW WE'RE USING LIVE BAIT.

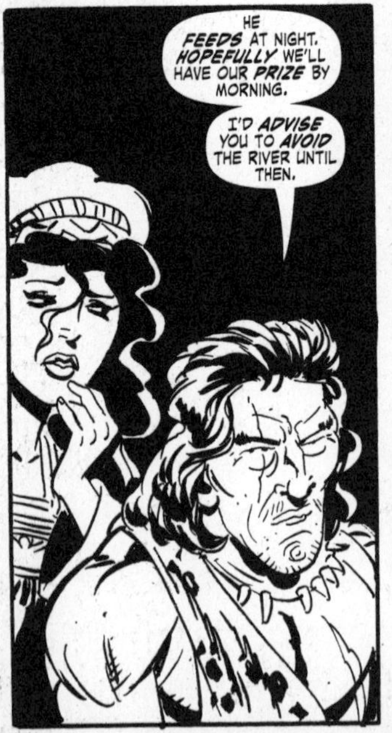
HE FEEDS AT NIGHT. HOPEFULLY WE'LL HAVE OUR PRIZE BY MORNING.
I'D ADVISE YOU TO AVOID THE RIVER UNTIL THEN.

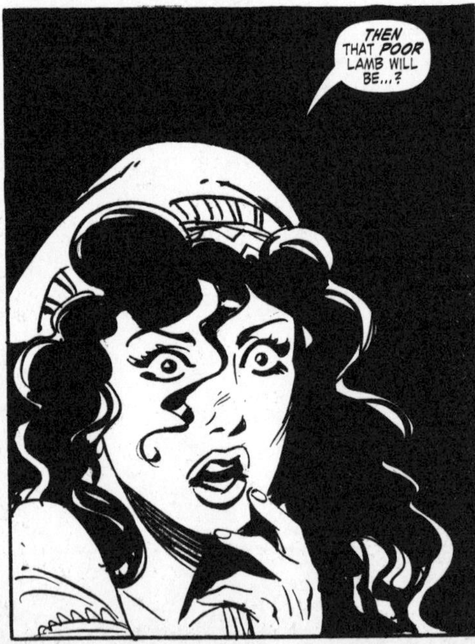
THEN THAT POOR LAMB WILL BE...?

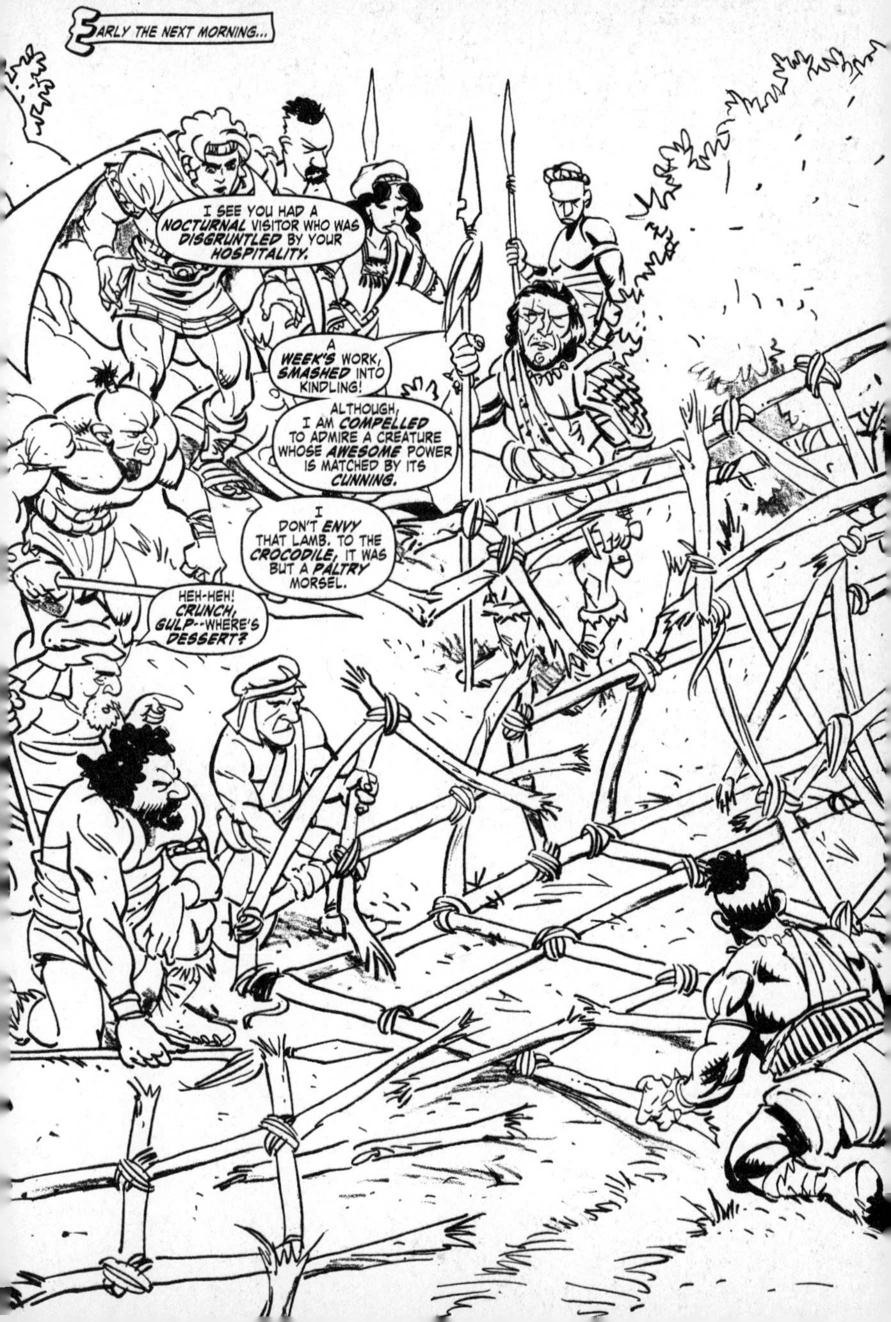
EARLY THE NEXT MORNING...
I SEE YOU HAD A NOCTURNAL VISITOR WHO WAS DISGRUNTLED BY YOUR HOSPITALITY.
A WEEK'S WORK, SMASHED INTO KINDLING!
ALTHOUGH, I AM COMPELLED TO ADMIRE A CREATURE WHOSE AWESOME POWER IS MATCHED BY ITS CUNNING.
I DON'T ENVY THAT LAMB. TO THE CROCODILE, IT WAS BUT A PALTRY MORSEL.
HEH-HEH! CRUNCH, GULP--WHERE'S DESSERT?

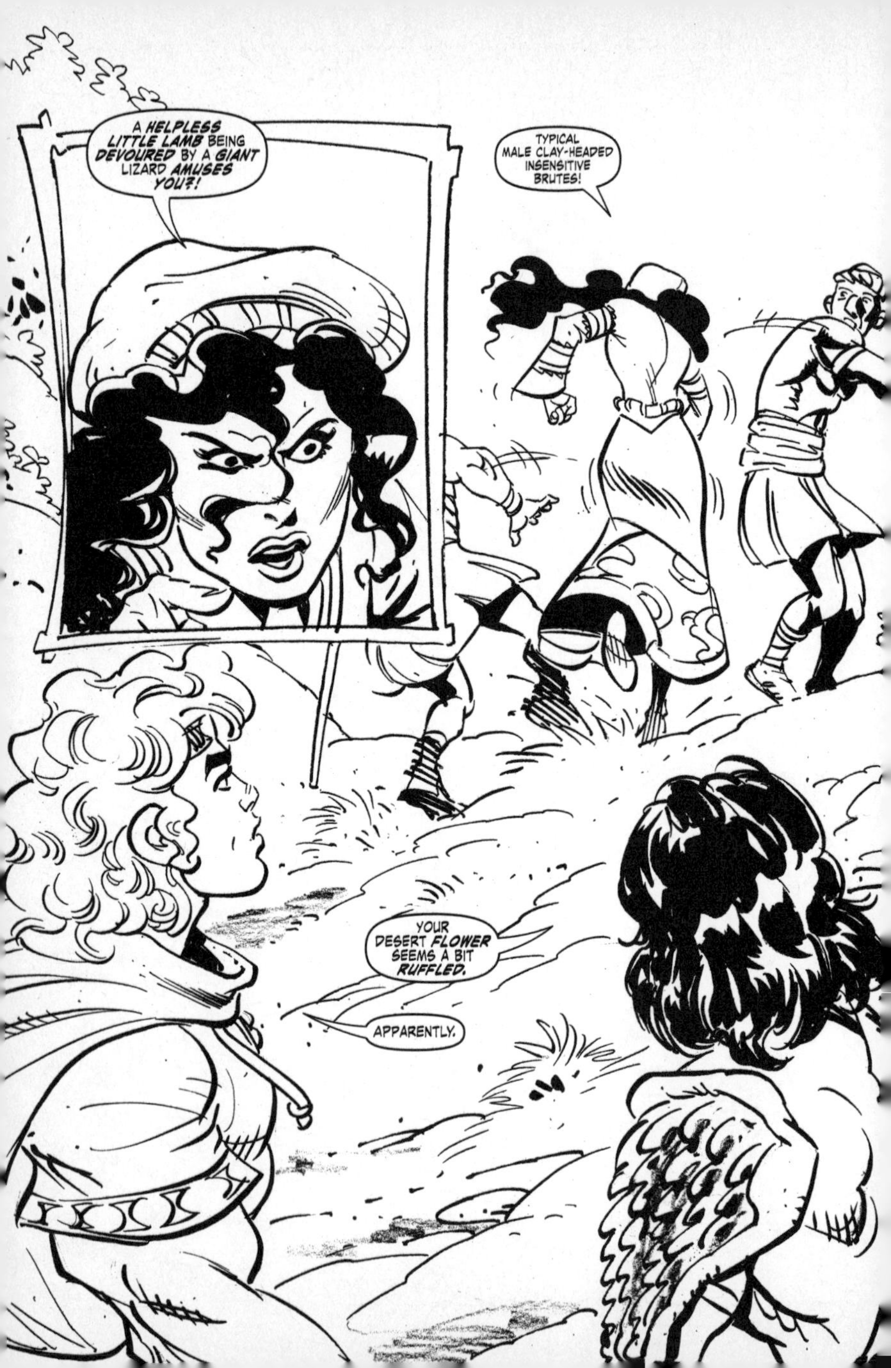
A HELPLESS LITTLE LAMB BEING DEVOURED BY A GIANT LIZARD AMUSES YOU?!
TYPICAL MALE CLAY-HEADED INSENSITIVE BRUTES!
YOUR DESERT FLOWER SEEMS A BIT RUFFLED.
APPARENTLY.

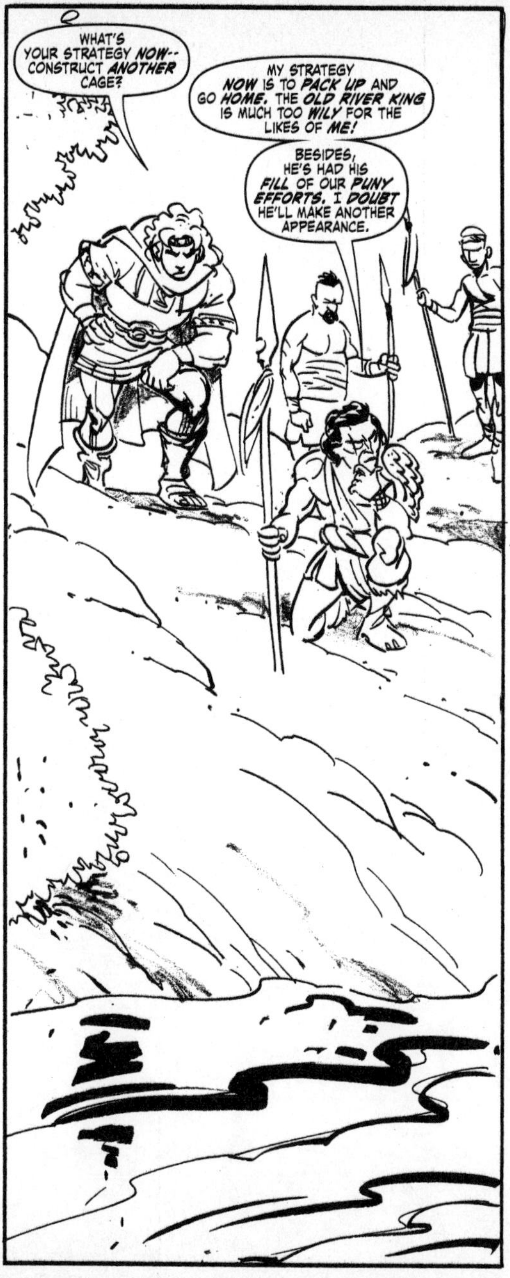
WHAT'S YOUR STRATEGY NOW-- CONSTRUCT ANOTHER CAGE?
MY STRATEGY NOW IS TO PACK UP AND GO HOME. THE OLD RIVER KING IS MUCH TOO WILY FOR THE LIKES OF ME!
BESIDES, HE'S HAD HIS FILL OF OUR PUNY EFFORTS. I DOUBT HE'LL MAKE ANOTHER APPEARANCE.

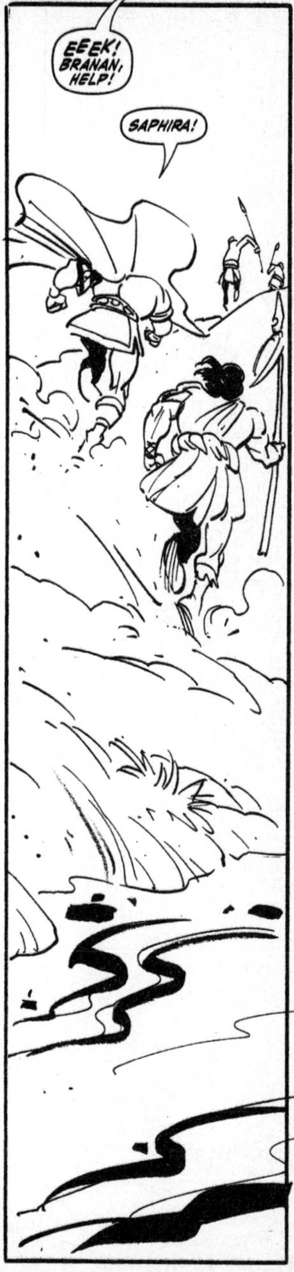
EEEK! BRANAN, HELP!
SAPHIRA!

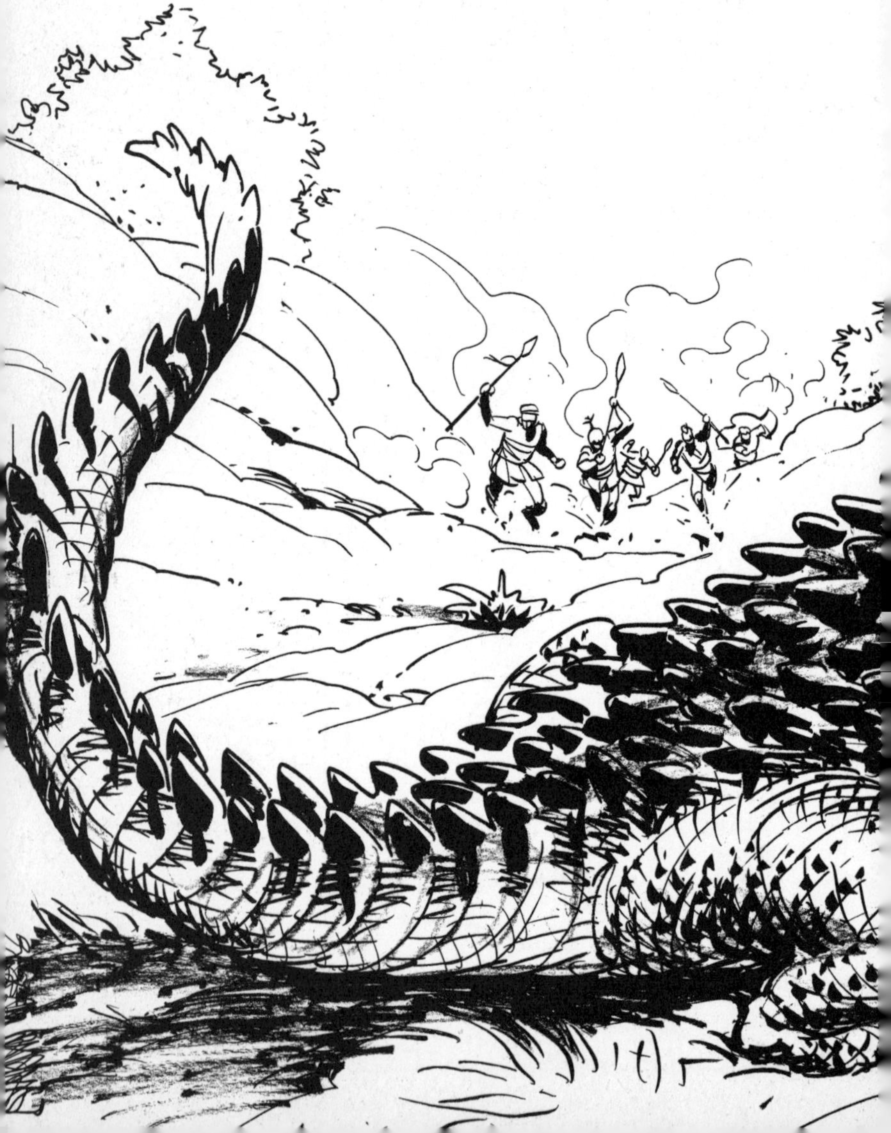

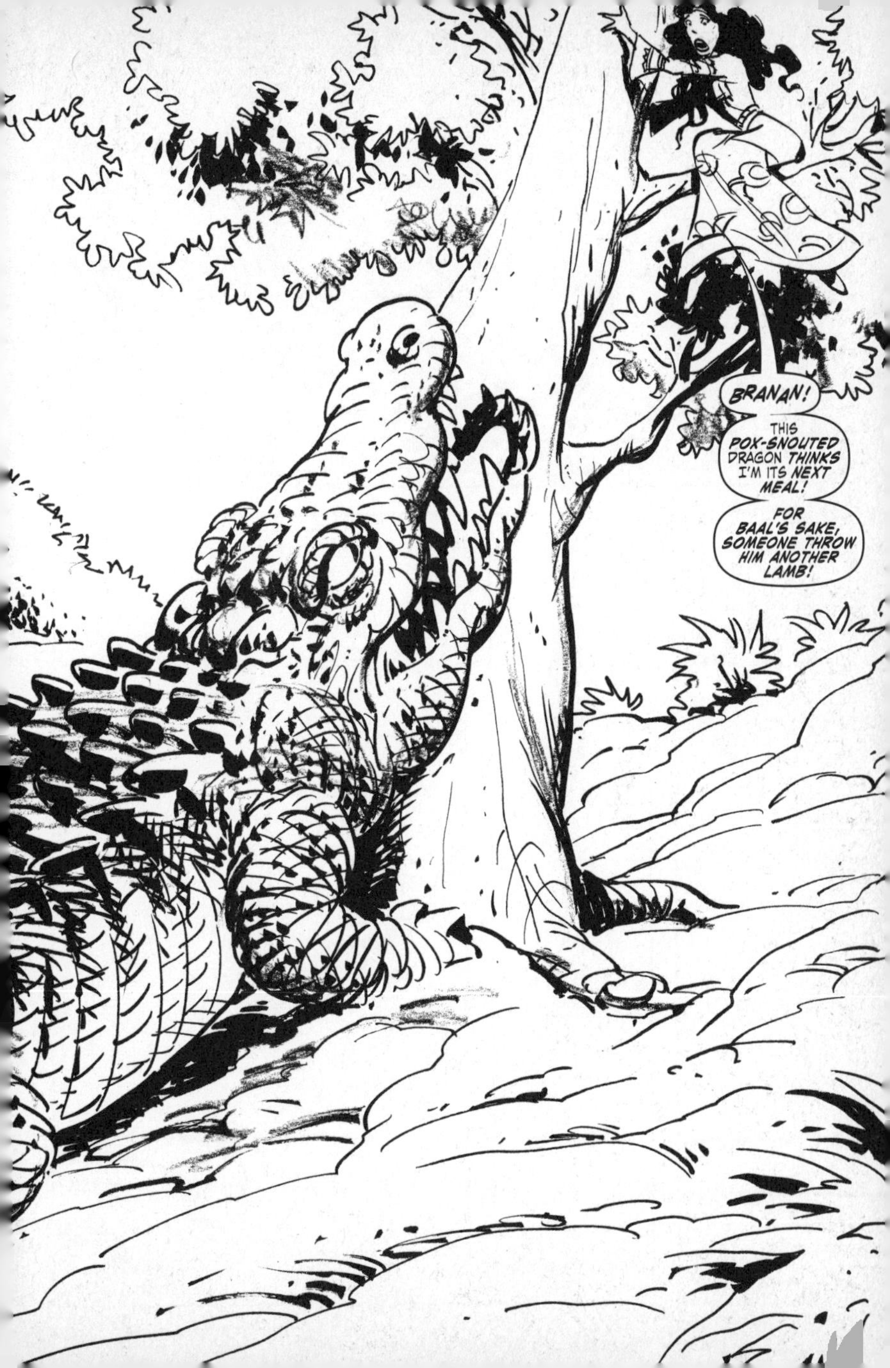
BRANAN!
THIS POX-SNOUTED DRAGON THINKS I'M ITS NEXT MEAL!
FOR BAAL'S SAKE, SOMEONE THROW HIM ANOTHER LAMB!

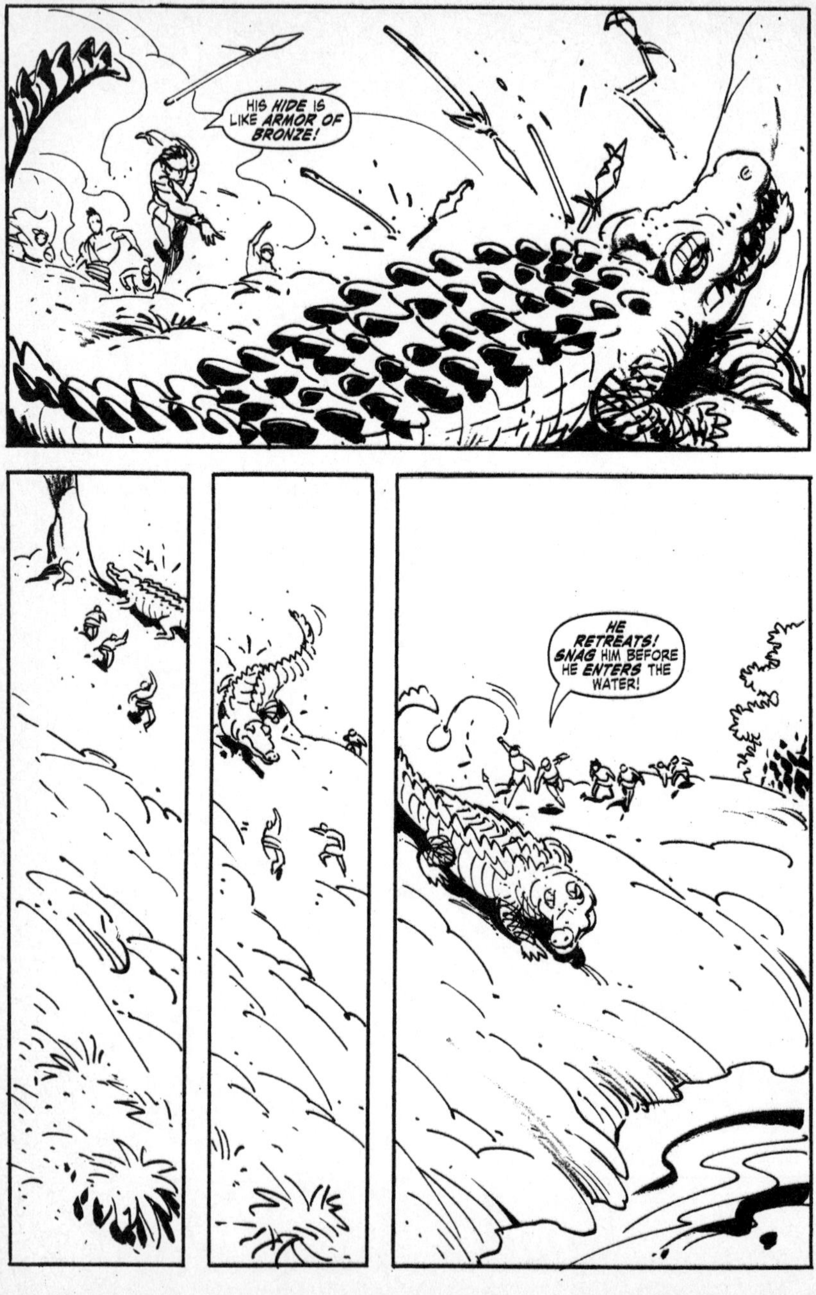
HIS HIDE IS LIKE ARMOR OF BRONZE!
HE RETREATS! SNAG HIM BEFORE HE ENTERS THE WATER!

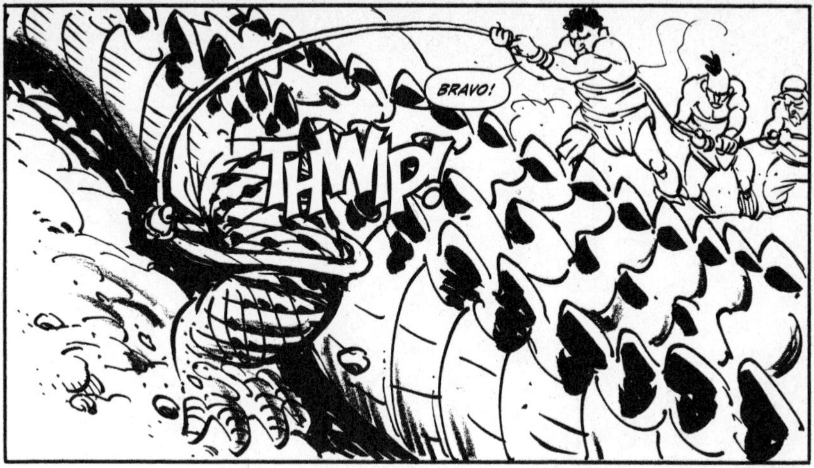
BRAVO!
THWIP!

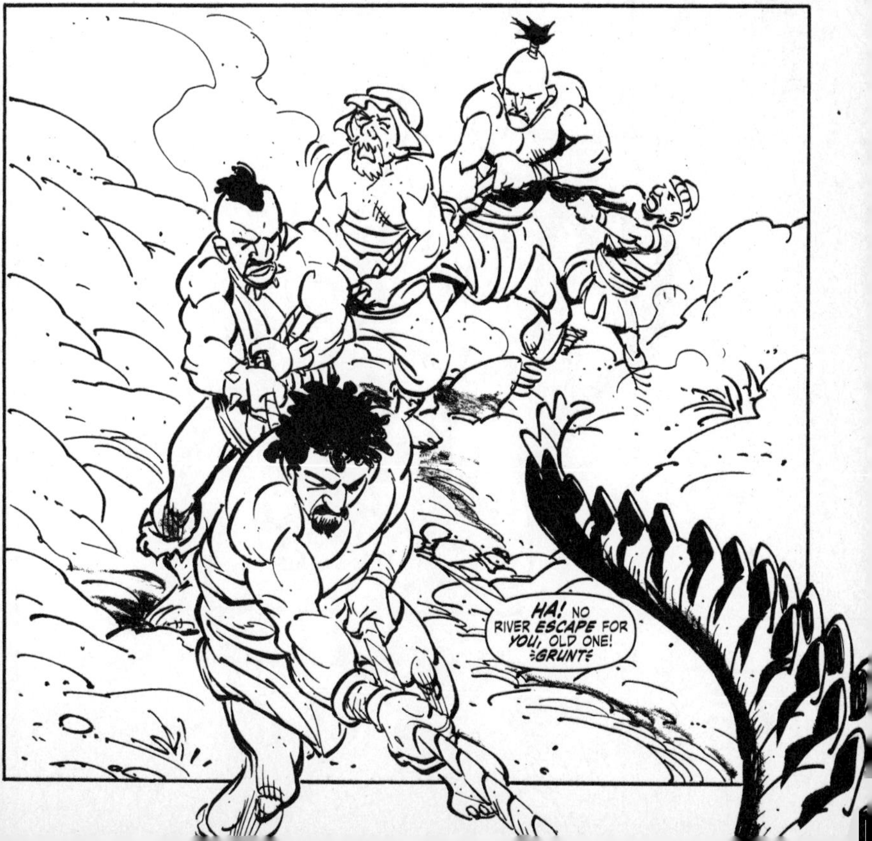
HA! NO RIVER ESCAPE FOR YOU, OLD ONE! GRUNT

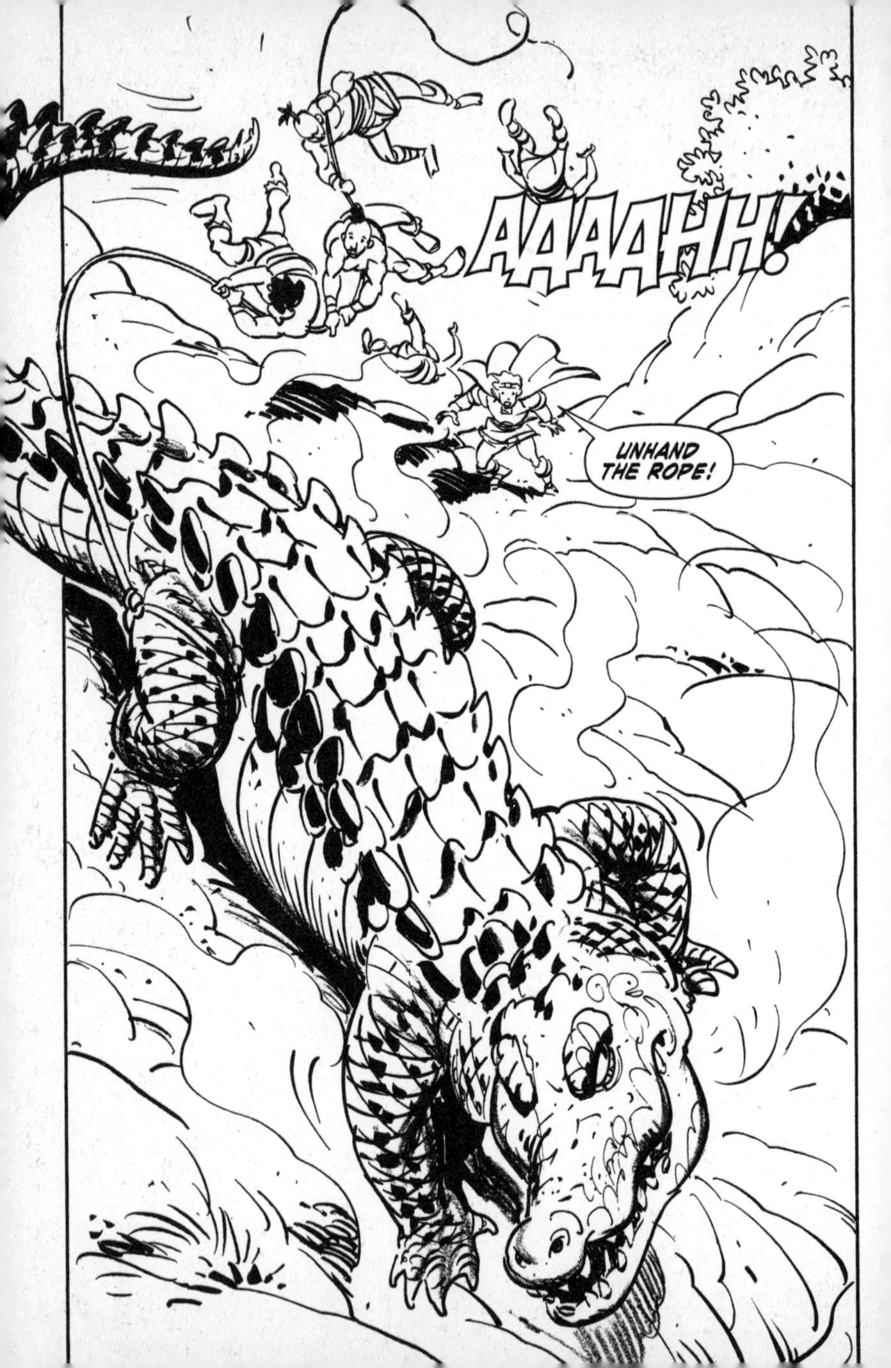
AAAAHH!
UNHAND THE ROPE!

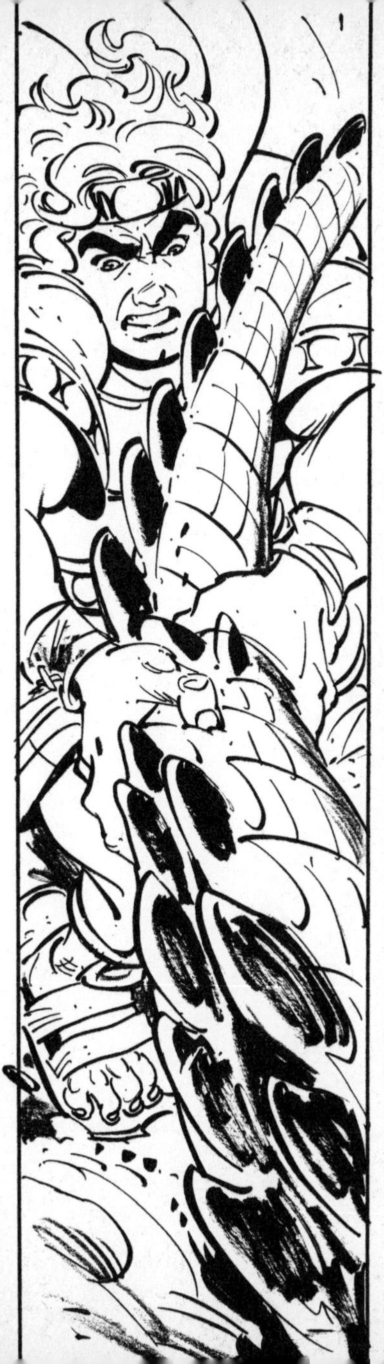

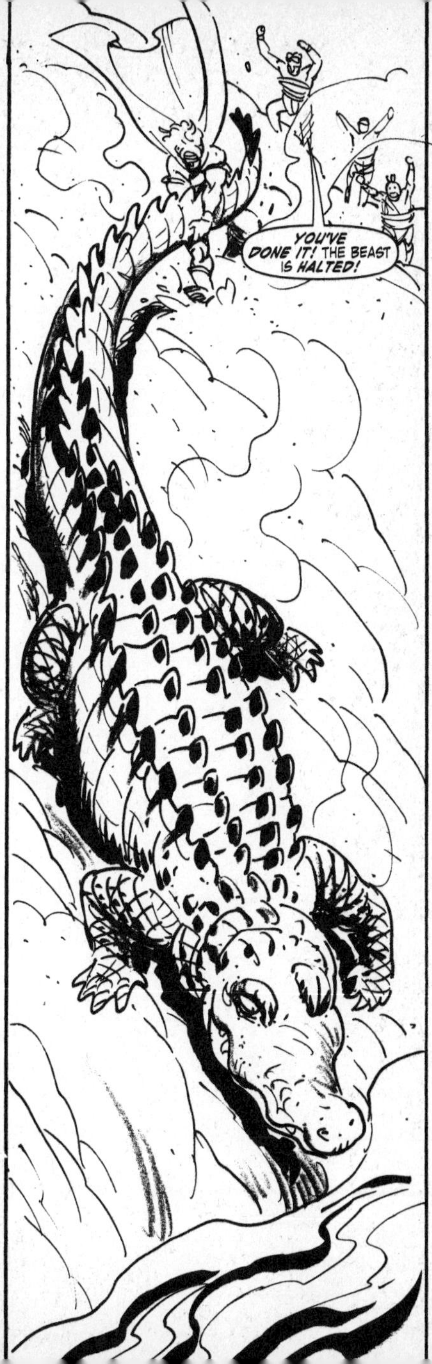
YOU'VE DONE IT! THE BEAST IS HALTED!

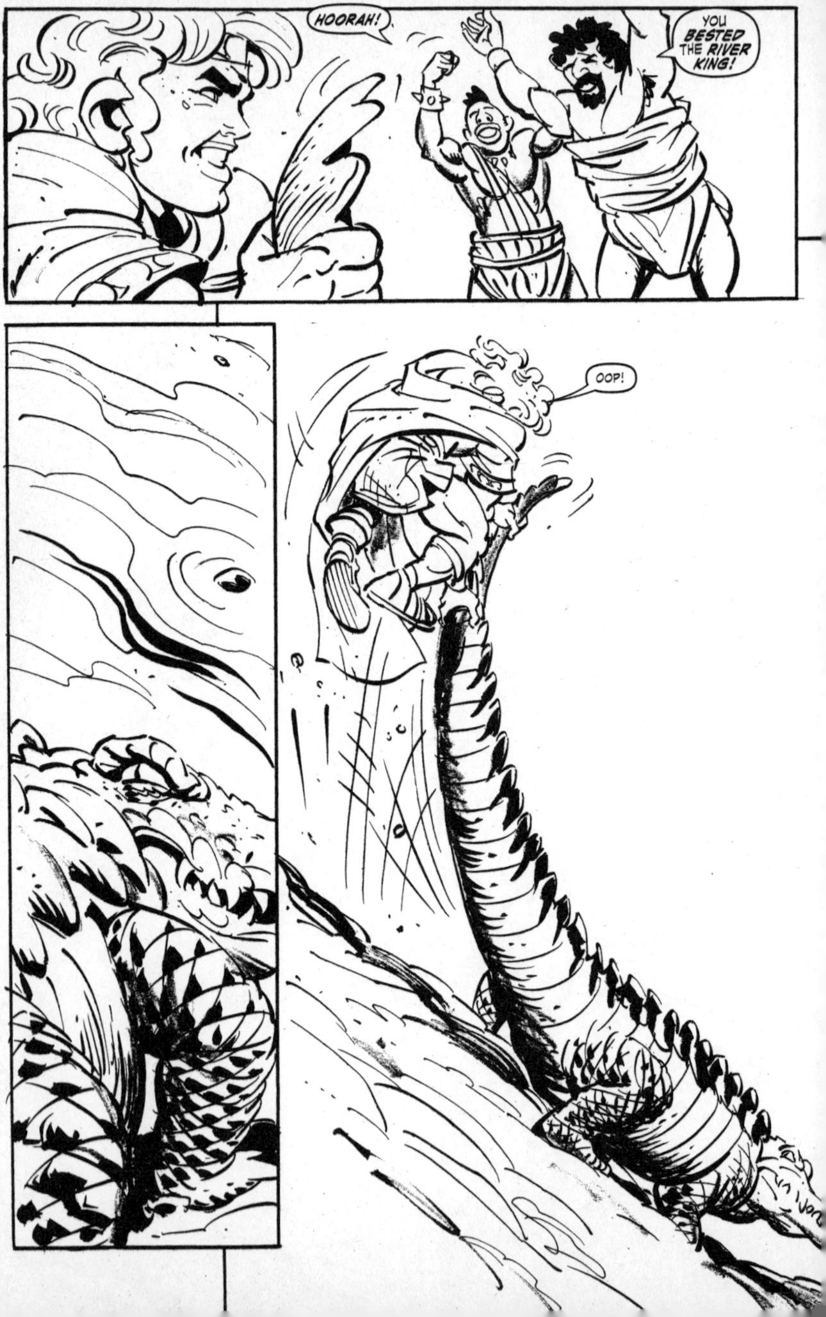
HOORAH!
YOU BESTED THE RIVER KING!
OOP!

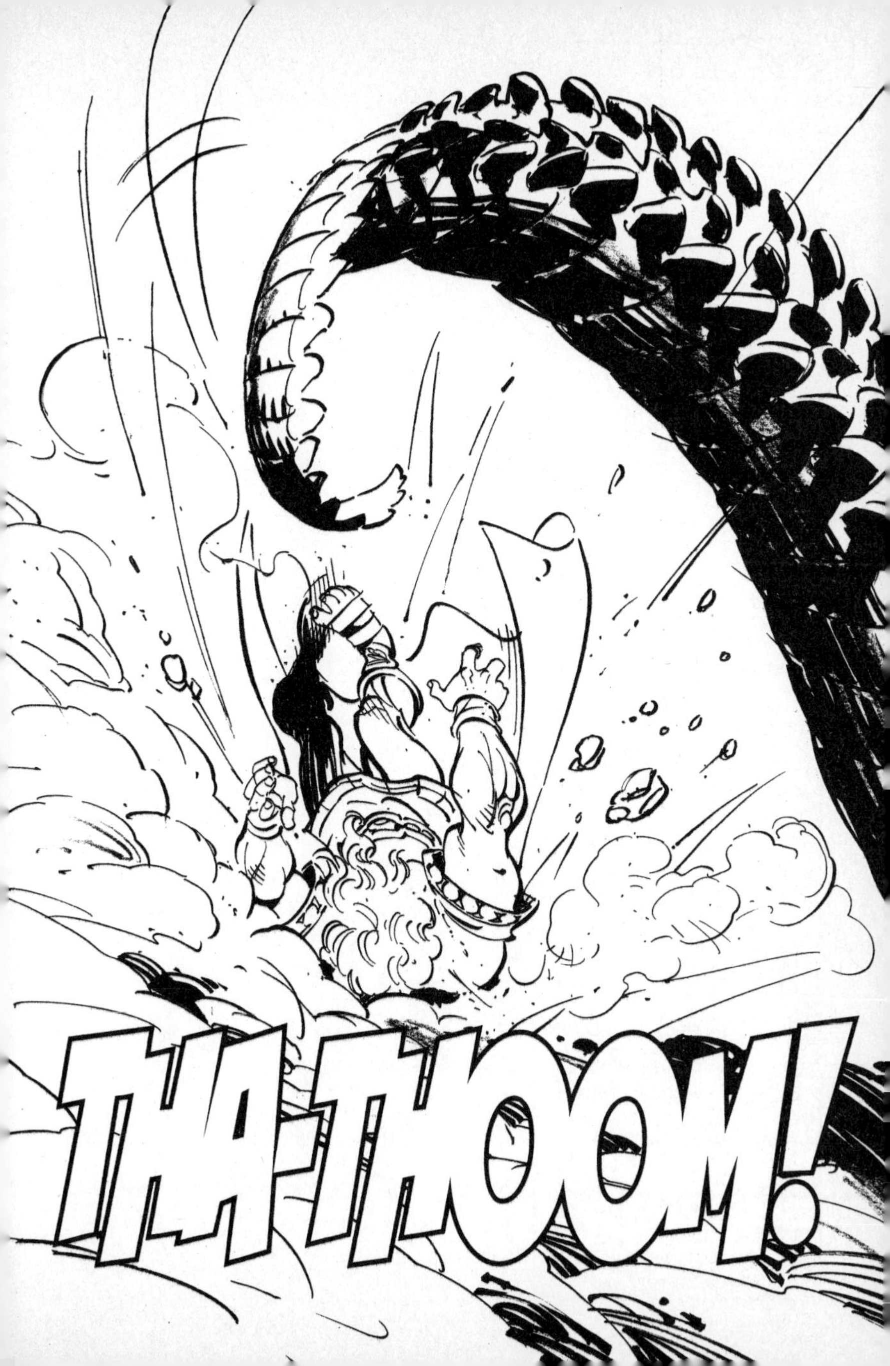
THA-THOOM!

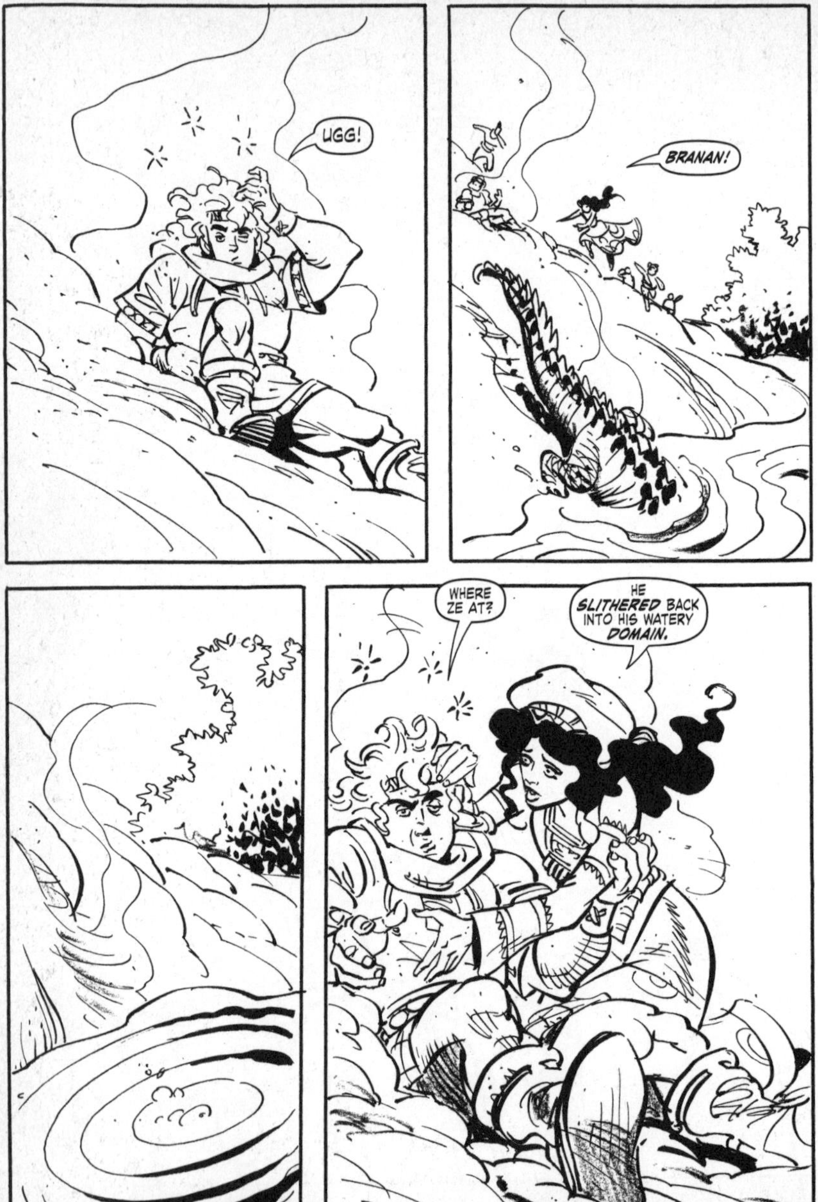
UGG!
BRANAN!
WHERE ZE AT?
HE SLITHERED BACK INTO HIS WATERY DOMAIN.

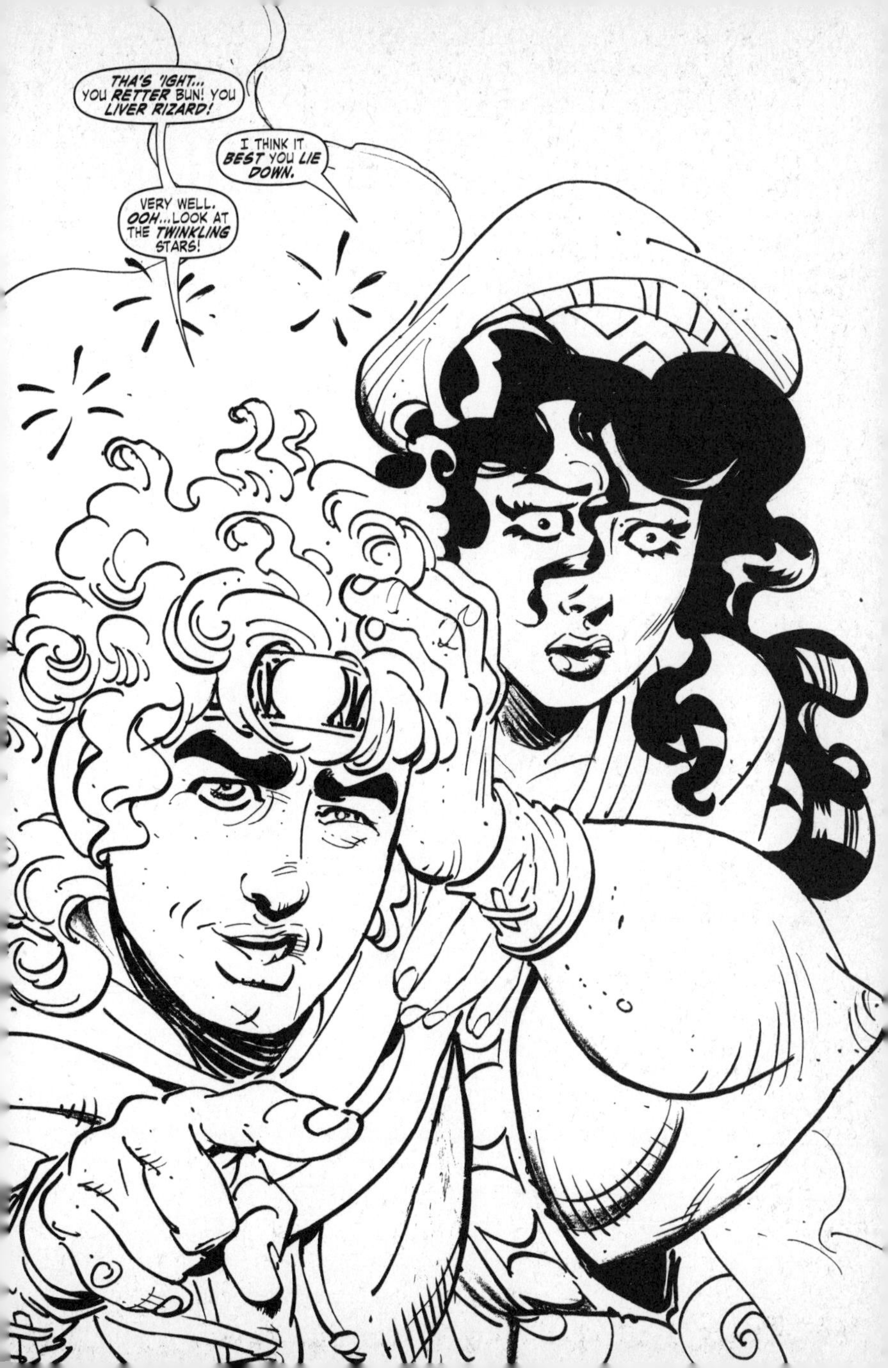
THA'S 'IGHT... YOU RETTER BUN! YOU LIVER RIZARD!
I THINK IT BEST YOU LIE DOWN.
VERY WELL. OOH...LOOK AT THE TWINKLING STARS!

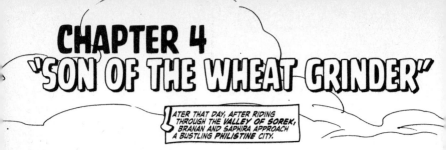

CHAPTER 4
"SON OF THE WHEAT GRINDER"

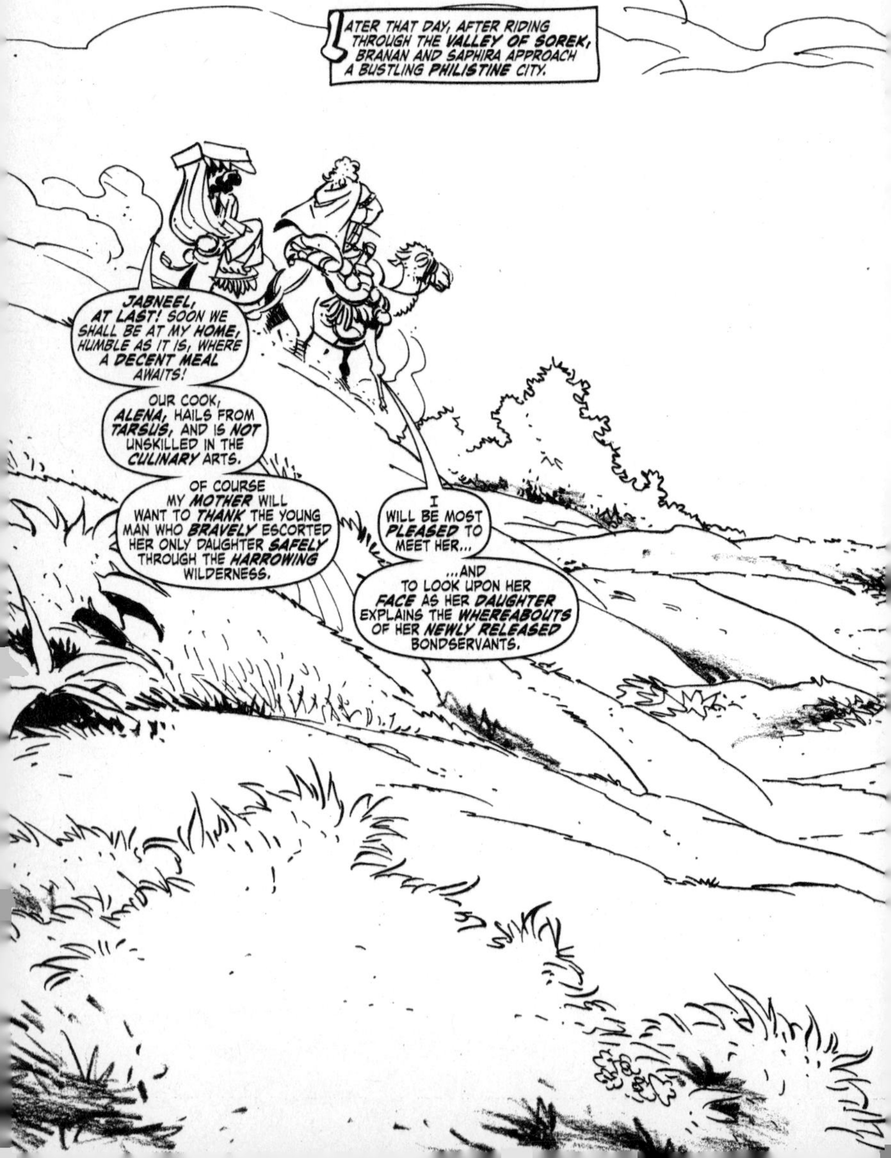

LATER THAT DAY, AFTER RIDING THROUGH THE VALLEY OF SOREK, BRANAN AND SAPHIRA APPROACH A BUSTLING PHILISTINE CITY.
JABNEEL, AT LAST! SOON WE SHALL BE AT MY HOME, HUMBLE AS IT IS, WHERE A DECENT MEAL AWAITS!
OUR COOK, ALENA, HAILS FROM TARSUS, AND IS NOT UNSKILLED IN THE CULINARY ARTS.
OF COURSE MY MOTHER WILL WANT TO THANK THE YOUNG MAN WHO BRAVELY ESCORTED HER ONLY DAUGHTER SAFELY THROUGH THE HARROWING WILDERNESS.
I WILL BE MOST PLEASED TO MEET HER...
...AND TO LOOK UPON HER FACE AS HER DAUGHTER EXPLAINS THE WHEREABOUTS OF HER NEWLY RELEASED BONDSERVANTS.

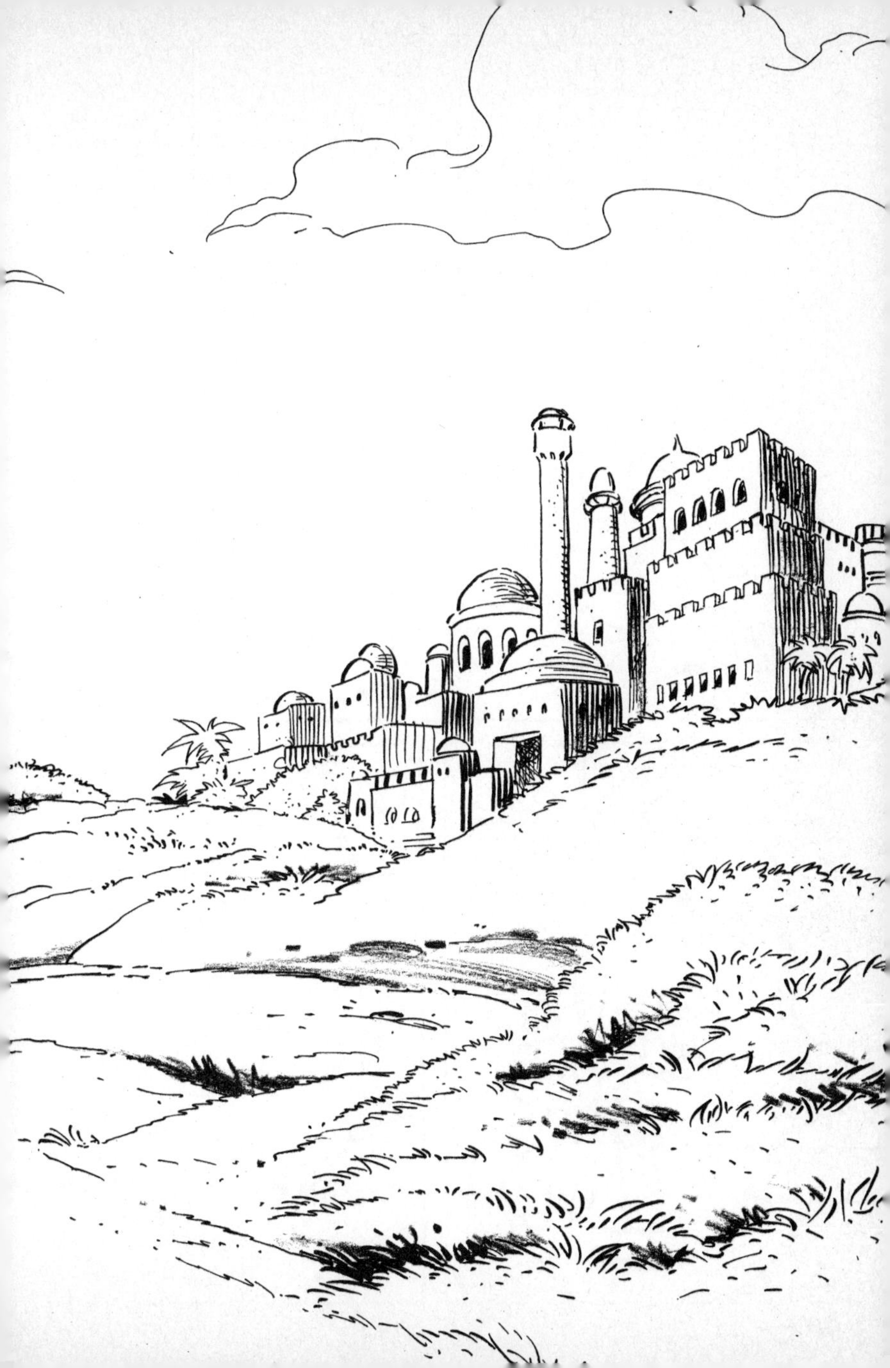

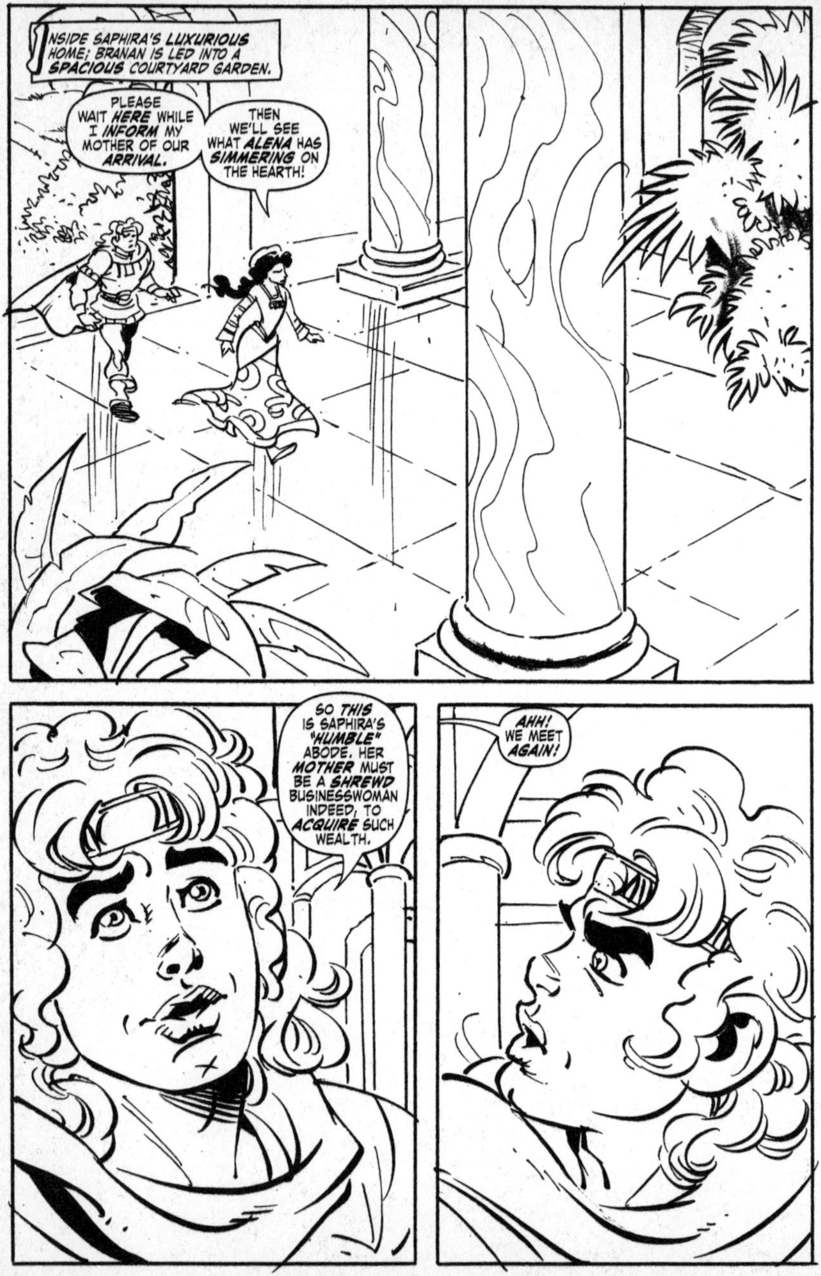
INSIDE SAPHIRA'S LUXURIOUS HOME; BRANAN IS LED INTO A SPACIOUS COURTYARD GARDEN.
PLEASE WAIT HERE WHILE I INFORM MY MOTHER OF OUR ARRIVAL.
THEN WE'LL SEE WHAT ALENA HAS SIMMERING ON THE HEARTH!
SO THIS IS SAPHIRA'S "HUMBLE" ABODE. HER MOTHER MUST BE A SHREWD BUSINESSWOMAN INDEED, TO ACQUIRE SUCH WEALTH.
AHH! WE MEET AGAIN!

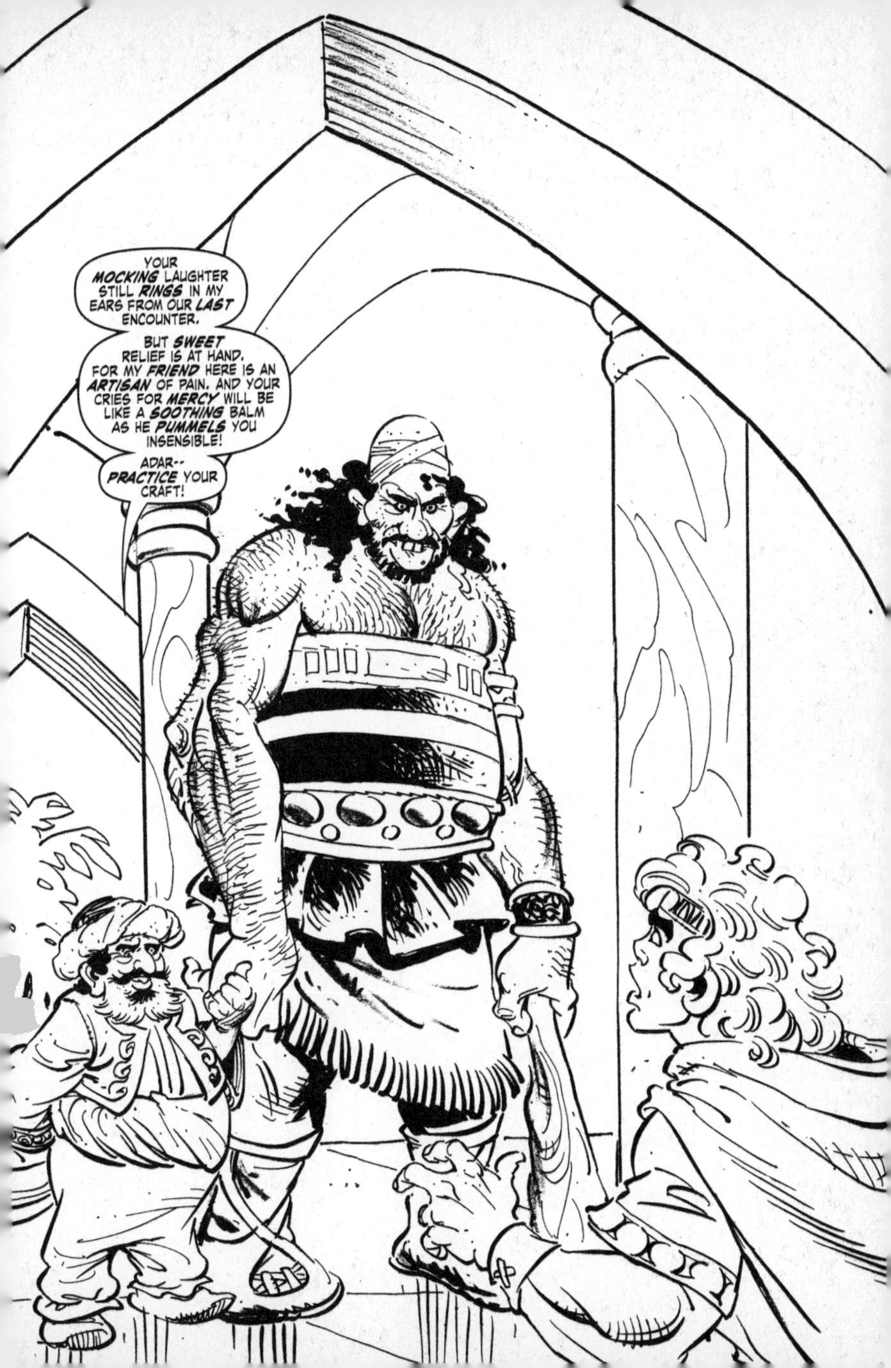
YOUR MOCKING LAUGHTER STILL RINGS IN MY EARS FROM OUR LAST ENCOUNTER.
BUT SWEET RELIEF IS AT HAND. FOR MY FRIEND HERE IS AN ARTISAN OF PAIN. AND YOUR CRIES FOR MERCY WILL BE LIKE A SOOTHING BALM AS HE PUMMELS YOU INSENSIBLE!
ADAR-- PRACTICE YOUR CRAFT!

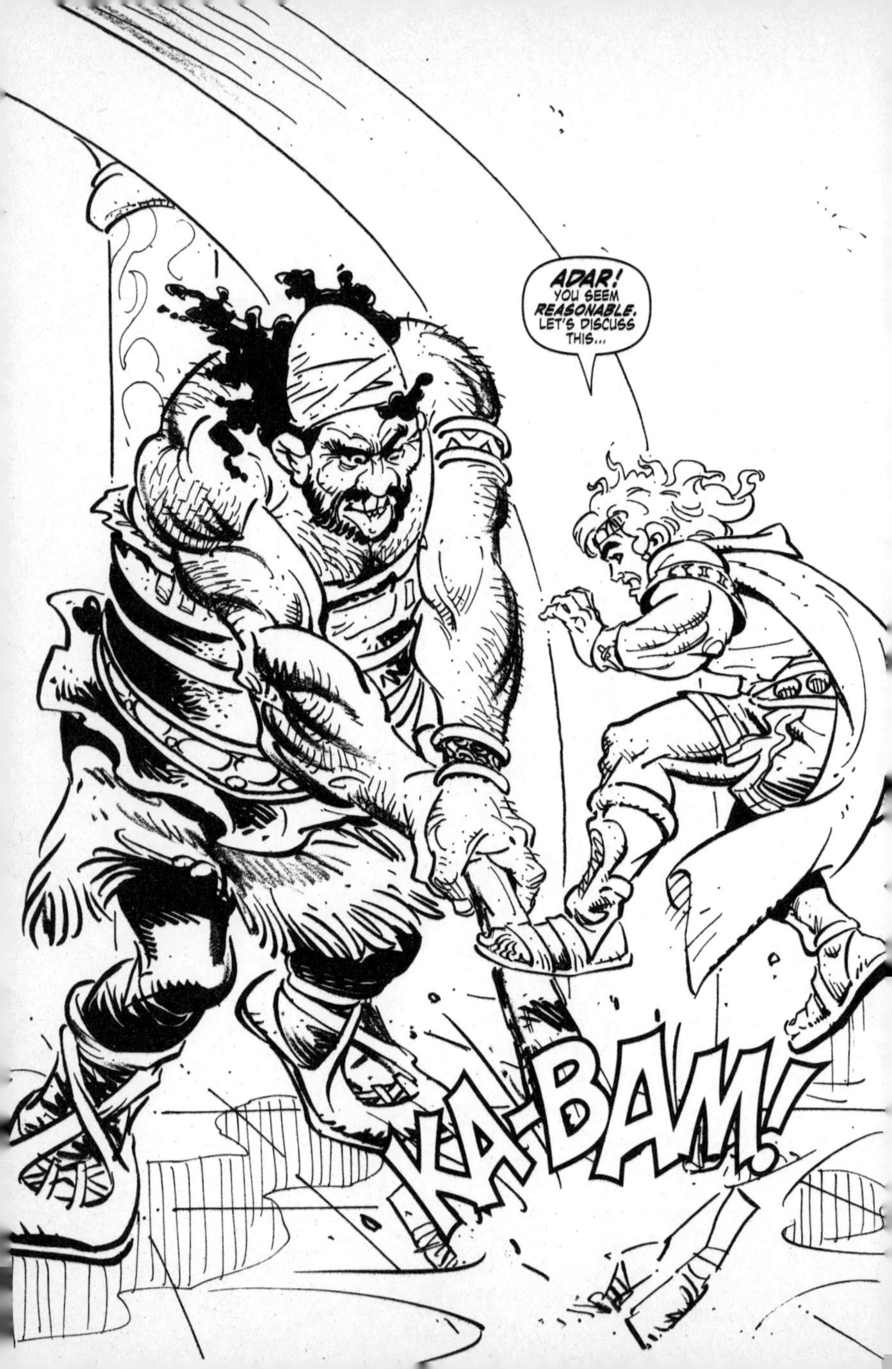
ADAR! YOU SEEM REASONABLE. LET'S DISCUSS THIS...
KA-BAM!

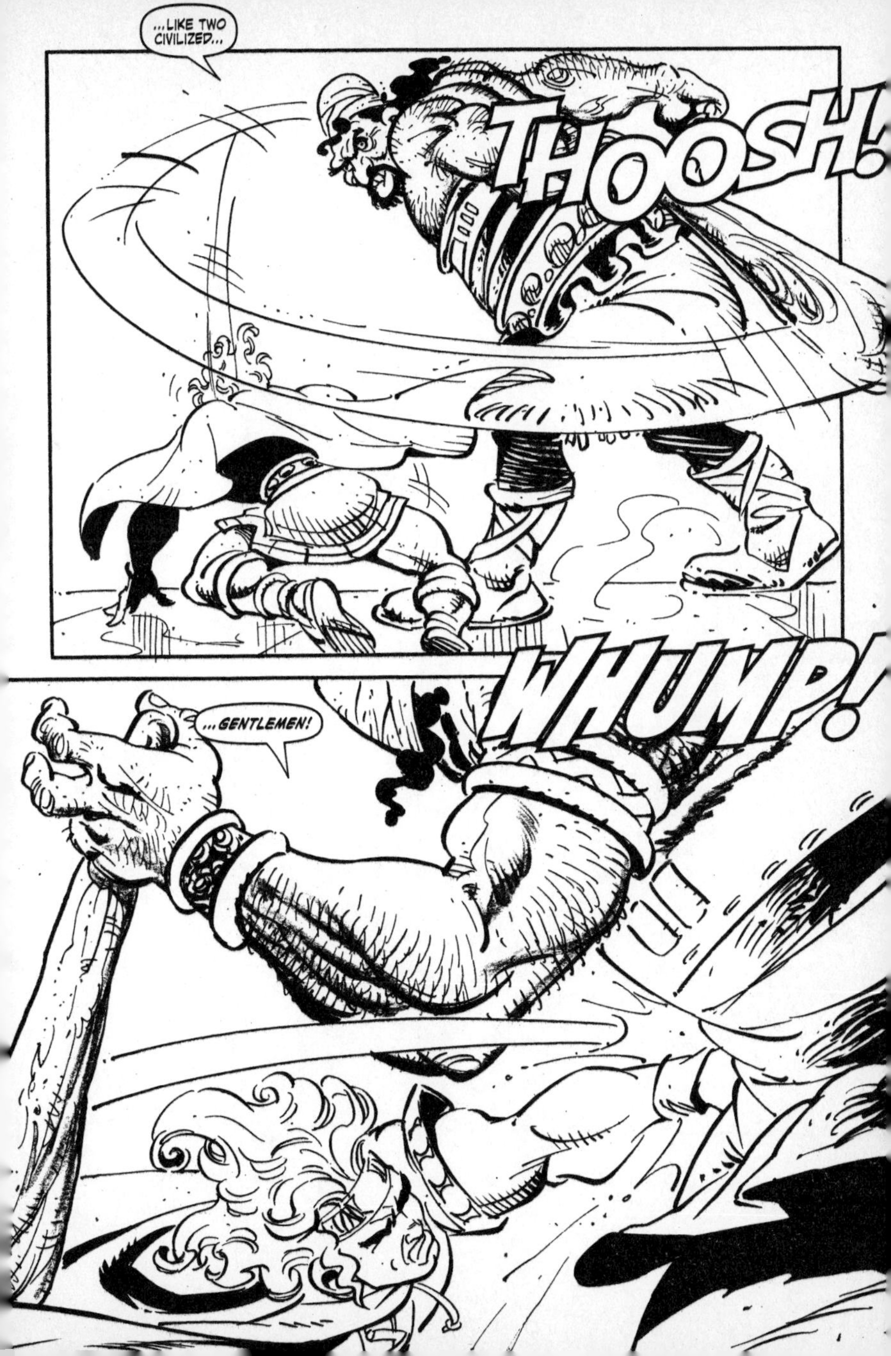
...LIKE TWO CIVILIZED...
THOOSH!
WHUMP!
...GENTLEMEN!

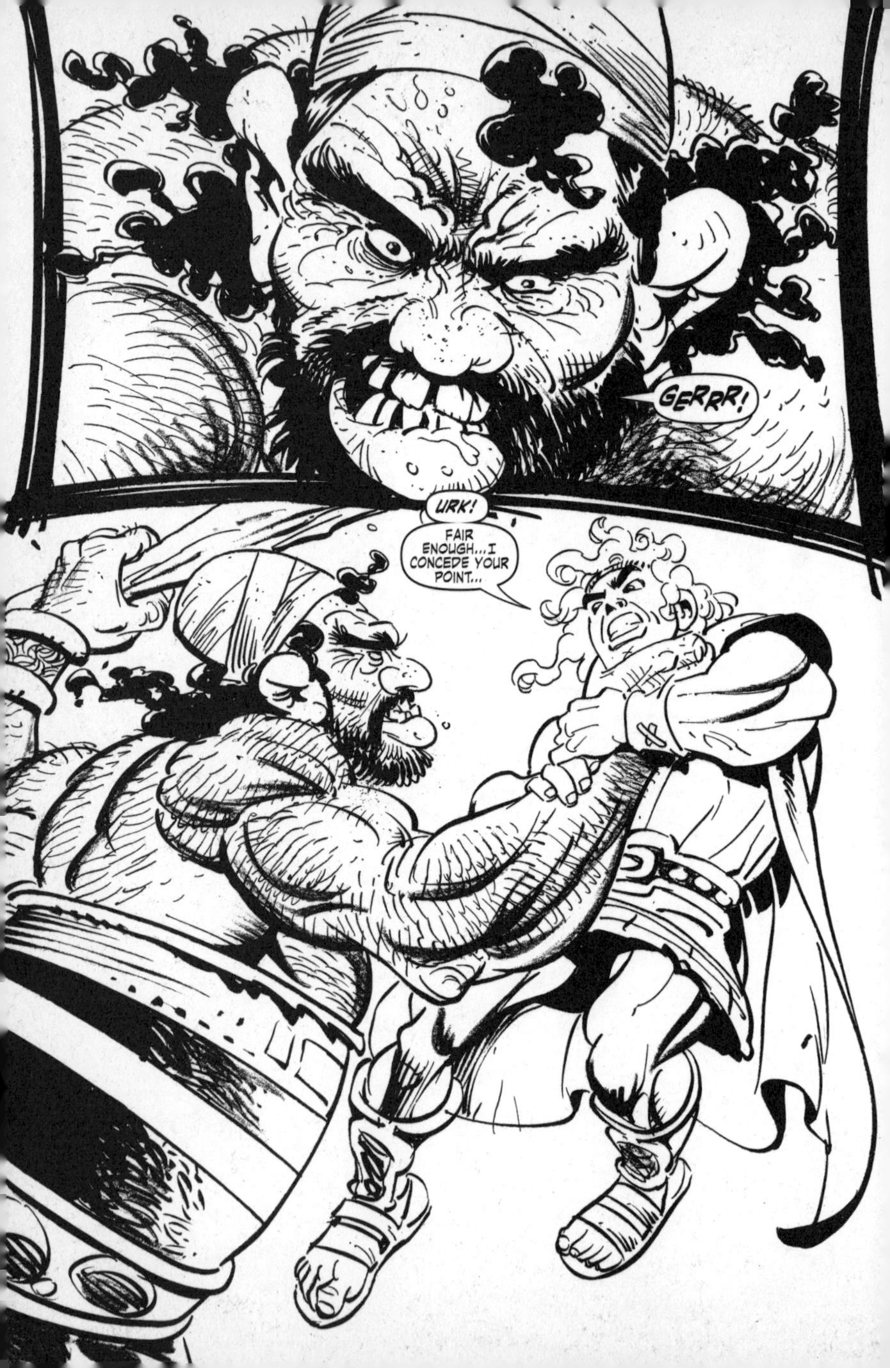
GERRR!
URK!
FAIR ENOUGH...I CONCEDE YOUR POINT...

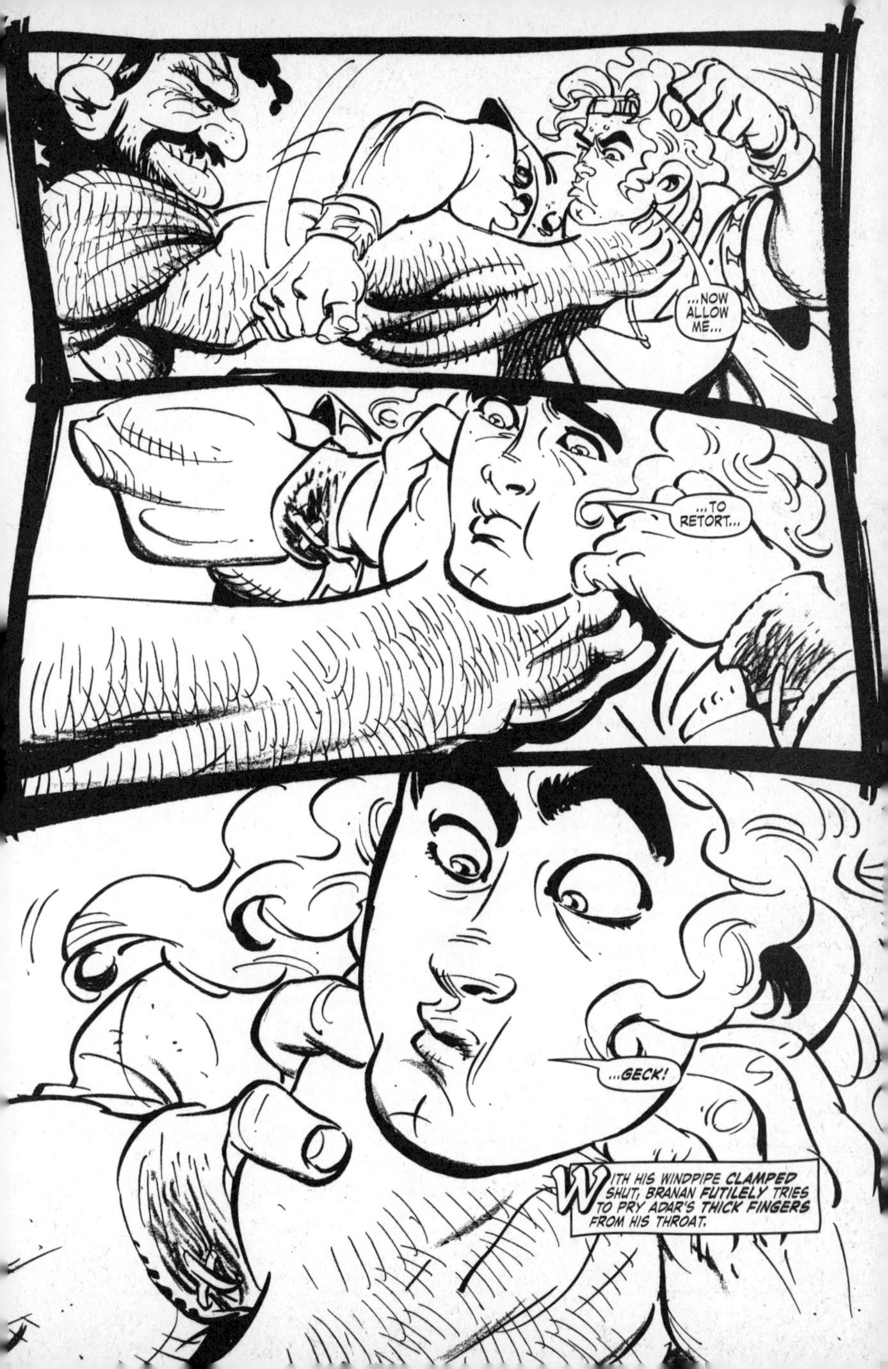

...NOW ALLOW ME...
...TO RETORT...
...GECK!
WITH HIS WINDPIPE CLAMPED SHUT, BRANAN FUTILELY TRIES TO PRY ADAR'S THICK FINGERS FROM HIS THROAT.

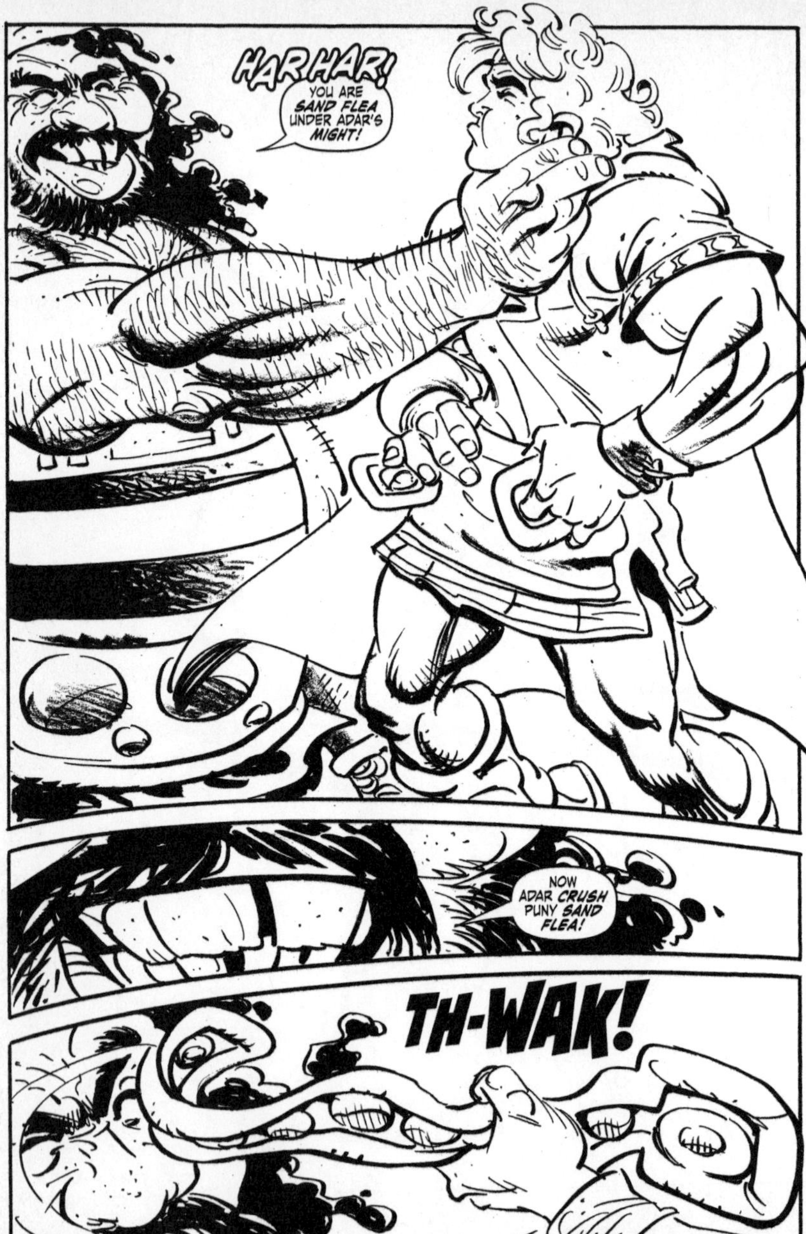
HAR HAR!
YOU ARE SAND FLEA UNDER ADAR'S MIGHT!
NOW ADAR CRUSH PUNY SAND FLEA!
TH-WAK!

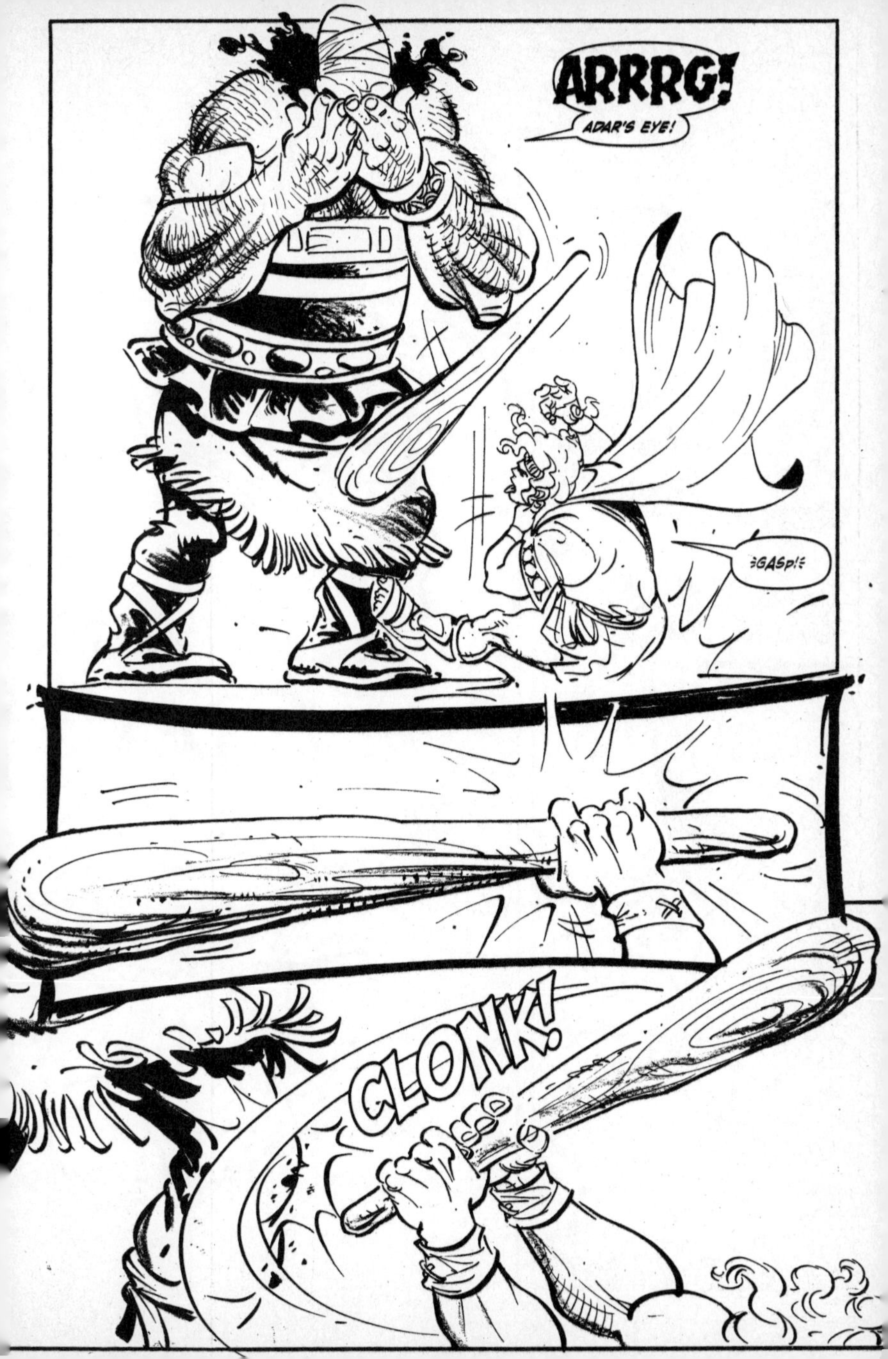
ARRRG!
ADAR'S EYE!
GASp!
CLONK!

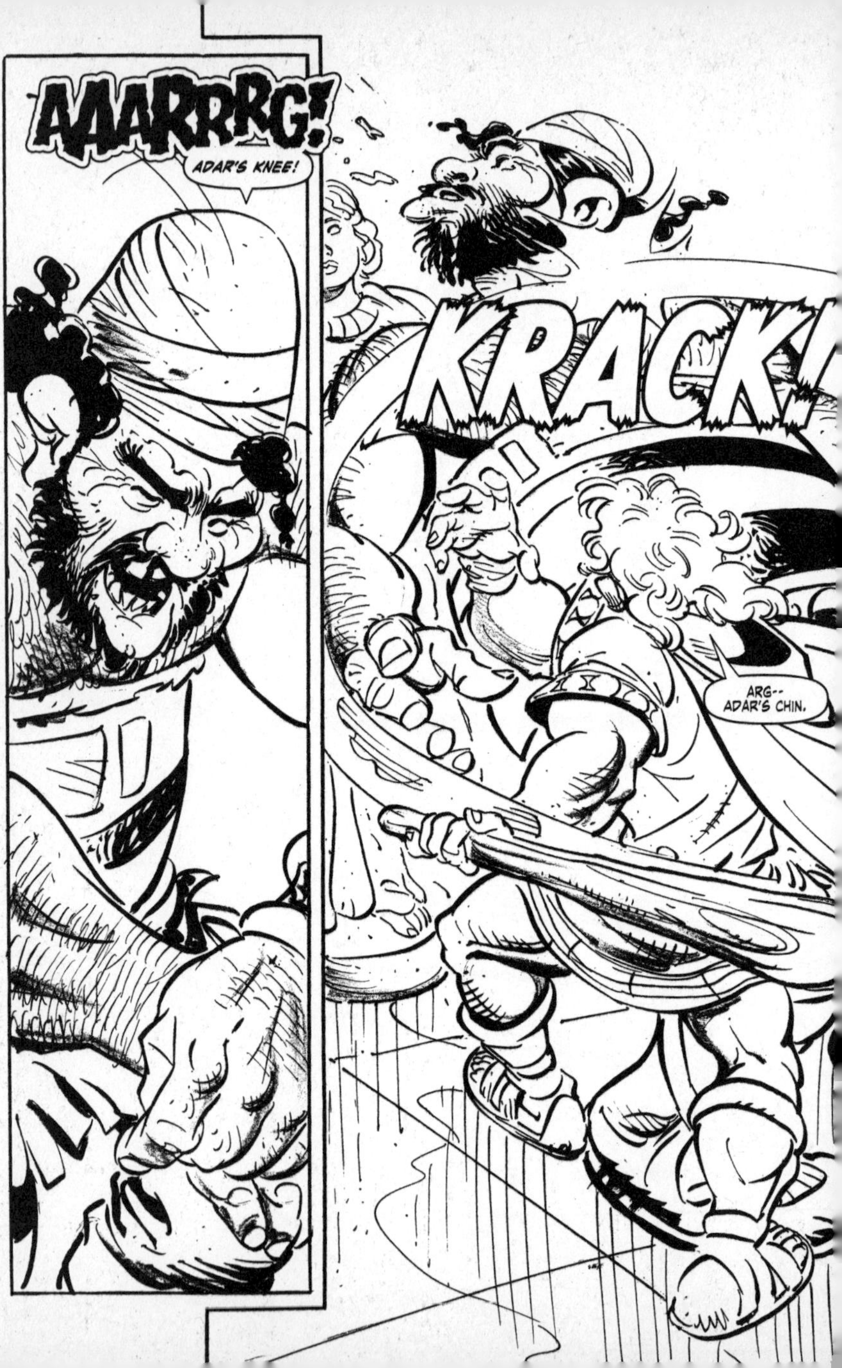
AAARRRG!
ADAR'S KNEE!
KRACK!
ARG--
ADAR'S CHIN.

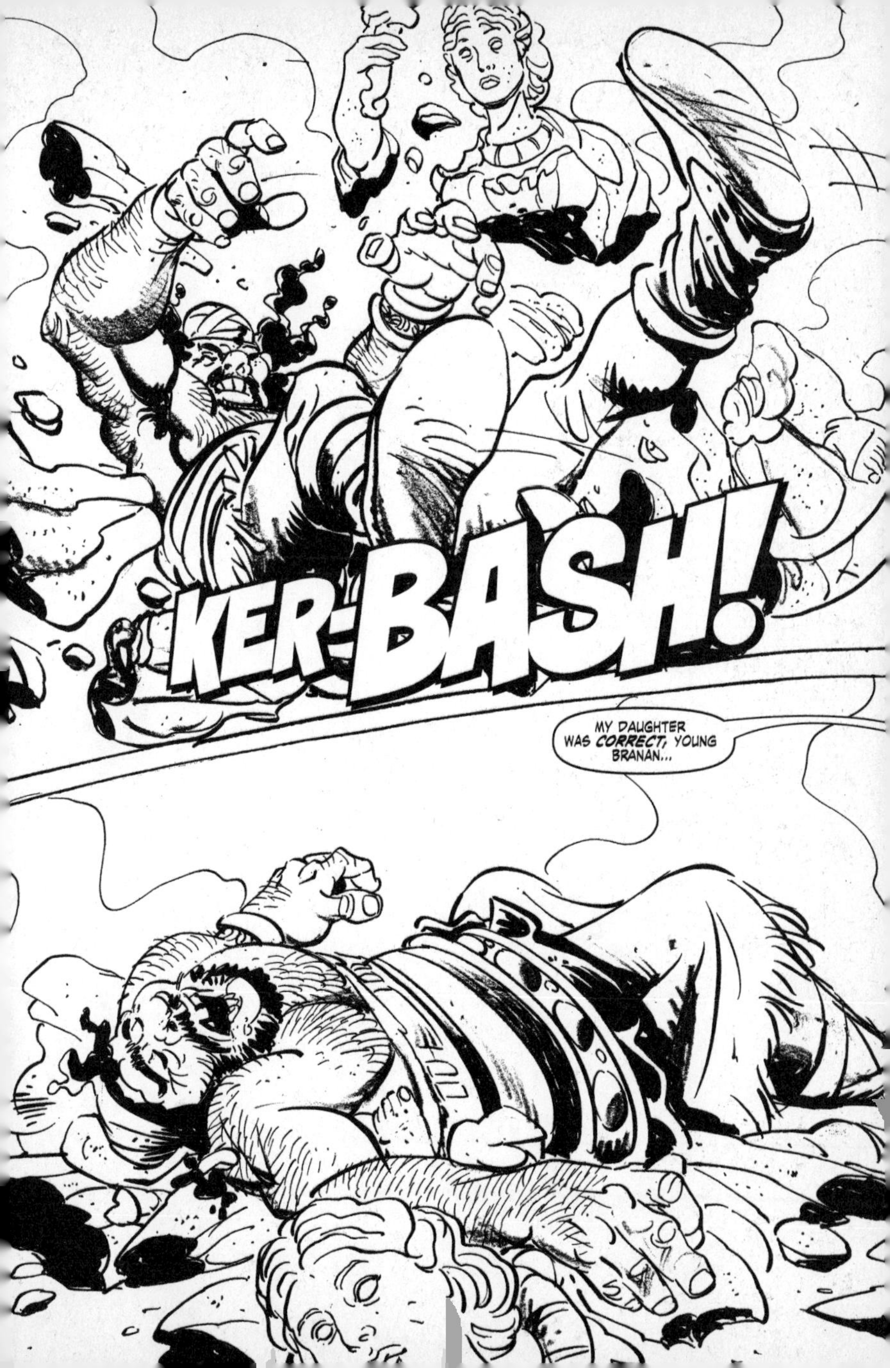
KER-BASH!
MY DAUGHTER WAS CORRECT, YOUNG BRANAN...

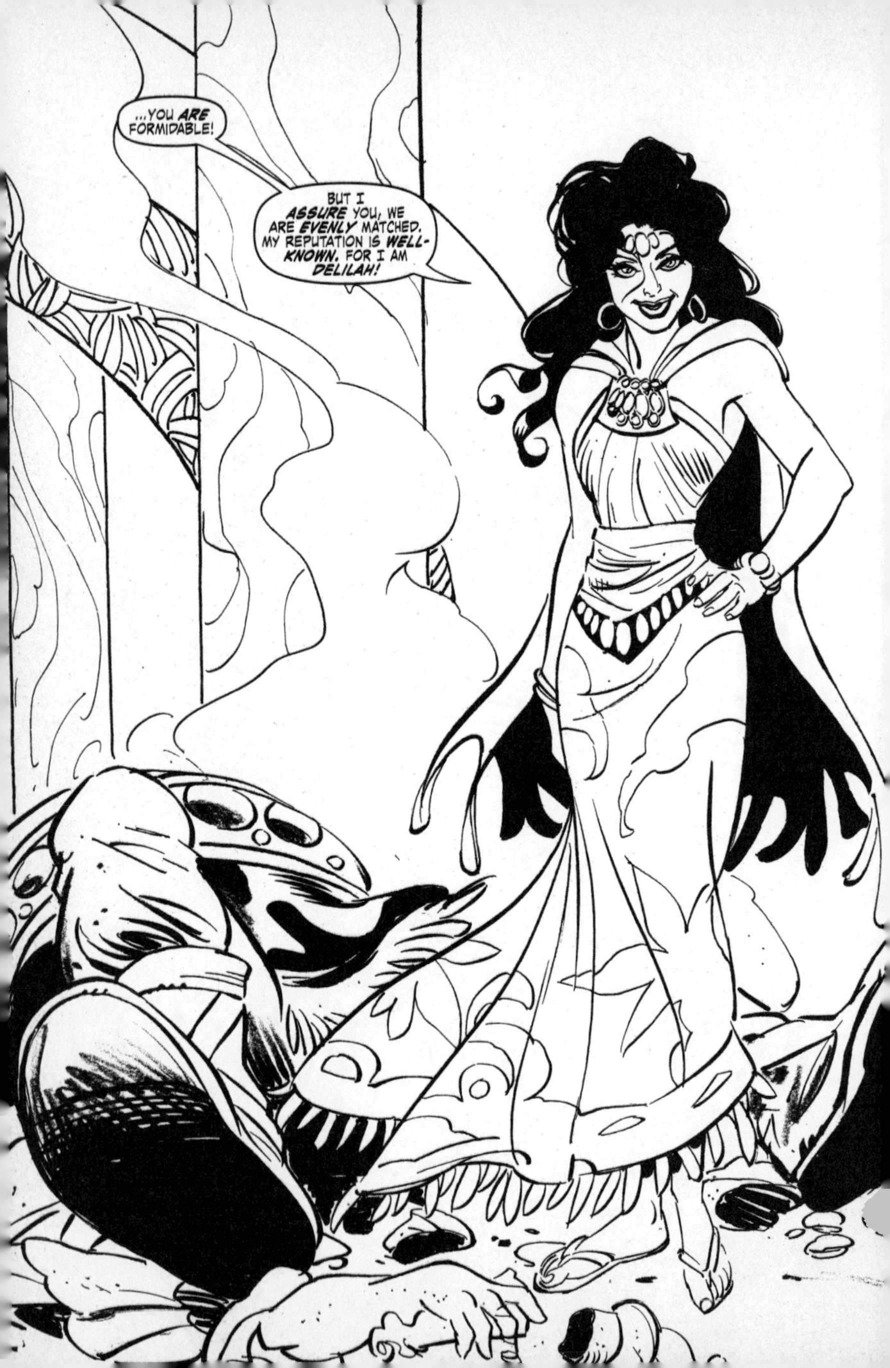
...YOU ARE FORMIDABLE!
BUT I ASSURE YOU, WE ARE EVENLY MATCHED. MY REPUTATION IS WELL-KNOWN. FOR I AM DELILAH!

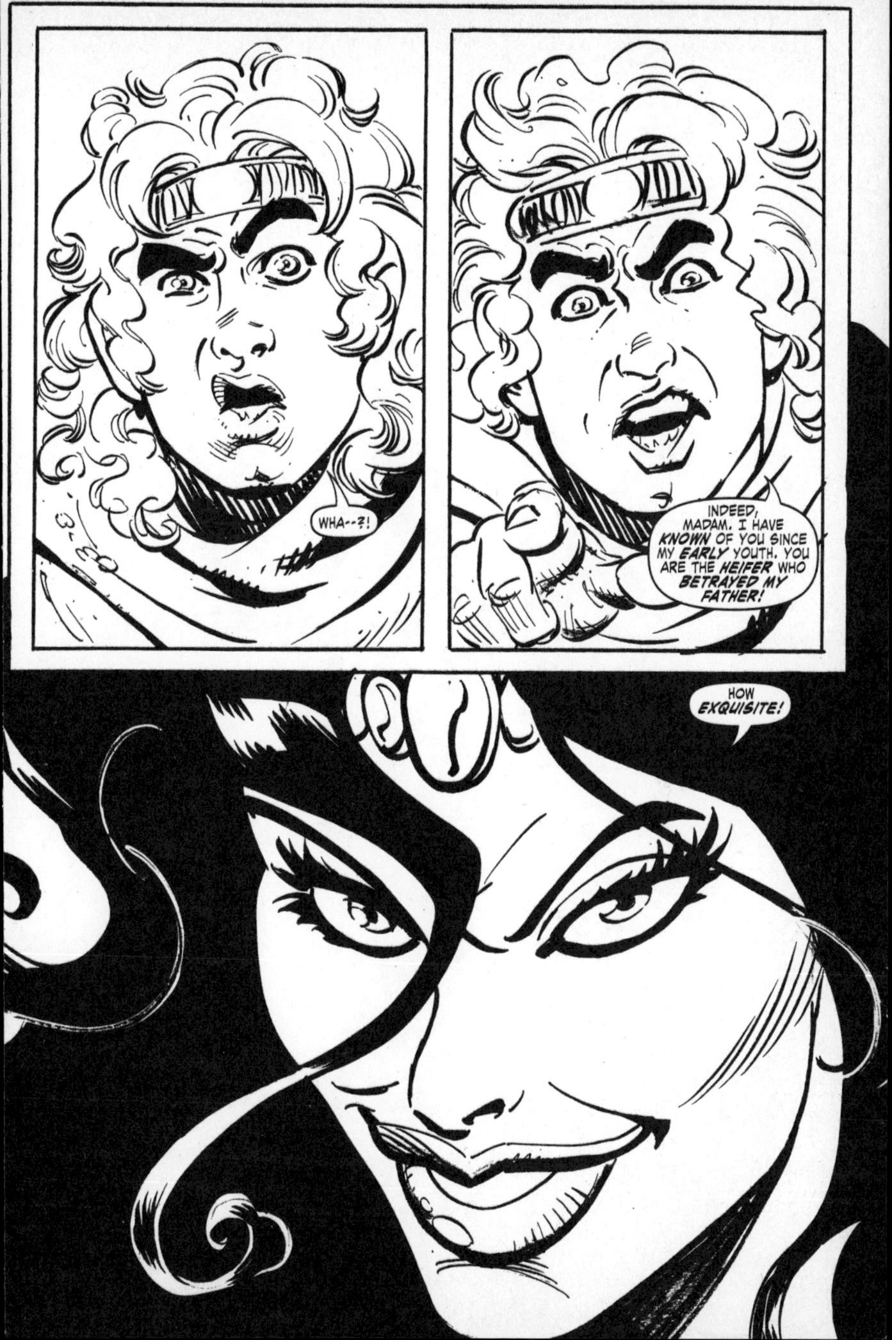
WHA--?!
INDEED, MADAM. I HAVE KNOWN OF YOU SINCE MY EARLY YOUTH. YOU ARE THE HEIFER WHO BETRAYED MY FATHER!
HOW EXQUISITE!

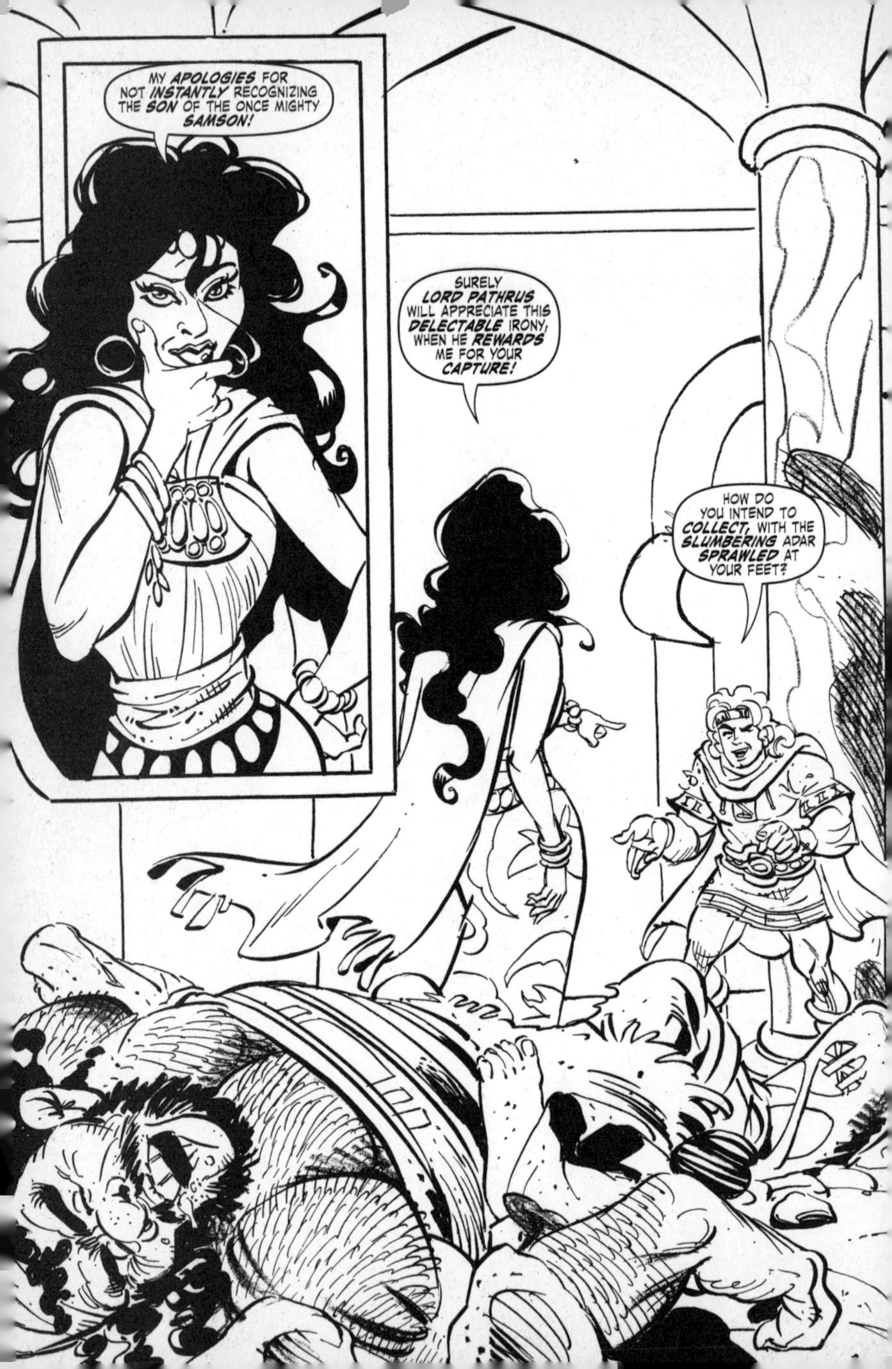
MY APOLOGIES FOR NOT INSTANTLY RECOGNIZING THE SON OF THE ONCE MIGHTY SAMSON!
SURELY LORD PATHRUS WILL APPRECIATE THIS DELECTABLE IRONY, WHEN HE REWARDS ME FOR YOUR CAPTURE!
HOW DO YOU INTEND TO COLLECT, WITH THE SLUMBERING ADAR SPRAWLED AT YOUR FEET?

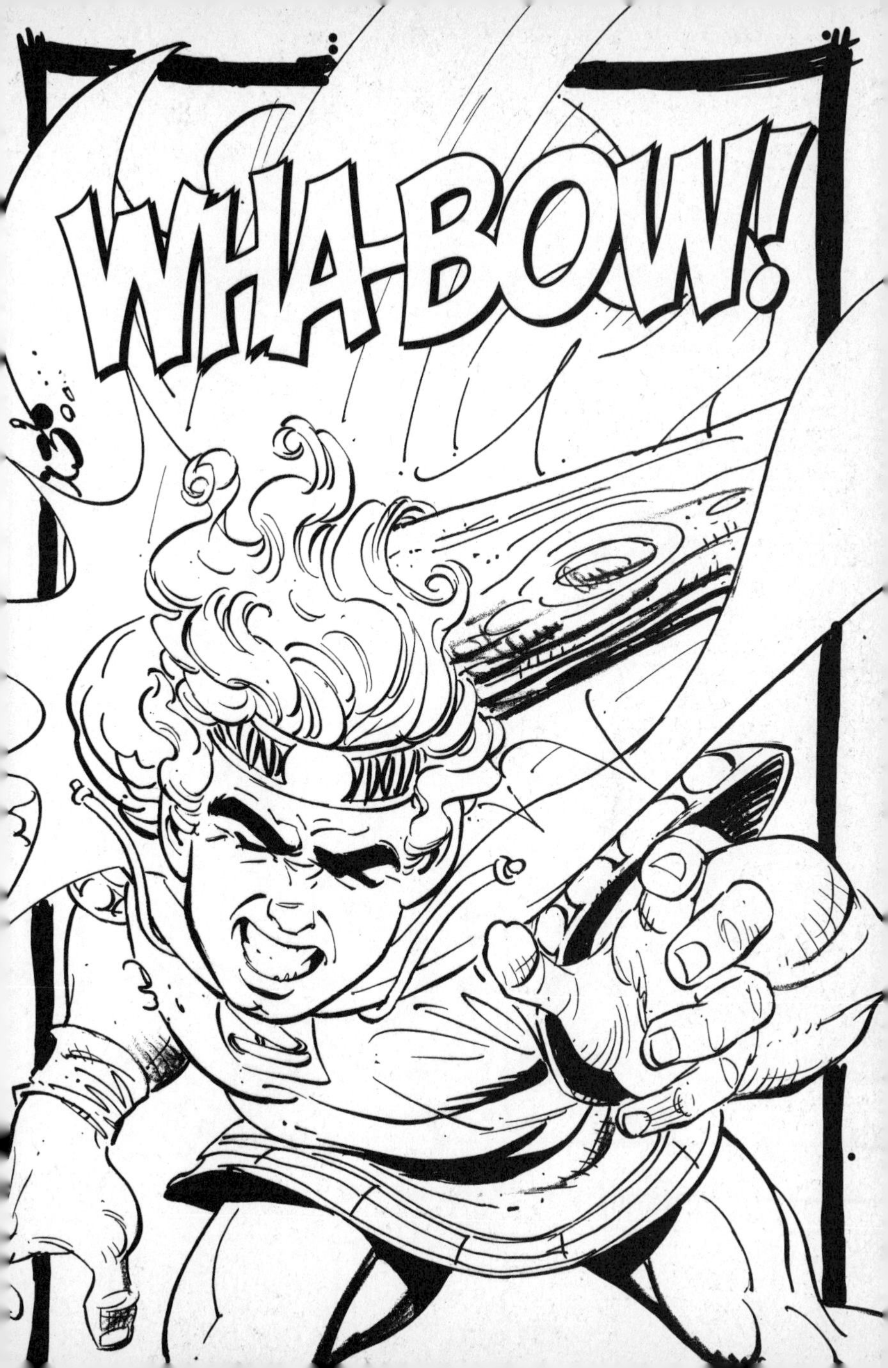
WHA-BOW!

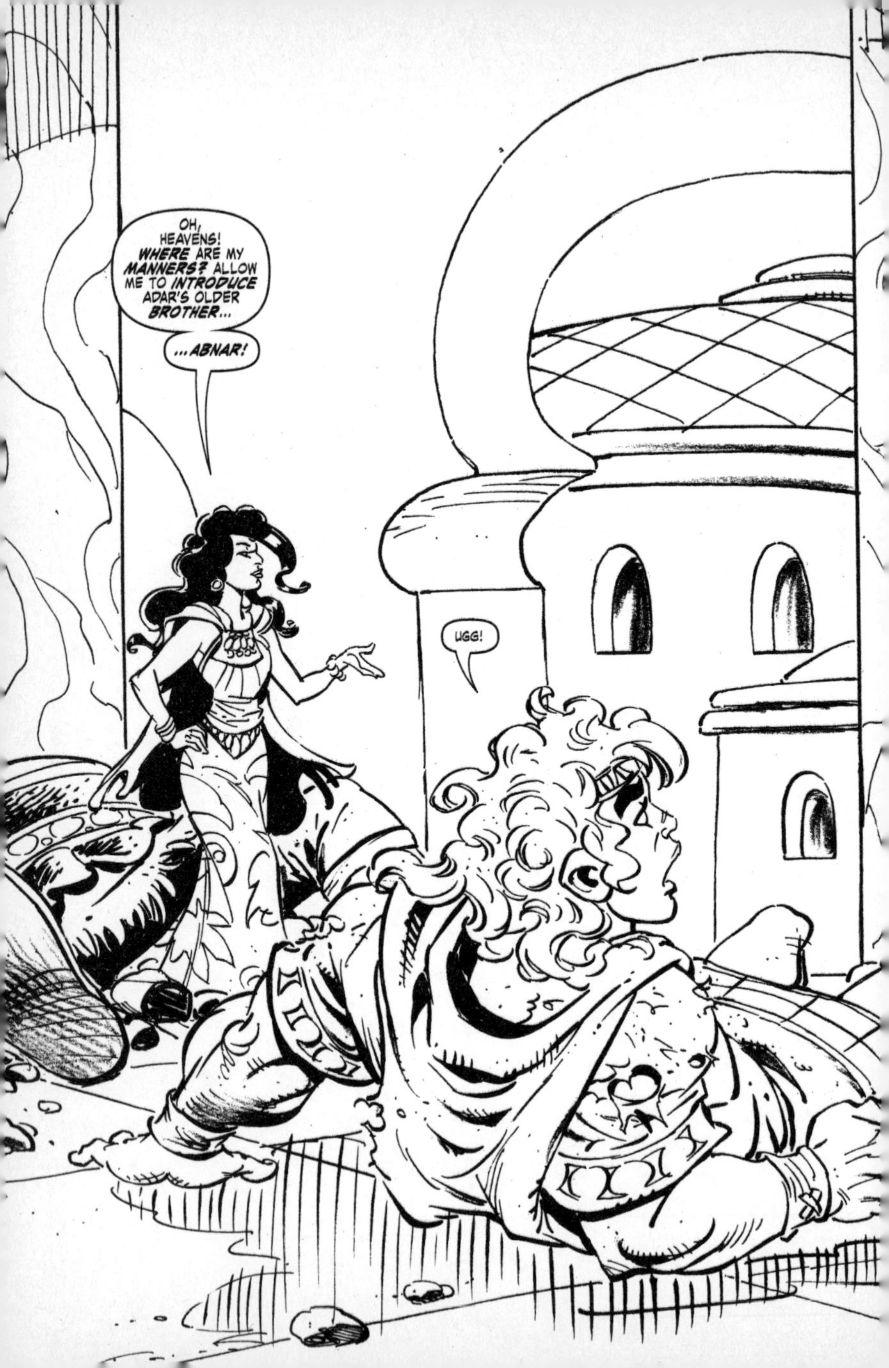
OH, HEAVENS! WHERE ARE MY MANNERS? ALLOW ME TO INTRODUCE ADAR'S OLDER BROTHER...
...ABNAR!
UGG!

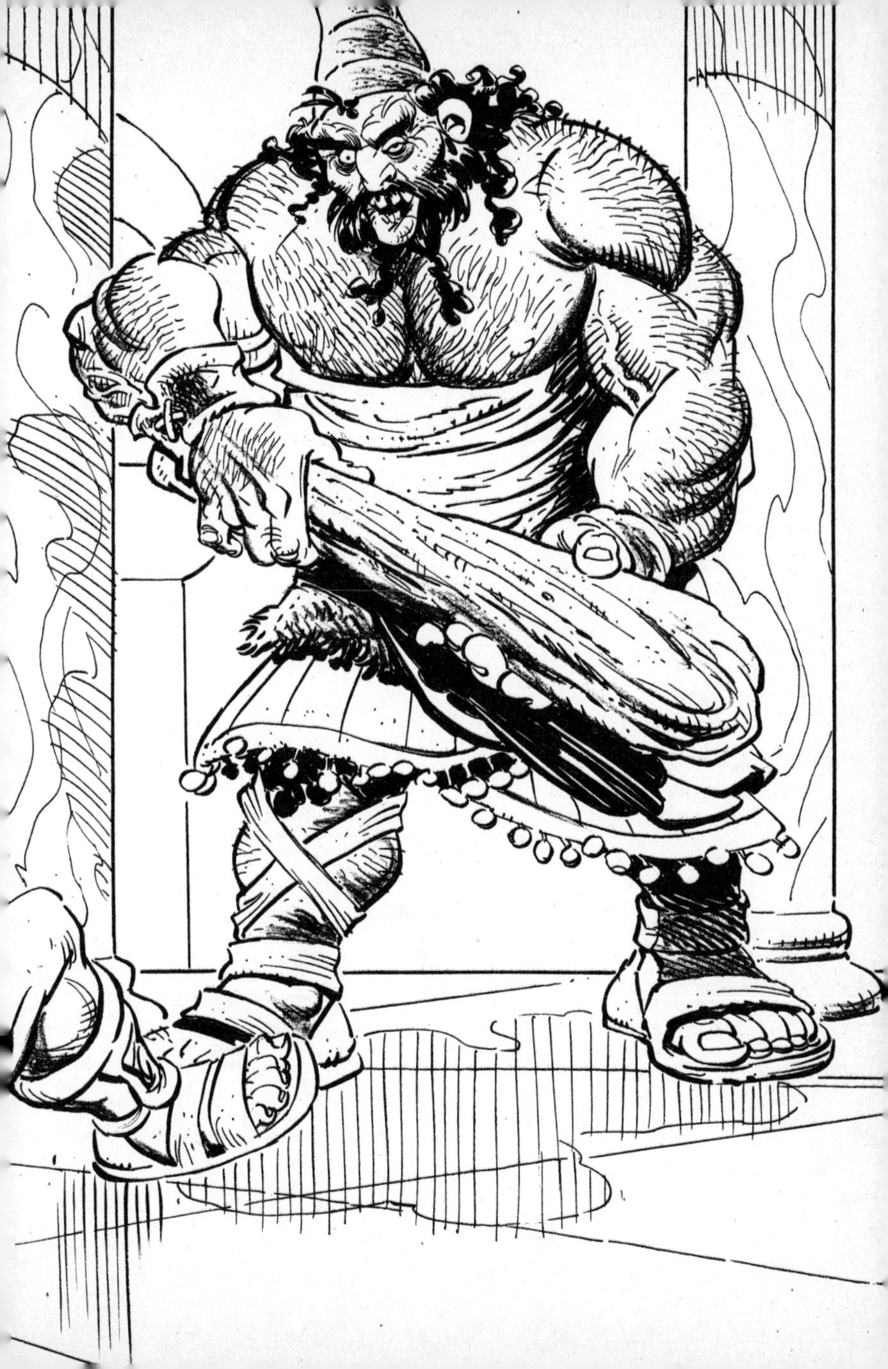

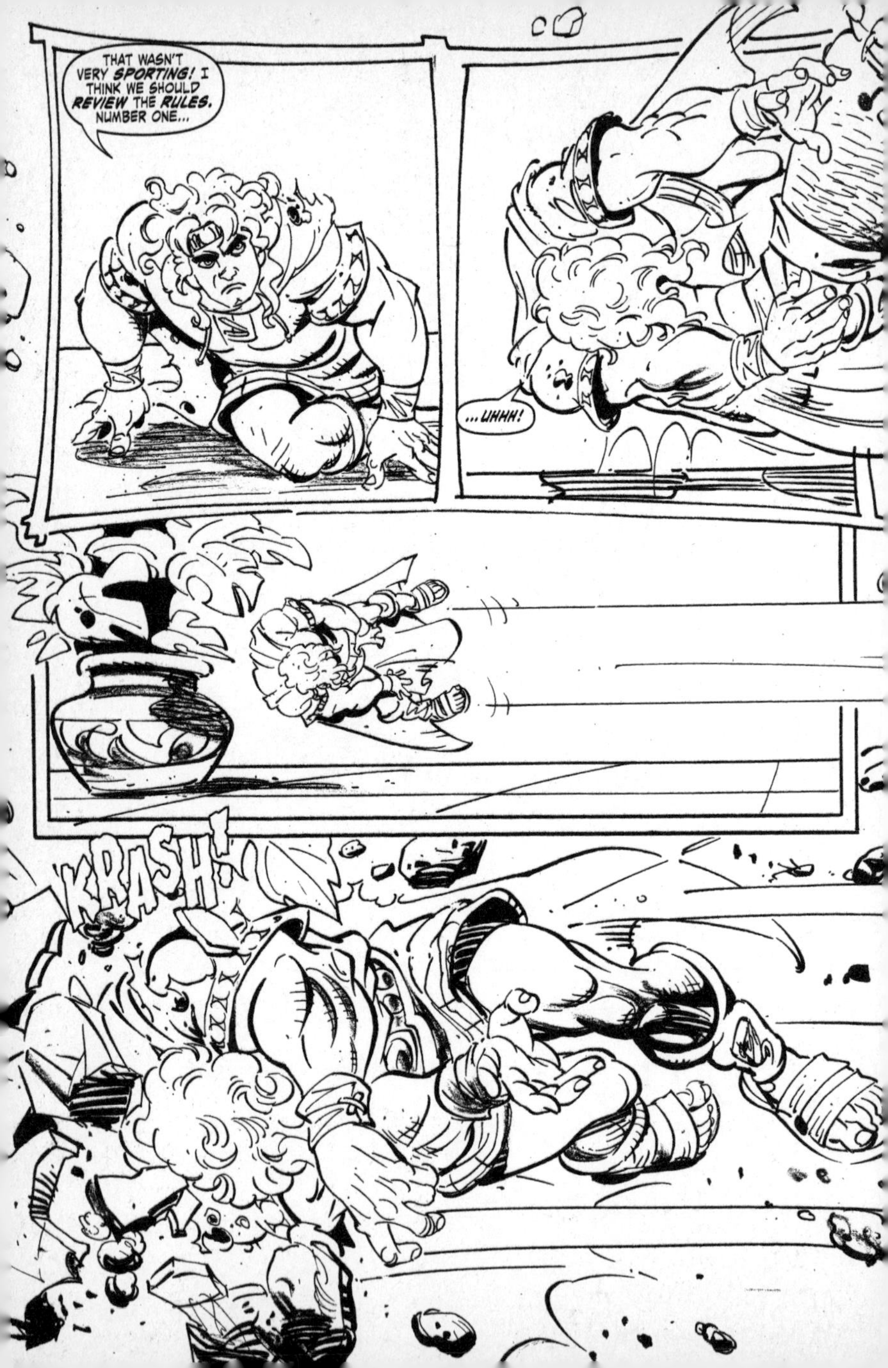
THAT WASN'T VERY SPORTING! I THINK WE SHOULD REVIEW THE RULES. NUMBER ONE...
...UHHH!
KRASH!

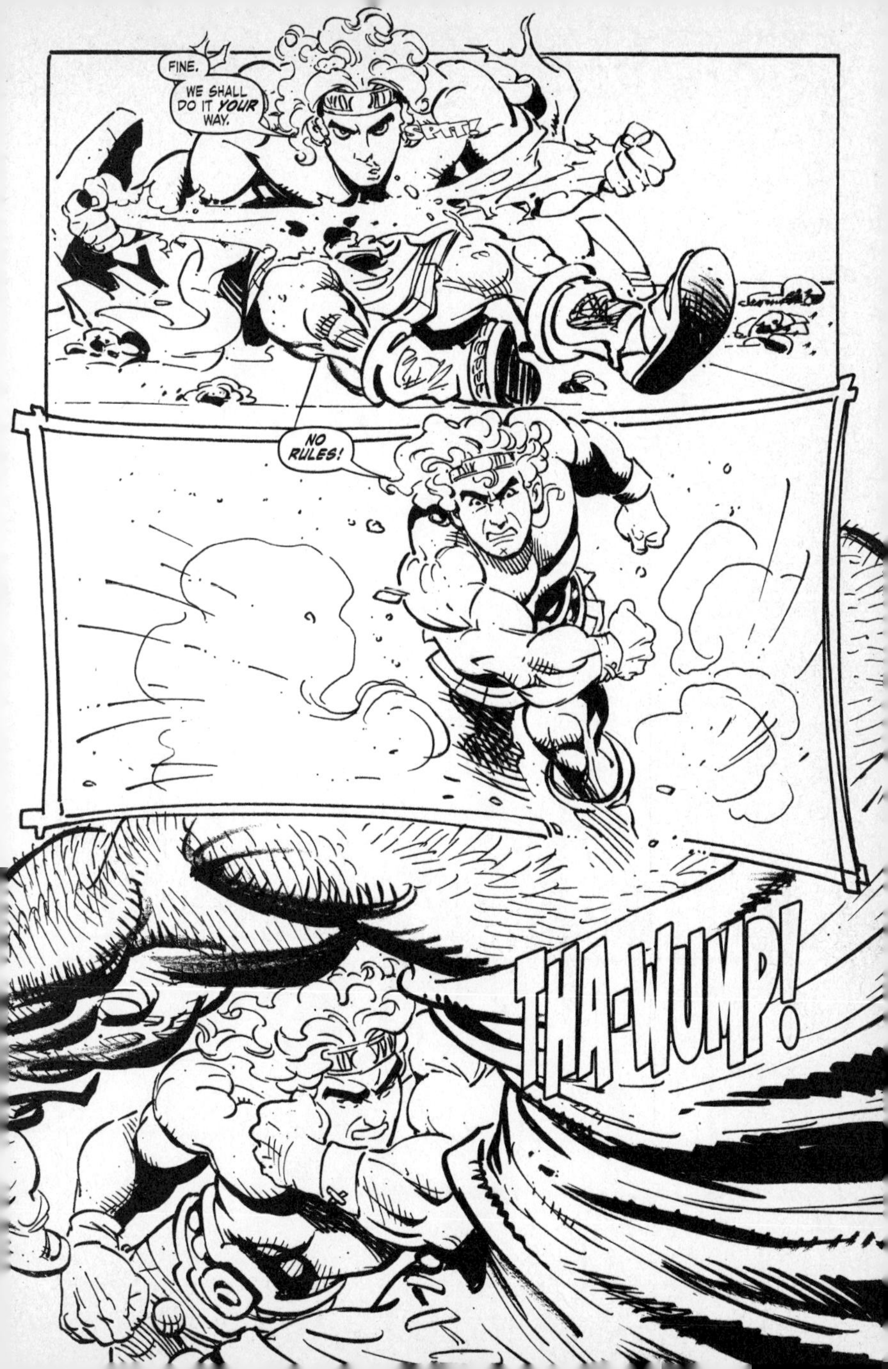
FINE.
WE SHALL DO IT YOUR WAY.
SPIT!
NO RULES!
THA-WUMP!

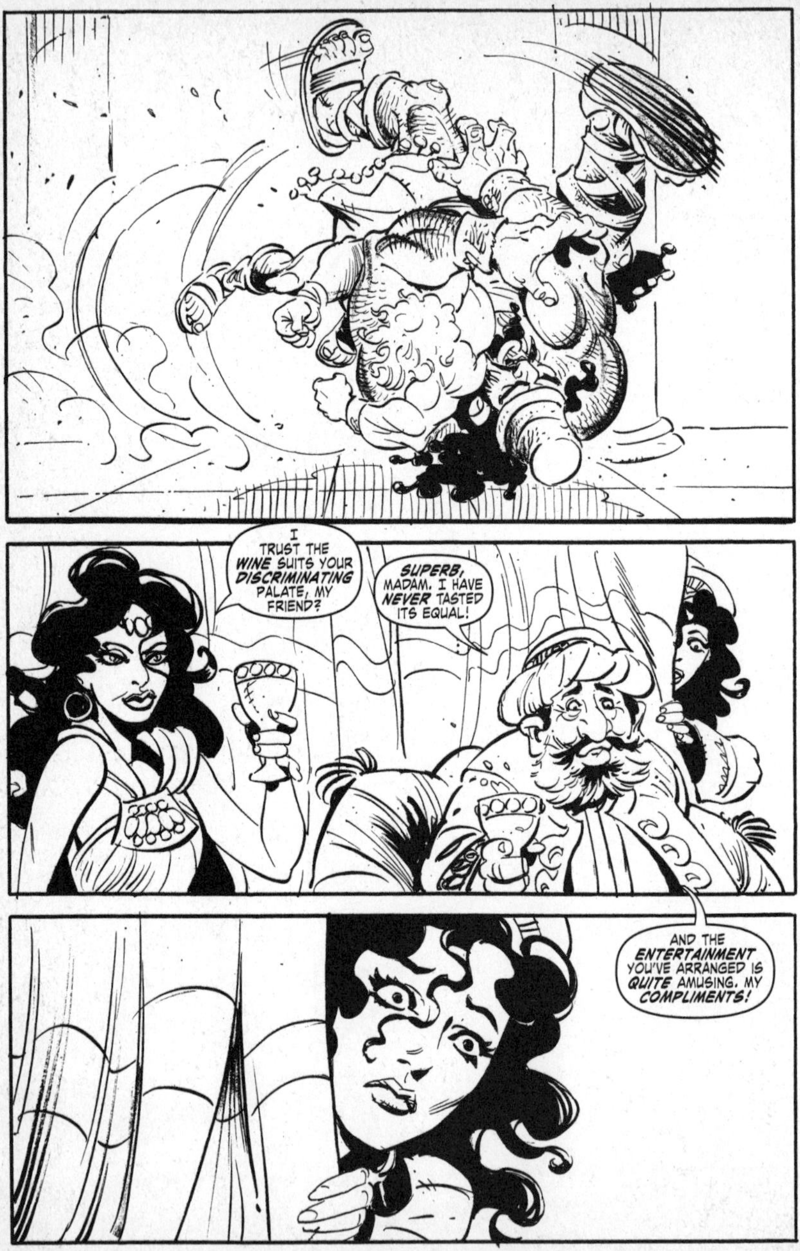

I TRUST THE WINE SUITS YOUR DISCRIMINATING PALATE, MY FRIEND?
SUPERB, MADAM. I HAVE NEVER TASTED ITS EQUAL!
AND THE ENTERTAINMENT YOU'VE ARRANGED IS QUITE AMUSING. MY COMPLIMENTS!

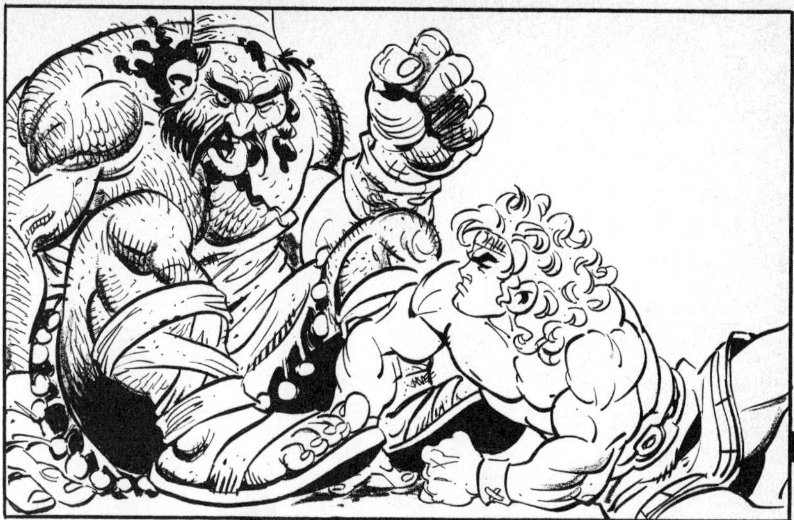

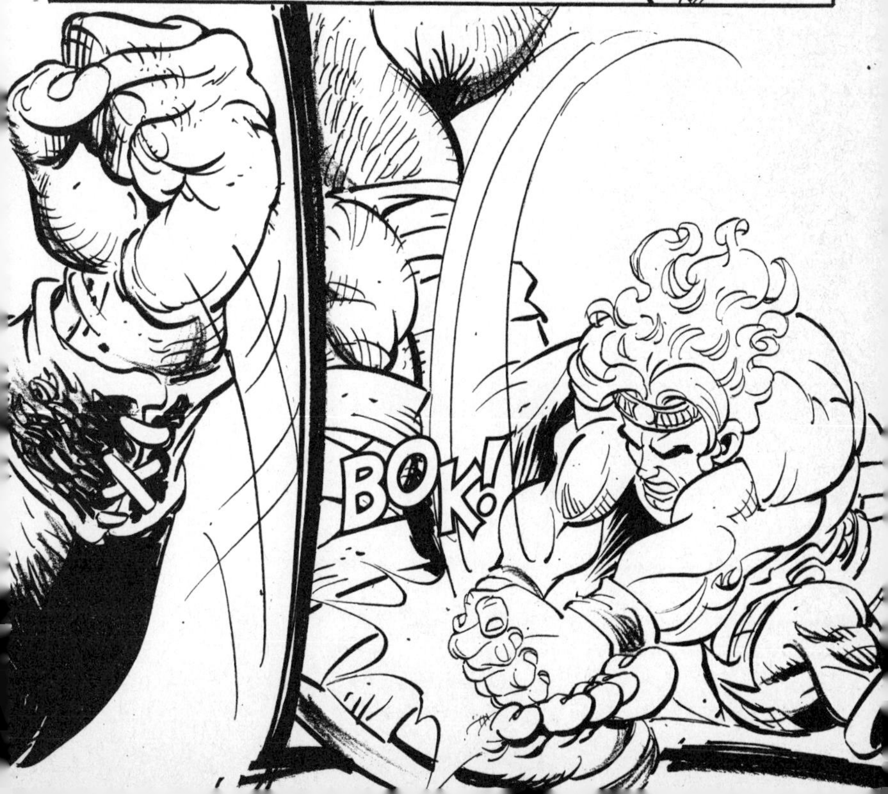
BOK!

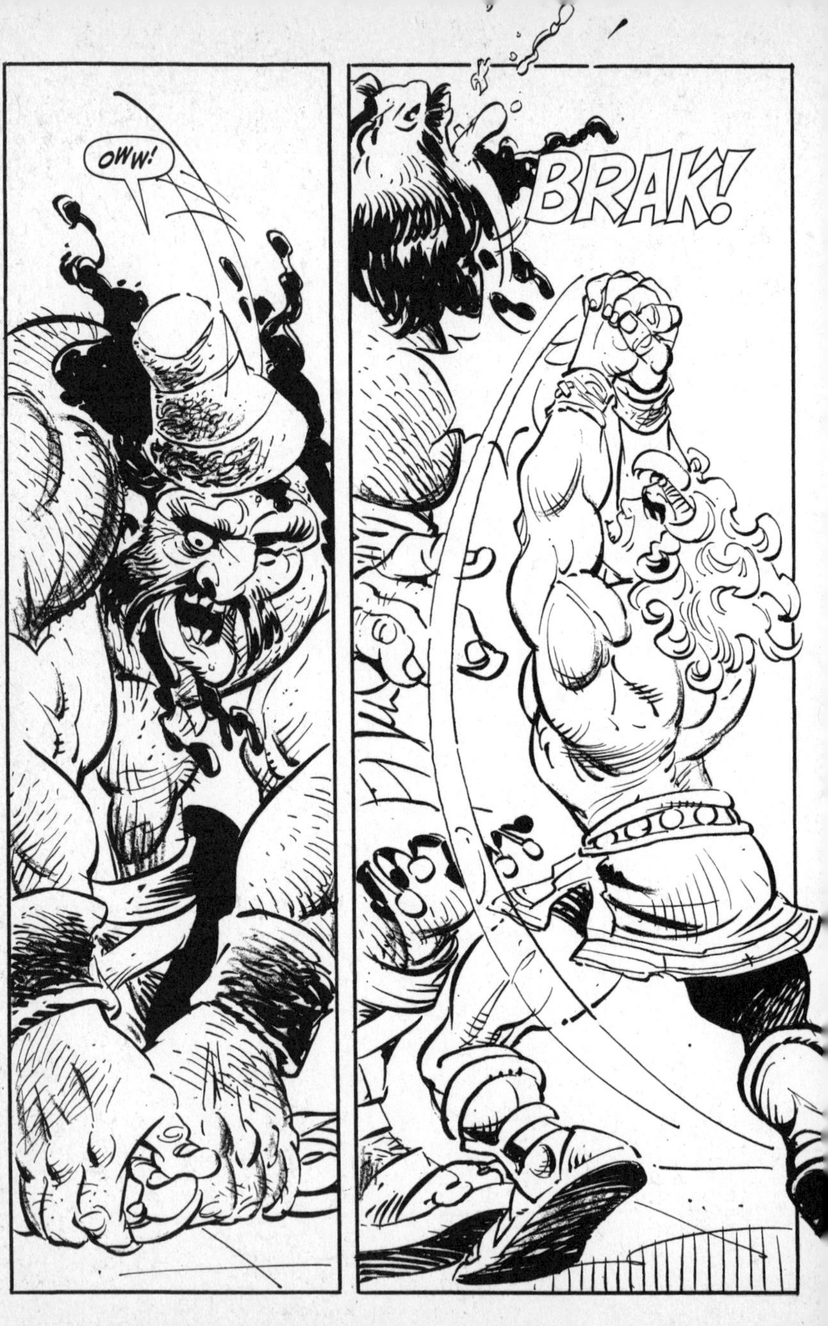
OWW!
BRAK!

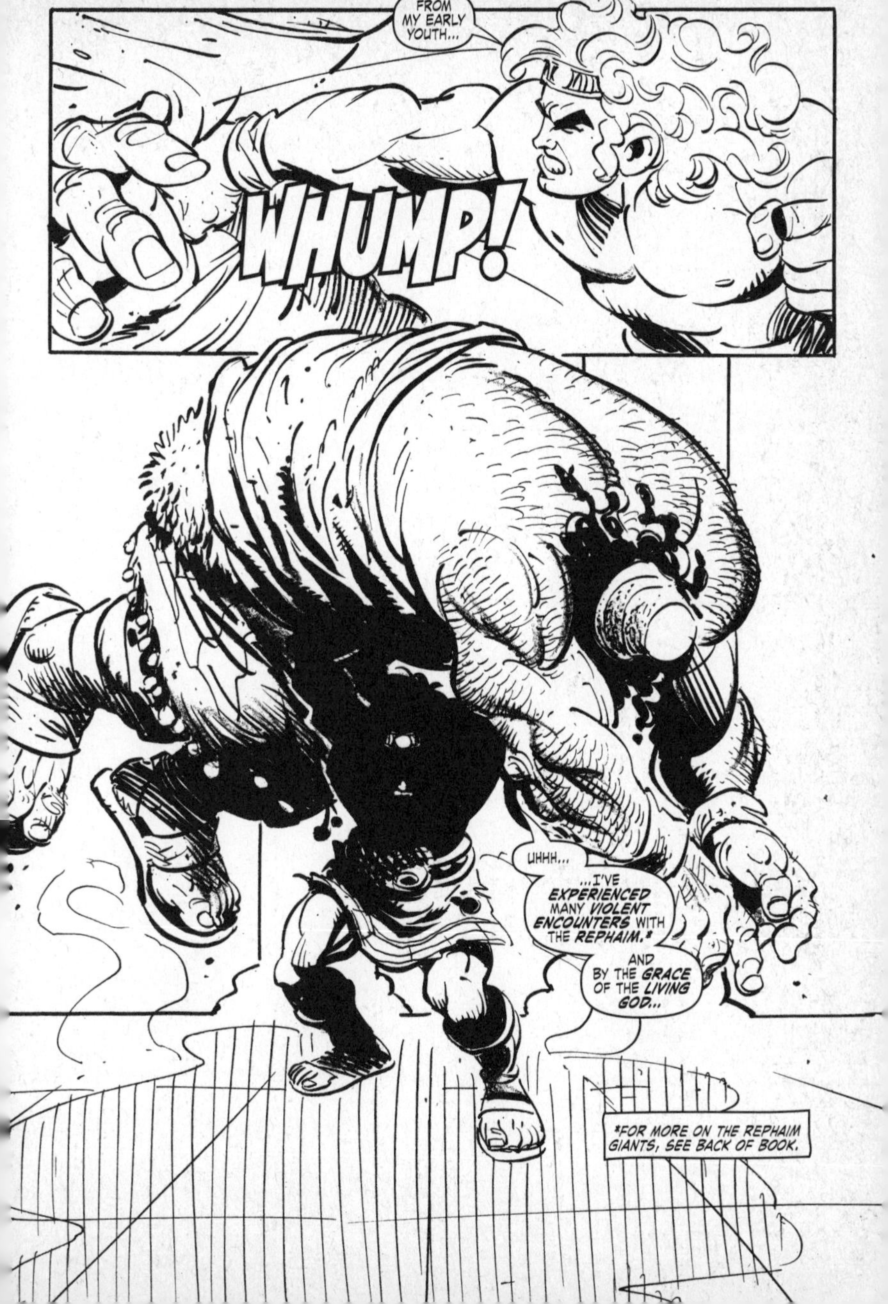
FROM MY EARLY YOUTH...
WHUMP!
UHHH...
...I'VE EXPERIENCED MANY VIOLENT ENCOUNTERS WITH THE REPHAIM.*
AND BY THE GRACE OF THE LIVING GOD...
*FOR MORE ON THE REPHAIM GIANTS, SEE BACK OF BOOK.

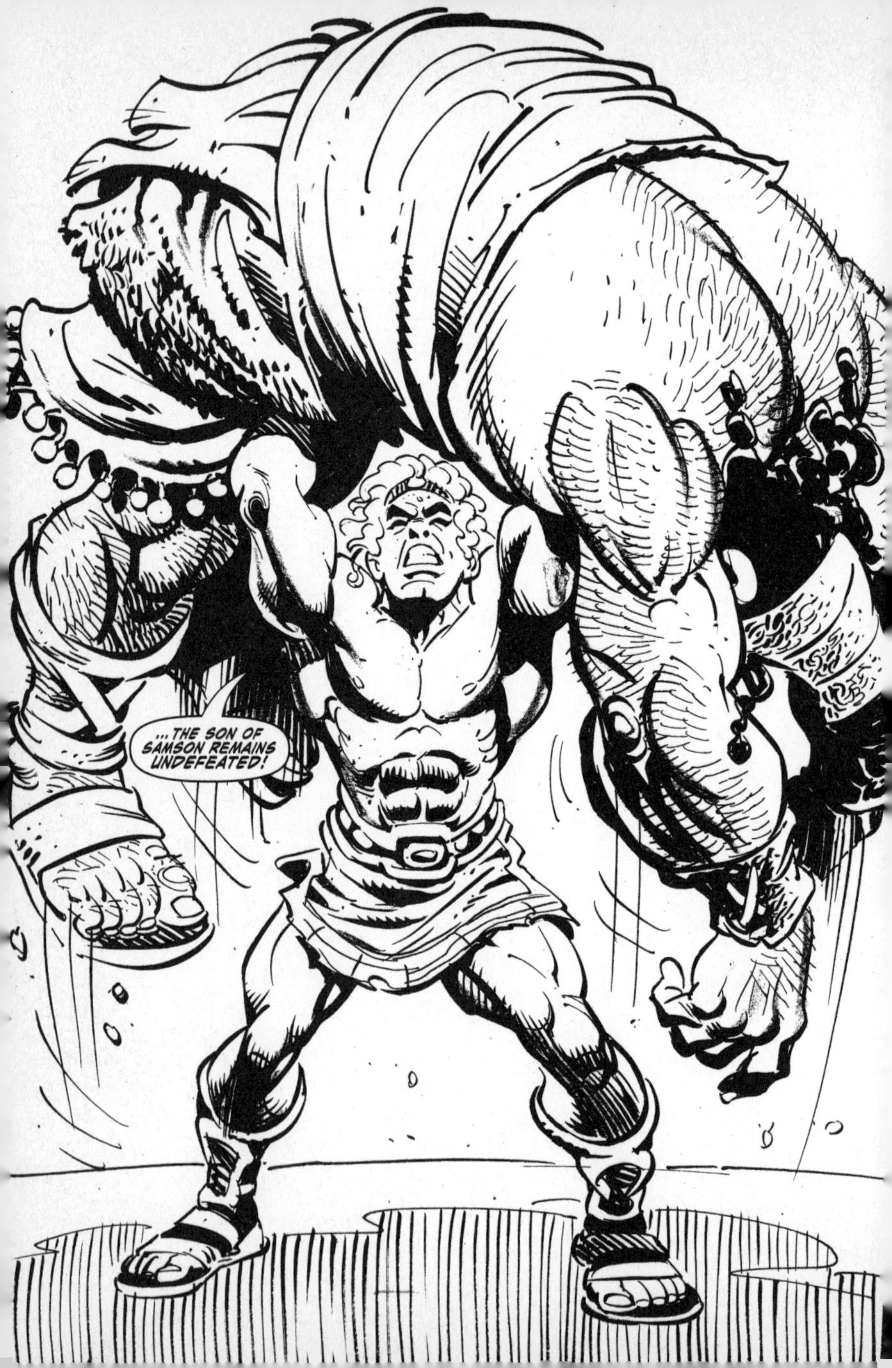
...THE SON OF SAMSON REMAINS UNDEFEATED!

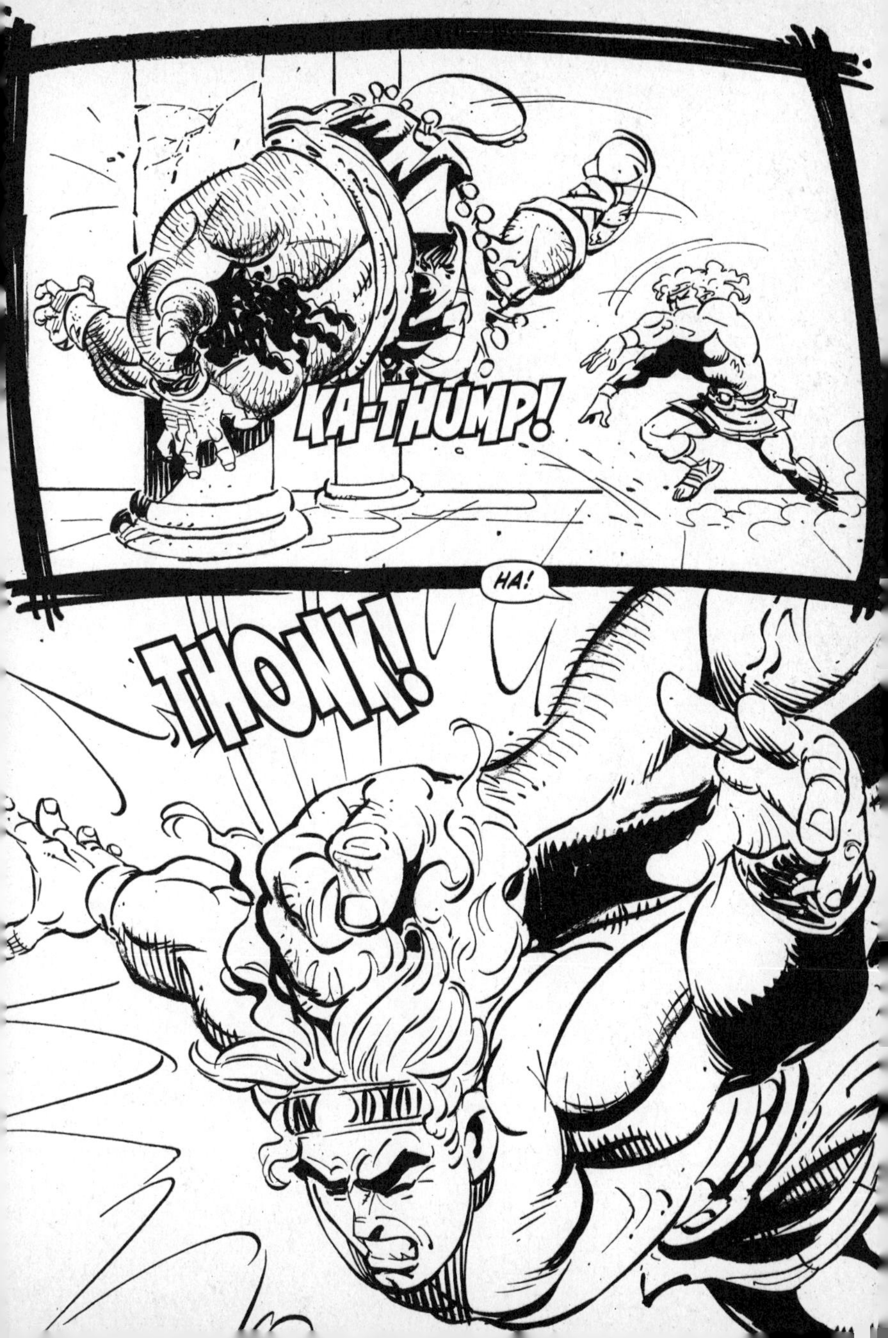
KA-THUMP!
HA!
THONK!

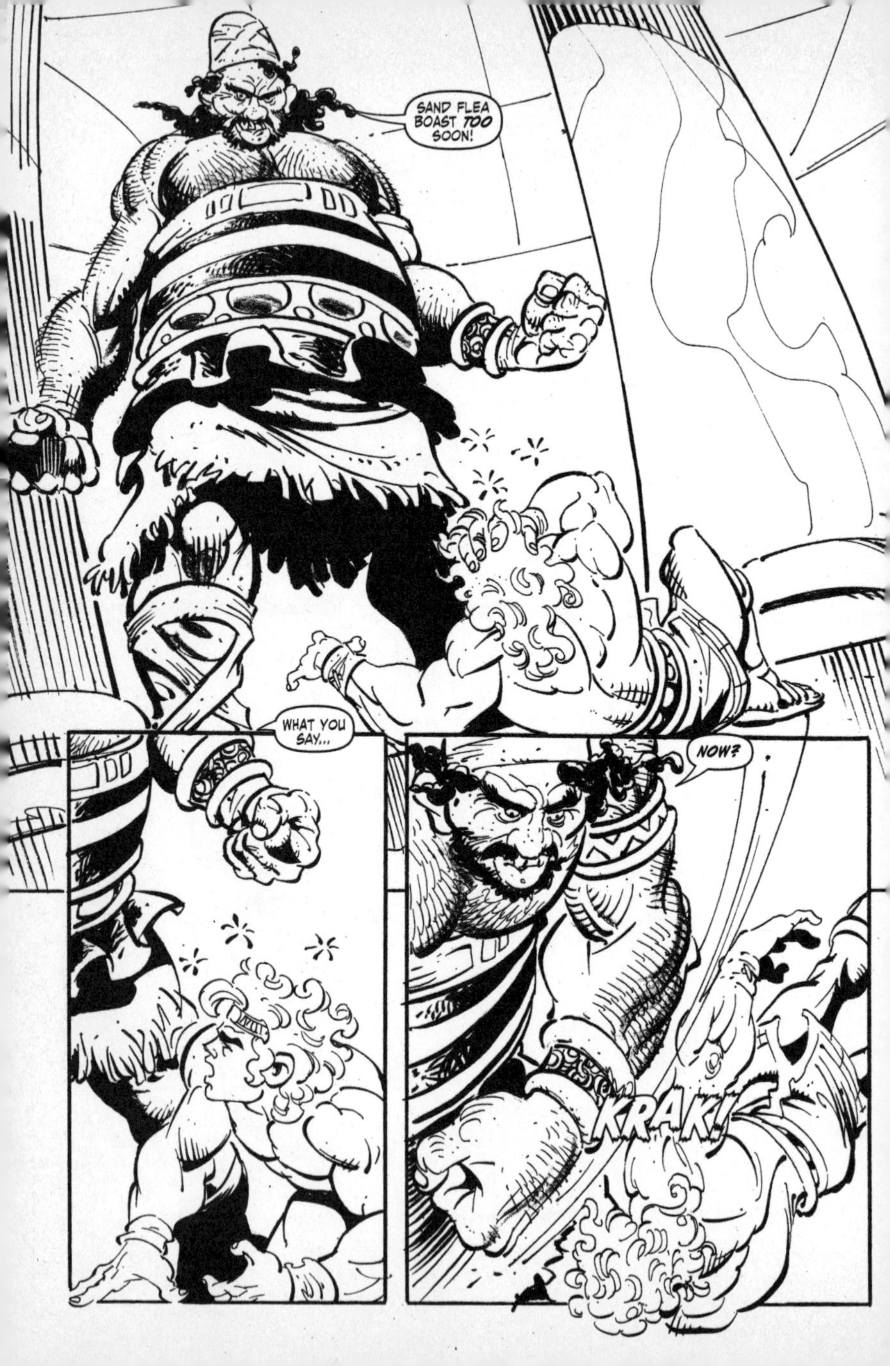
SAND FLEA BOAST *TOO* SOON!
WHAT YOU SAY...
NOW?
KRAK!

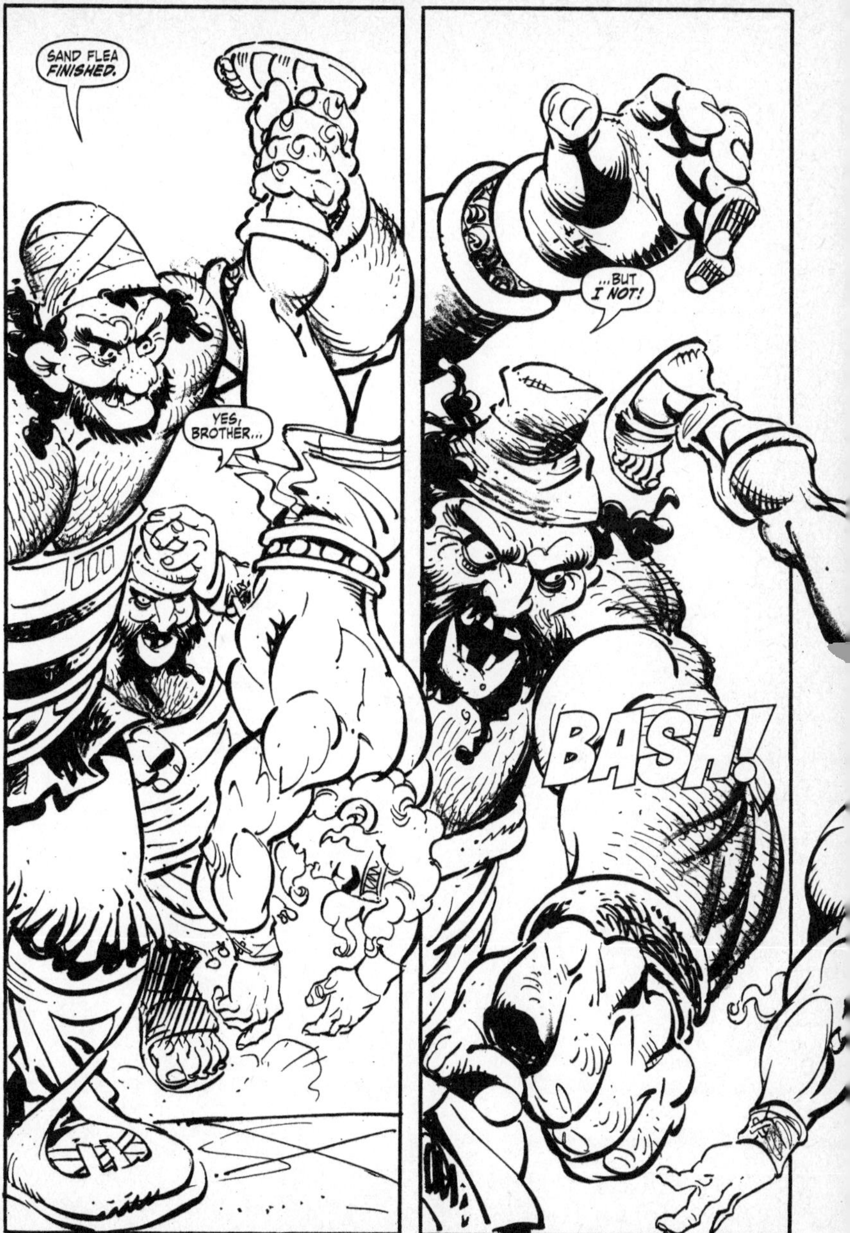
SAND FLEA FINISHED.
YES, BROTHER...
...BUT I NOT!
BASH!

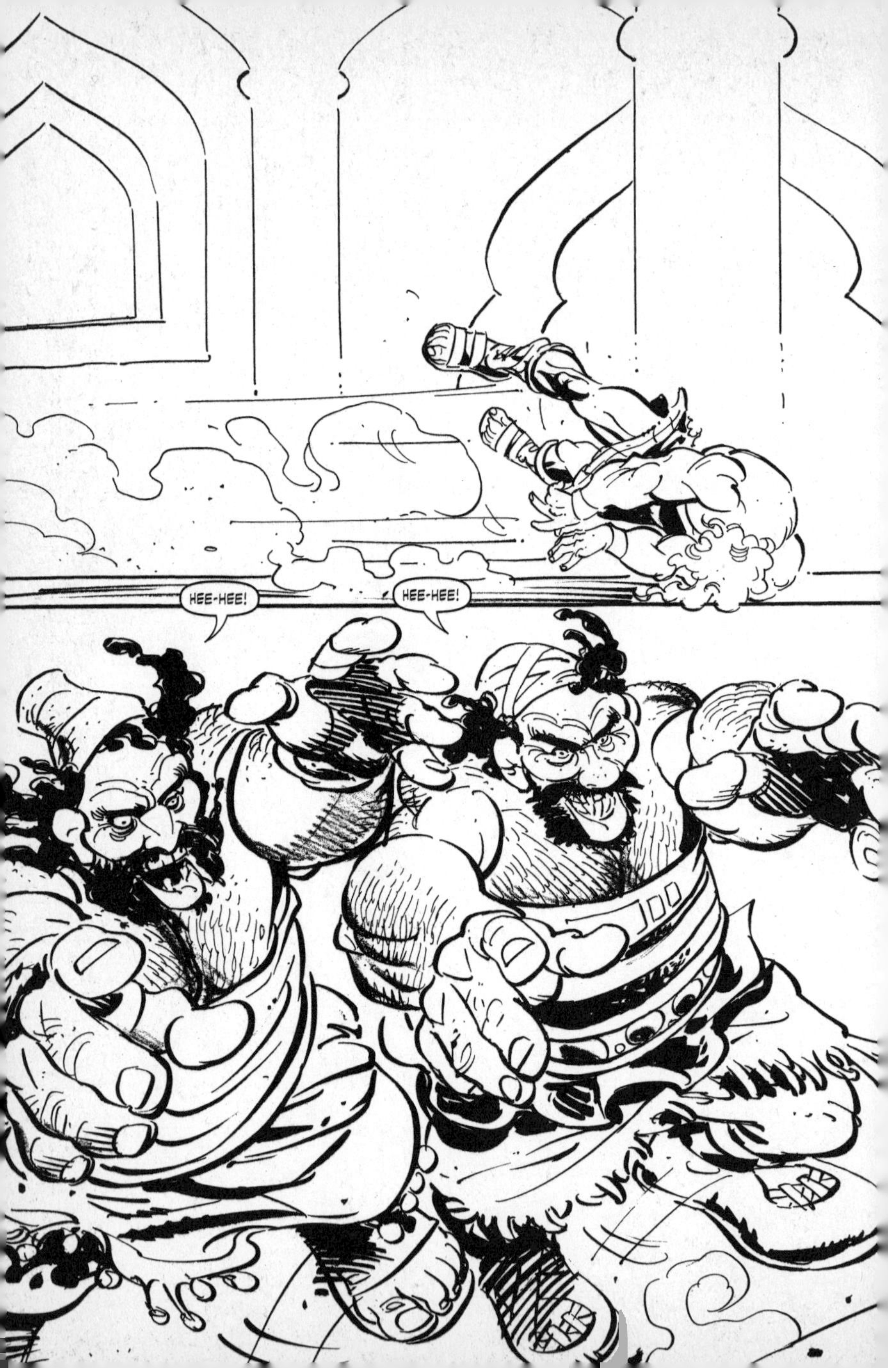
HEE-HEE!
HEE-HEE!

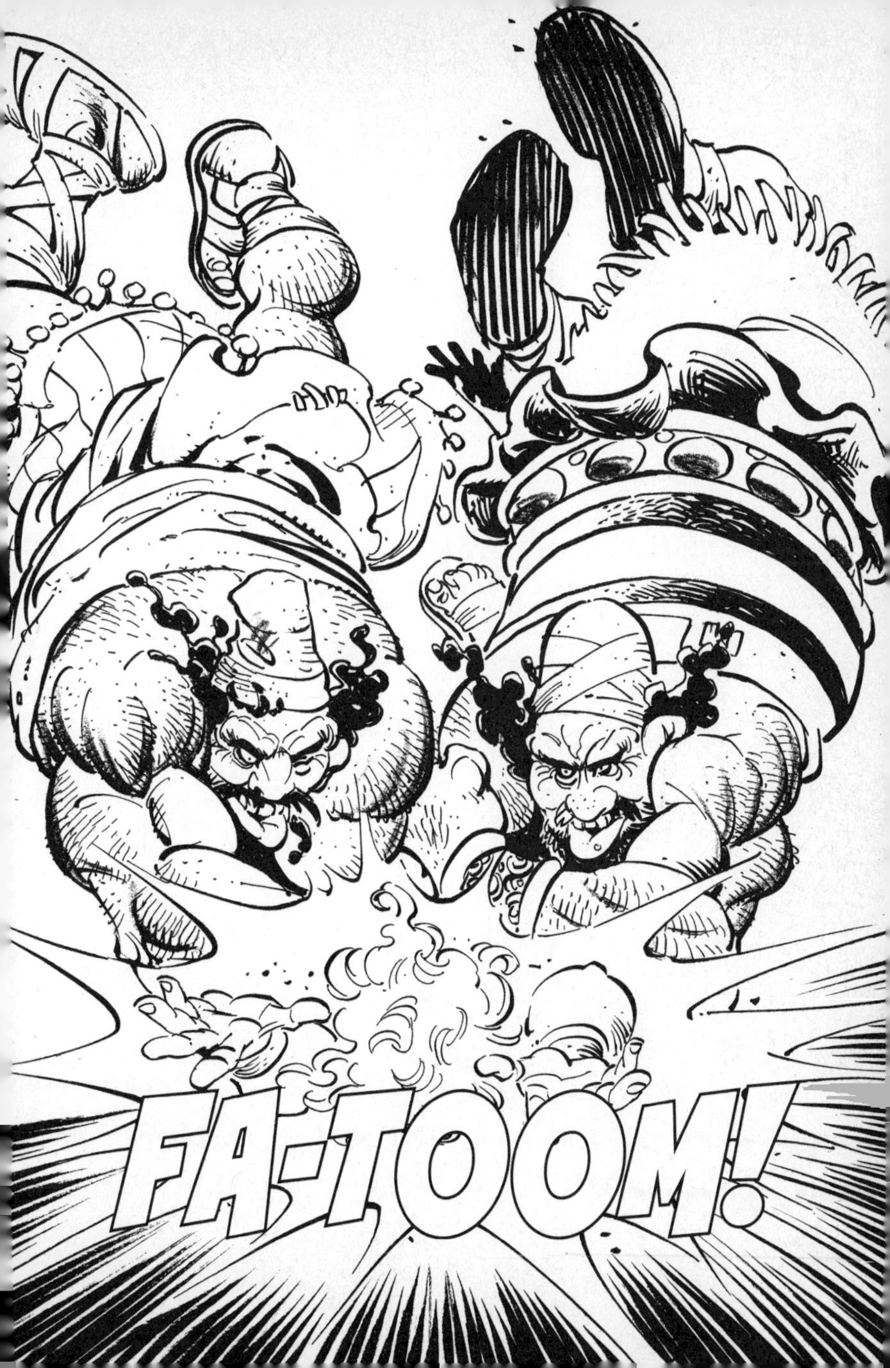
FA-TOOM!

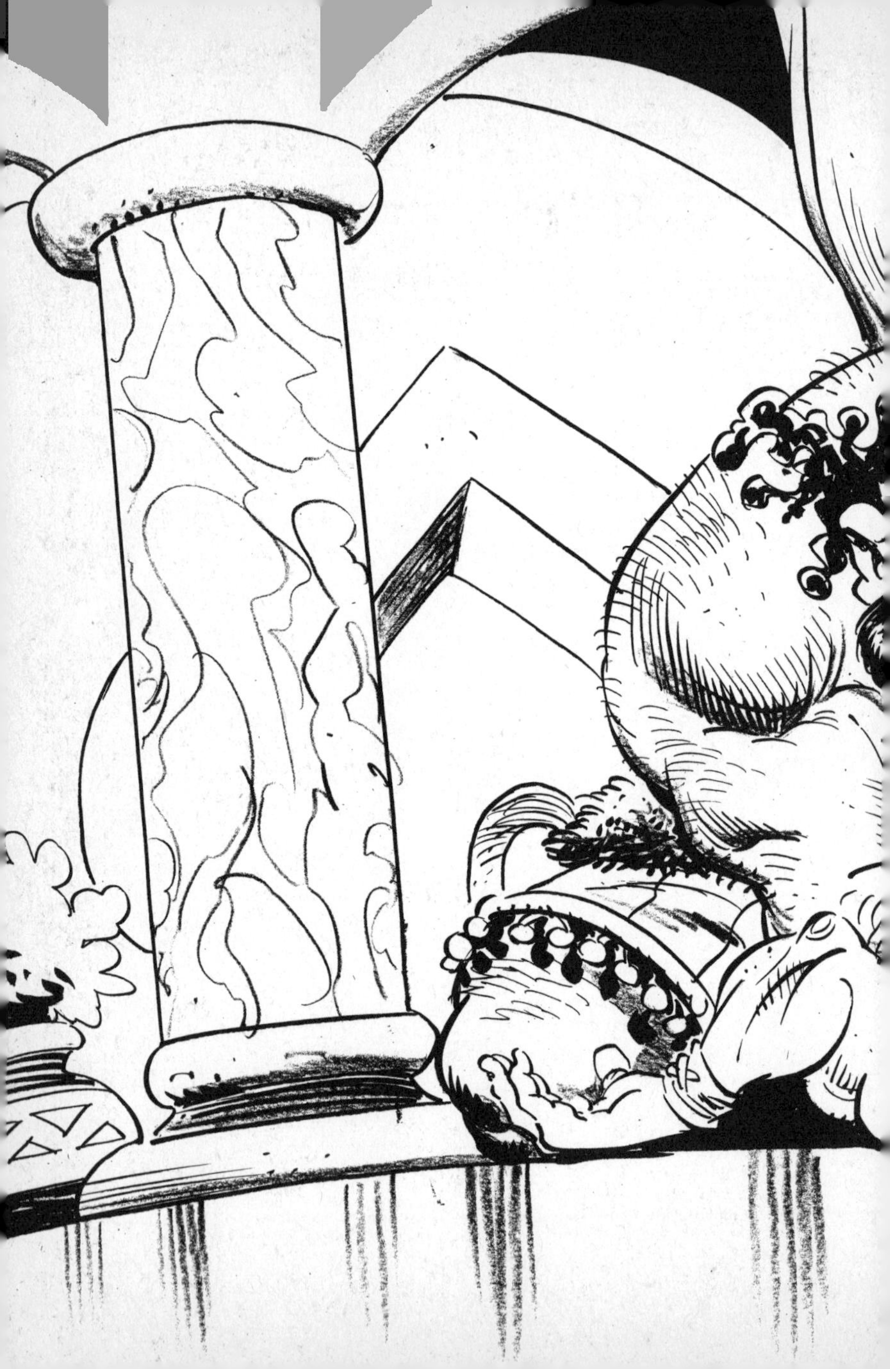

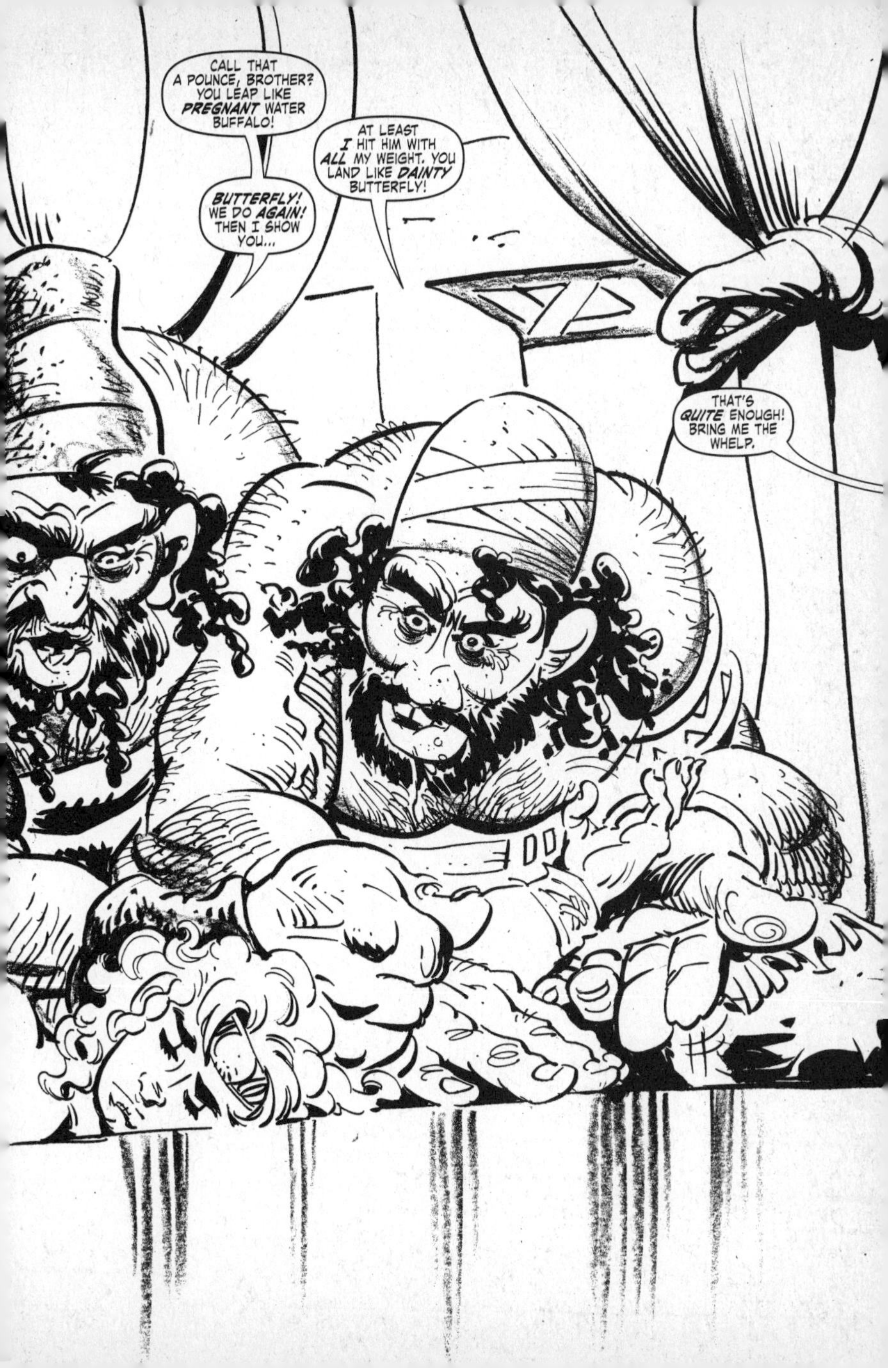
CALL THAT A POUNCE, BROTHER? YOU LEAP LIKE PREGNANT WATER BUFFALO!
AT LEAST I HIT HIM WITH ALL MY WEIGHT. YOU LAND LIKE DAINTY BUTTERFLY!
BUTTERFLY! WE DO AGAIN! THEN I SHOW YOU...
THAT'S QUITE ENOUGH! BRING ME THE WHELP.

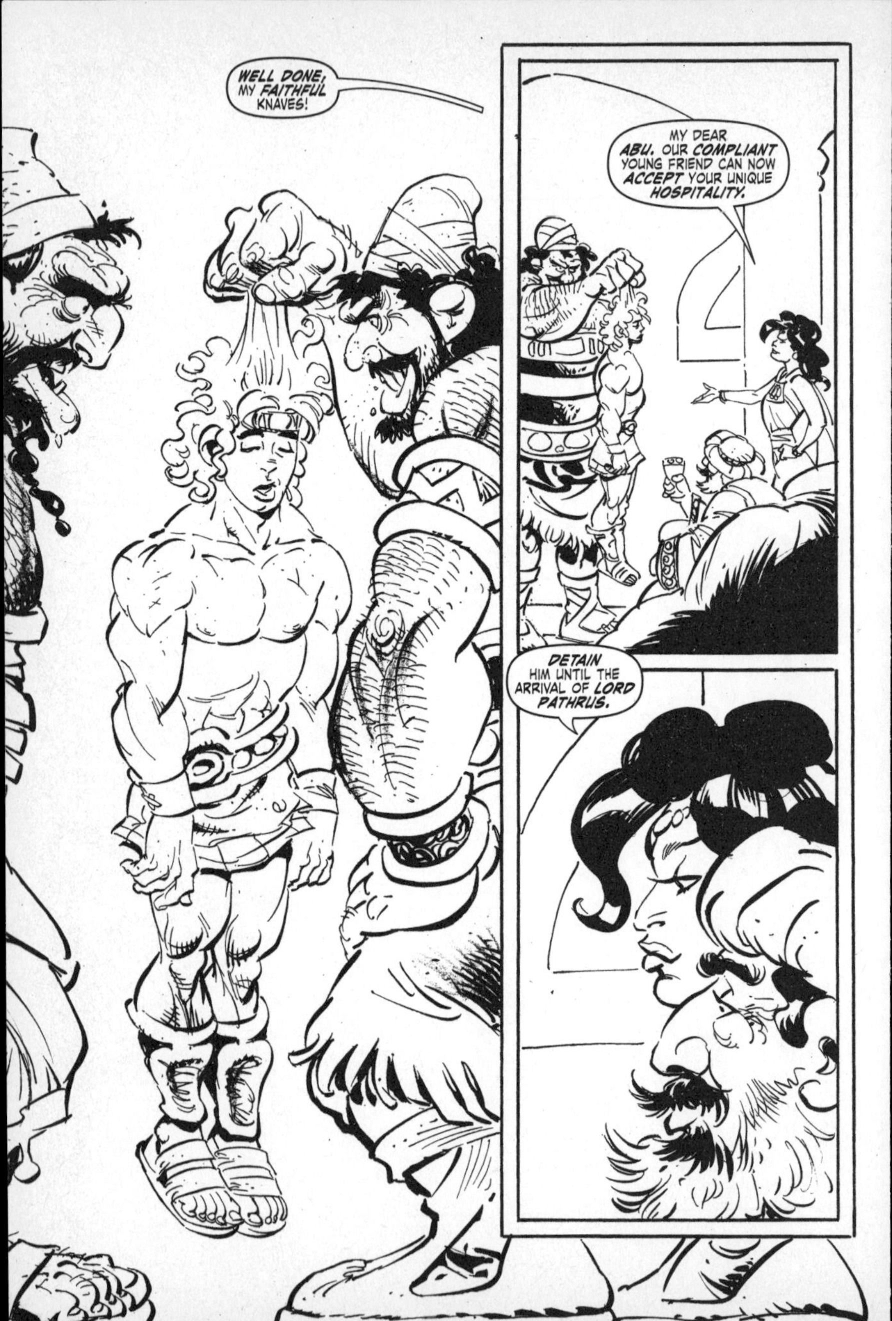

WELL DONE, MY FAITHFUL KNAVES!
MY DEAR ABU. OUR COMPLIANT YOUNG FRIEND CAN NOW ACCEPT YOUR UNIQUE HOSPITALITY.
DETAIN HIM UNTIL THE ARRIVAL OF LORD PATHRUS.

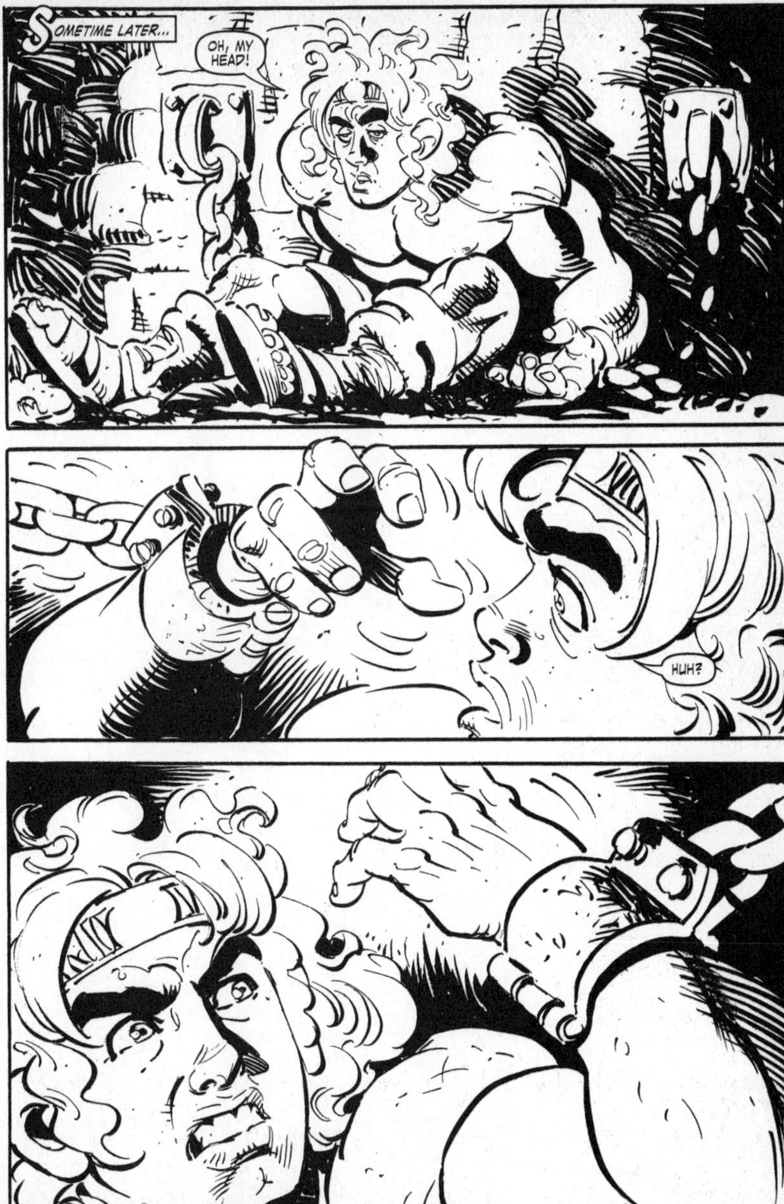
SOMETIME LATER...
OH, MY HEAD!
HUH?

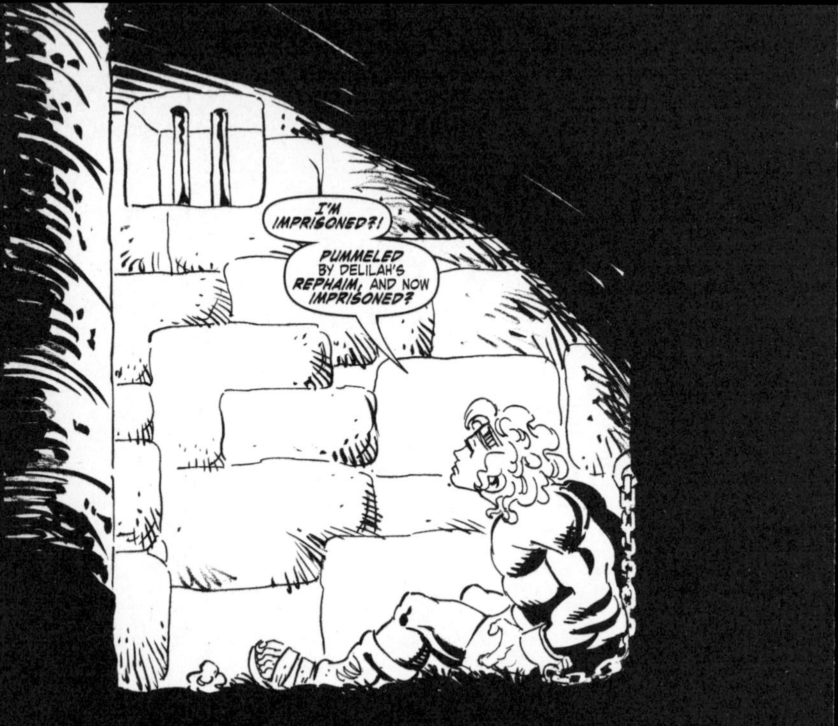
I'M IMPRISONED?!
PUMMELED BY DELILAH'S REPHAIM, AND NOW IMPRISONED?

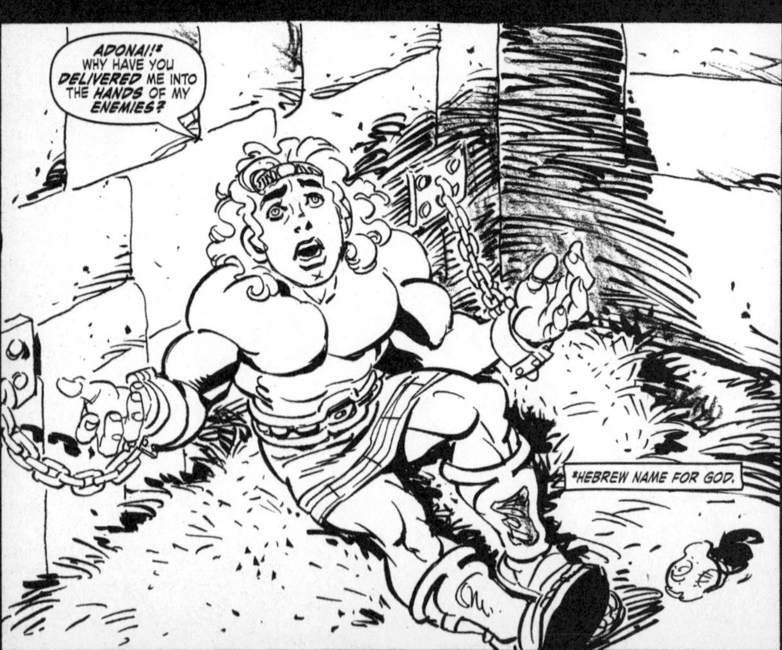
ADONAI!* WHY HAVE YOU DELIVERED ME INTO THE HANDS OF MY ENEMIES?
*HEBREW NAME FOR GOD.

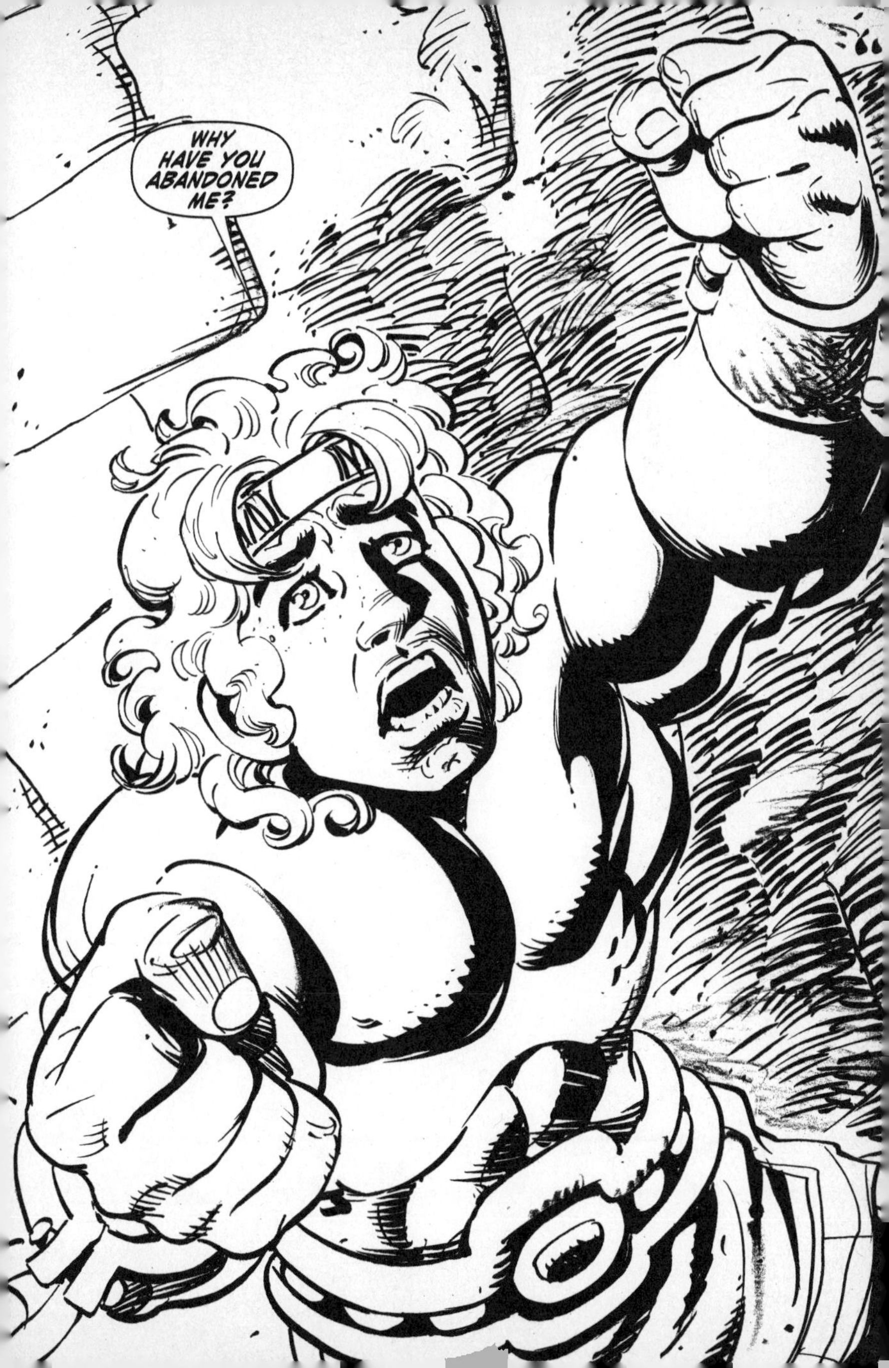
WHY HAVE YOU ABANDONED ME?

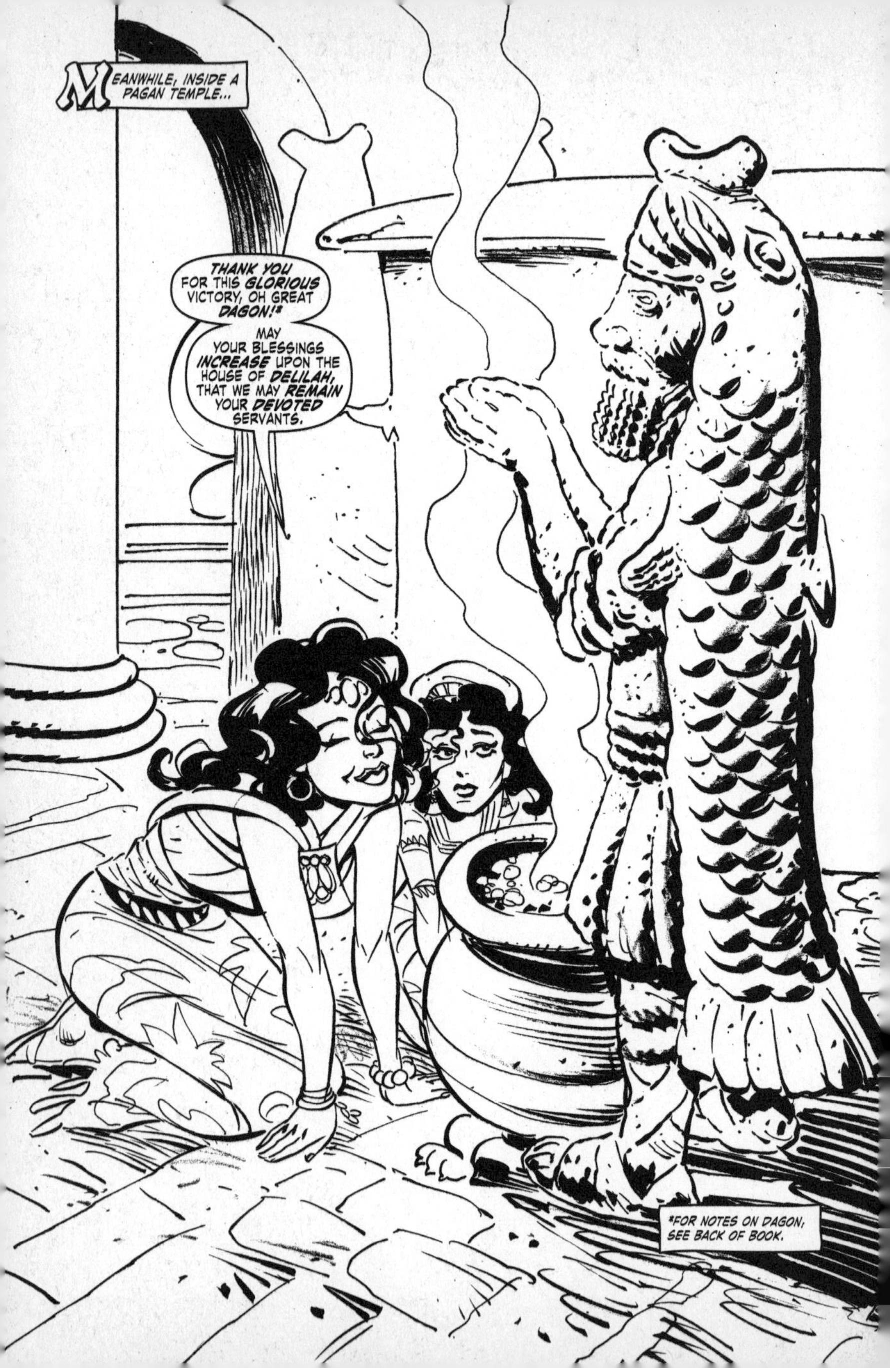
MEANWHILE, INSIDE A PAGAN TEMPLE...
THANK YOU FOR THIS GLORIOUS VICTORY, OH GREAT DAGON!*
MAY YOUR BLESSINGS INCREASE UPON THE HOUSE OF DELILAH, THAT WE MAY REMAIN YOUR DEVOTED SERVANTS.
*FOR NOTES ON DAGON; SEE BACK OF BOOK.

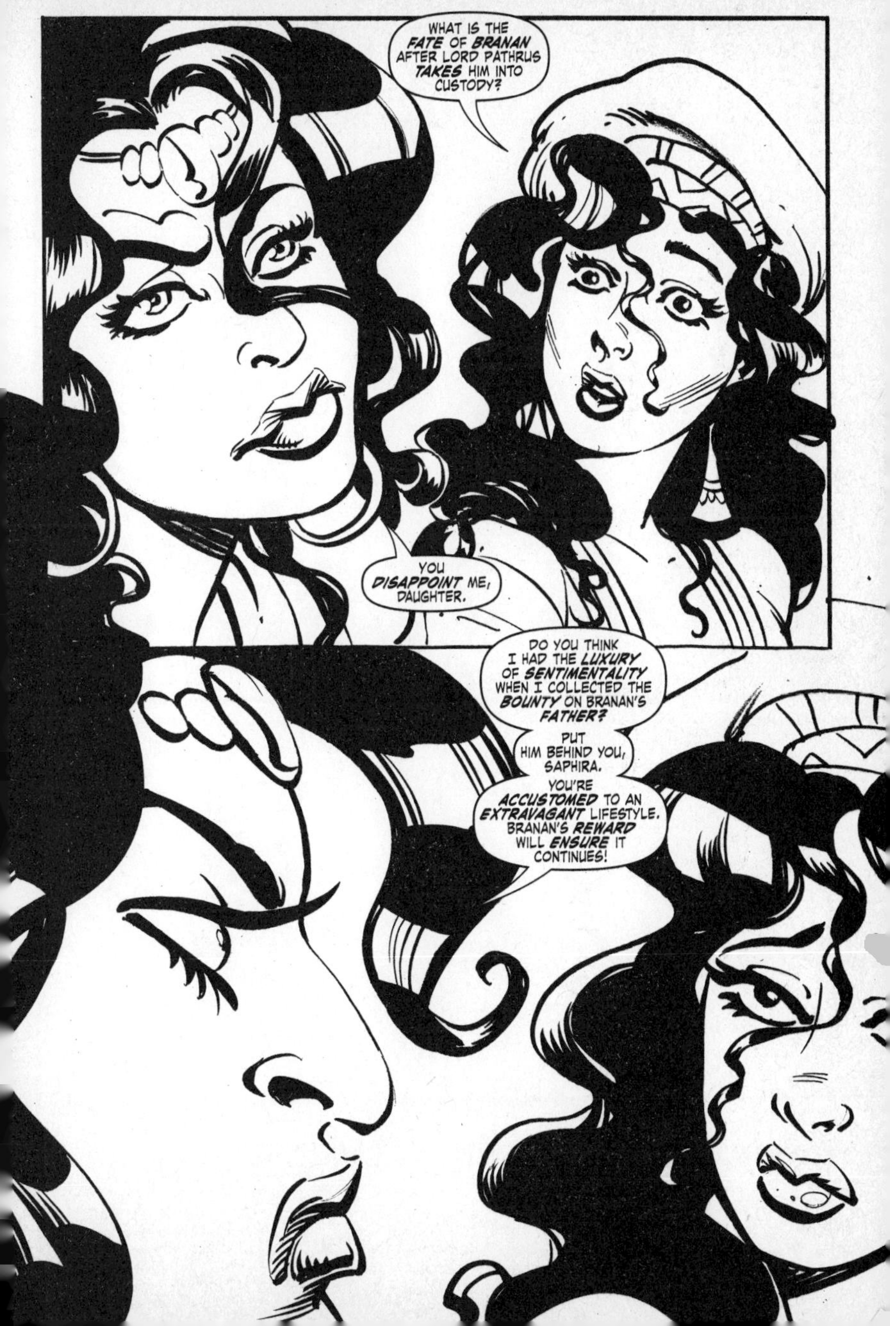
WHAT IS THE FATE OF BRANAN AFTER LORD PATHRUS TAKES HIM INTO CUSTODY?
YOU DISAPPOINT ME, DAUGHTER.
DO YOU THINK I HAD THE LUXURY OF SENTIMENTALITY WHEN I COLLECTED THE BOUNTY ON BRANAN'S FATHER?
PUT HIM BEHIND YOU, SAPHIRA.
YOU'RE ACCUSTOMED TO AN EXTRAVAGANT LIFESTYLE. BRANAN'S REWARD WILL ENSURE IT CONTINUES!

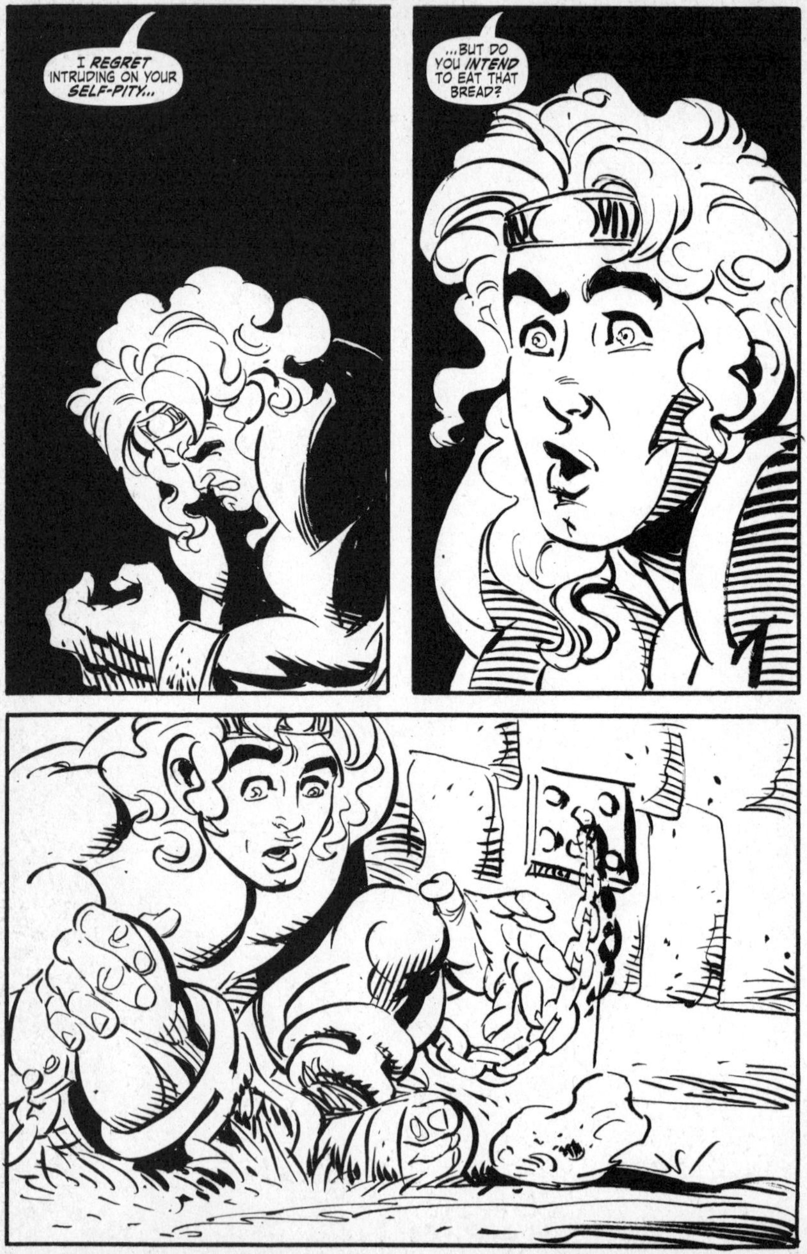
I REGRET INTRUDING ON YOUR SELF-PITY...
...BUT DO YOU INTEND TO EAT THAT BREAD?

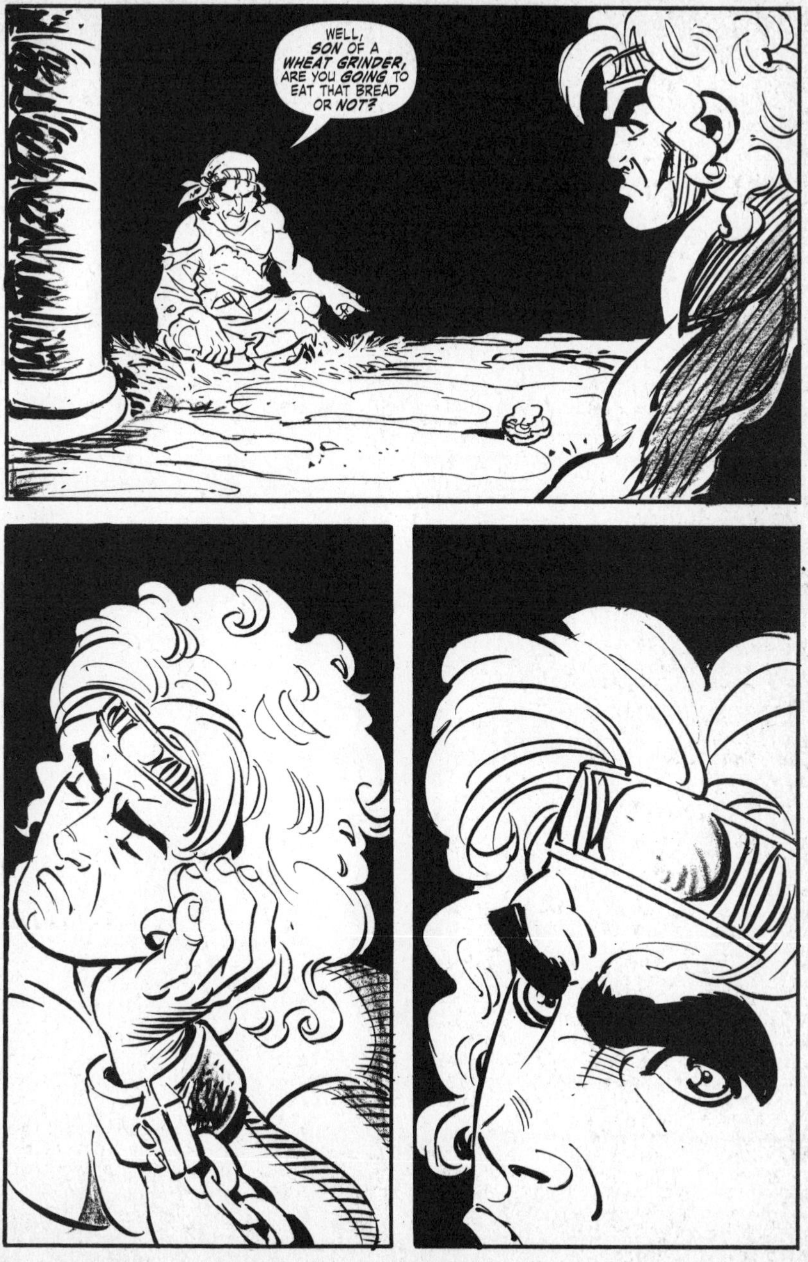
WELL, SON OF A WHEAT GRINDER, ARE YOU GOING TO EAT THAT BREAD OR NOT?

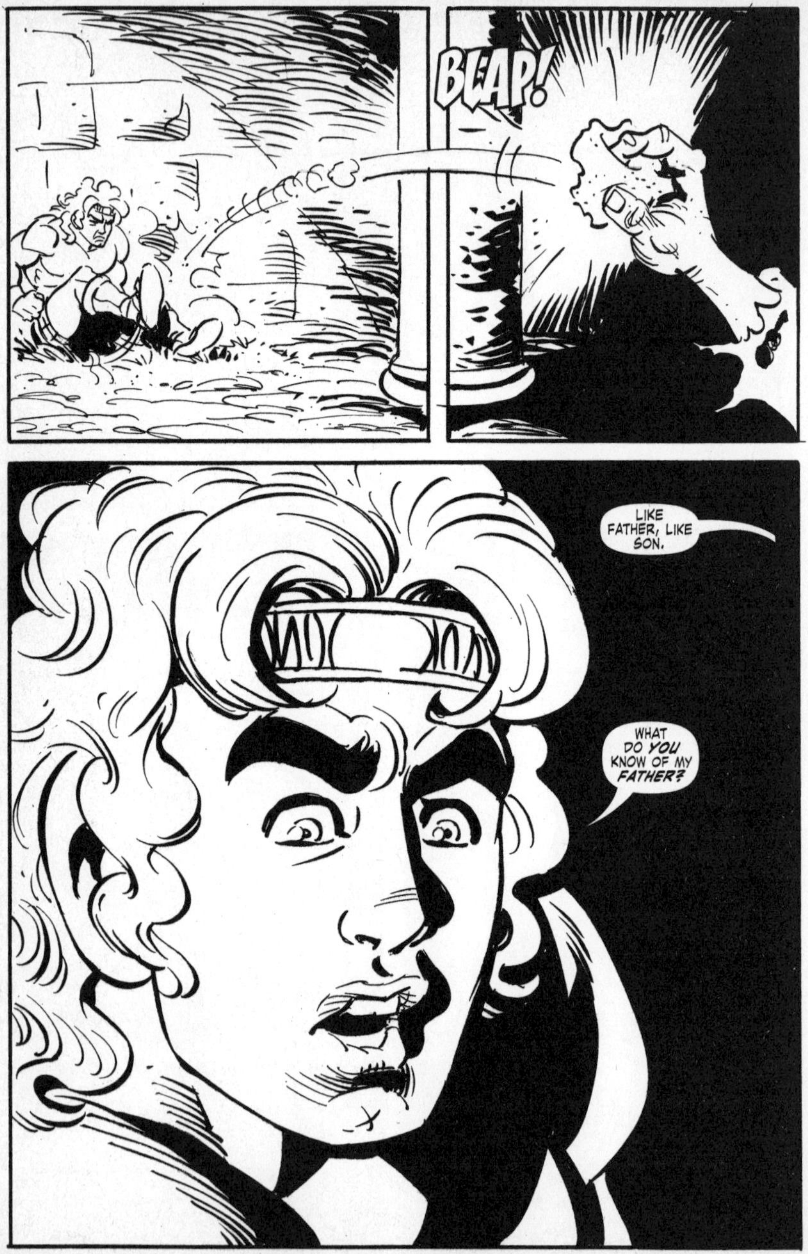
BLAP!
LIKE FATHER, LIKE SON.
WHAT DO YOU KNOW OF MY FATHER?

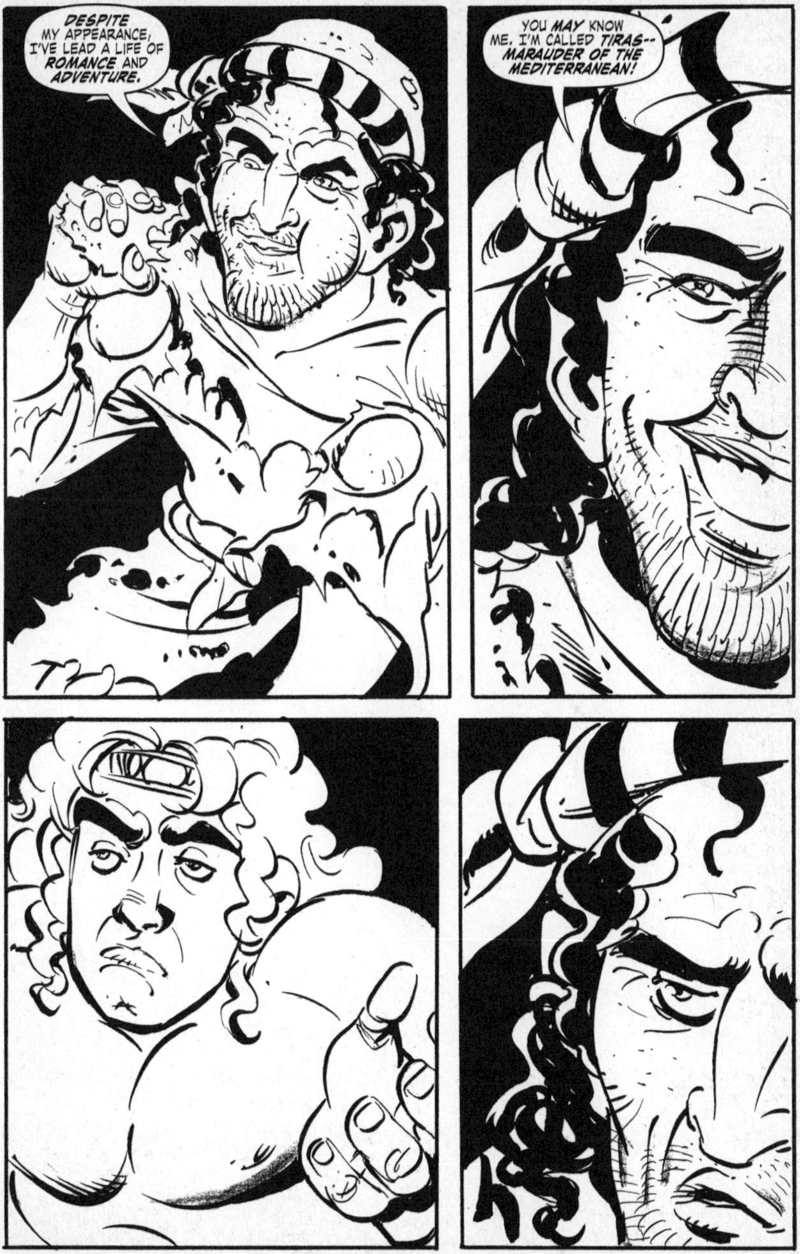
DESPITE MY APPEARANCE, I'VE LEAD A LIFE OF ROMANCE AND ADVENTURE.
YOU MAY KNOW ME. I'M CALLED TIRAS-- MARAUDER OF THE MEDITERRANEAN!

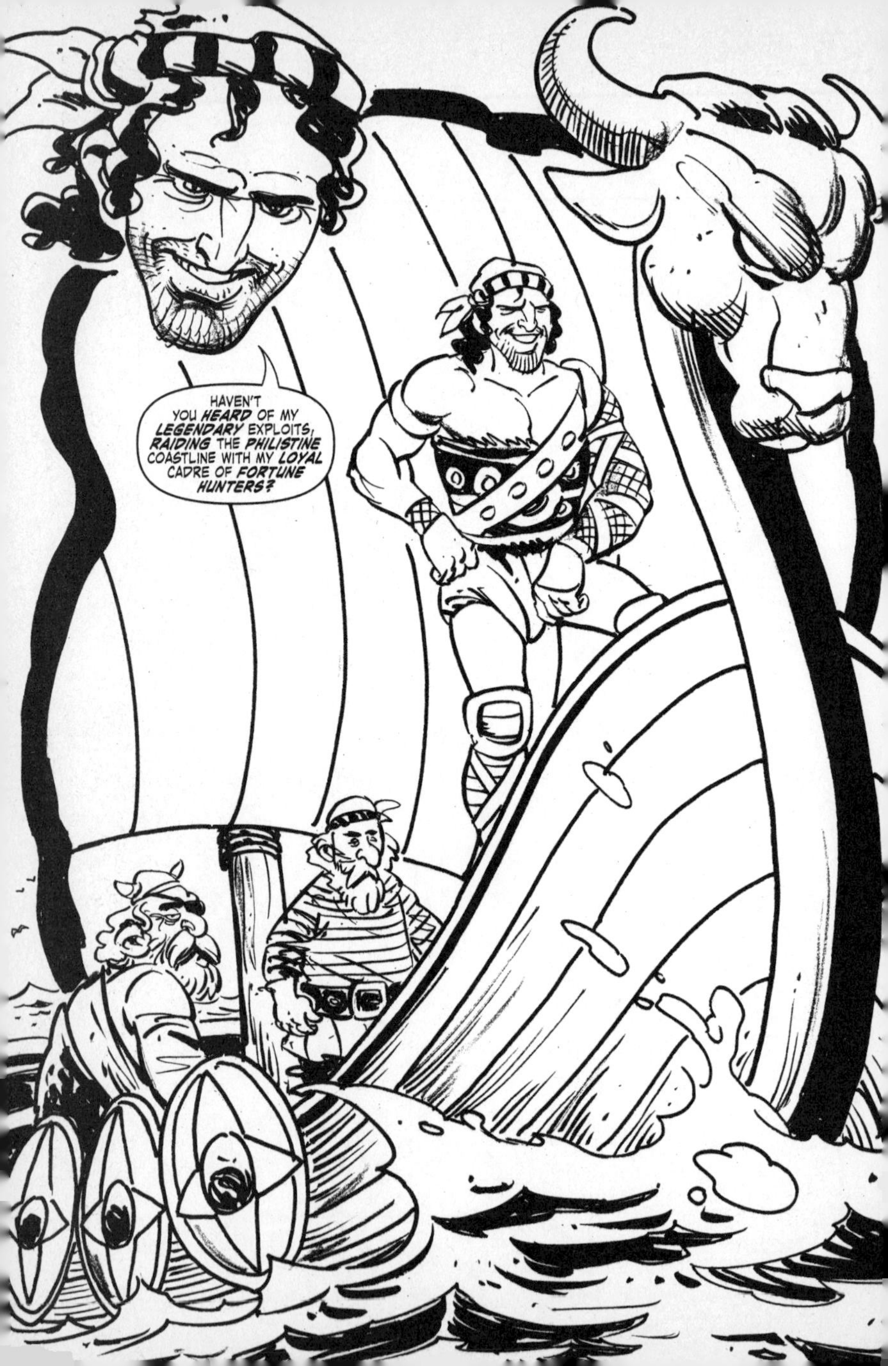
HAVEN'T YOU HEARD OF MY LEGENDARY EXPLOITS, RAIDING THE PHILISTINE COASTLINE WITH MY LOYAL CADRE OF FORTUNE HUNTERS?

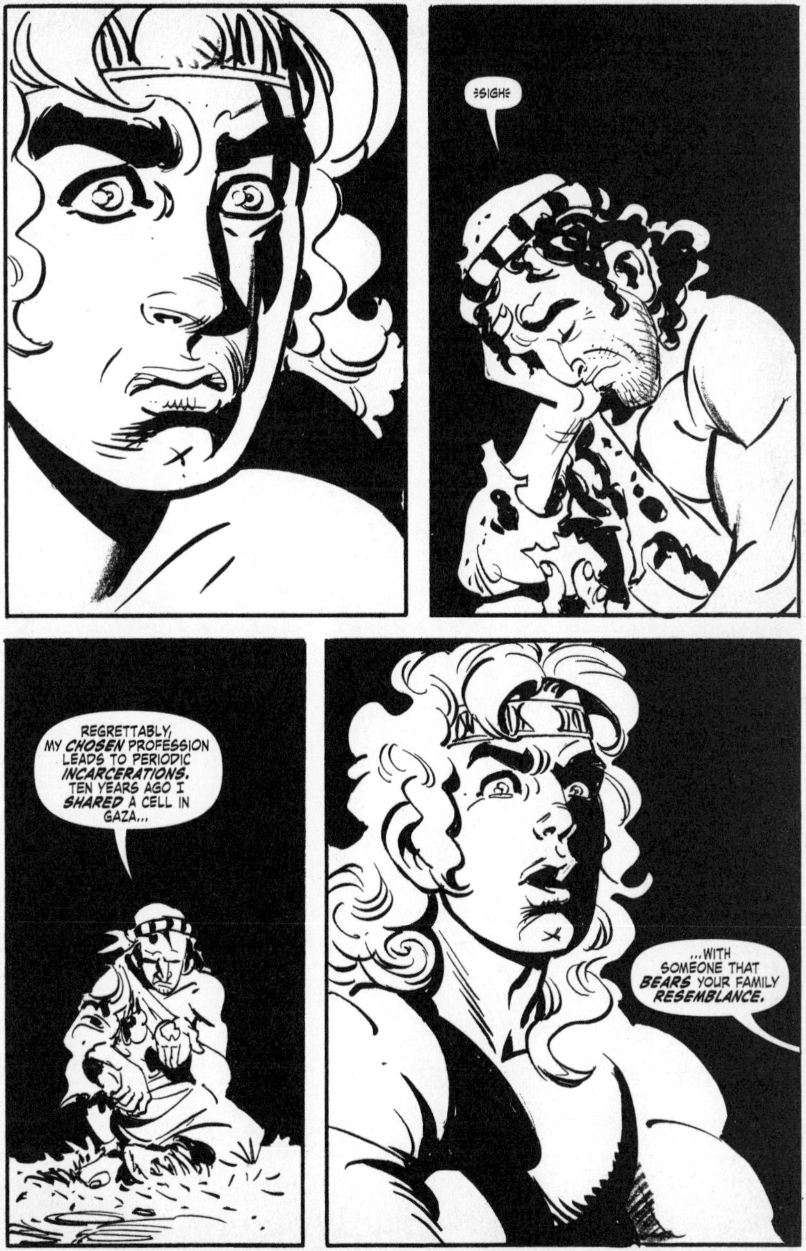

≋SIGH≋
REGRETTABLY, MY CHOSEN PROFESSION LEADS TO PERIODIC INCARCERATIONS. TEN YEARS AGO I SHARED A CELL IN GAZA...
...WITH SOMEONE THAT BEARS YOUR FAMILY RESEMBLANCE.

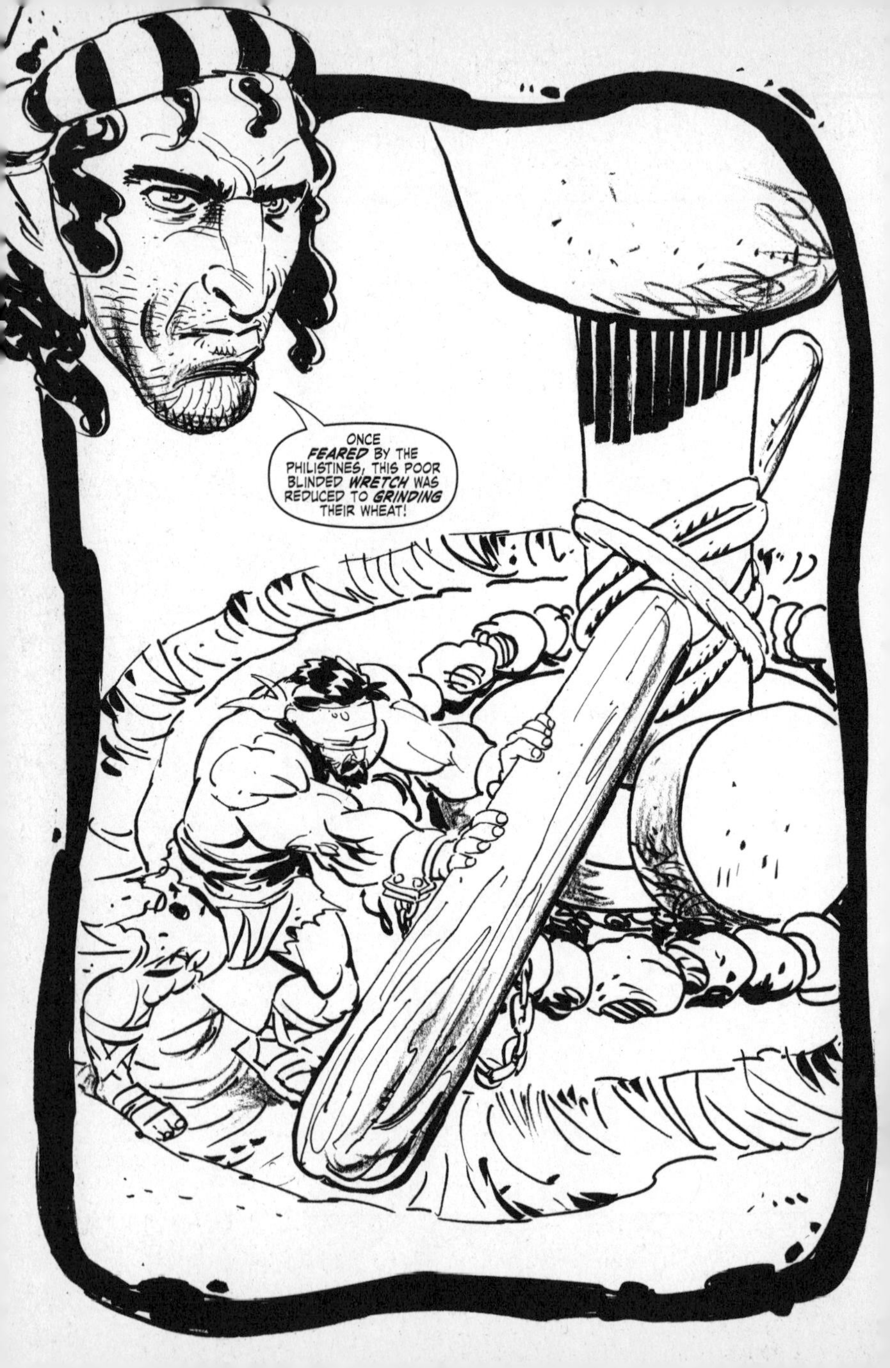
ONCE FEARED BY THE PHILISTINES, THIS POOR BLINDED WRETCH WAS REDUCED TO GRINDING THEIR WHEAT!

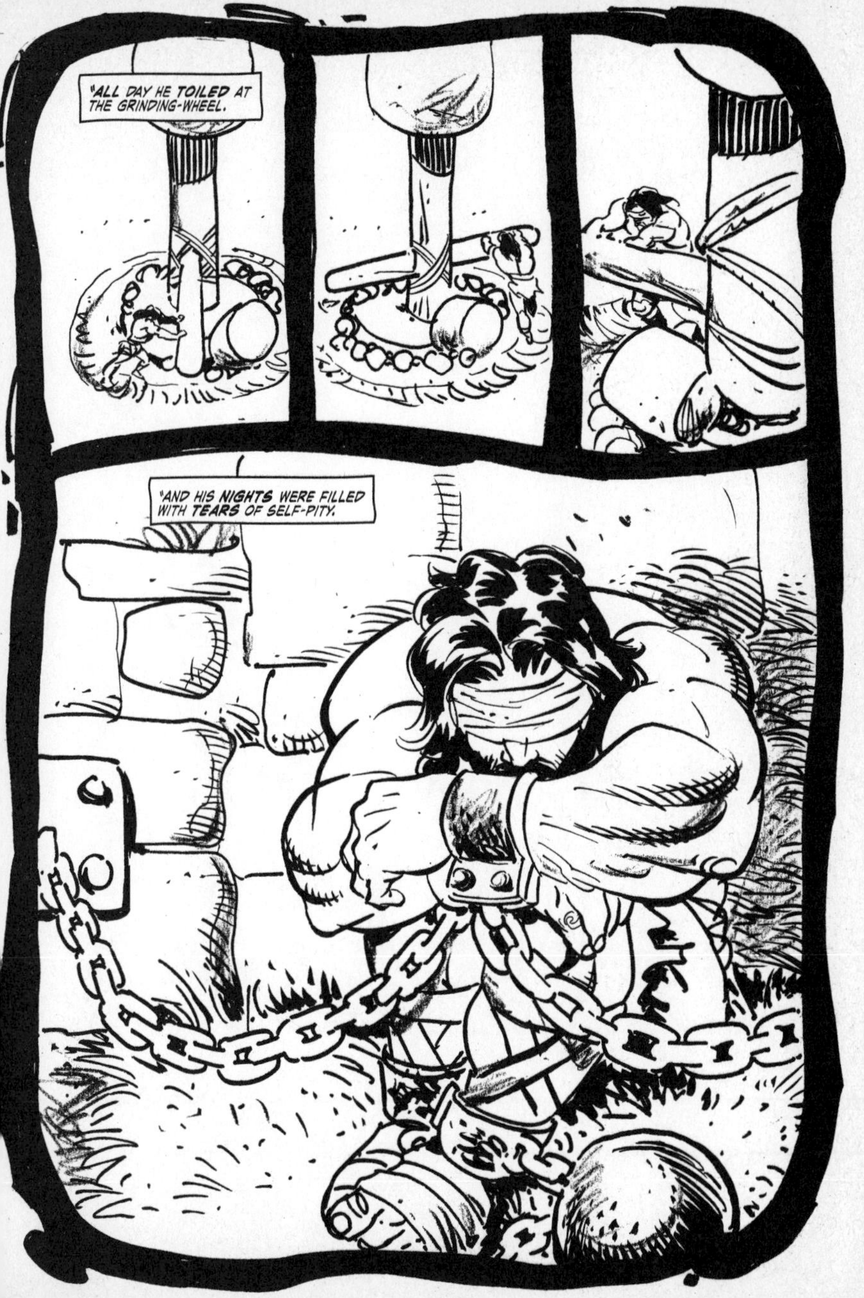
"ALL DAY HE TOILED AT THE GRINDING-WHEEL.
"AND HIS NIGHTS WERE FILLED WITH TEARS OF SELF-PITY.

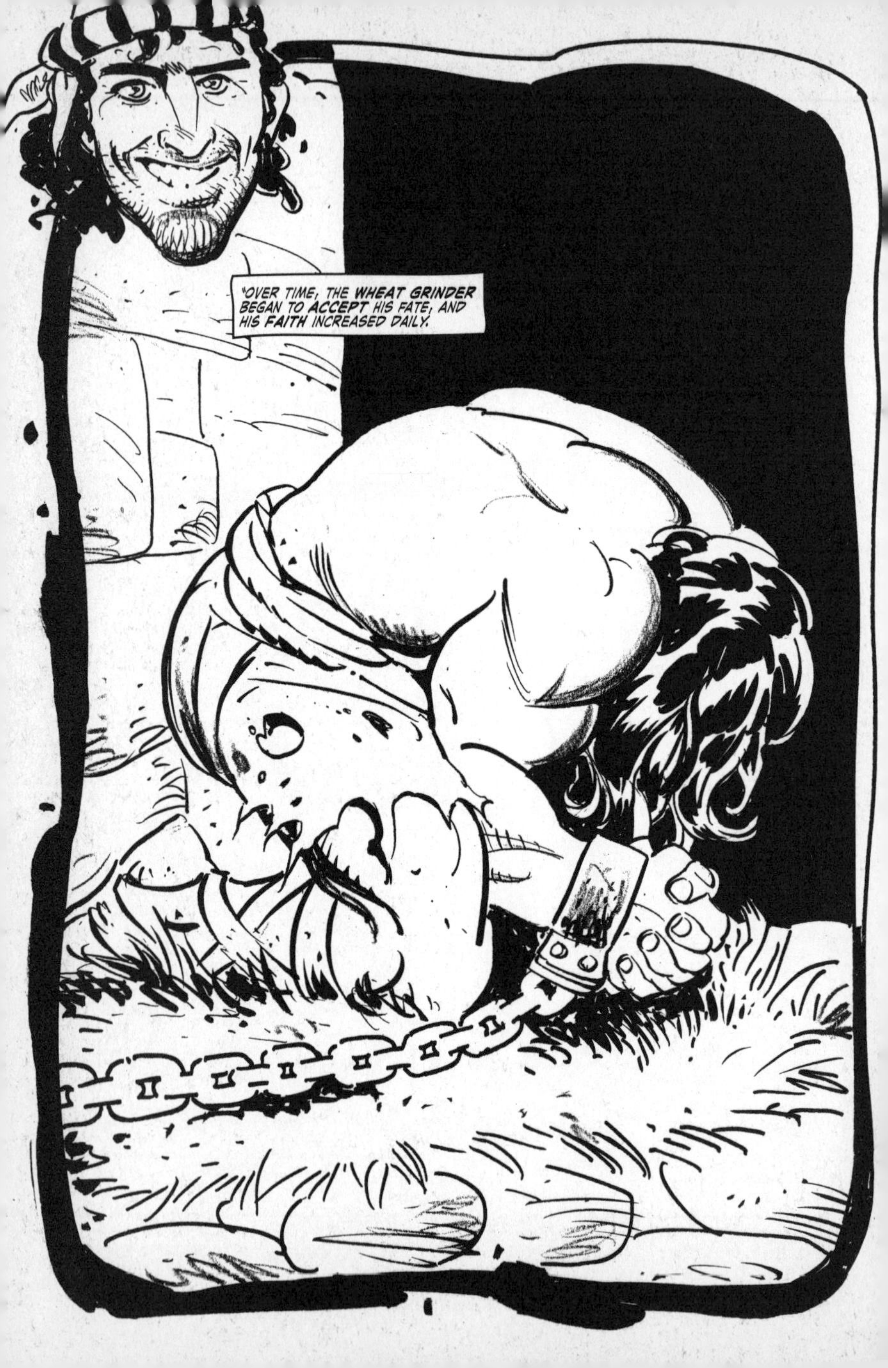
"OVER TIME, THE WHEAT GRINDER BEGAN TO ACCEPT HIS FATE, AND HIS FAITH INCREASED DAILY.

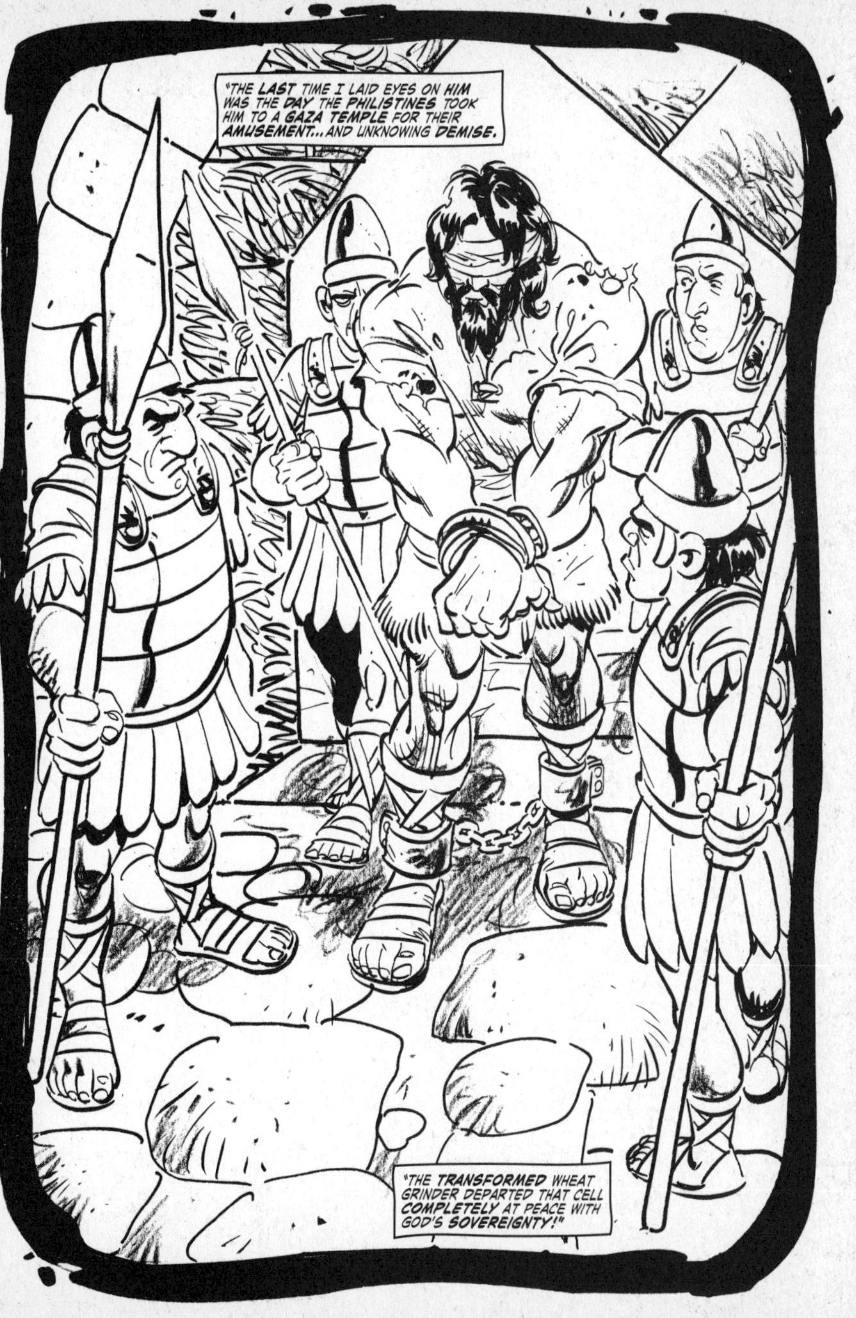
"THE LAST TIME I LAID EYES ON HIM WAS THE DAY THE PHILISTINES TOOK HIM TO A GAZA TEMPLE FOR THEIR AMUSEMENT... AND UNKNOWING DEMISE.
"THE TRANSFORMED WHEAT GRINDER DEPARTED THAT CELL COMPLETELY AT PEACE WITH GOD'S SOVEREIGNTY!"

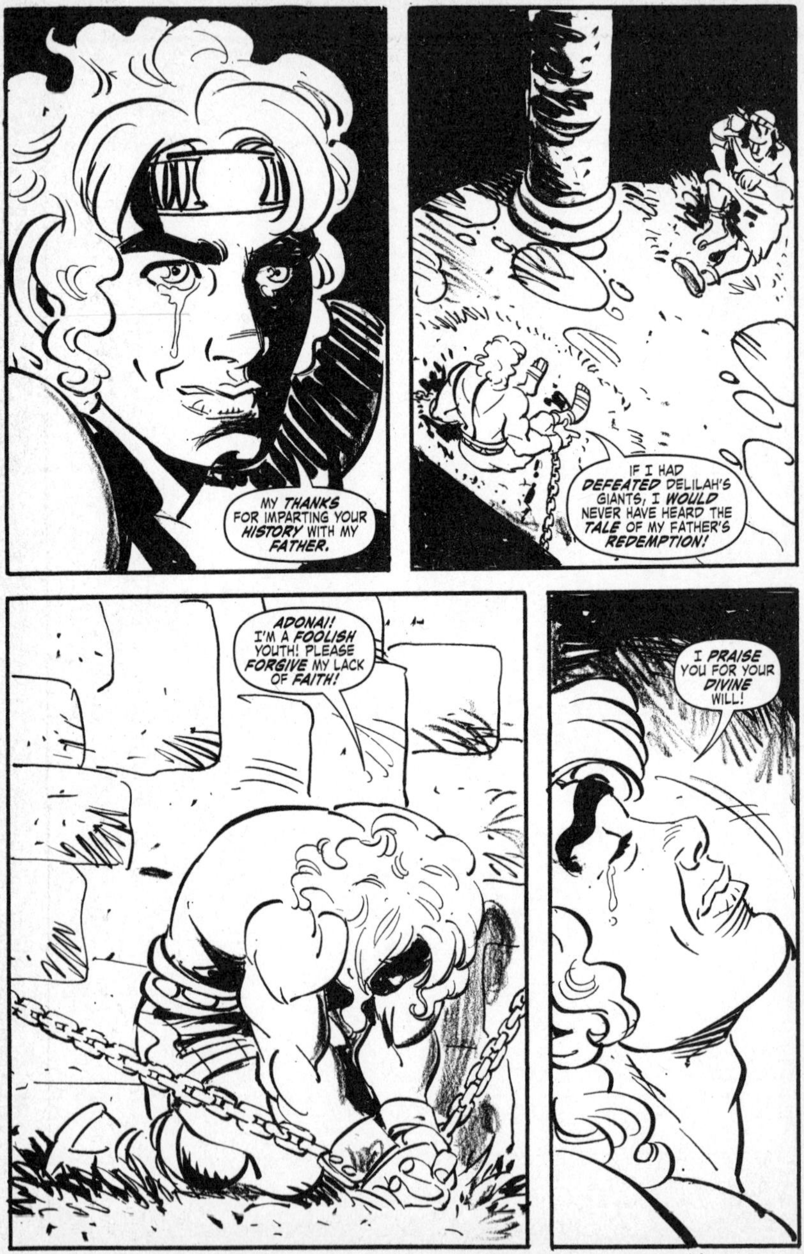
MY THANKS FOR IMPARTING YOUR HISTORY WITH MY FATHER.
IF I HAD DEFEATED DELILAH'S GIANTS, I WOULD NEVER HAVE HEARD THE TALE OF MY FATHER'S REDEMPTION!
ADONAI! I'M A FOOLISH YOUTH! PLEASE FORGIVE MY LACK OF FAITH!
I PRAISE YOU FOR YOUR DIVINE WILL!

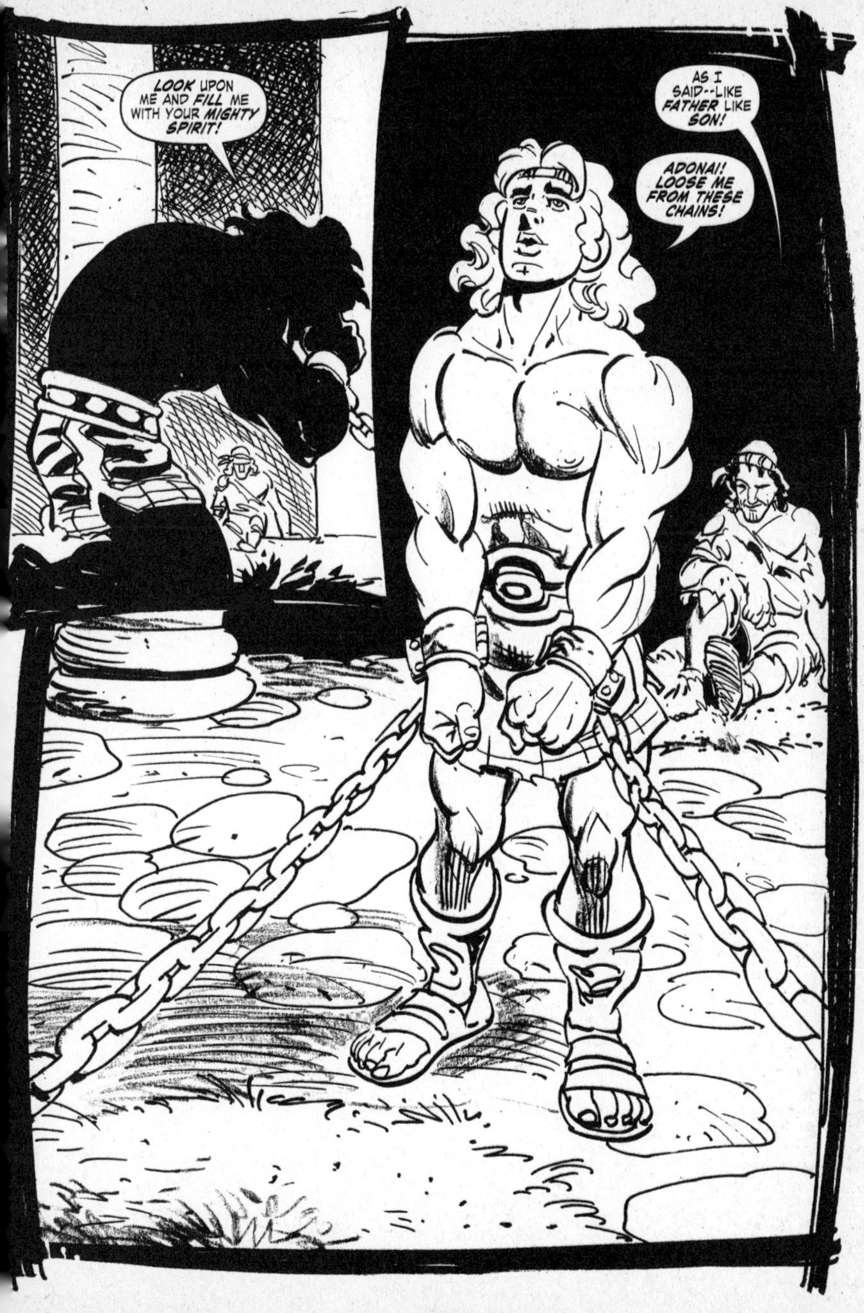
LOOK UPON ME AND FILL ME WITH YOUR MIGHTY SPIRIT!
AS I SAID--LIKE FATHER LIKE SON!
ADONAI! LOOSE ME FROM THESE CHAINS!

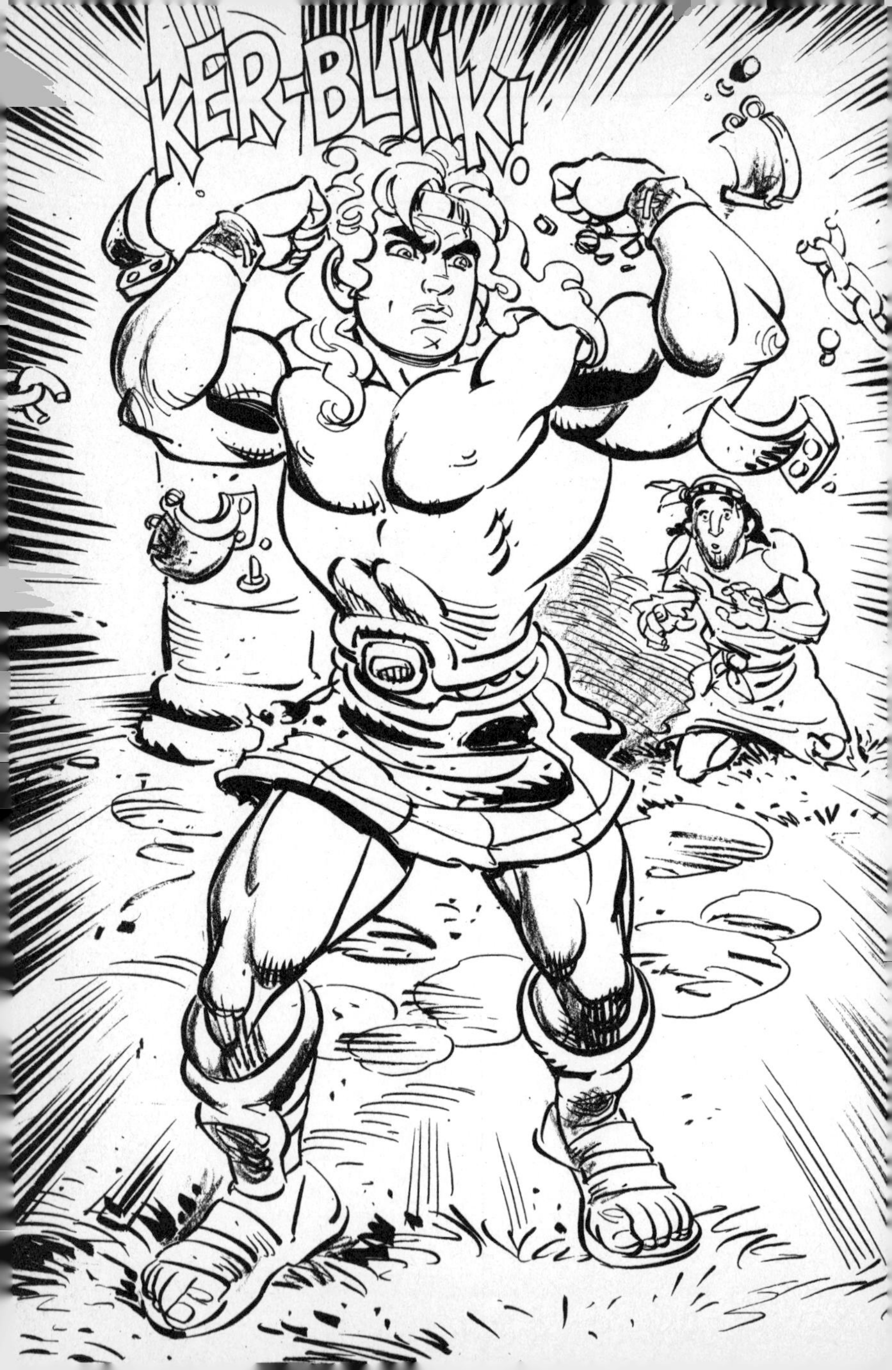
KER-BLINK!

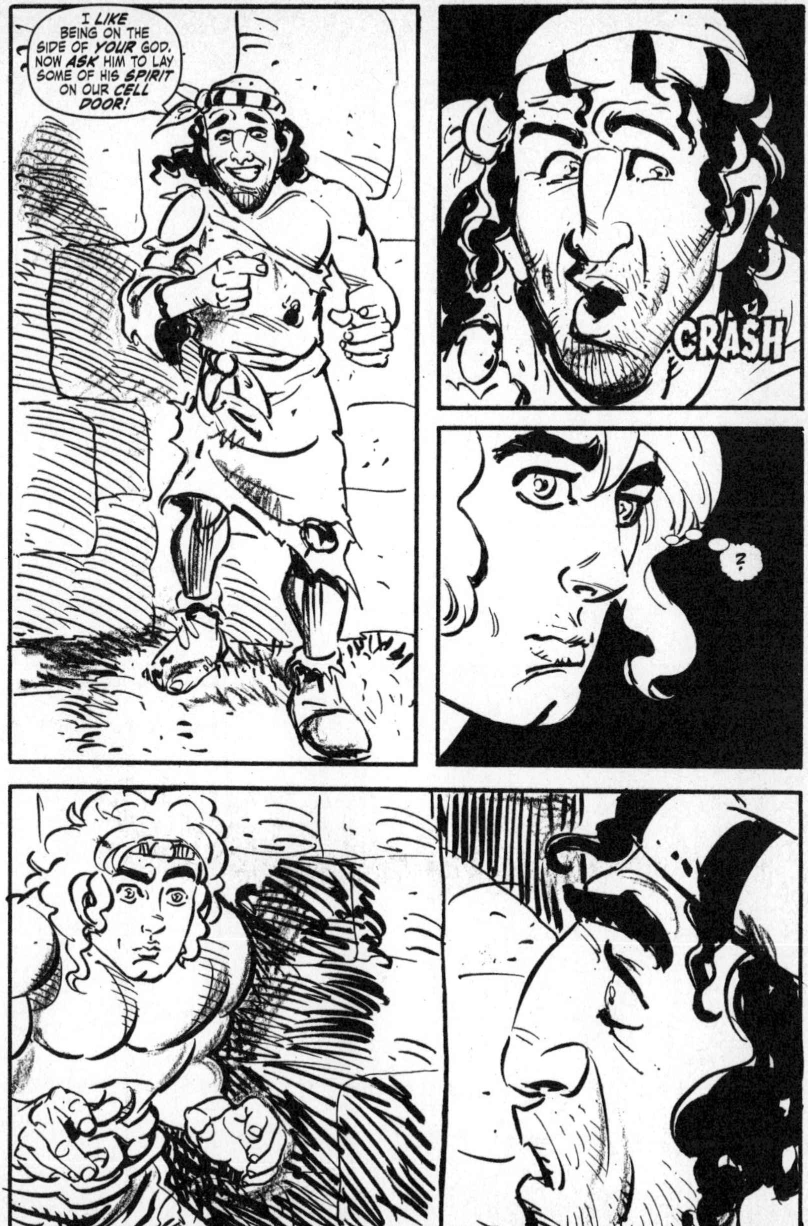
I LIKE BEING ON THE SIDE OF YOUR GOD. NOW ASK HIM TO LAY SOME OF HIS SPIRIT ON OUR CELL DOOR!
CRASH
?

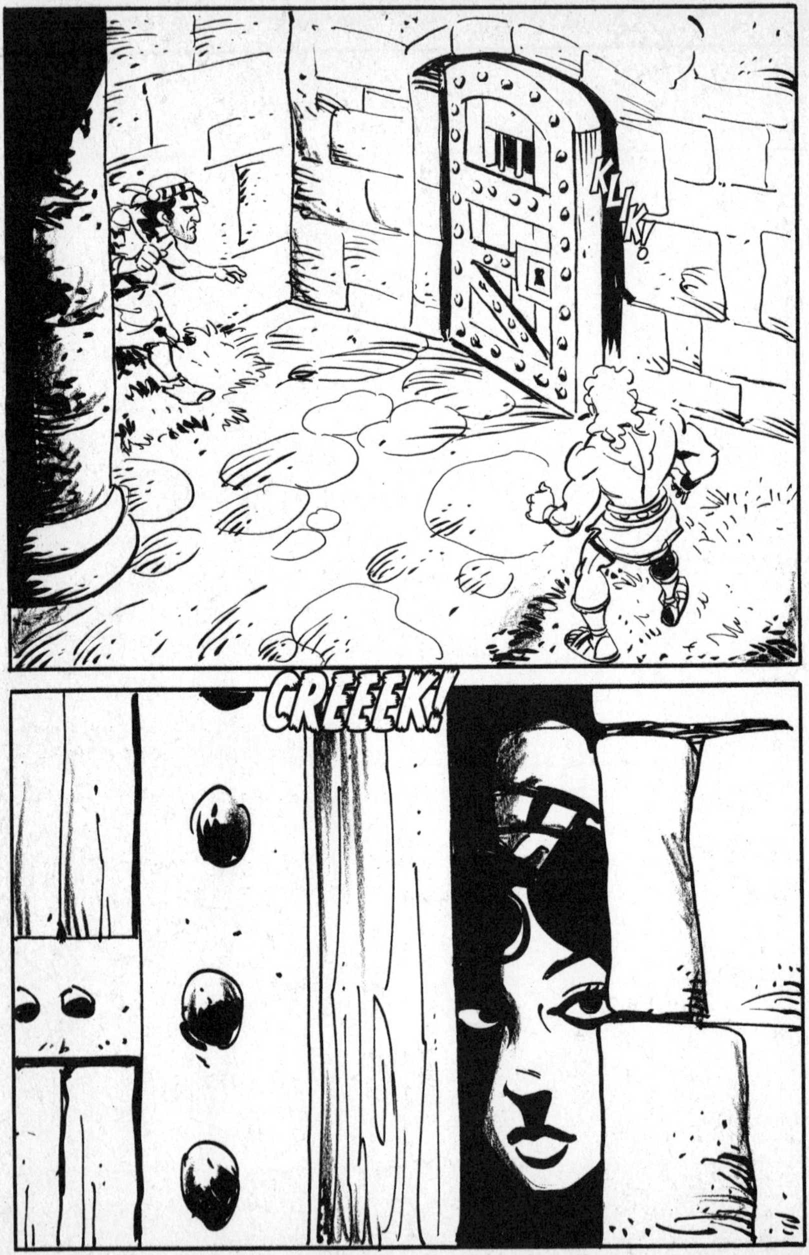
KLIK!
CREEEK!

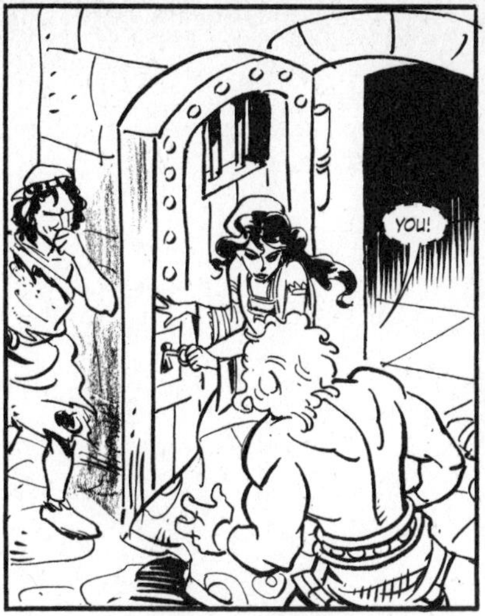
YOU!

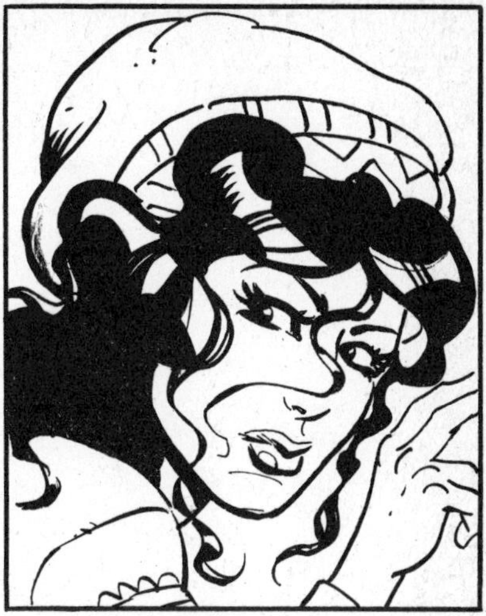

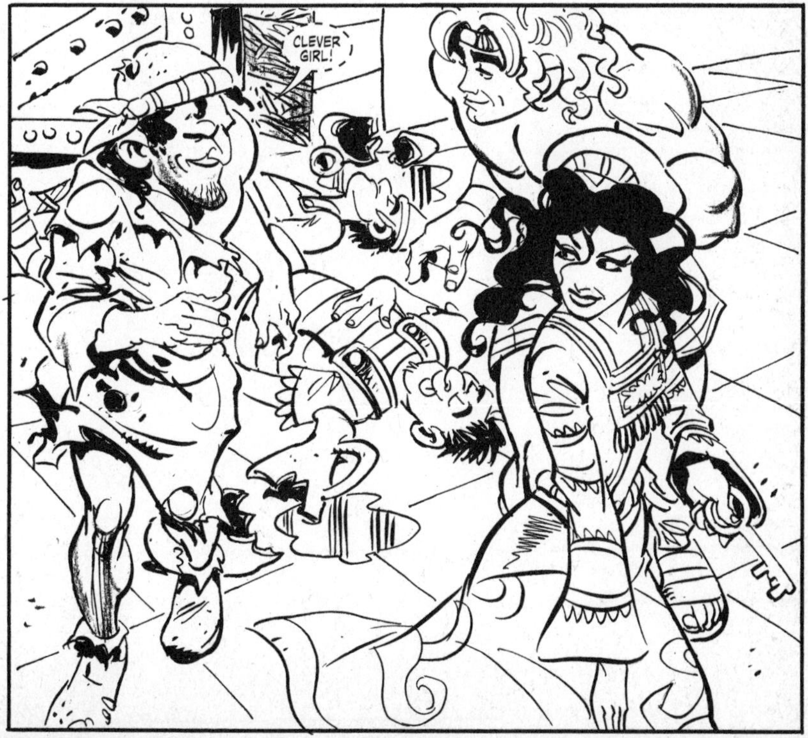
CLEVER GIRL!

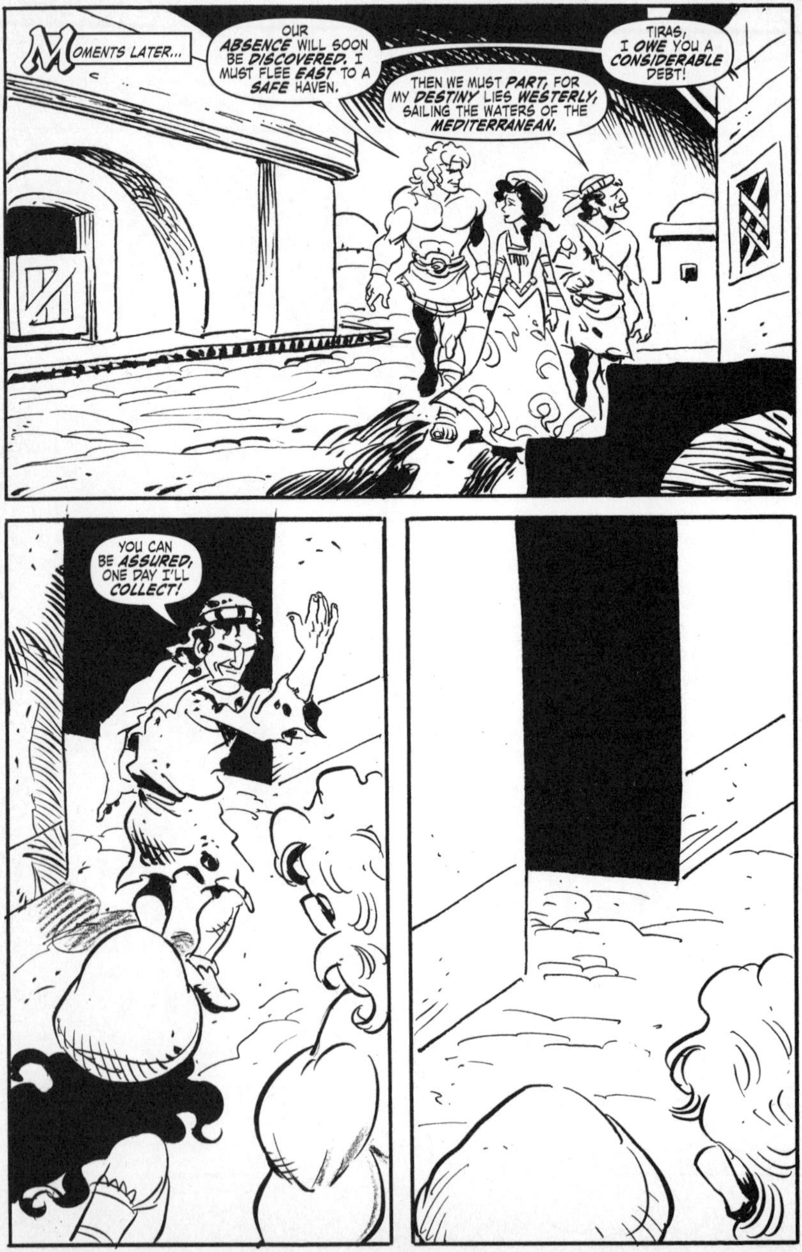
MOMENTS LATER...
OUR ABSENCE WILL SOON BE DISCOVERED. I MUST FLEE EAST TO A SAFE HAVEN.
TIRAS, I OWE YOU A CONSIDERABLE DEBT!
THEN WE MUST PART, FOR MY DESTINY LIES WESTERLY, SAILING THE WATERS OF THE MEDITERRANEAN.
YOU CAN BE ASSURED, ONE DAY I'LL COLLECT!

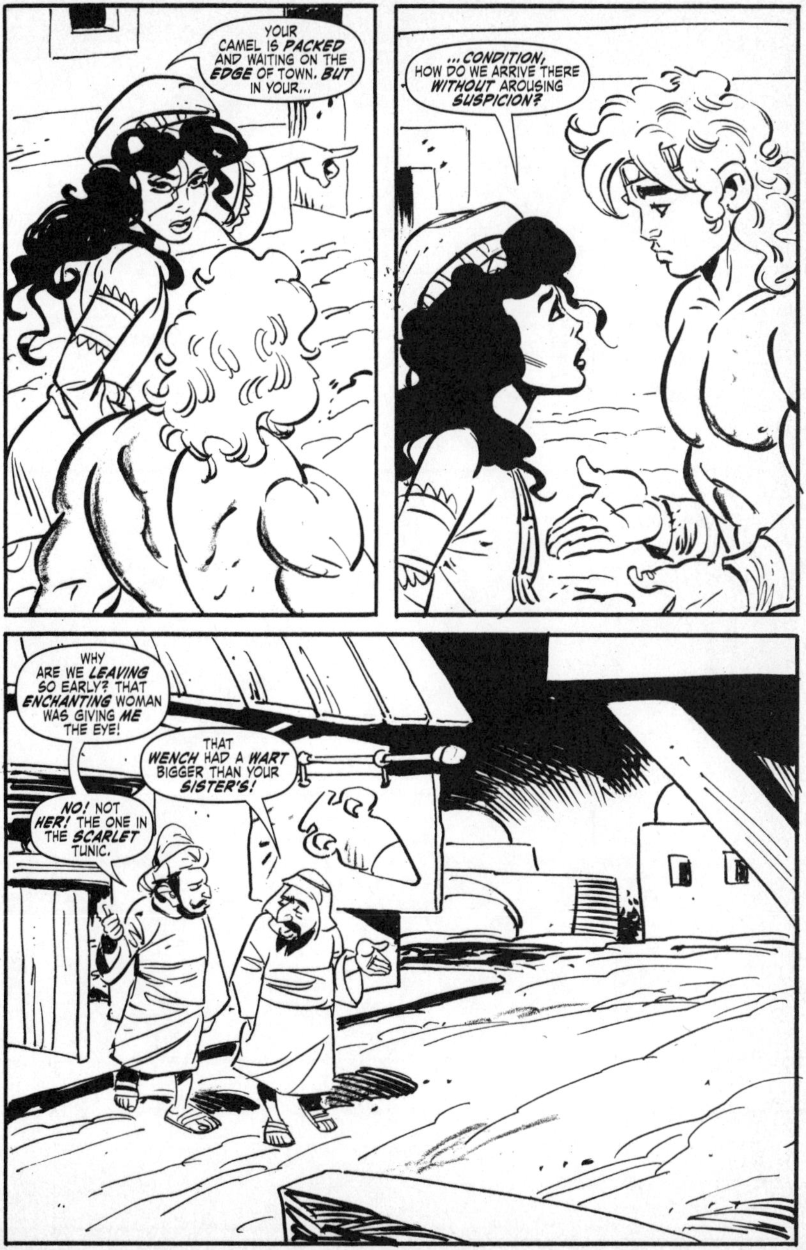
YOUR CAMEL IS PACKED AND WAITING ON THE EDGE OF TOWN. BUT IN YOUR...
...CONDITION, HOW DO WE ARRIVE THERE WITHOUT AROUSING SUSPICION?
WHY ARE WE LEAVING SO EARLY? THAT ENCHANTING WOMAN WAS GIVING ME THE EYE!
THAT WENCH HAD A WART BIGGER THAN YOUR SISTER'S!
NO! NOT HER! THE ONE IN THE SCARLET TUNIC.

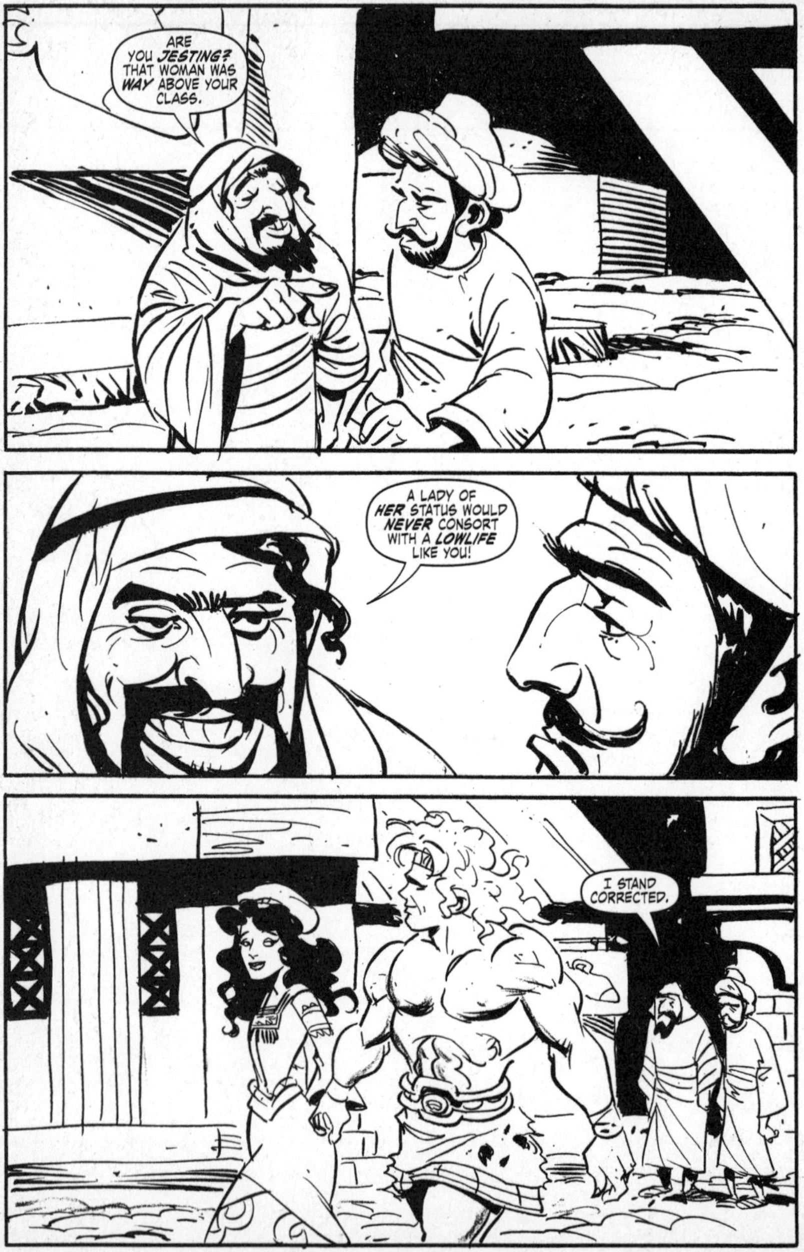
ARE YOU JESTING? THAT WOMAN WAS WAY ABOVE YOUR CLASS.
A LADY OF HER STATUS WOULD NEVER CONSORT WITH A LOWLIFE LIKE YOU!
I STAND CORRECTED.

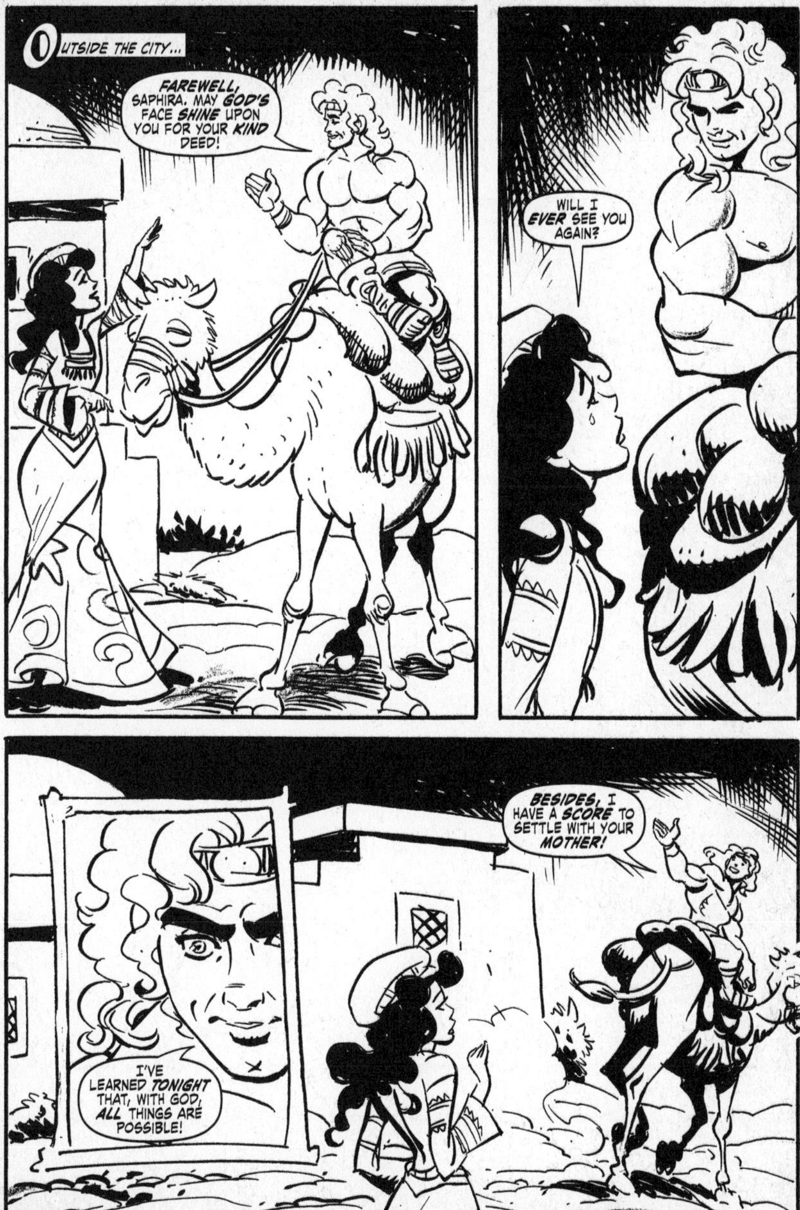
OUTSIDE THE CITY...
FAREWELL, SAPHIRA. MAY GOD'S FACE SHINE UPON YOU FOR YOUR KIND DEED!
WILL I EVER SEE YOU AGAIN?
I'VE LEARNED TONIGHT THAT, WITH GOD, ALL THINGS ARE POSSIBLE!
BESIDES, I HAVE A SCORE TO SETTLE WITH YOUR MOTHER!

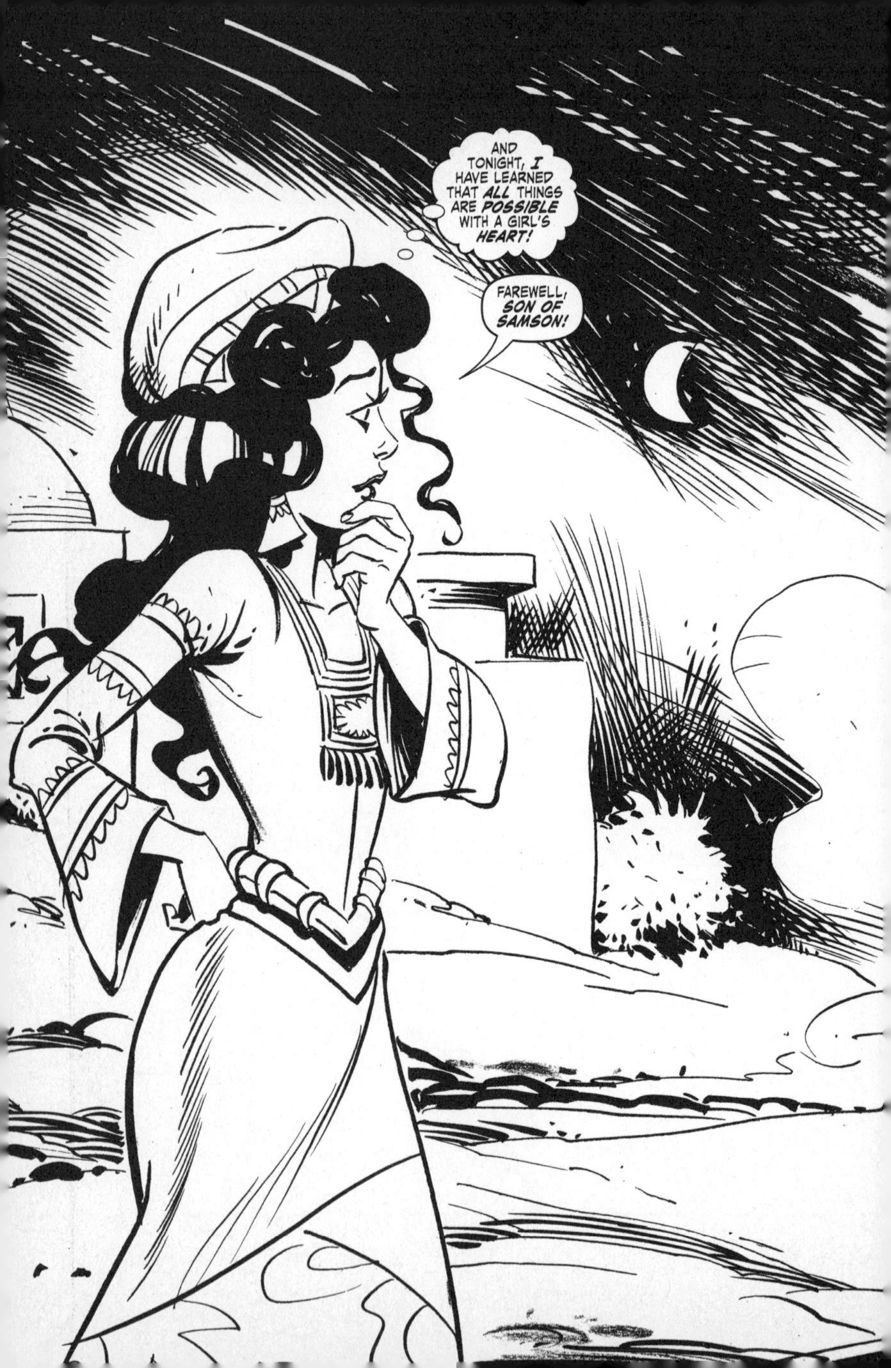
AND TONIGHT, I HAVE LEARNED THAT ALL THINGS ARE POSSIBLE WITH A GIRL'S HEART!
FAREWELL, SON OF SAMSON!

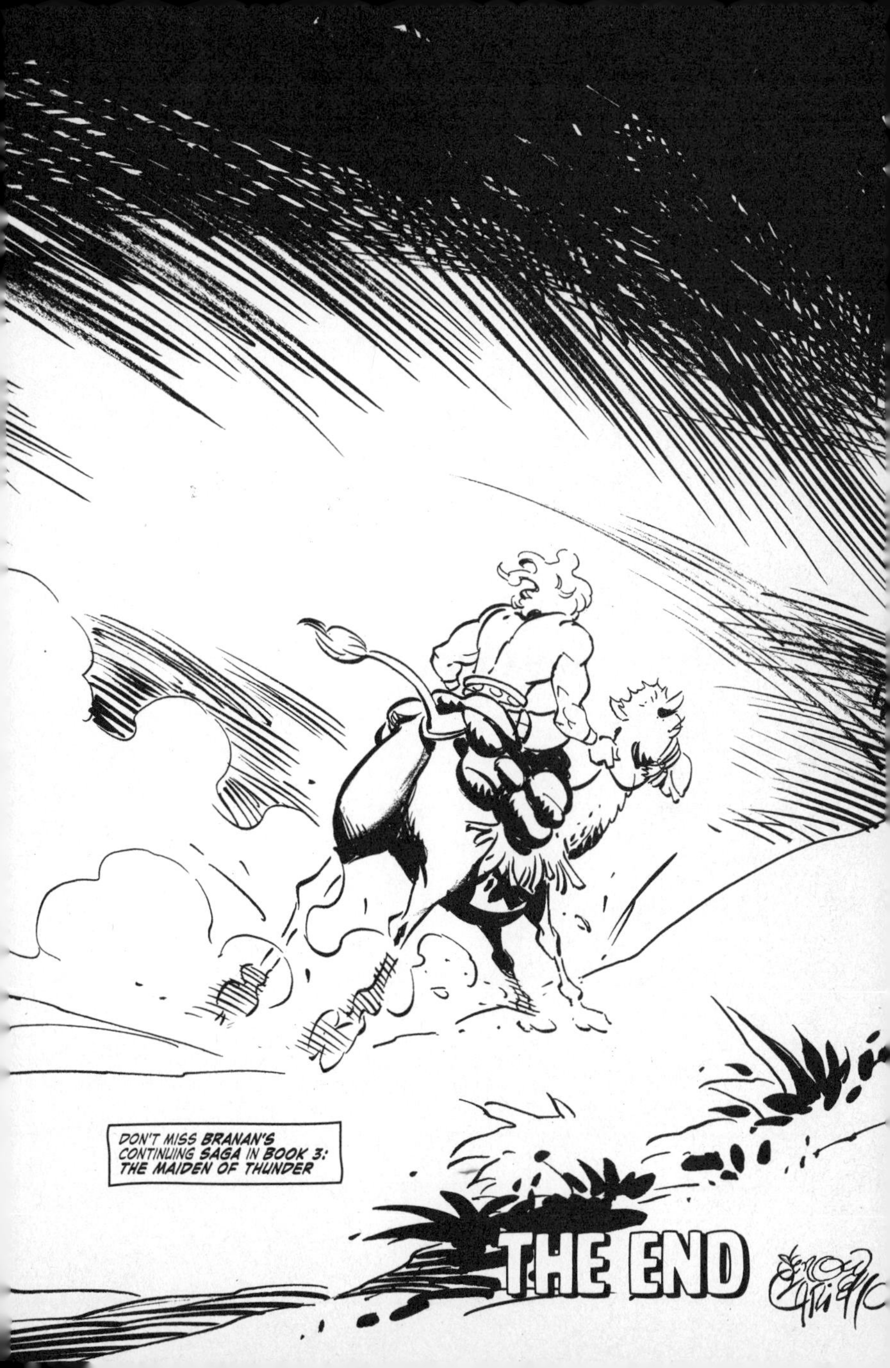
DON'T MISS BRANAN'S CONTINUING SAGA IN BOOK 3: THE MAIDEN OF THUNDER
THE END

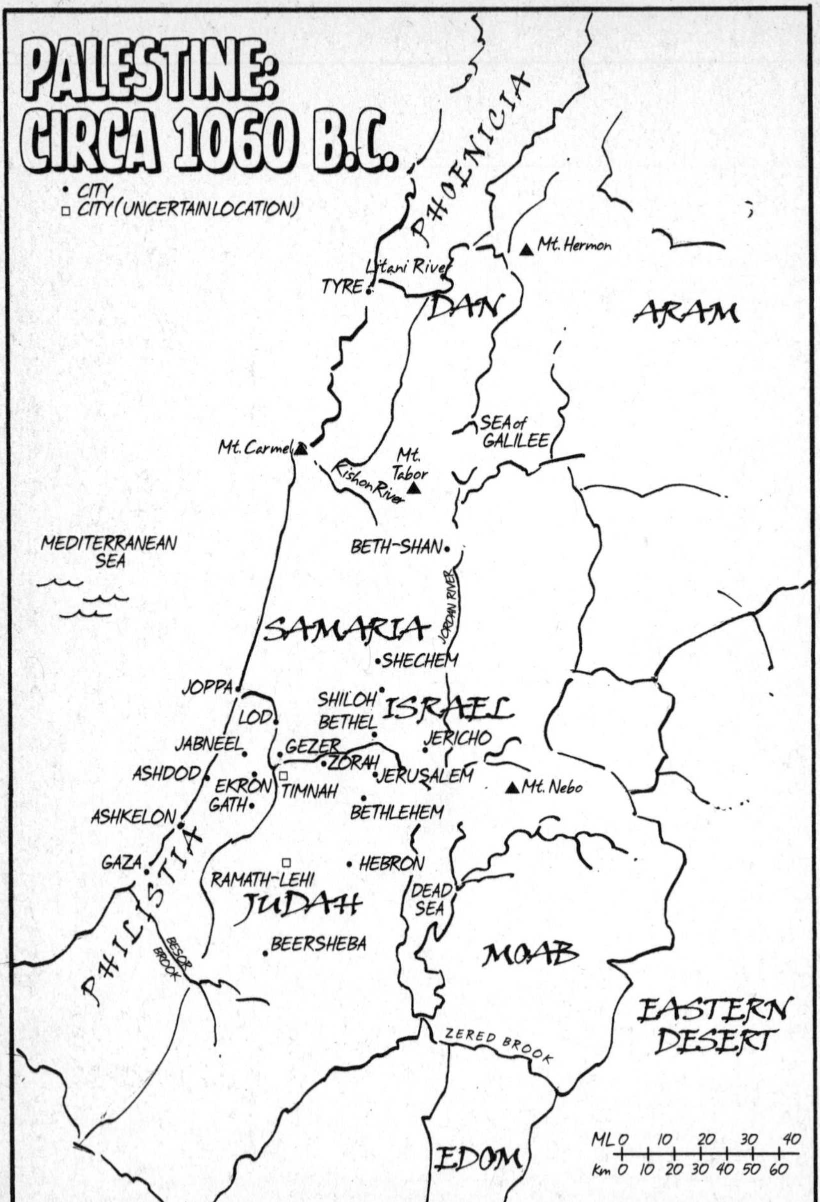
PALESTINE:
CIRCA 1060 B.C.
• CITY
□ CITY (UNCERTAIN LOCATION)
PHOENICIA
Mt. Hermon
Litani River
TYRE
DAN
ARAM
SEA of GALILEE
Mt. Carmel
Mt. Tabor
Kishon River
BETH-SHAN
MEDITERRANEAN SEA
JORDAN RIVER
SAMARIA
SHECHEM
JOPPA
SHILOH
ISRAEL
LOD
BETHEL
JERICHO
JABNEEL
GEZER
ZORAH
ASHDOD
EKRON
TIMNAH
JERUSALEM
Mt. Nebo
GATH
BETHLEHEM
ASHKELON
GAZA
HEBRON
RAMATH-LEHI
DEAD SEA
JUDAH
BEERSHEBA
PHILISTIA
BESOR BROOK
MOAB
EASTERN DESERT
ZERED BROOK
EDOM
ML 0 10 20 30 40
Km 0 10 20 30 40 50 60

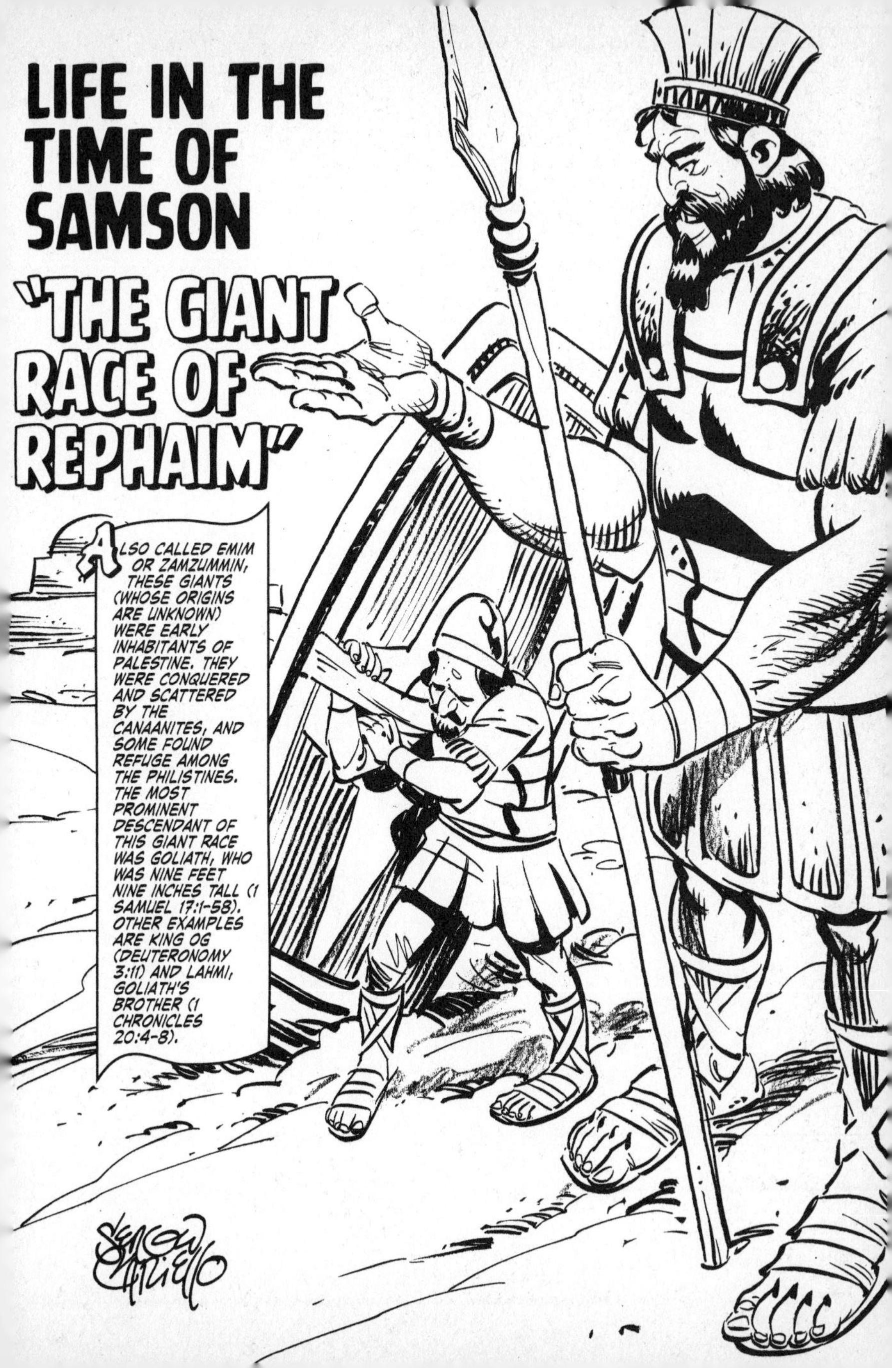
LIFE IN THE TIME OF SAMSON
"THE GIANT RACE OF REPHAIM"
ALSO CALLED EMIM OR ZAMZUMMIN, THESE GIANTS (WHOSE ORIGINS ARE UNKNOWN) WERE EARLY INHABITANTS OF PALESTINE. THEY WERE CONQUERED AND SCATTERED BY THE CANAANITES, AND SOME FOUND REFUGE AMONG THE PHILISTINES. THE MOST PROMINENT DESCENDANT OF THIS GIANT RACE WAS GOLIATH, WHO WAS NINE FEET NINE INCHES TALL (1 SAMUEL 17:1-58). OTHER EXAMPLES ARE KING OG (DEUTERONOMY 3:11) AND LAHMI, GOLIATH'S BROTHER (1 CHRONICLES 20:4-8).

LIFE IN THE TIME OF SAMSON

"SHIPS OF THE DESERT"

CAMELS ARE REMARKABLE CREATURES AND ARE WONDERFUL EXAMPLES OF GOD'S INTENTIONAL DESIGN. THERE ARE TWO SPECIES OF CAMEL. THE BACTRIAN HAS TWO HUMPS AND RESIDES IN ASIAN DESERTS. AND THE DROMEDARY (ALSO KNOWN AS THE ARABIAN) HAS ONE HUMP AND LIVES MOSTLY IN THE AFRICAN DESERTS. THESE INVALUABLE BEASTS OF BURDEN CAN CARRY LOADS UP TO 900 POUNDS AND TRAVEL FIVE TO TEN MILES PER HOUR FOR EIGHTEEN HOURS. THEY CAN GO WITHOUT WATER FOR WEEKS BEFORE REPLENISHING AND THEN DRINK FIFTEEN GALLONS IN TEN MINUTES! THEY DO NOT STORE WATER IN THEIR HUMPS. THE HUMP STORES FATTY DEPOSITS THE CAMEL USES FOR ENERGY ON LONG TREKS. WATER IS STORED IN BAGS THAT LINE THE INSIDES OF THEIR THREE STOMACHS. CAMELS EAT ALMOST ANYTHING, AND SIMILAR TO COWS, THEY REGURGITATE THEIR FOOD TO CHEW AS CUD. (WHICH IS AN EXCELLENT REASON TO STAY OUT OF A DISGRUNTLED CAMEL'S SPITTING RANGE!)

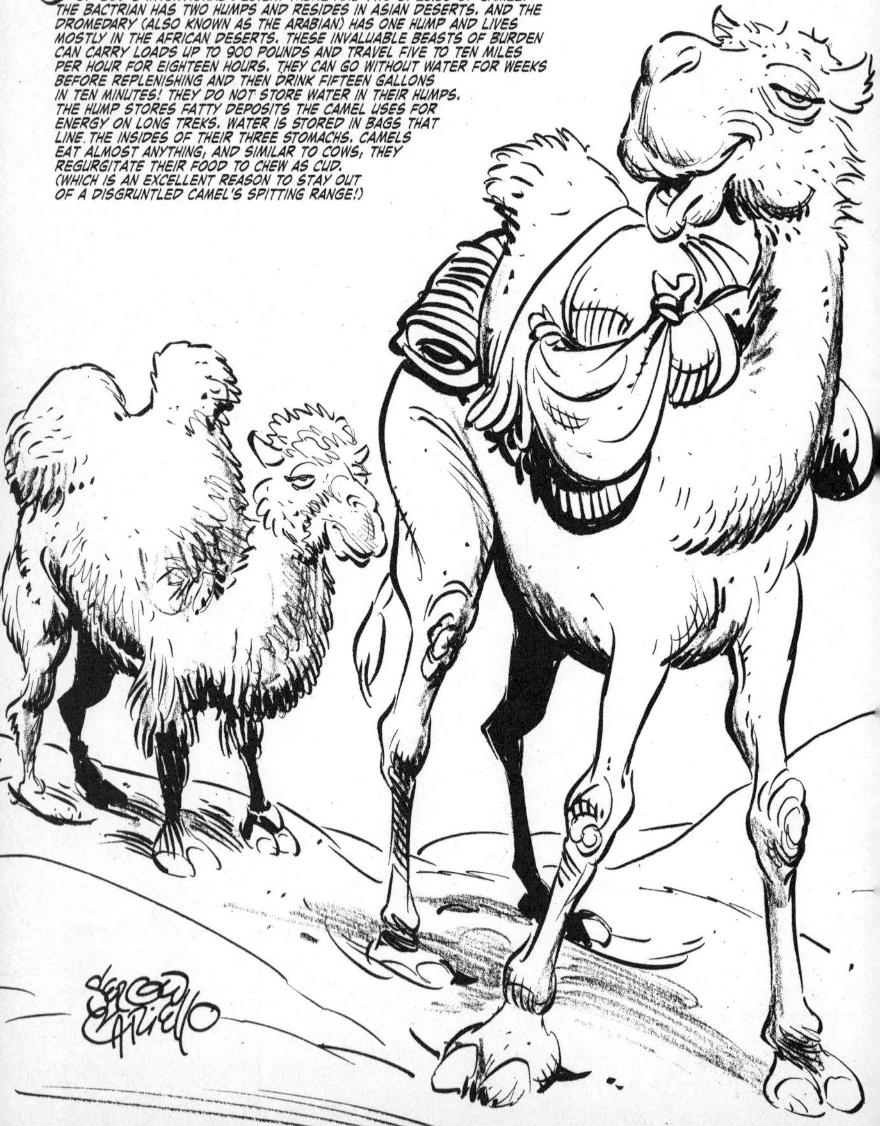
Sergio Cariello

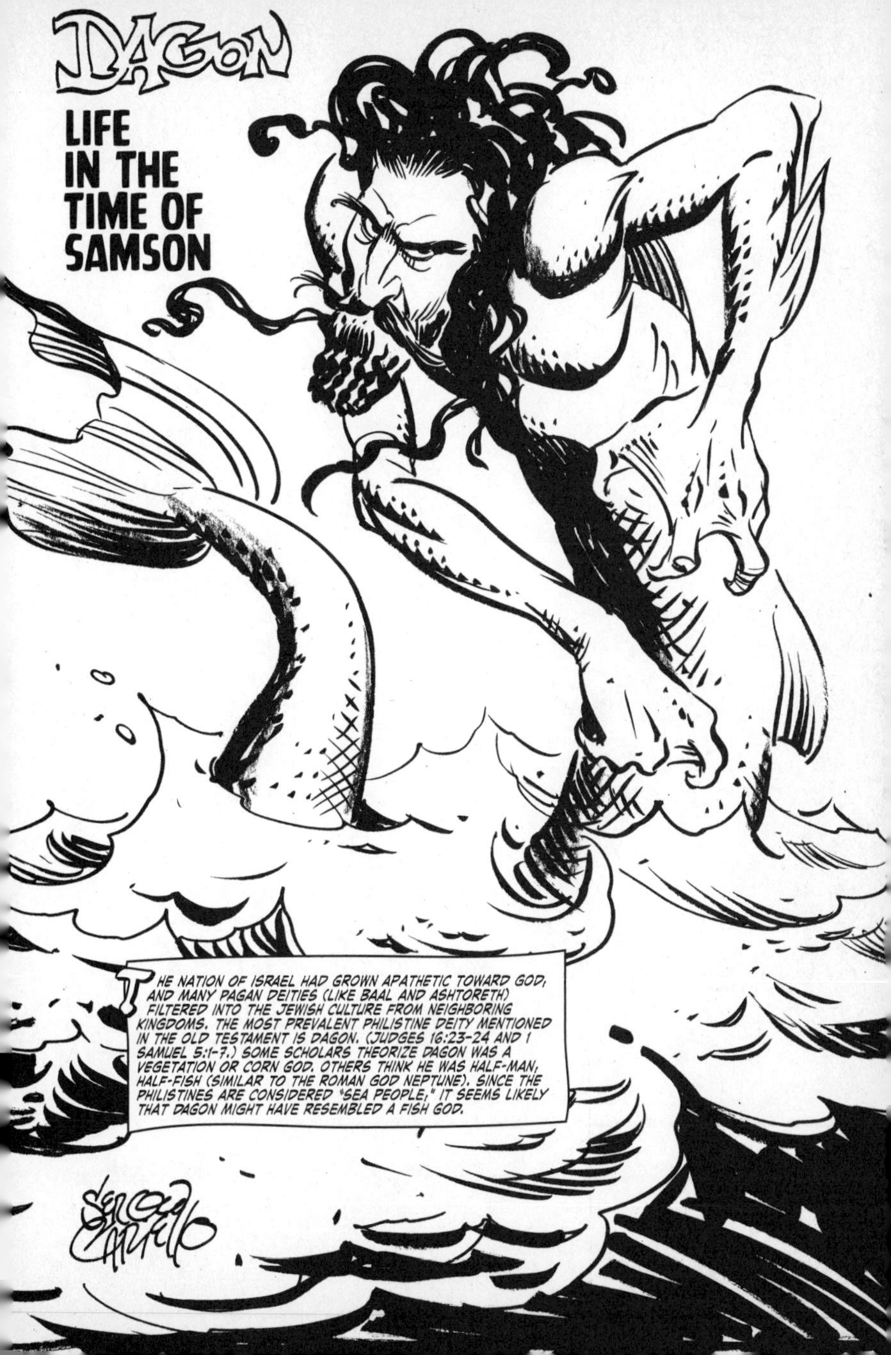
DAGON
LIFE IN THE TIME OF SAMSON
THE NATION OF ISRAEL HAD GROWN APATHETIC TOWARD GOD, AND MANY PAGAN DEITIES (LIKE BAAL AND ASHTORETH) FILTERED INTO THE JEWISH CULTURE FROM NEIGHBORING KINGDOMS. THE MOST PREVALENT PHILISTINE DEITY MENTIONED IN THE OLD TESTAMENT IS DAGON. (JUDGES 16:23-24 AND 1 SAMUEL 5:1-7.) SOME SCHOLARS THEORIZE DAGON WAS A VEGETATION OR CORN GOD. OTHERS THINK HE WAS HALF-MAN, HALF-FISH (SIMILAR TO THE ROMAN GOD NEPTUNE). SINCE THE PHILISTINES ARE CONSIDERED "SEA PEOPLE," IT SEEMS LIKELY THAT DAGON MIGHT HAVE RESEMBLED A FISH GOD.

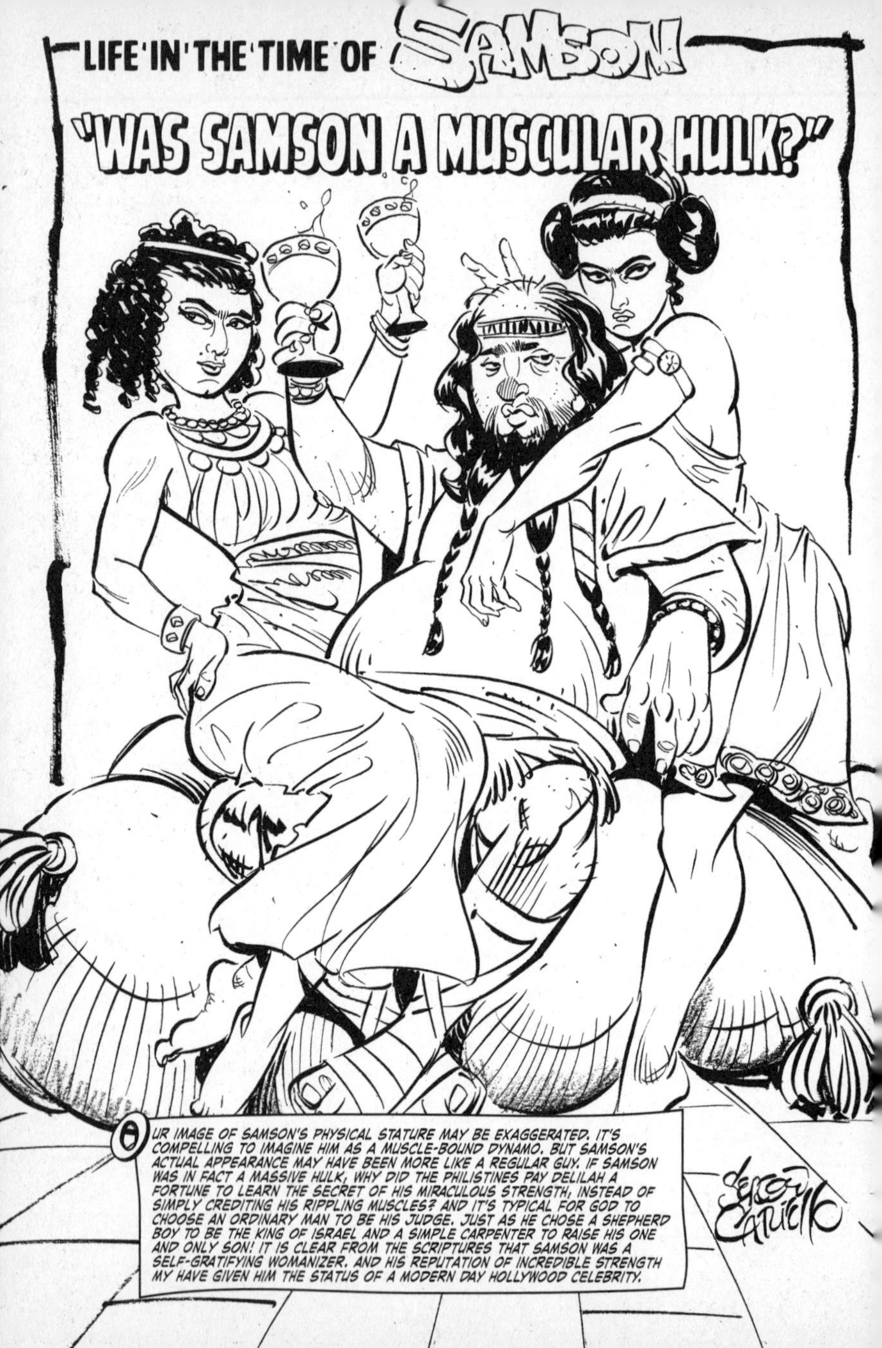
LIFE IN THE TIME OF SAMSON
"WAS SAMSON A MUSCULAR HULK?"
OUR IMAGE OF SAMSON'S PHYSICAL STATURE MAY BE EXAGGERATED. IT'S COMPELLING TO IMAGINE HIM AS A MUSCLE-BOUND DYNAMO. BUT SAMSON'S ACTUAL APPEARANCE MAY HAVE BEEN MORE LIKE A REGULAR GUY. IF SAMSON WAS IN FACT A MASSIVE HULK, WHY DID THE PHILISTINES PAY DELILAH A FORTUNE TO LEARN THE SECRET OF HIS MIRACULOUS STRENGTH, INSTEAD OF SIMPLY CREDITING HIS RIPPLING MUSCLES? AND IT'S TYPICAL FOR GOD TO CHOOSE AN ORDINARY MAN TO BE HIS JUDGE. JUST AS HE CHOSE A SHEPHERD BOY TO BE THE KING OF ISRAEL AND A SIMPLE CARPENTER TO RAISE HIS ONE AND ONLY SON! IT IS CLEAR FROM THE SCRIPTURES THAT SAMSON WAS A SELF-GRATIFYING WOMANIZER. AND HIS REPUTATION OF INCREDIBLE STRENGTH MY HAVE GIVEN HIM THE STATUS OF A MODERN DAY HOLLYWOOD CELEBRITY.

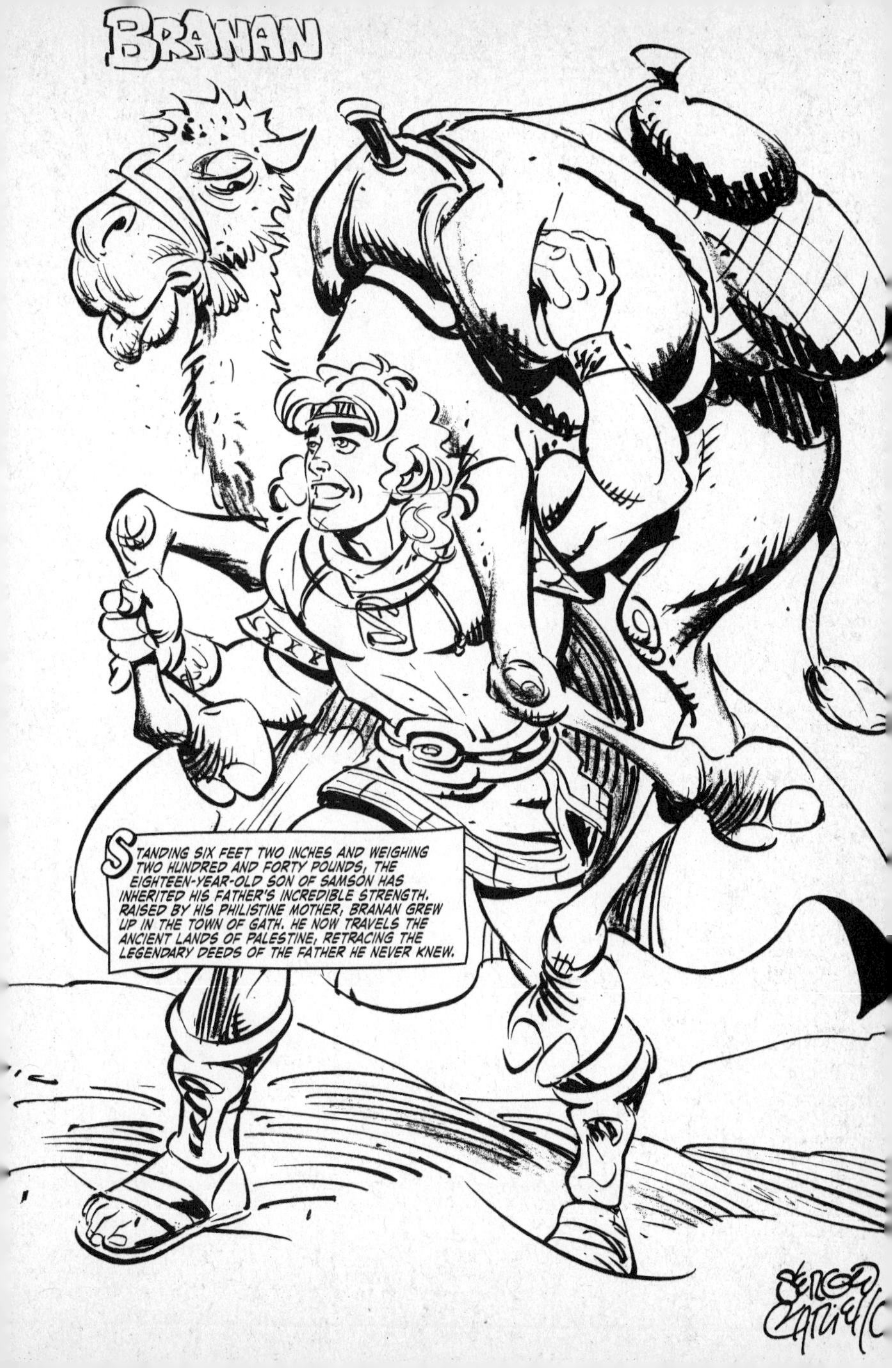
BRANAN
STANDING SIX FEET TWO INCHES AND WEIGHING TWO HUNDRED AND FORTY POUNDS, THE EIGHTEEN-YEAR-OLD SON OF SAMSON HAS INHERITED HIS FATHER'S INCREDIBLE STRENGTH. RAISED BY HIS PHILISTINE MOTHER, BRANAN GREW UP IN THE TOWN OF GATH. HE NOW TRAVELS THE ANCIENT LANDS OF PALESTINE, RETRACING THE LEGENDARY DEEDS OF THE FATHER HE NEVER KNEW.

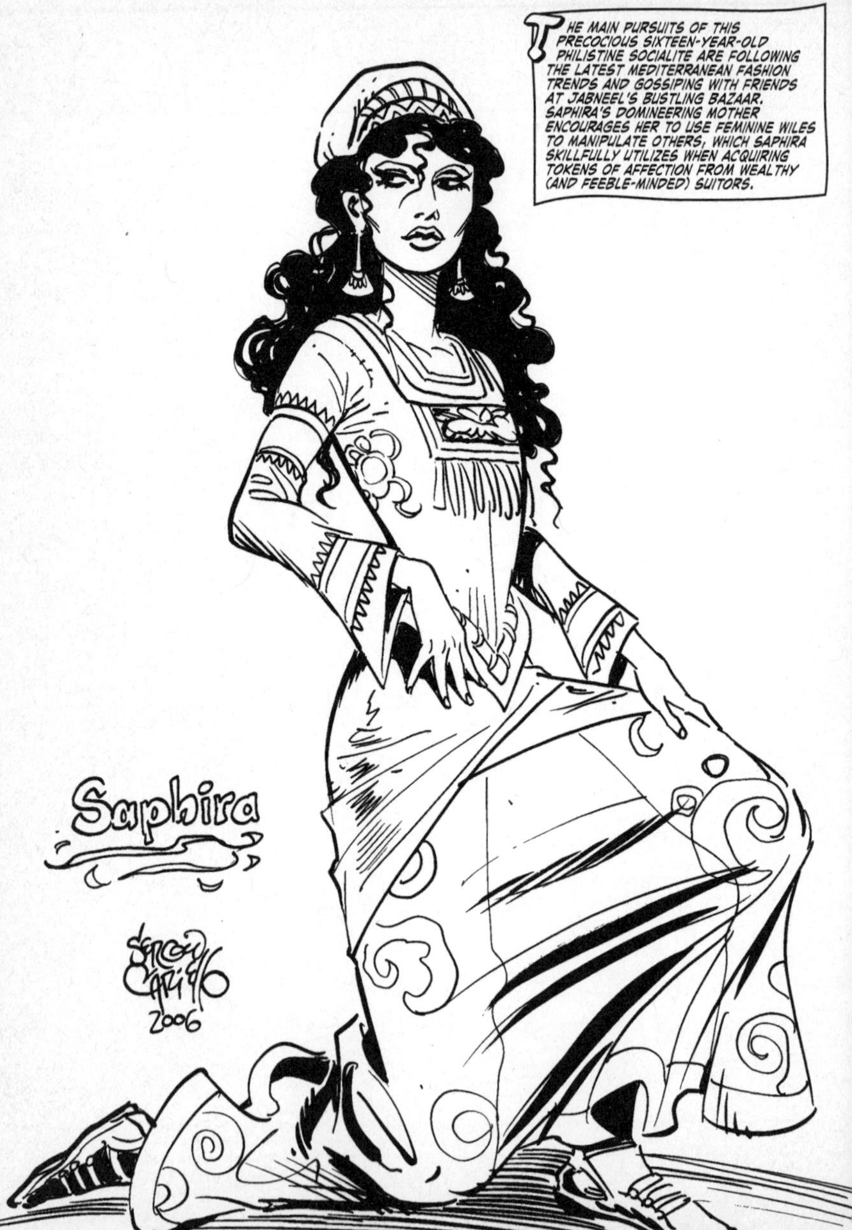
THE MAIN PURSUITS OF THIS PRECOCIOUS SIXTEEN-YEAR-OLD PHILISTINE SOCIALITE ARE FOLLOWING THE LATEST MEDITERRANEAN FASHION TRENDS AND GOSSIPING WITH FRIENDS AT JABNEEL'S BUSTLING BAZAAR. SAPHIRA'S DOMINEERING MOTHER ENCOURAGES HER TO USE FEMININE WILES TO MANIPULATE OTHERS, WHICH SAPHIRA SKILLFULLY UTILIZES WHEN ACQUIRING TOKENS OF AFFECTION FROM WEALTHY (AND FEEBLE-MINDED) SUITORS.
Saphira
2006

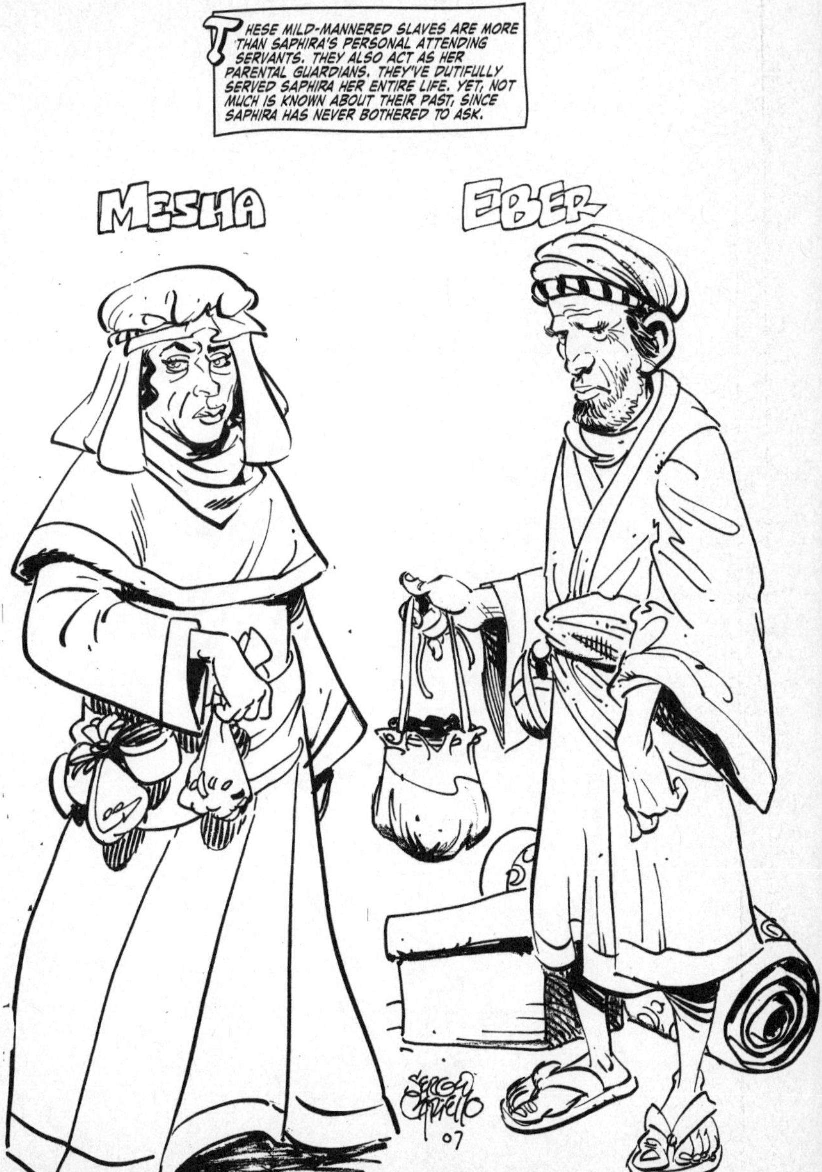
THESE MILD-MANNERED SLAVES ARE MORE THAN SAPHIRA'S PERSONAL ATTENDING SERVANTS. THEY ALSO ACT AS HER PARENTAL GUARDIANS. THEY'VE DUTIFULLY SERVED SAPHIRA HER ENTIRE LIFE. YET, NOT MUCH IS KNOWN ABOUT THEIR PAST, SINCE SAPHIRA HAS NEVER BOTHERED TO ASK.
MESHA
EBER
SERGIO CARIELLO 07

ABU

PLUMP WITH THE EXCESSES OF OPULENT LIVING, ABU THE SLAVE MERCHANT WILL NOT TOLERATE ANYTHING LESS THAN THE FINEST EXOTIC FABRICS TO ADORN HIS AMPLE BODY. BECAUSE OF ITS LUCRATIVE NATURE, ABU CONSIDERS HIS OCCUPATION AN HONORABLE TRADE, DESPITE THE UNTOLD MISERY IT INFLECTS ON THE WRETCHED SOULS HE BUYS AND SELLS.

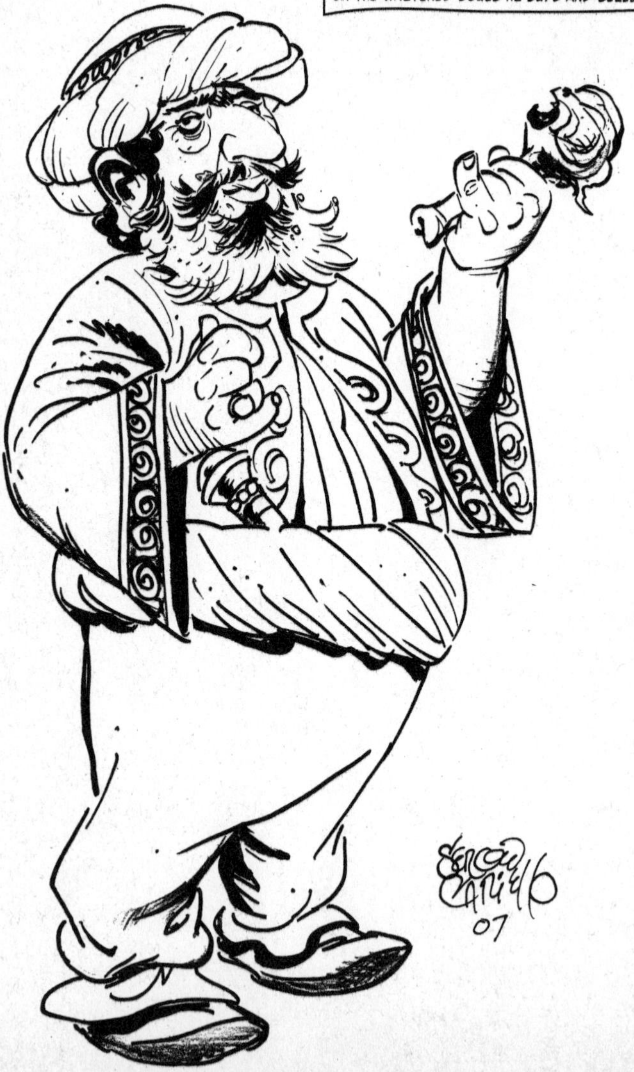

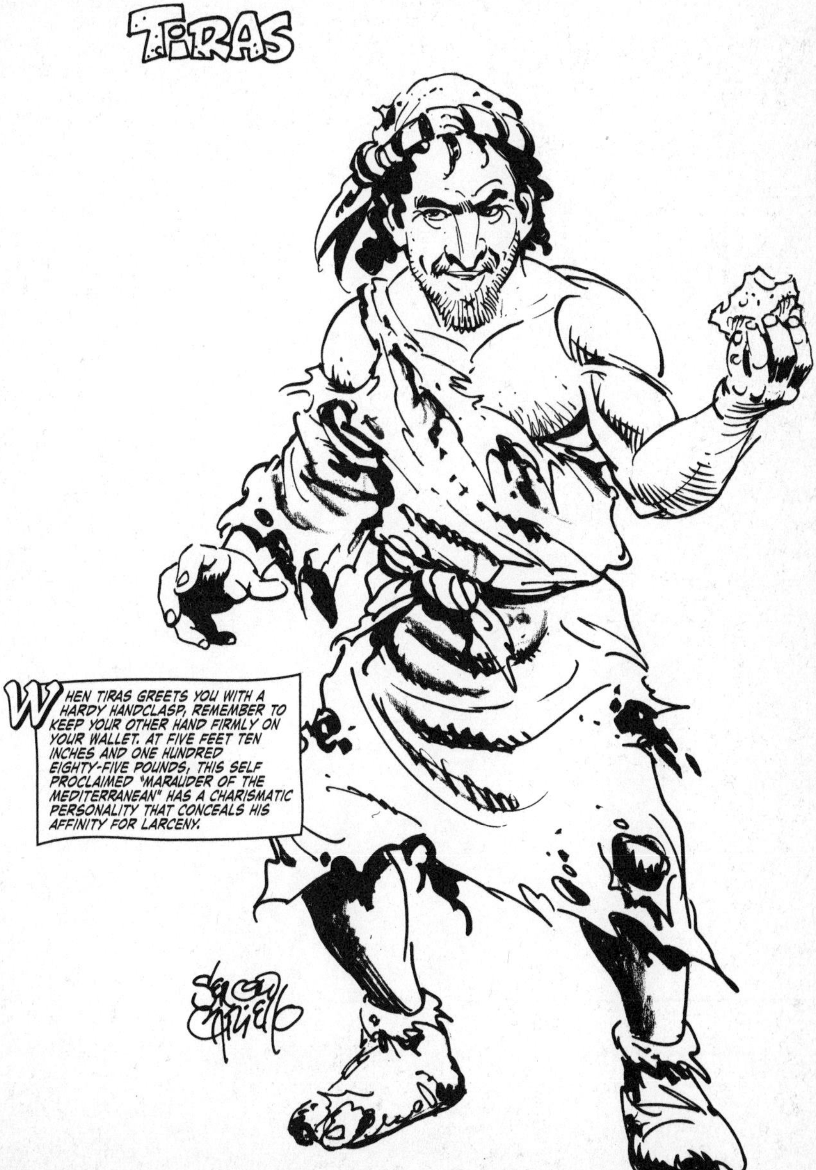
TIRAS
WHEN TIRAS GREETS YOU WITH A HARDY HANDCLASP, REMEMBER TO KEEP YOUR OTHER HAND FIRMLY ON YOUR WALLET. AT FIVE FEET TEN INCHES AND ONE HUNDRED EIGHTY-FIVE POUNDS, THIS SELF PROCLAIMED "MARAUDER OF THE MEDITERRANEAN" HAS A CHARISMATIC PERSONALITY THAT CONCEALS HIS AFFINITY FOR LARCENY.

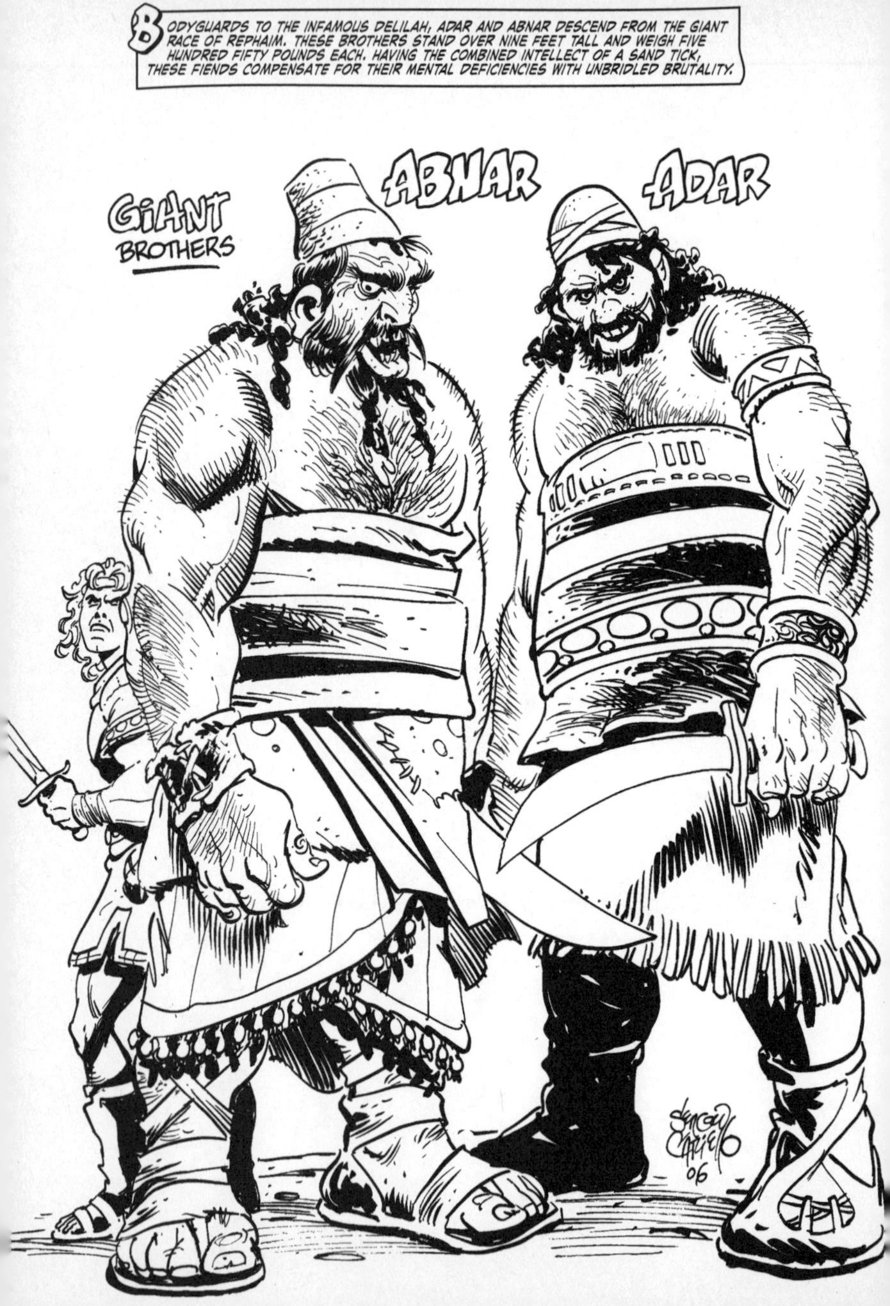
BODYGUARDS TO THE INFAMOUS DELILAH, ADAR AND ABNAR DESCEND FROM THE GIANT RACE OF REPHAIM. THESE BROTHERS STAND OVER NINE FEET TALL AND WEIGH FIVE HUNDRED FIFTY POUNDS EACH. HAVING THE COMBINED INTELLECT OF A SAND TICK, THESE FIENDS COMPENSATE FOR THEIR MENTAL DEFICIENCIES WITH UNBRIDLED BRUTALITY.
GIANT BROTHERS
ABNAR
ADAR

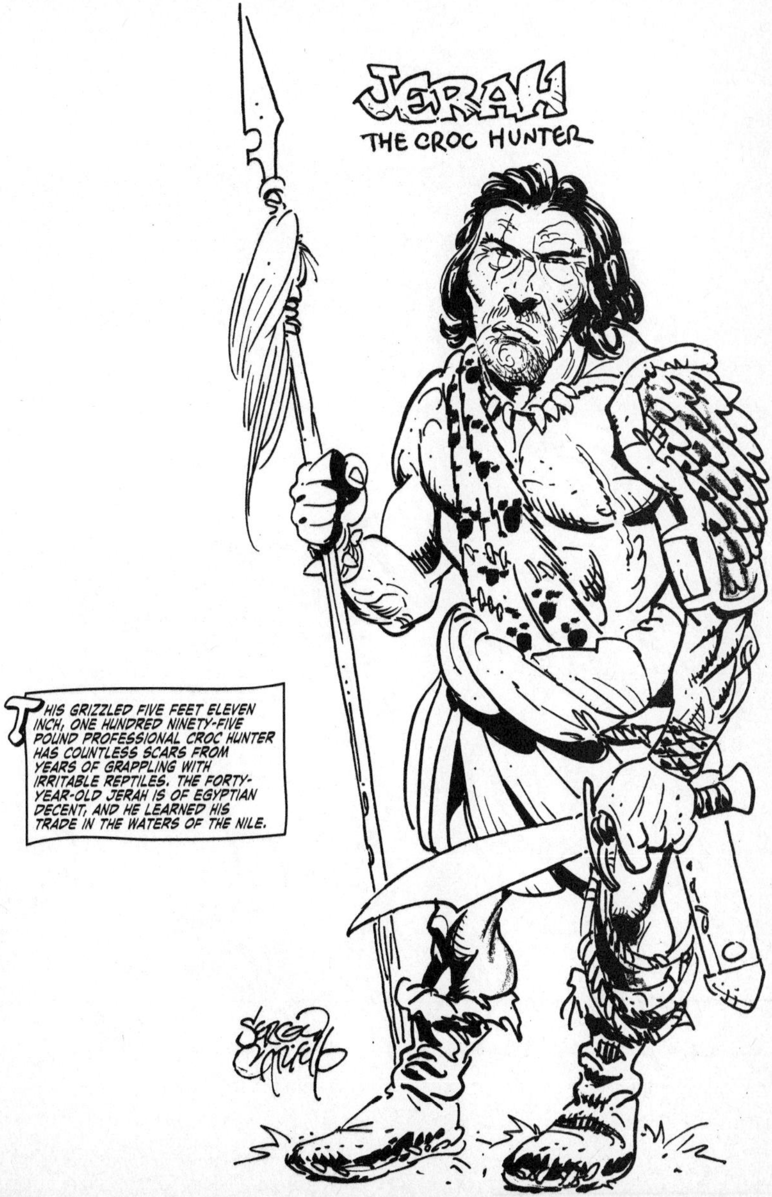
JERAH
THE CROC HUNTER
THIS GRIZZLED FIVE FEET ELEVEN INCH, ONE HUNDRED NINETY-FIVE POUND PROFESSIONAL CROC HUNTER HAS COUNTLESS SCARS FROM YEARS OF GRAPPLING WITH IRRITABLE REPTILES. THE FORTY-YEAR-OLD JERAH IS OF EGYPTIAN DECENT, AND HE LEARNED HIS TRADE IN THE WATERS OF THE NILE.

Sergio Cariello

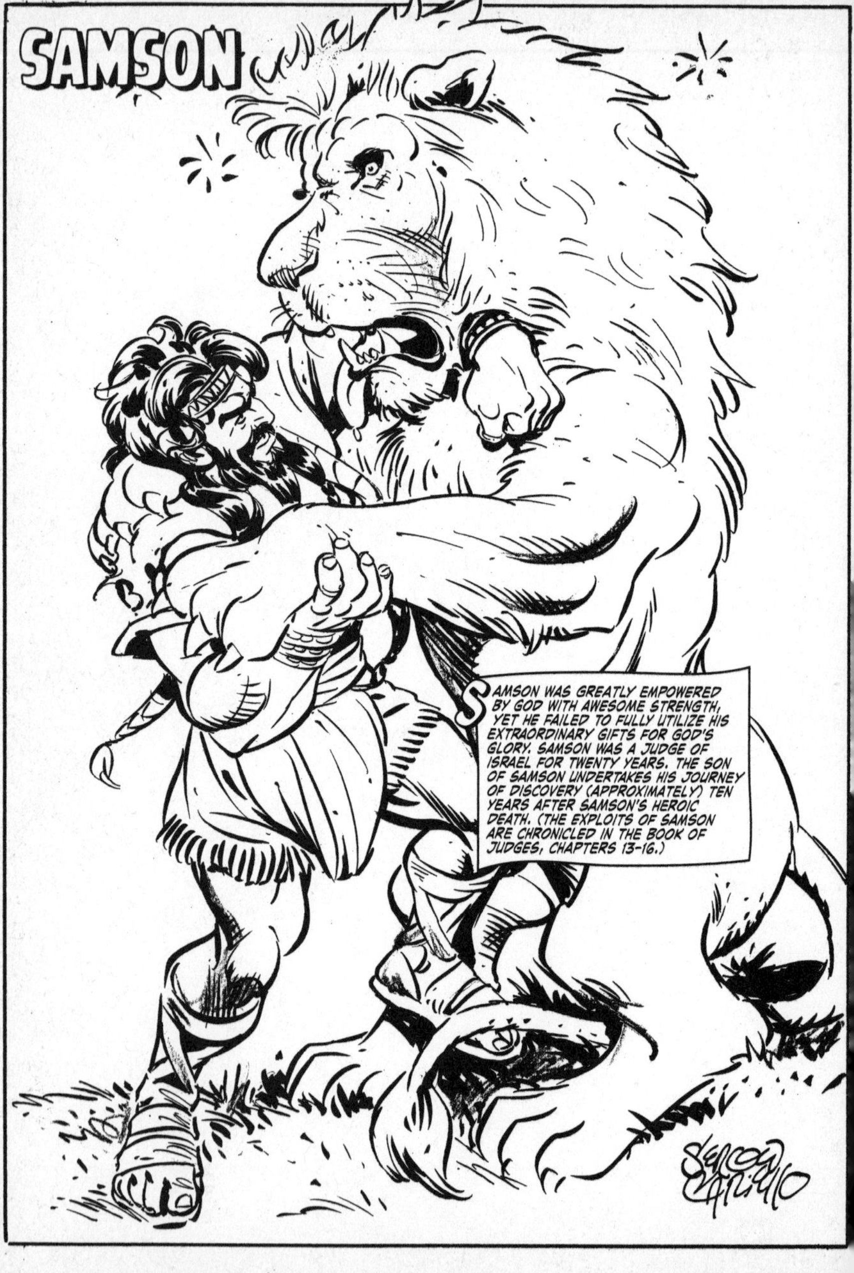
SAMSON
SAMSON WAS GREATLY EMPOWERED BY GOD WITH AWESOME STRENGTH, YET HE FAILED TO FULLY UTILIZE HIS EXTRAORDINARY GIFTS FOR GOD'S GLORY. SAMSON WAS A JUDGE OF ISRAEL FOR TWENTY YEARS. THE SON OF SAMSON UNDERTAKES HIS JOURNEY OF DISCOVERY (APPROXIMATELY) TEN YEARS AFTER SAMSON'S HEROIC DEATH. (THE EXPLOITS OF SAMSON ARE CHRONICLED IN THE BOOK OF JUDGES, CHAPTERS 13-16.)

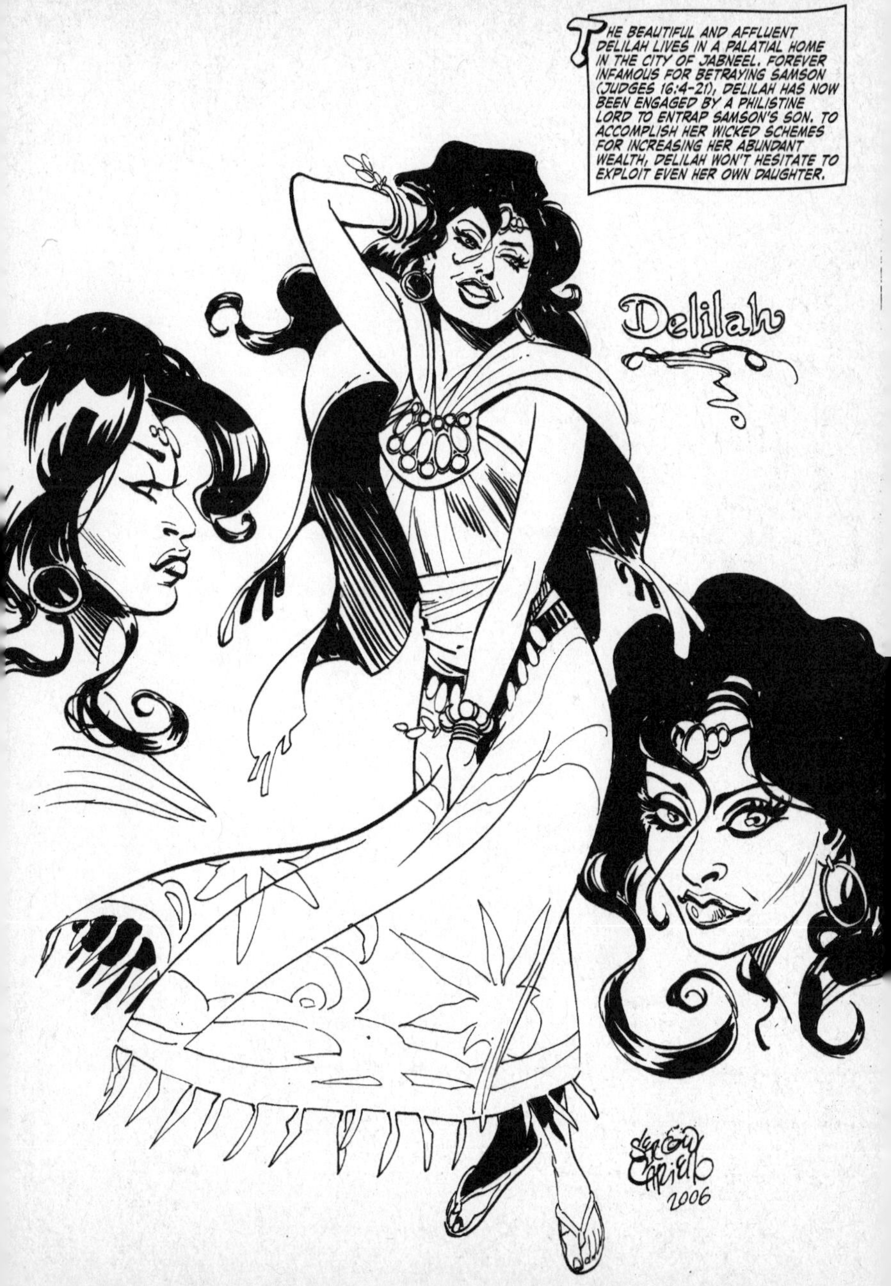
THE BEAUTIFUL AND AFFLUENT DELILAH LIVES IN A PALATIAL HOME IN THE CITY OF JABNEEL. FOREVER INFAMOUS FOR BETRAYING SAMSON (JUDGES 16:4-21), DELILAH HAS NOW BEEN ENGAGED BY A PHILISTINE LORD TO ENTRAP SAMSON'S SON. TO ACCOMPLISH HER WICKED SCHEMES FOR INCREASING HER ABUNDANT WEALTH, DELILAH WON'T HESITATE TO EXPLOIT EVEN HER OWN DAUGHTER.
Delilah
2006

GROWING UP IN SAN JOSE, CALIFORNIA, GARY MARTIN'S DREAM WAS TO BECOME A COMIC BOOK ARTIST. AT AGE 24, HE PACKED UP HIS DRAWING BOARD AND MOVED TO NEW YORK CITY, HOME OF MARVEL AND DC COMICS. LIFE IN NEW YORK WAS NEVER DULL FOR THE CALIFORNIA BOY. EVEN A MUNDANE COMMUTE BY SUBWAY INTO MANHATTAN COULD TURN INTO AN ENTERTAINING RENDITION OF THE *JETSONS* THEME SONG BY AN ECCENTRIC PASSENGER. AFTER GARY'S SIX-YEAR STINT AS A STARVING ARTIST (LITERALLY), HE LANDED A REGULAR GIG AS AN INKER, AND WAS ABLE TO SAY GOOD-BYE TO THE BIG APPLE.

IN 1986, GARY MOVED BACK TO THE WEST COAST, AND HAS BEEN A FREELANCE COMIC BOOK ARTIST AND WRITER EVER SINCE. HE'S WORKED FOR ALL THE MAJOR COMPANIES, INCLUDING MARVEL, DC, DARK HORSE, IMAGE, AND DISNEY, AND ON SUCH TITLES AS SPIDER-MAN, X-MEN, BATMAN, STAR WARS, AND MICKEY MOUSE. GARY IS BEST KNOWN FOR HIS POPULAR HOW-TO BOOKS ENTITLED *THE ART OF COMIC BOOK INKING*. RECENTLY, GARY WROTE A COMIC BOOK SERIES CALLED *THE MOTH*, WHICH HE CO-CREATED WITH ARTIST STEVE RUDE. GARY'S HAPPY DAYS ARE NOW SPENT INKING AT HOME (IN HIS PJS AND FUZZY SLIPPERS), WRITING SON OF SAMSON STORIES, AND TRYING TO TEACH HIS LOVELY BRAZILIAN WIFE, MARIA, THE THEME SONG TO THE *JETSONS*.

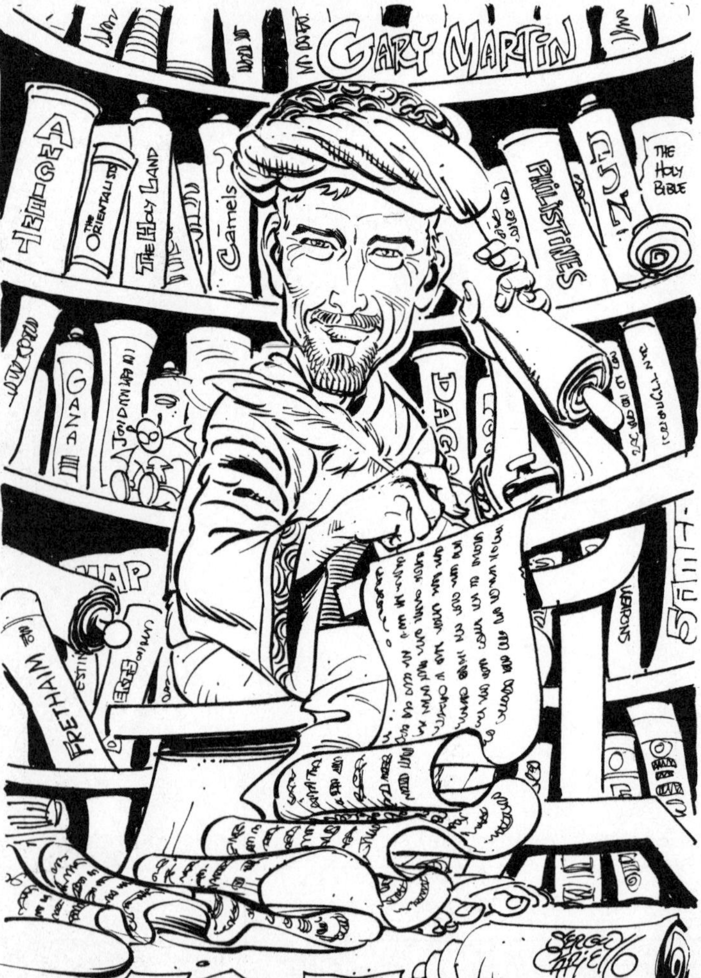
GARY MARTIN
THE ORIENTALISTS
THE HOLY LAND
Camels
Philistines
THE HOLY BIBLE
FRETHAIM

SERGIO CARIELLO WAS BORN IN 1964. HE BEGAN HIS CAREER AT THE AGE OF ELEVEN, WRITING, DRAWING, AND LETTERING HIS OWN COMIC STRIP, *FREDERICO, THE DETECTIVE*, FOR A LOCAL NEWSPAPER IN BRAZIL. HE MIGRATED TO THE USA IN 1985.

IN 1987, HE ATTENDED THE JOE KUBERT SCHOOL OF CARTOONS AND GRAPHIC ARTS IN NEW JERSEY. DURING HIS SECOND SCHOOL YEAR, HE WAS HIRED TO LETTER BOOKS FOR MARVEL COMICS, AND HE WAS QUICKLY MOVED ON TO DRAW SOME OF THEIR MAIN CHARACTERS SUCH AS SPIDER-MAN, DAREDEVIL, AND THE AVENGERS. HE ALSO ILLUSTRATED MANY OF DC COMICS' CHARACTERS LIKE SUPERMAN, DEATHSTROKE, WONDER WOMAN, THE FLASH, AZRAEL, AND BATMAN.

IN 1997, SERGIO REJOINED THE JOE KUBERT SCHOOL TO TEACH FOR SEVEN CONSECUTIVE YEARS, CONTRIBUTING TO PRODUCE MANY OF TODAY'S LEADING CARTOONISTS. IN 2005, SERGIO JOINED FORCES WITH ACCLAIMED WRITER CHUCK DIXON TO LAUNCH HIS FIRST CO-CREATOR-OWNED PROPERTY, THE IRON GHOST, A MINISERIES PUBLISHED BY IMAGE AND ATP COMICS. SERGIO ALSO WON FIRST PRIZE IN THE FIRST INTERNATIONAL CHRISTIAN COMICS COMPETITION FOR *NO PROFIT*! (A TWO-PAGE COMIC BASED ON ECCLESIASTES 5).

SERGIO CARIELLO AND HIS WIFE, LUZIA, LIVE IN SUNNY FLORIDA WITH THEIR ADORABLE DOG, CALLED MONIQUE. LEARN MORE ABOUT SERGIO CARIELLO BY VISITING WWW.SERGIOCARIELLO.NET

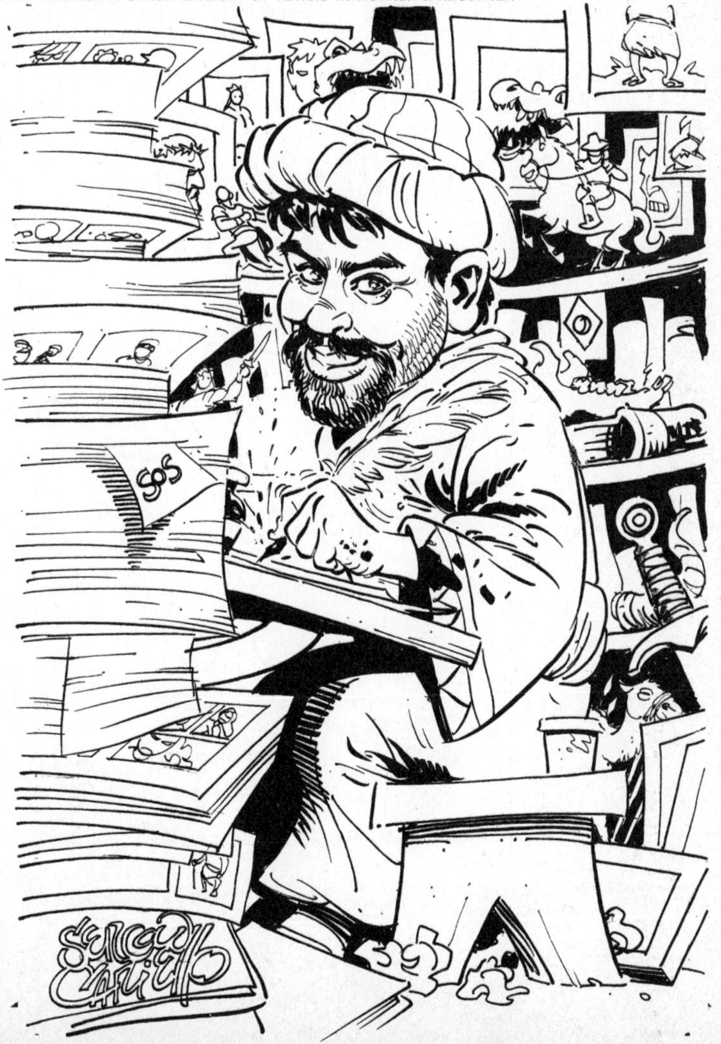
SOS

SON OF SAMSON'S LETTERER ***DAVE LANPHEAR*** HEADS ARTMONKEYS STUDIOS. YOU CAN FIND ARTMONKEYS' WORK AT MANY PUBLISHERS, INCLUDING MARVEL, DC'S CMX, DISNEY, URBAN MINISTRIES, DARK HORSE, NACHSHON PRESS, AND ZENESCOPE, AND FUTURE PROJECTS WITH MANY MORE STUDIOS.

AS A COMIC BOOK LETTERER, IT'S ESTIMATED DAVE'S LETTERED OVER 40,000 PAGES, ENOUGH TO TILE THE LARGEST COMIC BOOK CONVENTION'S FLOOR FOUR TIMES. IN HIS 15 YEARS AS A LETTERER, HE'S WORKED IN THREE MAJOR STUDIOS–MALIBU COMICS, COMICRAFT, AND CROSSGEN COMICS–AT THEIR MOST PROLIFIC TIMES, AND HE'S RECEIVED SEVERAL AWARDS FOR HIS LETTERING. HE'S BEEN BLESSED TO WORK WITH TALENTED WRITERS, ARTISTS, AND EDITORS, COUNTING MANY AS FRIENDS, AND HAD THE PRIVILEGE TO WORK ON NUMEROUS PRESTIGE PROJECTS STILL SOLD TODAY.

DAVE IS A THREE-TIME EDITORIAL CARTOON WINNER, AND HAS ALSO BEEN A CARICATURIST, COMIC STRIP CARTOONIST, NEWSPAPER ILLUSTRATOR, STORYBOARD ARTIST (NOTABLY PBS'S *DRAGON TALES*), MAGAZINE DESIGNER, TALENT COORDINATOR, AND PUBLISHING CONSULTANT. BUT DAVE LIKES HIS CURRENT WORK BEST: STAY-AT-HOME DAD AND HUSBAND WITH HIS BEAUTIFUL WIFE NATALIE AND THEIR TWO SONS, DAWSON AND KEATON.

COME READ *BEHIND THE LINES*, THE ARTMONKEYS BLOG AT HTTP://ARTMONKEYS.BLOGSPOT.COM, OR SEE THEIR GALLERY AT WWW.ARTMONKEYS.COM.

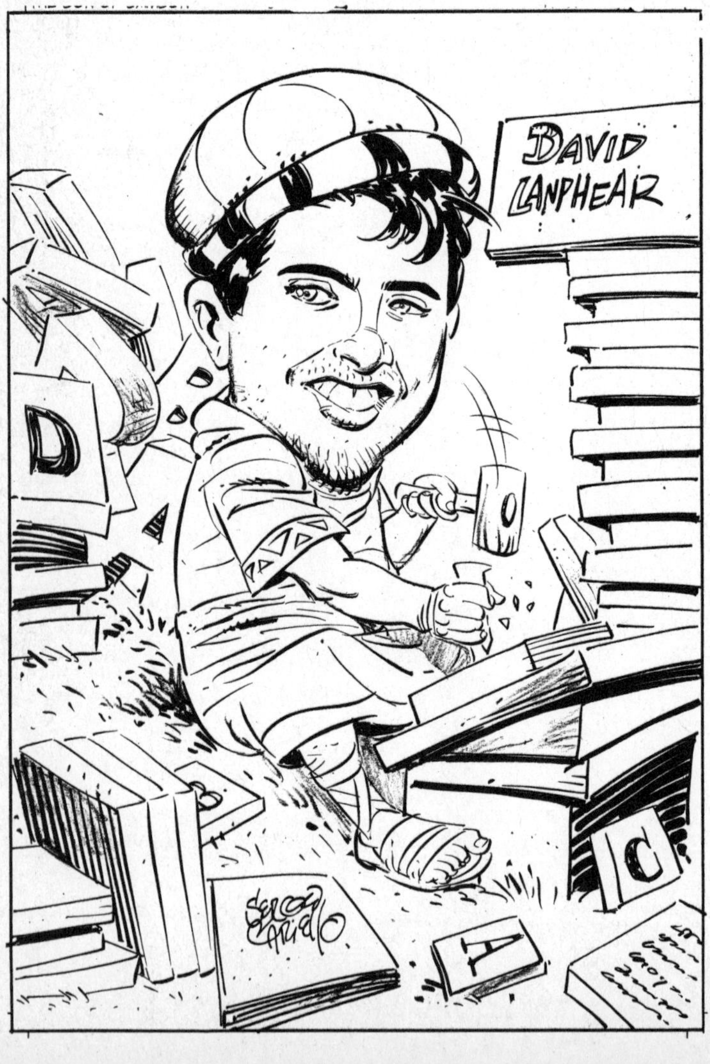
DAVID LANPHEAR
D
A
C
A